PRAISE
THE FRID

"*The Friday Girl* is an absolute triumph, and certainly the best thing R.D. McLean has written. He has captured the grim essence and fading glory of Dundee excellently. Corruption in the police is no great surprise, but the way it is portrayed in the book is terribly believable, as is the misogyny. Hard men living through hard times and taking it out on the women as much as each other. R.D. McLean does for Dundee what Ian Rankin did for Edinburgh, fixing it firmly in the pantheon of Scottish crime fiction destinations."

JAMES OSWALD

"Late '70s Dundee is evoked in all its grit and glory in this compelling noir novel. A city where the only thing harder than being an honest cop is being an honest woman cop. Combining the dark delights of a serial-killer thriller with an unflinching corruption tale, *The Friday Girl* is R.D. McLean on the very finest form."

EVA DOLAN

"Gripping and fiendishly twisted, *The Friday Girl* had me rooting for the gutsy Burnet from page one. A superbly crafted, dark and twisty read that transported me deep into 1970s Dundee."

D.S. BUTLER

THE FRIDAY GIRL

THE
FRIDAY
GIRL

R.D. McLEAN

Black&White

Black&White

First published in the UK in in 2025 by
Black & White Publishing Ltd
Nautical House, 104 Commercial Street, Edinburgh, EH6 6NF

A division of Bonnier Books UK
5th Floor, HYLO, 103-105 Bunhill Row,
London, EC1Y 8LZ

Owned by Bonnier Books
Sveavägen 56, Stockholm, Sweden

Copyright © R.D. McLean 2025

All rights reserved.
No part of this publication may be reproduced,
stored or transmitted in any form by any means, electronic,
mechanical, photocopying or otherwise, without the
prior written permission of the publisher.

The right of R.D. McLean to be identified as Author of this
work has been asserted by him in accordance with the
Copyright, Designs and Patents Act, 1988.

This is a work of fiction. Names, places, events and incidents
are either the products of the author's imagination or used fictitiously.
Any resemblance to actual persons, living or dead, or actual
events is purely coincidental.

A CIP catalogue record for this book is available from the British Library.

ISBN: 978 1 78530 731 7

1 3 5 7 9 10 8 6 4 2

Typeset by Data Connection
Printed and bound in Great Britain by Clays Ltd, Elcograf S.p.A.

MIX
Paper | Supporting
responsible forestry
FSC® C018072

www.blackandwhitepublishing.com

For Dot McLean
(AKA "Mad Mum")
(and once AKA "Girl Friday" – so how could
I not dedicate this title to you?)

DUNDEE
APRIL-MAY 1978

1

ELIZABETH BURNET PULLS HER COAT TIGHT. Not simply for the cold. She's being watched.

High-heeled shoes clatter on concrete slabs. She might topple. Doesn't like heels. Never has.

But:

You need to look the part.

Christ.

Feeling foolish. *Done up like a hoor*, her mother would say. So much for her 'respectable' profession.

Dudhope Park should be safe. But in the past four weeks, several women have been approached. The man's behaviour escalates with each encounter.

No rapes.

Yet.

But:

It's a possibility.

Eyes on her.

Walk faster.

The heels make it difficult.

Someone approaching. Didn't see him on the main path earlier. Maybe waiting in the bushes?

Male. Mid-thirties. Dark hair. Big coat. Holding it closed. Maybe – like Burnet – protection against the bitter cold.

Aye. Right.

Instinct: *get away from him.*

But Burnet tells herself:

Just a man going for a stroll through the park. Heading home after work.

Until he proves otherwise.

Closer. Clock bare ankles and calves, feet in brogues. Pale sticks rising out of the shoes. A few inches of flesh beneath the trailing edges of the coat.

Keep walking.

Don't run.

Look up. Stare straight ahead.

Not her first flasher. Ask a room full of women: most will raise their hand if asked about being approached by a man with ill intentions, or with his dick in his hand.

First time for Burnet: age eleven.

She ran away. He shouted after her. All the things he wanted to do.

Eleven years old.

Don't do anything to antagonise him. You're just walking to work. You haven't seen anything unusual. This goes better if you just act normal.

Close now. Wanting to make eye contact.

Burnet looks away.

He steps in front of her.

Here we go.

The coat opens. Erect. Wild grin.

4

Eyes rolling in their sockets. Groin pumping: a bad parody of John Travolta.

More *John Revolting*.

Burnet can't see anyone nearby. Just lines of bushes and trees. No people.

Oh, Christ.

Her heart does a pitter-patter rhythm. Bad jazz syncopation.

"You're doing this to me," the man says. "Allayouse cunts do this to me. Not my fault."

He shrugs off the coat. Comes at her. Wiry and strong.

He reaches out.

She can't move.

Instincts kick in.

Literally.

Boot in the balls.

"Fuck!"

On his knees. Retching.

Now: footsteps. Male voices.

About time!

She stops herself putting a heel through his eye. Or anywhere lower. These heels could puncture his ballsack.

The Detective Sergeant is in his forties, panting, out of shape. Red face. A coronary on legs.

"Where were you?" Burnet asks.

He points back to the bushes.

Two uniforms cuff the pervert. He screams and yells as they haul him to his feet. Burnet notes his dick is no longer proud.

The pervert's eyes blaze. "Bitch could have ruptured my balls!"

Detective Sergeant Coronary recovers his breath, straightens up, gets in the pervert's face. "The least you deserve." Slams his forehead into the man's nose. The pervert falls back.

DS Coronary shakes his head. "Rapists... worse than bloody poofters." Low laughter from the other officers. At least one of them nervous.

Burnet remains impassive. No point saying anything.

The uniforms keep the pervert on his arse. He looks like a tortoise turned over on its shell. Except the tortoise has more dignity.

"Cold weather," DS Coronary says. "Best to watch out. The ground can get slippery. What do they call it?"

A uniform nods in agreement. "Black frost."

"Aye," Coronary says. "Black frost."

The uniforms get the perv back up onto his feet, haul him out the park, and into the back of the wagon.

Coronary comes over to Burnet. Hand on her shoulder. "You all right, love?"

She almost corrects him – *constable* – but decides he doesn't know what he's saying. *Choose your battles.* "Aye. Just, for a moment, I thought maybe no one was watching."

"Lass like you?" Stepping back, looking her up and down. "Come on! How could we not watch?"

Deep breath. Tight smile. "Can we go back to the station?" she says. "These shoes are killing me."

* * *

The newly built HQ on West Bell Street. Brutalist. Intimidating.

On the third floor, Burnet changes back into uniform.

She washes off makeup. Pauses. A long look in the mirror. Better without the slap. More real. Like herself. But Coronary – can't even remember his real name; just another DS – insisted she wear it during the operation.

The kind of girls this wacko goes for, he'd told her, *all of them dressed like they were asking for it.* Shaking his head. *Honestly, what is it with you girls? Need to take better care of yourselves. Think how you look, what kind of message it sends.*

Burnet's seen the files. The Pervert doesn't care whether his victims are tarted up, dressed down, young or old. Not what it's about for men like him. But what would she know? Just a bloody woman, isn't she?

The door opens. Another WPC. Looking tired. Maybe just off shift. Checks herself in the mirror beside Burnet.

"Heard you were on flasher detail," the WPC — Caroline, that's her name — says.

Burnet nods. Keeps looking at her reflection. Something's missing. She doesn't know what.

"They put you in the hoor getup?"

"Apparently, that's the only thing these men go for."

"You know i's bollocks, right?"

"Oh, aye."

Caroline finishes. "For their own pleasure more than for bait."

"They're the ones in charge."

"Aye. Unfortunately." Caroline nods at Burnet's reflection, then leaves.

Burnet stays. Thinks about the things women say to each other in these situations. Why they don't talk about it to the people who might be able to make a difference.

Not that she's unaware of the answer.

* * *

The canteen. Quiet.

Burnet grabs a bacon roll, still nervy from the encounter with the pervert. Skin jangling. One question dominating her thoughts – *what took them so long to react?*

She imagines: DIs behind the bushes sneaking a fag break (with hip-flask chaser). DIs watching the guy get his dick out; having a good old laugh, all boys together, taking bets on whether the perv has the balls to follow through. On whether Burnet panics. Or screams.

"This taken?"

DS Dow. Early fifties, built like a collection of tangled pipe-cleaners. A shock of hair so pure white you'd swear he was born with it.

Her fists unbunch.

Dow's good people. One of the few. The uncle you wish you had. He served in the war, but discusses it fleetingly. Did his duty, but would rather forget he ever had to.

Sometimes the men who were too young to be called up rattle on about the war like a glorious crusade. Dow never corrects them, but it's clear from his expression he thinks they're talking out of their arses.

He takes a sip of tea. Looks at her with bright blue eyes that belong to a man several decades younger. Crow's feet crinkle.

Dow has a son. Grown, now. Never mentions him. Never talks about his home life.

Burnet doesn't mind. Makes believe that he thinks of her like a daughter. Maybe true, maybe not.

"I heard you were the lucky one today," he says.

"How could I say no? You know about this one, right?"

"I heard. Escalating attacks. Exposure to assault. You got him before he moved to rape."

"Today could have been the day." Still thinking: *what took the DIs on backup so long to intervene?*

"But it wasn't."

Dow's concerned; it's in the way he looks at her. But he can't understand how it *felt*, in that moment. "You booted him in the balls?"

That makes her smile. "Aye."

"See, he didn't have a choice."

She shakes her head. "Maybe," she says.

Dow stands. "I just wanted to check in. Supposed to be in a briefing but needed a cup of tea first. When you get to my age, no one cares if you sneak in a few minutes late." He lingers for a moment, brow crinkling again like he's trying to work out if he said what he needed to. Then: "I'm an old dodderer, I know. But if you need someone to talk to, all that shite ..." He seems to think about that for a second. "I've a young one of my own. You know that, aye?"

She nods.

Dow clears his throat. "That's all it is. I'd be proud if they did something like you. Choosing a career, I mean."

She lets him leave.

Thinks about her own father. Every night, when she gets home: *Girls your age don't need careers. They need to get married.*

Her father. Younger than Dow, yet somehow more old-fashioned and out of touch.

She used to think Dow represented hope. But beneath that, a more cynical part of her wonders if he's just a tease, the universe showing her what she wants, and telling her that it'll never really be there.

2

MICKEY KNOX, ARMS FOLDED, lips twisted into what might be a sneer, stares across the table at Kelley.

Kelley takes the stare and the attitude. "So . . . this is how we're going to do it, eh?"

Mickey stays still.

Mickey's got a sheet longer than your arm. First break in: age six, with his brothers. First arrest: twelve. A little fish allowed back into the pond. Youthful hijinks, according to the arrest report.

Kelley's brought Mickey in more than once in the last three years. Twenty-one now. No longer a little fish. But keeps getting thrown back anyway.

Sometimes he gets as far as court. Mostly what happens is: a slap on the wrist, then back out onto the streets with a promise to change.

The problem with break-ins is evidence. Stony silence serves these ones best. That's what they're told. That's what they do.

Say nothing. Admit nothing.

So, what's a polis to do? Get them to open up. Or just make a stupid fucking mistake.

One way to do it:
Meet silence with silence.
People hate silence.
Especially in the room.

Kelley writes in his notebook: *All work and no play makes Kelley a dull* ...

That book in his head lately. More than just a ghost story – the author talking about something else even if it was eluding Kelley as he read.

He's thinking about the book more than about Mickey Knox. They can take their time in the room. Not like there's a solicitor rushing down to the station.

Mickey's falling for it. Can't help himself.

Kelley writes the phrase a few more times. He stands up. Nods at DS Dow, who's standing at the door. *This is it. We're out of here.*

Dow's eyebrows raise, but he follows Kelley's lead.

"What'd you write?" Mickey asks. Slight tension. Nearly a squeak.

"Nothing."

"What'd you write?" Insistent, now.

Kelley pretends to read. "Suspect uncooperative. Recommend we follow the evidence. Throw the book at him."

"What evidence?"

Kelley sits down again. "You've been at the game a long time, Mickey. Back then, you were a skinny wee bastard, and what they'd do – your brothers – they'd send you through partially opened windows or other tight spaces, get you in where others couldn't or wouldn't go. Good work until you grew up a little. That late growth spurt was something of pain in the arse, am I right?"

"What evidence?" Mickey's mind one-track, now.

Kelley continues, careful. "Here's the thing, Mickey," he says. "This is 1978. Two years and it'll be 1980. You believe that? 1980. We're living in the bloody future. And so what's happening is that the police force is moving forward, too. Have you heard of forensic evidence?"

Dow's gaze is burning into the back of his head. But the older detective keeps quiet. Lets Kelley keep control.

Of course, if he fucks up ...

"Frenzied *what*?"

"Forensic evidence." Deep breath. Keep it going. He's started, so he'll finish. "Right, you know about fingerprints?"

"I know that any thief worth his salt wears gloves. Like, that's common knowledge. They do it on the TV."

"Aye, that's right."

"My fingerprints weren't at the scene."

Kelley wags a finger. "Close to a confession, Mickey."

"Tell it in court, then. I'm just saying, your man – whoever the fuck he is – leaves fingerprints behind, he's a fucking eejit."

Kelley allows himself a smile. "Fingerprints – they're going to be passé, soon."

Kelley's not losing him yet, even showing off with the French.

Mickey makes a show of being cool.

But look at his eyes. See the worry.

Kelley stands. Like a teacher. Or the gaffer at morning briefing. "DNA. Your skin's made of the stuff. Don't ask me what it stands for. Sounds like it should be a new rank, doesn't it? Anyway, full name of it's something more scientific, but it's a bit technical to remember offhand. Think *Panorama* did something about it – this DNA – a while back. You watch

Panorama, Mickey? You really should. Broaden your horizons. Get something of an education."

"See," Mickey says, "you can't trust everything on the BBC. *Panorama*, they're the ones did that Spaghetti Tree shite. Spaghetti grows on trees? My mum was convinced it was true, you know. Eat your fucking vegetables, Mickey, she'd say, whenever we had it. Fucksakes. She even phoned the helpline, you know? Put a sprig of spaghetti in a tin of tomato sauce, like they said. Hope for the fucking best. They actually said that to her. And because it was the BBC, and because it was Dimbleby, she believed it, too."

"It was April the First when they aired that one."

"All the same—"

"DNA's like fingerprints. But it's in every flake of skin, every lock of hair, every fleck of spit. I mean, I'm no scientist, but I think this is the way the world is going. Never mind chasing criminals through back alleys or waiting to catch them in the act ... we're going to be able to prove they were in the room. This stuff, it's in its infancy now ... you can try all you like, but you'll always leave behind some skin or saliva at the scene. Gloves aren't enough. A balaclava won't cut it."

Mickey's sweating now. Light, but visible. Clears his throat before speaking. "So what're you—?"

"What I'm saying – and I know you're a smart man, Mickey – what I'm saying is that you left behind a tiny flake of skin. Maybe from your hands. Maybe your cheek – like brushing against a wall. I mean, I'm not the scientist here, but we found something. And the university ... well, you know the university here's getting known for science, right? We send it to them, they do us a favour ..."

"I'm ..."

"When we processed you, we took your DNA. A little bit of contact from your skin, when we made you do the prints."

"No one—"

Hook.

"We wouldn't ask you. You're a thief, Mickey. You broke into those shops when they were closed, you cracked the safes and took the goods, and now we know for sure that it was you. They've matched the DNA. Like fingerprints, DNA is unique to each individual. So there's no room for mistake."

Line.

"Fuck."

Sinker.

"Fuck indeed."

"What now?"

"You can go into court, go in front of the sheriff and deny it. We can go to trial and you can have a solicitor waste his time when we have this evidence. Or ... you can admit it all now, and you know, maybe things'll go better for you."

Mickey weighs things up. His brow creases. He looks at Kelley, then at Dow. And then he reaches a decision.

* * *

The photo on Detective Constable Kelley's desk: his old man in uniform, looking proud.

Not too much older than Kelley is now. Maybe there's some resemblance, but Kelley is wirier, with hair that never quite settles. People say, though, that their eyes are the same. Kelley isn't so sure.

He isn't his father.

No matter what the papers say.
That headline still haunting him.

HERO COP'S SON FOLLOWS FATHER'S FOOTSTEPS

He could do without it. This blessing and this curse.

"Earth to Constable Kelley..." Dow, his hand on Kelley's shoulder.

One last look at dear old Dad. Then back to work.

"Sorry," Kelley says. "Away with it. Haven't been sleeping well lately."

Dow raises his eyebrow. But doesn't ask.

Instead: "DNA? What the fuck is that?"

Kelley grins ear to ear. "I was serious. *Panorama* really did do a piece. Wave of the future. Next import from the Yanks, and all that."

"And all that shite you fed Mickey...?"

"I think it's mostly true. There was something about some people shed their DNA, where others don't. But I thought... if you say it with enough conviction, is someone like Mickey going to know what you're talking about?"

"It's better than beating it out of him." Then: "Speaking of getting a beating, you hear they got the pervert?"

"The flasher? Aye." Kelley feels relief. Keep it business, keep it cop-shop-talk.

"He's sweating it out in the room just now. They're sending someone in later once he's good and basted."

"Who's on?"

Hesitation. "It was Mollison's case, but Garner's going to be the one in the room."

"Then it's not an interview, is it?"

Dow grimaces. "They drew lots. It's the way things happen, sometimes."

"But not the way they're supposed to." Kelley feels tight, from his chest all the way down his groin.

Light sweat.

Heat.

Anger.

Keep it down.

Dow says, "Come on, let's get a coffee. Maybe somewhere outside. Just in case you have the urge to try and lend a hand or something."

The bad blood between Kelley and Garner runs deep. Dow keeps saying: *play the long game.*

Planning ahead isn't Kelley's strong suit. Even when he knows it's the only option he has.

He's self-aware, knows it's a flaw.

Combine with it his father's sense of duty, and you'll know why Kelley's tour in CID got off to a bad start.

* * *

Now:

Kelley and Dow grab coffee and bacon rolls at a greasy spoon down Union Street. Sit in the green vinyl-backed booths at plastic-topped tables.

Dow speaks first. "You shadowed him, didn't you? Your first few days in CID?"

Kelley nods. Bites roughly at his roll. Rips flesh and dough.

Dow gives him a moment. "I'll be honest with you – Garner's almost as bad as some of the pricks we put away."

"You don't say." Speaking between chews.

"But there are ways that things work. You know why I'm the only one who'll work with you?"

"I wanted to work with the best, but I don't know why you hang around." Keeping it light. But he knows what this is about.

Dow waits a moment. Holding eye contact. "You know, coming in, people were wondering how like your father you were. A lot of us, we remember the old man."

"Aye, so Garner told me." Kelley puts down the roll, holds up his right hand, and twists the middle finger round the index. "Like that, he said."

Which was a fucking lie. Like everything Garner says. Maybe they worked together, but Kelley's father wouldn't have tolerated Garner's shite. Certainly wouldn't have encouraged it.

His father had been polis through and through.

Passed that down to his son.

Dow says. "Your father didn't want you to become polis like him. You know that, right? Part of that being ... he didn't want you to be disappointed."

"In him? In the job?" Doesn't say: *In myself.*

"We've all done things that maybe we'd regret if we thought about them too much. It's the nature of the job."

"No. The nature of the job is—"

"Upholding the law? Catching criminals? Aye. Well, maybe that's part of it. But to do that ... you know the old saying, don't you? Set a thief and all that?"

"Fire with fire," Kelley says. "That's another." Shakes his head. "All shite, though. An excuse, really."

"Maybe. But ... it's how things work. Or maybe ... how it works for my generation, your dad's generation." Dow sips his tea. "Maybe how it's meant to work, too. I see young men like you coming through, and they burn out or they fuck up. Because they have this idea of being a police officer that comes from what they've been told. Men like ... your dad ... me ... even Garner ... we work from the gut. Do you understand?"

"You approve of the way he works?"

"I respect that he gets results."

"My dad was good polis."

Those first few days – partnered with Garner – Kelley refused to believe some of the things that thug told him about his old man.

"He had a good record," Dow says before stopping suddenly, the speech half-finished. "But he was a man like the rest of us."

"What are you saying?"

"There are things that your father did ... we all make compromises. Part of the job. He did, too. He was human."

Kelley stands. Doesn't want to hear it.

Thunder in his head.

Anger. Impatience.

"Please," Dow says. "I'm not here to soil your father's memory. I'm not going to tell you he was in someone's pocket or he murdered someone, or whatever the fuck it is that you think is about to happen here. But he knew well enough to leave well enough alone. Do you understand?"

Kelley sits.

The thunder quiets.

Force of will.

Kelley's inheritance from his old man: a quick temper. One he learned to control.

Dow says, "This thing ... you putting in a complaint against Garner. I understand why. What happened at the high rises that first day on the job ... the thing with the Huns, it was a stupid fucking move. A chest-beating piece of bullshit."

Anger again. In the chest. The stomach.

Head buzzing.

Keep it clear.

But the memory's always there, ready to remind him.

Kelley's first day in CID, Garner taking him out to bring in one of the gang leaders for a wee "chat". The two of them got separated when they got inside the building. Kelley walked into a trap and a beating. Two days in hospital. Knowing Garner had arranged the "accident" to send a message: idealists like Kelley weren't going to usurp Garner's rule in CID or on the streets.

"Men like Garner," Dow says, "they have friends. Your father knew it. I know it. They're embedded in the system. The political system and the streets. If you try to rock the boat, what's going to happen is you're going to get tossed out before you get the chance to make a change."

"So what's the point?"

"That's the question you have to answer for yourself. Your dad did it. I did it. But no one can tell you. All I can do is give you advice. Whether you're polis to the bone, or just some wee lad playing out fantasies he saw on the telly, you need to decide who you are."

What can Kelley say?

Kelley wants to fight back against men like Garner. Make the police what it should be. What his dad had made him believe in.

Fighting a losing battle is noble. Right up to the moment you realise that there's no final reprieve, no universal justification. The polis should offer hope: justice and mercy and hope. But they're just people. Just an organisation. Good men. Bad men. Everything in between.

3

THE KEILLER'S FACTORY IN ALBERT SQUARE is due for demolition.

Frank Gray, sitting on a stool just inside the entrance to the NCR building, glances up over top of his paper to check who's walking past. Clocks a suit, a face he's seen before, and then glances back down.

Empty feeling in his stomach.

A sense of loss.

Why? He never worked there. Never cared much for their marmalade either. His son had loved the books about that bear, though – the one who loved marmalade, wore the daft bastard hat.

Another little hole. Right in the centre of his stomach.

More loss.

His son. Seventeen, now. A waster.

Just like his old man.

Ignore the voice. Fucking *ignore* it.

The voice has been stronger in recent months. He never used to hear it. Not when he was the Beast of Balgay – too many years ago now to put a number on them. Not when he was a new father, distracted by crying, the fear that there might be something wrong with this wee thing who looked so frail and whose mother kept talking about how he was going to have a different life from them, as though they'd somehow failed but they could make up for it through this boy.

The voice has come only recently. Only after Frank first realised his son really is a waster.

A wimp.

He'd been bullied at school. Frank suspects some of the local lads still give him a hard time, even if the boy doesn't say anything. Spending all his time in his room. Sometimes, the look of him, as though he's been in a fight. And Frank's sure it's not one where he was the victor.

Boys need to grow up strong. Boys need to grow up tough.

Boys need to learn early about what it means to fall on your arse.

He thinks of his own dad. The moustache, the hard ice eyes, the cruelly twisting scar down one side of his face. Frank on the dining table. His dad encouraging him to jump, saying, "Don't worry, I'll catch you."

His dad. Letting him fall.

"Here endeth the lesson."

What Frank wanted to say to his own son. The words he swallowed – bit down – so hard he tasted blood in his mouth every time the lad fucked up.

Whose fault was it? Ask Frank, and he'd blame the wife. Say she spoiled him.

Jeannie meant well, but she was also naïve. Take the incident the other night with the music; his son blaring music from his room so loud it took Frank back to the bad old days when every loud noise had been a potential fucking Nazi bomb.

The kind of 'music' you could have used as torture. Some prick growling about being an 'antichrist' over guitars making a sound God never intended.

Frank had pulled the plug. Thrown out the offending cassette.

His son had simply stood there, eyes red with tears.

Fucking *tears*.

Frank's son.

Wanting to be an anarchist and weeping like a bairn.

The state of his generation. Little wonder the world was going to waste.

"End of an era."

Frank turns. The man in the suit beside him, looking at the paper – at the picture of the old Keiller's factory.

The suit, uninvited: "We're the last ones standing."

Frank doesn't say anything.

"Count yourself lucky. We're future proof here."

Frank wonders who the suit thinks he is. English accent. Air of entitlement. Talking to Frank with a tone that screams: *And be fucking grateful for it!*

The Beast of Balgay would have broken the bastard's bones, speaking like that.

But Frank Gray – a citizen, now – sits on his stool, nods, and ignores the itch from his cheap shirt.

22

4

DOMESTIC VIOLENCE COMPLAINT OFF BLACKNESS ROAD. PC Lincoln shouting, "I need a WPC!" and then: "Burnet, you're it!"

Always the same. Domestic violence call? Bring a WPC. Tell her to hold the victim's hand. But stand back, love, and don't worry your wee head about us giving the perp a kicking before saying he "fell down" or "resisted arrest". That one's for the men. You just make sure the victim's got a cup of tea, okay? A shoulder to cry on. Girl talk helps, doesn't it?

Jesus.

Taking down the flasher – even as bait – should have *meant* something. But she's still a glorified secretary.

And it's back to: *I need a WPC, because someone's got to make a cup of tea on this one!*

Lincoln drives. Taking his eye off the road when she pulls down the hem of her skirt after getting in.

Maybe thinking she's fine with the attention.

Lincoln drives erratically. Burnet can smell beer on his breath. Her fingers flex, seeking something to grab onto.

Lincoln parks arse-end out on the street, wheels mounting the kerb.

"Police business, right?"

She follows him to the front door. Unlocked. Easy access to the stairwell. "Second floor," he says. "What the call said, aye?"

He has to ask?

From above, she hears yelling. Crying. The thump of someone punching a wall.

Burnet grits her teeth.

Up two flights, Lincoln hammers on the door. "Police!"

Something smashes. A dinner plate?

Lincoln shoulders the door. Knocks off the interior chain.

The front room: poky. Drawn curtains. Musty smell. A man standing over a woman, fists raised. She's curled into a ball, back to him.

The man turns, jaw dropping like he's offended by them entering. Maybe five-eight. Barrel chested. Big arms and big hands. Eyes too small for his face.

The woman's hair's matted and untidy. Her skin's a breakout of spots that wouldn't look out of place on a teenager. She looks ill. Her makeup is smeared. Bottom lip bleeding. One eye blackening.

The man forces his jaw back under control. "What the fuck is this?"

Too late. He's lost the power in the room.

Lincoln steps up to him. Burnet gets an arm around the woman's shoulders. The woman resists. Burnet persists.

The two men focus their attention on each other. An overflow of testosterone.

Lincoln locking eyes with the husband. *Put all your attention on me.* "Sir, we had a report of a disturbance at this address."

"Jesus fuck," the man says, rolling his eyes. "She's the fucking disturbance!"

"Sir, I can see evidence of a physical confrontation—"

"Come on, pal! The wee bitch was with another man. On the ran-dan with her bitch of a sister, thinking I wouldn't know what she was up to."

Burnet and the woman almost out the door.

Too slow.

"Ask her!" Stopping them in their tracks. "Fucking ask the bitch! A man's got his pride, right?" Turning back to Lincoln. "You understand, aye? A man's got to look out for what's his. Can't let women go getting ideas. Jesus, I was just teaching her a lesson."

"All well and good," Lincoln says. "But you were disturbing your neighbours."

Burnet chokes down a laugh of disbelief. Tightens her grip round the woman's shoulders, leans into her. "Come on." Speaking soft, "Let's get you out of here."

"You're going nowhere!" The man turning again. No longer surprised, no longer in shock. A step forward. "Fucking bitch!" Eyes flicking to Burnet: "Bet you're one of these feminist lesbians, too. Giving women ideas above their station, burning your fucking bras, all that shite."

Burnet removes her arms from the woman's shoulders, steps in front of her. Wondering why the fuck Lincoln isn't doing anything to take this guy down.

Her hand drops down to her truncheon.

The man makes his move.

Burnet sidesteps, then clobbers him. Hard as she can. Maybe harder than she should. The wooden stick smashes into his jaw. A crunch. He's down. Spitting blood on the carpet.

Lincoln kicks the man in the kidneys. He stays down.

"I'll talk to this fuck," Lincoln says. "Maybe make this woman a wee cup of tea, calm her nerves?"

Cup of bloody tea.

* * *

The woman's name is Gloria. The ape in the front room – her husband, Alec.

Gloria shakes on the edge of the bed. Burnet stays standing.

From the front room, they can hear Lincoln having a wee word with Alec. Burnet thinks about why Lincoln didn't try and stop the man earlier. Thinks about the size difference between the two men. *Jesus.*

Maybe make this woman a wee cup of tea.

Burnet shrugs off anger. Gets down in front of Gloria, like she would a child. Takes the woman's hands and wraps her own around them.

Gloria's eyes are wide.

"Is this the first time?"

"That he's hit me?" Gloria shakes her head. "Naw."

"Why haven't you come forward?"

"Why the fuck d'you think?" She laughs. Bitter. "Complained the first time it happened. The polis come round, nice woman like you, and this other officer. And you know what, she takes me through here, and himself and the officer stay there in the front room, laughing about dirty jokes. The man comes in here, maybe, what, ten minutes later, tells me it was all a misunderstanding, that Alec was sorry for what he did, but I had to understand that I was the one who made him that way."

Burnet's face burns. Shame. Recognition. Old story. Does it ever change?

"What the fuck can you do?" Gloria says. Then, "You seem like a nice lass. You're young, and all, but you get married, you'll learn. Men get carried away sometimes. When they get jealous and that. It's how they are. They can't help it."

Words feel useless.

"I wasn't seeing anyone. I would never cheat on Alec. Not just his temper ... I love him, like. I know how that sounds and all, but it's true. When he's not drinking or nothing, he's a sweet man." Deep breath and she lets it go. Like the very act of speaking has been helpful. "Just the way it is, right? Men and women. I know the young girls like you are all about equality and all that, but it's never gonnae happen. It's just the way we are, men and women. Nothing we can do but try and make sure they're happy ... and if we do that, they'll keep us happy, too."

Burnet says, calmer than she expects, "I'll get you that tea, shall I?"

* * *

Alec's cuffed in the front room, quietly speaking in monosyllables. He's on the sofa, and he's shaking.

Lincoln's taking down details. "Night in the cells"—Scribbling in his little notebook—"that'll calm you down. Give you time to think before assaulting an officer of the law."

Burnet moves quietly into the kitchen. Trying not to laugh – but it's either that or give Lincoln a slap round the back of the ear. Jesus, what they saw when they came in, and Lincoln's concerned about Alec's reaction to the police?

Not her place. He's a senior officer. She's just along to make the tea.

Busying herself with the kettle, she earwigs:

"You get it, don't you? I love that bitch, I really do ... But she's been acting out of sorts lately."

"I understand," Lincoln says. "You want to make sure she doesn't go off the rails."

"It's for her own good."

"Aye, well, you need to think about how you tell her that. Can't go slapping your wife around like that, it's only going to drive her away."

"Worked for my old man."

"Aye?"

"Aye."

"He and your mother still together, then?"

"She's dead."

"I see."

"Her fault, aye? She didn't listen to him. He was trying to protect her. For her own good, you know? And, aye, well. Not that anyone gave a fuck."

"Where'd he end up?"

"Perth. Still fucking there, too."

The kettle whistles. Burnet finds the teabags.

"Night in the cells is what it'll have to be," Lincoln says. "Can't avoid that."

Burnet – with two cups of tea – walks back past the men. Alec's eyes follow her. She sees the hate. If Lincoln weren't here, the guy would be kicking off.

Jesus. A night in the cells? And then back to his wife? No prizes for guessing what happens then.

And Lincoln's talking to him cool and calm? Empathising with the arsehole?

Christ.

In the bedroom: Burnet hands the tea to Gloria. "Milk and two sugars. Like you asked."

Gloria nods.

"He's going to the cells," Burnet says.

"Because he tried to attack you?"

Burnet realises what the other woman's saying. Shrugs her answer away.

Thinking: *keep to the job. Keep to the procedures.*

"You have somewhere you can go?"

Gloria takes her first sip of the tea. Makes a face like it's not right, but looks up and smiles at Burnet. A thin smile.

"I know places," Burnet says.

"Shelters? Nah, that's where women go when they're turfed out, when their man doesn't want them no more."

"Have you looked in the mirror? Have you seen what he's done to you?"

Gloria tenderly touches her blackened eye. Traces down to her busted lip. "I've had worse," she says. "I suppose it was the noise this time, wasn't it?"

Burnet's stomach churns. "At least see a doctor, just to check—"

"No doctor," Gloria says. "He spends a night in the cells, he'll calm down. And when he comes back, things'll be better. You'll see. You'll see." She looks up at Burnet, eyes wide like she's pleading. "We can forget it and move on. Everything'll be fine."

Burnet sips her tea. Stays schtum. Waits for Lincoln to be done with the ape in the other room.

After that, there's nothing more they can do here.

5

THAT AFTERNOON, LINCOLN TELLS HER she's needed on another call.

In the locker room, a nudge from one of the other girls: "I think he likes you."

She knows about the pool some of the male officers have going. The one about who'll get into her uniform first. Pathetic and juvenile. Besides, they want the Friday Girl, not Elizabeth Burnet.

The *Dundee Herald*'s fault.

She hadn't wanted it. They'd insisted.

Not just the paper, her new bosses.

First day in uniform: a photographer from the *Herald* asks if she'd want to be in their Daily Girl feature.

Her shift sergeant said yes for her.

First day. Don't make any waves. Dream job. Don't ruin it. She didn't say no.

What was the Daily Girl? *Here's a lass doing a job. Isn't she pretty? See another one tomorrow.*

She'd gone in on the Friday, in her uniform:

Elizabeth Burnet, 21. A new cadet with Tayside Police.

Nothing salacious. The picture slightly unfocused, like a snapshot from a photo album.

And yet ...

She knew what people called her: *The Friday Girl*. How they thought of her: a wee bit of totty to make the force look good. Modern, even. Yes, even pretty girls can be WPCs. All they really need to do is make cuppas and fill in arrest forms.

Jesus.

Burnet turns on the radio. Blondie singing "Denis".

In the car, Lincoln turns down the volume, and says: "I hear from sources that you were one of the most popular Friday Girls ever."

Subtle. Or just awkward. Maybe not a fan of Blondie.

"That so?"

"Oh, aye. The editor himself called the Chief. Never had so many letters praising a girl as you. Statistically, the prettiest girls tended be on a Monday, so you were an outlier. Bet you didn't know that?"

Burnet concentrates on not biting her upper lip. An old habit. One she developed in school. A way of dealing with exams, surprise tests, dance nights.

"Good for our image, right? I mean, for the polis to look like we're progressive and modern and all."

"Having a woman dolly herself up for the papers? Oh, aye. That's progressive."

He laughs at that. "Woman? You're a slip of a girl. That's why they wanted you, right? Not some hacket old bint like, say, Annie down the cells."

Burnet takes in a deep breath though her nose.

Lincoln, unable to take the hint, keeps talking: "I mean, she's experienced and all ... but Jesus, imagine looking at that mug over your morning cornflakes? Never mind if you're just starting out the week."

Burnet looks out the window. They're leaving the Kingsway. The call had come from Birkhill, out near Templeton Woods.

At least it's not a domestic. Some OAP concerned about her pet, apparently. Wasn't that the fire brigade's area of expertise, usually? Getting kittens out of trees?

Except this kitten was dead. Murdered by a fox, maybe. Something like that. They had to go out, take a statement. Half the time in uniform, the job was more social than foiling criminals.

Lincoln, after a few moments of silence says, "Nearly there. Drew the short straw on this one, though. Already know whatdunnit. Christ, all we're doing is going out to hold this woman's hand."

Burnet shrugs. "Can't always be murders and beatings and thieves."

"Oh, but she said on the phone, like ... this is a murder. So now we have to go out."

"A cat can be a loved one. When I was a girl, one of our neighbours had a cat she used to take out for walks in a baby stroller."

"You know this is a waste of time. Arrest a fucking fox, why don't we? Jesus."

They turn onto the street: low bungalows, new builds.

No need to look at house numbers. Old woman on the road, waving them down. Rinse perm, spotted pinny over her brown dress and white blouse.

Lincoln parks carefully beside her. Careful not to mount the kerb this time. Aye, talk your way out of running over a sweet old woman.

"You want to take the lead here?" he says. "Use that Friday Girl charm, and this'll all be over in a jiffy. We can get back to real police work." A hesitation. "Think we can squeeze a cup of tea out of her? She looks like she might have some cake, too."

Burnet's on the same side as the woman when she gets out.

"Annie McDiarmid." Too distressed to offer her hand. "I'm so glad you're here. I can't believe anyone would do this to little Fluffs."

Burnet can almost hear Lincoln's eyes go wide. Hopes Mrs McDiarmid isn't looking at him.

"Where is she, now?"

"He. He's where I found him." Mrs McDiarmid turns and starts up the neatly paved path that bisects her equally neat lawn. There's a bundle lying at the front step.

"I covered him with a towel," Mrs McDiarmid says. "So children wouldn't see him on the way to school." Her forehead creases with worry. "That was the right thing to do, wasn't it?"

"It's fine," Burnet says. Looks at the towel bundled on the step. A paw sticks out from underneath. Orange and white fur. Blood, too, dried onto the front step.

So close to home.

Brave bloody fox, leaving its kill right here.

Lincoln hangs back. Making it clear that this not important enough for him to engage unless he has to.

Keeping a professional head, Burnet asks, "How old was ... Fluffs?"

"Oh, coming up for ten. A ripe old age."

"And he was an outdoor cat?"

"Aye. But every night, without fail, he's in by eight for his evening cuddles. He watches the news with me, you know. On my lap. He loves it in the winter, when the fire's on."

"I'm sure." Burnet can't take her eyes off the towel, the paw, the dried blood. "Has he ever been in trouble before? Not with the law, I mean. But maybe ... has he got into fights with other cats – or maybe dogs – in the area?"

"He's not a scrappy cat," Mrs McDiarmid says. "That wee Jack Russell two doors down, at Mrs Maine's, he's a yappy little thing, and every time he starts off, Fluffs runs scared. I've asked her, you know, to keep the dog quiet. But she doesn't do a thing. If it was me, I'd muzzle it."

"But you can't think of anything unusual? I mean ..." Burnet sees the trees nearby. The nearness of the woods. "Could Fluffs have got in a fight with something else ... say a fox?"

"No, no, no. Never had any trouble like that before ..." She stops, then. "I mean, there's been a few things in the last year ... don't you have files on that?"

"On what?"

"Mrs Lochhead at twenty-two, her dog went missing in January. Then there was Mr Tibbs, this adorable black and white who moved in at fourteen, he went missing too."

"A rash of pet disappearances?"

"Aye."

Burnet considers her response. "But this is the first animal found that's been mutilated—"

"Murdered!"

"... Murdered, yes. This is the first one?"

"Aye. My Fluffs. Who could have done this?" A shake of the head. White curls bounce. "Shouldn't you look at the body?"

Lincoln's keeping his distance. Neutral expression, but his eyes say more than enough.

Burnet hunkers down. Lifts the towel.

She can't help herself: "Jesus!"

"Please," Mrs McDiarmid says, "don't take the Lord's name in vain!"

"I'm sorry," Burnet says, dropping the towel again. "I wasn't expecting ..."

Burnet's seen death before. A call about a woman who hadn't been answering her door – Burnet arriving to a close stinking of decay, breaking into the flat to find her decomposing in the bathtub. Heart attack. When Burnet found her, skin was discoloured, flesh was bloated. Almost half of her flooded away down the plughole when the bath emptied.

Why is this worse?

A fresh corpse. A small animal. Belly ripped, guts exposed.

"Something's chewed on the corpse." Not meaning to say it out loud.

Mrs McDiarmid *wails*.

Lincoln shrugs.

Great. Of course this is why he brought her along.

Make the tea.

Burnet tries not to clench her fists.

The old woman collapses against Burnet. Each sob shaking hard.

Lincoln gives a thumbs up and walks over. Finally.

Now he's had time to prepare himself, he doesn't show a reaction when he lifts the towel. Playing it cool. The big man in charge, while Burnet plays the role of the comforting woman.

Burnet slowly lets Mrs McDiarmid go. The old woman looks at Burnet with wet eyes that carry sad gratitude.

Lincoln says, "I know you don't want to hear this, but I believe that Fluffs has been the victim of an animal attack."

"What kind of animal?"

"WPC Burnet here already suggested foxes on the way over. Suppose I'd agree. Could be them. Or wildcats. They sometimes form communities in the woods. Much more vicious than domestic moggies."

"Well, what can you do about it?"

"We can't arrest foxes, I'm afraid. Or wildcats."

"You must be able to do something!"

"Nothing we can do, I'm afraid."

Mrs McDiarmid looks back to Burnet. "You looked at Fluffs, didn't you? An animal wouldn't do that. Not even a fox."

Burnet considers carefully. There's a line here. "You seem convinced that this wasn't an animal attack, Mrs McDiarmid. I wonder if you maybe have another reason for believing that perhaps a person or persons was behind what happened here?"

Mrs McDiarmid sags – all the air has escaped her in an instant. "At night," she says. "There's someone in the woods."

Lincoln looks at Burnet with a pained expression, careful that Mrs McDiarmid can't see.

Burnet says, "Someone in the woods?"

"He's out there." Pointing to the treeline. "At night, I can see him running through the trees. Not someone out for a jog, or whatever it is that the young people do nowadays, but someone actually hiding in the trees."

"What do you think they're doing out there?"

"Watching," Mrs McDiarmid says. "I see him watching the houses. I see him looking into the windows. Waiting."

"For what?"

"You've seen Fluffs," Mrs McDiarmid says. "I think we all know what he was waiting for."

6

FHQ. THE CAFETERIA. DOW BRINGS TEAS, shaking his head.

A voice from just behind Kelley: "Room for one more?" Kelley looks up.

WPC Burnet. They've crossed paths a few times. She's friends with Dow. Good friends. Department gossip has the older detective putting the moves on her. Kelley's pretty certain that's not the case.

Dow gestures for her to sit. "Surprised you aren't off for another photo shoot. Aren't you hero of the hour for bringing in the flasher?"

Burnet takes a breath before answering. "I think CID's the hero of the hour. Me? I just dressed in heels and had my hair down for a stroll through the park. Or that's how they see it, I suppose. Back on patrol. Back in uniform. Back to domestics and . . ." She stops, thinking about something. Then says, "Dead cats. Well, one dead cat. Reported as murder. A call out from an old lady in Birkhill."

Dow instantly says, "Foxes."

Burnet shrugs; not so sure.

Kelley says, "So what, then?" sensing she has more to say, doesn't know whether she should.

Dow says, "No wrong answers here."

Burnet takes a long breath. "I think it was a human being."

"With a knife?" Dow says. "You get some sick fu—"

"No," Burnet interrupts, suddenly forceful. "No knife. I ... I took the corpse down to the hospital, just to be sure. They took a look – after telling me they weren't vets – but they confirmed what I thought I'd seen."

"Which was?" Kelley asks, even though he thinks he knows the answer.

"Whoever did this ... they chewed at the cat's entrails. The marks confirmed it. Human. Whoever killed the cat, they tried to eat it, too."

Sick bastards in this world. Kelley thinks of them hiding in the shadows, hoping no one sees them.

His jaw tightens.

Dow says, "So why aren't we hearing about it?"

It wasn't a crime, per se. But horrific enough that it should be the talk of the station.

"Because Lincoln wrote up the report."

"And he doesn't agree with you?" Kelley says. "I mean, we could have a cha—"

"No," Burnet says. "Just leave it. No one's going to want to get involved when it's just a cat, are they?"

Kelley wants to say that he would get involved. Instead, he stays quiet.

* * *

End of shift. Kelley out of the suit, in civilian clothes. Important to dress differently off-duty.

Polis/Kelley.

Kelley/Polis.

Mark the lines. Don't let them bleed.

What his dad told him, shortly before his death.

He's inclined to believe Burnet about what happened to the cat. She's good polis. Good instincts. Doesn't matter she's a woman or that she had her picture taken by the papers on her first day of work. If she says it, then there's a good chance she's right.

Kelley's heard stories from other officers about the kind of thing people do to stray cats. Trapping them in bins, setting them alight, but this is something different.

What do you charge them with? Cat deaths don't make front pages. Making animal cruelty charges stick is difficult.

The unwritten rule of policing: law in action differs from law on paper.

Kelley splashes water on his face. Through the streaked mirror, sees bags under his eyes. When did he last take a day off? What else does he have in his life? What would be the point? There's the job, and then there's—

Nothing.

So much for Polis/Kelley, Kelley/Polis.

No girlfriend. No friends outside the force. Not even family. Dad dead as long as he's been, and Mum ... Last time they spoke? At his father's funeral. Most of the words between them were four letters.

Kelley splashes more water to wash memories out of his mind.

Time to go home. Maybe stop in at a pub along the way. Sink a couple. Stop his brain spiralling. Always the same at the end of a shift. Faulty fucking wiring up there. Constant need for stimulation. No off switch.

Stairwell down to ground level. Couple of uniforms on the third-floor landing. Kelley stops just above.

"—the noise coming out of Interview One?"

"What do you reckon?"

"Whatever, he deserves it. He's a pervert, right?"

"Aye, but—"

"But what? He tried to rape a WPC."

"I mean, aye, he exposed himself, but he didn't—"

"Look, whatever the fuck DS Garner's doing in there, he deserves that and more."

Kelley's stomach knots. Tight and hard. Almost enough to double over.

Fuck it.

Most people might think the pervert deserves what he gets. But Garner's *police*.

There are rules when you're police. What's the point if you just ignore them?

It's not the beating that angers Kelley.

There's a difference between bending and breaking rules. Garner's as much of a crook as anyone in the cells, even if he's protected by the thin blue line.

It's been simmering a while. All those implications about Kelley's father, that there was something else in the way he died, something darker than the news reports and the official investigation ever revealed.

Fuck it.

Push past the uniforms. Out the stairwell. Down the corridor: Interview One.

Pause outside the door.

A moment of doubt?

The noise from inside sounds muffled in the corridor.

This isn't the time.

Aye? Then when is the time?

The definition of madness – Kelley read somewhere – is doing the same thing every time and expecting different results.

If no one stands up and demands change, then it doesn't happen.

Through the door.

Garner with the guy on the table, holding him down with one hand, punching kidneys with the other.

Pause.

"Finally grow a pair? You want a piece of this arsehole?"

Kelley moves fast. His dad taught him to box, took him the gym when Kelley was a little older. The reflexes don't leave. He's got a right hook, but more, he's fast.

Garner's big, but moves slow. Kelley ducks under and inside.

Jabs for the midriff, slides behind to kick the bigger man's knees out. There's a difference between fighting in the ring and the real world.

Garner goes down. Head cracking the side of the table.

The flasher flees into a corner. Disoriented. The door's open. He could escape. But he's thrown, can't see the obvious.

Kelley, finding time slowing for a moment, thinks: Maybe Garner's beating shook the prick's brain.

Garner pulls himself up, using the table for balance.

Kelley keeps his distance. His heart pumps faster. On his toes. His old man's boxing lessons play in his head on a loop. Instincts had been drilled into him.

All he can see is Garner.

Garner also keeps his distance. Spits. "This isn't your problem."

"You were beating a suspect."

"Who deserved to be fucking beaten."

"Jesus *fuck*, Garner! We're polis!"

"And we do what we have to, to get the job done. You think he doesn't deserve a wee slap in the puss?"

"I think he deserves to be dealt with within the law."

Garner shakes his head. "That first day, that was kind of a test, aye? An initiation. See what kind of polis you were." He leans on the table, like he's out of breath. It's a small gesture, but Kelley sees it. "What happened was, I saw you were a fucking spastic. No head for police work. Your old man'd be so fucking disappointed to know what an eejit you turned out to be. Maybe he dropped you on your head when you were a bairn. He knew how it worked. Someone needs to show these bastards what's what."

Kelley simply says: "Leave him alone." Trying to ignore the roaring in his skull. Anger – the mention of his father a blindside jab. Should have seen it coming, but still fucking hurts.

Garner's head turns slightly, towards the door.

Kelley lets himself glance in that direction. Sees other officers and detectives waiting there. None of them coming inside. But they're gathering.

Kelley says, "You want to do this with an audience?"

Kelley forces himself to relax. Knows whose side the other coppers will take if he wades in first.

Garner's on Kelley fast, grabbing the smaller detective's head in both hands and throwing him back so his skull cracks off the wall. The world shakes and shudders. Kelley's vision goes. There's no pain at first, and then it seeps through his brain and down his spine. He tries to fight back, but for some reason he can't move. Stuck in treacle.

Flashbacks.

The ring.

First losing fight.
His father telling him: go low, get under the punches.

But every impact slows him. Every punch paralyses him enough for Garner to get another in.

He's against the post. Knows he's going down.

And he's on the floor.

Back in the interview room.

Dow in the room now. Pulling Garner back.

Other officers shout their disapproval, braying that the fight's over too soon.

Kelley wipes his face with the back of his hand. Sharp pain in his nose. Vision fritzing. Blood on the back of his hand. In the back of his throat, too; thick when he swallows. He tries to breathe through his nose. That taste washes even thicker down into his throat, and he thinks he could drown.

He's heard about it before, people drowning in their own blood.

Kelley looks up again. DCI Redman's in the room now. The shouting from the other detectives has stopped. Dow lets go of Garner.

Redman looks at the two men.

First Garner.

Then Kelley.

He walks out the room. Not a word. No need.

Kelley closes his eyes.

7

BURNET COMES IN OFF THE BEAT when the news hits.

The station is buzzing.

Gossip is the lifeblood of any building. Burnet worked that out in school; no surprise the adult world functions similarly.

People love a good narrative. Especially one that makes them feel superior.

Renate Hutton's at the front desk, perusing paperwork. The civilian assistant's eyes glow when she sees Burnet. Bursting to say something.

Burnet beats her to the punch. "What happened?"

"Rammie in CID." Her tone is clear: this isn't just any brawl. This is juicy.

Renate beckons. Burnet leans in. Hush-hush confidential.

"Who?" Burnet whispers.

"Your friend Dow." Burnet's heart hammers in her ribcage. Hard to picture the old man in a fight. "It was his other friend, that young one. Handsome. His dead dad got him on the job?"

Kelley. Makes sense. That look in his eyes: always on the verge of losing control. Like he thinks the rest of the world is drowning in stupidity and only he has the answers.

Never trust someone who has all the answers. Usually, they're the wrong ones.

"Him and Garner," Renate says. "Like we didn't know it was coming."

Burnet's heard whispers. Kelley's first day in CID, his beating in the multis. Garner claiming their separation was accidental. Kelley saying otherwise. The two men avoiding each other after that.

CID taking sides.

Mostly with Garner.

"How'd it happen?"

"Your flasher. Garner was having a wee word with him. The detective constable, he goes into the room and lamps him one. For no reason."

"No reason?"

There was a reason.

Most likely? Garner being an arsehole.

Stranger things in Heaven and Earth, Horatio . . .

"So I hear. Although . . . he's taking it higher . . . making a real case out of it."

Renate says, "He's an eejit, that boy. Garner was going to give the pervert a hard time – we all know it. But . . . he'd been going to rape you. So he deserves whatever's coming."

"But he didn't rape me. We stopped him raping another woman."

"But he could have raped you. If the other officers hadn't been there. He meant to. He meant to rape those other girls, too. Men like that, once they get confidence, you know . . ."

Burnet pulls back and heads through the double doors into the main building.

* * *

Locker room: civvies on, clock-off time. After a full day on the beat, even fresh clothes feel sweat-drenched.

Outside, in the corridor, she sees Dow. Touches his elbow as they pass.

He stops. "Is it true?"

He knows instantly what she's talking about. Probably the only thing anyone's been talking about since it happened. "About the fight? Aye. Was coming sooner or later. Wee hothead, he is."

"Really? I mean, Garner's been pushing Kelley from day one."

"He didn't push him today. This was unprovoked."

"You've been working with Kelley for months now. You know that he—"

He shakes his head. "Lad's a walking contradiction. Misplaced anger and righteous conviction in one package. I think even he doesn't know why he does things." He pauses for a moment, thinking about what he's just said. "Heart's in the right place, like. He sees where the force is heading. Where it should be heading. Problem is, he wants to take it there before anyone else is ready."

"No one's listening to him. Bound to make anyone a little cranky, right?"

"Guess you'd know how that feels." A hand lightly placed on her shoulder, then removed fast like she's burned him somehow. "More young men like him on the force, I think they'll help women move forward."

"More young men will help women?"

"Change has to come from within. You know how it is already, even with old duffers like me. Are we really going to change the habits of a lifetime because people tell us to?"

"You're not so bad."

He smiles, but there's no humour there. "Guess it means there's an opening in CID. The boy's in with Redman now, making his case. But you know which way that prick's going to swing."

"An opening?" Burnet says. "Let me guess. For some young buck?"

"Guess so."

But there's a look in his eyes Burnet thinks she might just have imagined. Something that could be encouragement.

8

DCS REDMAN ENTERS THE ROOM.

Kelley sits and stares.

Silence. For maybe a minute.

Redman grabs a chair. The desk forms a barrier between the men. "You don't have anything to say?"

"I've said what I need to."

"Publicly, too." Redman takes a deep breath. Leans back, locks his hands behind his head. Hisses through gritted teeth – a mechanic deciding how to pad his estimate.

Kelley says, "Everyone knows about Garner. And no one does anything."

"Garner knows the city," Redman says. "Knows the difference between how things should work and how they do work."

"That sounds like an excuse."

Redman leans forward now. Keep his eyes locked with Kelley's. "It's a fact, son. Look, I know you and him have bad blood—"

"He paid off a bunch of thugs to beat seven shades of shite out of me."

"So you say. His story is that you got separated, and that you ran into trouble on your own. That neck of the woods? I can believe it. I should never have assigned you to shadow him."

"Because of my father?"

"He thinks you blame him for what happened."

Kelley stifles a laugh. "The thought has crossed my mind more than once."

"They were friends. Not grab-a-pint-after-a-shift friends, but they worked well together, Garner and your father. Singing from the same hymn sheet."

Kelley clamps down his instincts. No inch will be given. "I didn't blame him ... not until ... I mean, you know there were questions to be asked about what happened to my father."

"We caught the bastard who stabbed him."

"And he killed himself, right?"

"Maybe we leaned on him a little hard."

"*We?*"

"What are you saying?"

"I saw the files. Garner was the one who interviewed him. And then, just a few hours later, he happens to kill himself?"

"This is a serious charge."

"Add it to the list."

Kelley sits back. Folds his arms.

Redman stays stock still. Basilisk.

"We're supposed to be an example," Kelley says, breaking first. "As police officers, we should be showing people that the system *works*."

"The system does work. And you know, it's best if Joe Public thinks it works differently to the way it does. The people we're after, son, they're *criminals*. And what that means is not that they break the law, but that they make life worse for people

50

out there. When you're on the street, what you're supposed to learn is that there's a difference between what we want to work and what really works."

Kelley doesn't respond. Giving as good as he's getting.

"But that's neither here nor there. And you can think what you like if it makes you feel better about what happened to your old man. But you assaulted a senior officer in the execution of his—"

"He was beating a suspect."

"The pervert ... pardon me, the *suspect* ... was being interviewed, yes. He admits that Garner was intimidating him, but he has not lodged a formal complaint."

"Because his jaw had been wired shut."

Redman shakes his head. His lips stretch into what might be a smile. "His jaw was wired shut, because he got caught up in the fracas between yourself and DS Garner. Had you not interfered... intent on battering a fellow officer, no less ... in such a confined space ... then he would not have had to write out his statement on lined paper." Deep breath, then. Eyes fixed on Kelley. "Which would have been a relief for all of us, because, frankly, my four-year-old's handwriting is more comprehensible. But we got there in the end. And his statement supports DS Garner's version of events."

Kelley gets it now: this meeting is about sending a message: *Let other coppers do the job their way. Do not create a scene.*

The thin blue line.

On one side the polis, on the other side everyone else. You're supposed to keep everything bad on the right side of the line, so that the citizens know nothing about it. Cop problems are dealt with internally and quietly. And you always yield to those with experience and power.

An old saying pops into his head: *Who watches the watchmen?*
Pretend two and two make five. For the sake of your career.
Pretend that everything's all right.
Think of the bigger picture.

But the bigger picture for Kelley is what his old man used to tell him:

The police should be better than the criminals.

And Kelley's forced to wonder: was that a lie? Like saying Santa Claus is real?

"But I can't ignore facts," Redman says. Calming it now, adjusting his tone. He reaches into his desk drawer. Takes out a pack of cigs. Lights up. Sits back.

No longer the arsehole boss; now the avuncular father-figure.

What he's saying: All of this is being done for Kelley's own good. Redman really cares for him. Cares for all the detectives under his command.

"I can't just sweep this under the carpet. It wasn't just confined to CID – uniforms, civilian staff, all kinds of people witnessed you attacking another detective for no good reason."

"Have you asked them what they saw?"

"They all say the same thing," Redman says. "That there was no reason for you to burst into that room, that there was no reason for you to yell at Garner, much less try and lamp him one."

Kelley gets a twinge in his ribs. Still sore, even after a day. Bruising, luckily. Nothing worse.

"So I have a decision to make," Redman says, taking a drag. "And it's not an easy one." A pause. Kelley thinks he can hear the whole station hold its breath. "A lot of people have asked that I discharge you from the force. It might surprise you to learn that DS Garner was not among those who supported the move."

It does surprise Kelley. He tries to remain impassive.

"In light of that – and in light of the fact that in the eyes of the press you're the son of a hero, and therefore good for Tayside Constabulary's public image – I'm going to defuse the situation by removing you from the department."

"What do you mean?"

"You're back in uniform. On the beat. Back to responding to muggings and old ladies whose cats get stuck up trees. You'll take a pay cut, of course. And you'll be suspended for the next three weeks as a disciplinary measure." He regards Kelley for a moment, maybe searching for a hint of reaction. "After that ... we'll make a formal decision regarding your future career. I mean, if you wanted to hand in your notice right now – for the good of the force, of course, to show that it was *your* choice to admit to a mistake – then I wouldn't object—"

Kelley stands. "Let me see if the uniform still fits."

He doesn't want to leave.

Redman says nothing. Taps ash into the tray on his desk.

Kelley's hands form tight fists as he leaves, down the stairs, out the back entrance. Waits until he's out of sight of the building before punching the nearest wall.

* * *

Kelley bellies up to the bar. Money in hand. Blood still wet on his knuckles. "Wee heavy," he says. "And a half-n-half."

The bartender looks about to say something, then decides the better of it and gets to work. Drinks down, money taken without a word.

The pub's mostly empty. A couple of regulars huddle in a corner. Old duffers playing dominoes and slowly rotting.

Kelley downs the whisky from the half-n-half. Burning in his throat like paint stripper. But that's the point. Strength, not taste.

How Kelley learned to deal with bad news: *Be a man. Drink it up and get the fuck on with life.*

So much for progressive ideas.

Drink. Don't think.

Except all he can do is think.

When he gets angry, he gets sloppy, stupid. Act first, think later.

He's not a thug. He's smart. But he's ruled by impulse when he allows it.

Old weakness.

Why he went into CID, thinking it was the thinking copper's place where impulse wouldn't rule.

What he expected: solving crimes, mysteries, out-thinking crooks.

Truth: it more was more of the same. The crooks were never smart. The work wasn't mentally taxing. He was no Sherlock Holmes. Didn't need to be.

Which was why men like Garner could advance beyond their means. Getting confessions became a game of who could punch the hardest.

Both Garner and Redman implying his father knew this.

Tolerated it.

Was maybe even involved?

His father's death never added up. Kelley used to tell himself it was just dumb luck, the way he died. Could happen to any copper on the beat.

Kelley joined up in his memory.

But his father's death never sat easy.

He used the opportunity to look into the arrest reports, the transcripts. Real detective work: following evidence and finding the trail.

Look at the arrest reports: his father and Garner pursuing a suspect in several muggings. The suspect runs. They split to catch him in a pincer movement. Suspect runs into an alley. Garner goes round the building. Kelley's old man runs in direct pursuit.

The suspect produces a knife to "defend" himself against the approaching detective. There's a struggle – this part conjecture, as the suspect's own testimony seems confused – and the blade pierces the officer's side.

Wounds. Eviscerates. Rips through.

Kelley's father falls. Internal bleeding. Organs ruptured.

Garner finally arrives from the other direction. Tackles the suspect. The suspect gains concussion and three broken ribs, tries and escape. Garner gives chase, gets him in the cuffs. Returns to his fellow officer.

Finds him close to death.

The ambulance arrives twenty minutes later.

Eighteen minutes too late.

Garner insists that Kelley's father "told him to pursue".

It doesn't feel right. No one on the committee sees that, however. The arrest is *righteous*. The charge of murdering an officer is added to the suspect's sheet.

Garner leads the interviews.

The transcripts read wrong. Garner polite but firm, and never coming close to being physical.

Not someone Kelley recognises.

And then there's the confession – there, in black and white, but still feeling wrong. The speech patterns changing, the suspect being matter of fact where before he was fuzzy. Again, like the words had been typed up by a different person.

The final notes give Kelley real pause.

The suspect commits suicide in custody. Hanging by their own shoelaces. The coroner's report confirms the death by strangulation. Notes other injuries that may be "historical" but discounts them.

Nothing in the reports adds up.

Not enough for Kelley.

Not enough for anyone who might have half a brain cell.

Kelley has considered confronting Garner. But Garner has friends in the right places. Kelley does not. His father's name isn't enough.

His plan became:

Change through example.

Show a better way.

But don't rock the boat.

So what happened the other day?

Did the dam just burst?

Jesus, stop thinking about it.

He downs the half pint. Closes his eyes. Listens to the noise of the pub.

The bartender's listening to the radio. There's chatter about Scotland entering a team for the world cup in Argentina. Speculation, this far out, but they sound excited, like it's a real possibility. Maybe it is, too. Kelley doesn't follow the football too closely these days. Something about guarding the matches at Dens and Tannadice the last few years putting him off. The beautiful game? The ugly aftermath.

He opens his eyes.

A second half-n-half waiting.

He didn't ask.
But:
Fuck it.
Drown it all out.
Wake up tomorrow. Pretend everything's back to fucking normal.

9

OLD MAN HANNIGAN GESTURES FOR MARTIN to take a seat.

Back room of Hannigan's Autos. The sound of motors, drills, local radio, muffled through too-thin walls.

Papers stacked up on shelves. MOT certificates pending, bills of sale, part numbers and more. No apparent order, but maybe he has a system.

Martin takes the seat. The springs squeak. He worries that it might fall apart.

Old Man Hannigan perches on the plywood desk.

"Me and your da go way back."

Prepared. He's practised this.

Martin wonders how it's going to happen. Is this a threat, or is this a firing?

"And I know he can be tough to talk to."

Unexpected. Martin shifts in the seat. Springs squeak.

"I know you're not interested in being a mechanic. But it's a decent job, and in this economy ..." Hannigan shrugs.

Martin nods like he understands.

But he doesn't.

What's the old man trying to say?

"He just wants what's best for you. I know you don't want to be here. But maybe you can make the best of it? Till you figure things out?"

Martin thinks:

Who grassed?

Someone telling the old man how he'd been late the last few weeks. Not his fault. Sleep coming hard at night. The scratching at the window. The wolf outside, wanting to be let in. The only way to keep it out is to stay awake, stay vigilant.

Or else ...

You end up like Mrs McDiarmid's cat.

Prey.

"I ..." Throat closing around the words. Cough and try again: "I think I'd rather be working with animals."

Hannigan's brow creases. The lines go deep, his leathered skin loose around his skull. "You tell your dad this?"

Martin spits back, "Think he'd understand?"

"Maybe." A pause. Then, gentle: "Tell you what ... You buck up your ideas round here, I'll have a chat with him for you? See if we can't work something out?"

"Why?"

"Why what?"

"Why not just fire me?"

"Like I said, me and your da, we go back a long way. And he asked me to take care of you. Because he's worried. He doesn't want his son to become a waster."

Martin nods.

He's here because he has no choice.

He's here because he knows – no exaggeration – his dad would kill him otherwise.

"Me and your old fella, we go back, so we do. Back to the docks, you must know. I was his cut man, then. You know what a cut man is?" He doesn't wait for an answer. "The man who cleans up the blood, makes sure the fighter's getting some water down him between rounds. That's what I did. Now, bare knuckle, it's tough stuff. The stuff you see on TV – Ali floating like a butterfly and stinging like a bee – that's good and all, but bare knuckles're where a man proves he's a man. That's the problem, you see? Take a sport, clean it up, make it safe. It's not supposed to be ..."

Martin's nodding, but he's no longer listening.

He's thinking about his dad.

His dad – a man of violence, even in the way he talks.

No wonder Martin's always had nightmares.

His dad inside.

The wolf outside.

He daren't sleep.

And he wants to. So, so very badly.

Just close his eyes.

And disappear.

10

FOUR WEEKS LATER.

Burnet walks out of the interview, forcing herself to stay upright. Trying to banish the idea that this is the worst day of her life.

They pushed hard. Asked about her ambitions, and her stance on working with men who may not have previously worked so closely with "the fairer sex".

Stating that most women who join CID are happier in the squad room or working more mundane cases like traffic. Warning her that female detectives could be a target for certain types of criminals.

Like she didn't already know. Like it wasn't in her files, what happened with the flasher, or that time a suspect tried to rape her when she placed him under arrest for causing affray.

The interview panel: five men with white hair and beer bellies who hadn't walked the beat in decades.

She had expected them. And she'd expected to speak up for herself and other women in front of them.

The truth? She sat across the desk and took their shite.

Why?

Fuck it. They wanted her to fail, that's what she thinks.

A deep breath outside the women's toilets. Into a stall, rest for a moment.

She doesn't cry.

Doesn't breathe heavy or feel panic.

Just disappointment. In the world and in herself.

* * *

Dow's waiting in the canteen. Smiles, then falters. "It can't have been that bad." Can't even convince himself.

What can she say? "They make it tough on everyone."

They join the line for coffees.

Dow says, "When I went in for my interview, they put me right on the spot. You know what they said? I was too soft. Too *soft*. Jesus, but right then and there I thought I'd messed up before I even set foot in the room. I wondered why they even wanted to talk to me. Maybe just to humiliate me."

"But you got the job."

"Aye, but what I'm saying is that I didn't think I had. Same as you, now."

She tries to nod but can't. Dow's heart is in the right place, but he doesn't understand that being a man has advantages.

"I put in a good word. For what it's worth."

"It's the feeling of anticlimax," she says. "You know? When you've done something, and you should feel something afterwards, but all you really feel is like there's a missed opportunity, like ... *is that it?*"

Dow pays for the coffees. They grab a table.

"You won't know," he says, "until the word comes in." His blue-grey eyes are clear and encouraging.

Burnet thinks about her father. What he said to her the night before: *prepare yourself for disappointment.* Like he wanted her to fail.

Dow brushes his hand over hers. The kind of gesture her father would never give.

But he pulls back quickly. In this station, she understands. The gossip. A male detective showing affection to a female colleague? That'd have the tongues wagging.

One of the other reasons they don't want her in CID. They didn't say, but she knew what they were thinking all through the interview:

The Friday Girl? Who'd be able to resist that? A distraction for the red-blooded males in the department.

Enough to drive someone mad.

* * *

Home that night – up to her room straight from the front door.

The walls are bare. Pop star pictures long gone – she almost misses the comfort of Donny Osmond looking down on her – but nothing has replaced them. On the bedside table is a picture of her at five or six, sitting on a fence next to her father. A country walk.

The little girl smiles broadly. Not a care in the world. Daddy loves her.

Downstairs, she finds Mum laying out the cutlery. She looks at Burnet and smiles. "Elizabeth," she says, "your dad's on his way home."

Mum knows what today was. She's waiting for her daughter to broach the subject.

Or else she already knows the answer and doesn't need to say anything.

Burnet sits. Looks at the cutlery, perfectly shiny, perfectly placed on a perfectly ironed tablecloth.

The front door opens.

"Alan!" Mum yells. "It's all ready. Hang up your coat and I'll be through. Elizabeth's already home."

Noises from the hall as her dad hangs up his jacket, takes off his shoes and replaces them with slippers. Burnet doesn't turn round in her chair.

When he comes in, they look at each other for a moment. It's odd, almost challenging.

He sucks in a quick breath and says, "Well?"

"Well?" she says in return.

"Come on," he says. "I'm asking, aren't I? I'm supposed to be interested, right?"

"I haven't asked yet, Alan!" Mum's voice sails through from the kitchen. "I thought she wanted to wait until you were home."

Dad locks eyes with daughter. "Well?"

"I won't know until tomorrow."

Mum comes in from the kitchen, a smile painted across her face. Steaming dishes of vegetables are laid in the centre of the table. Like a Sunday lunch. "I'm sure she did well." She looks at Dad. "As your father is, too, I'm sure."

Dad says, "You're certainly ambitious."

"That's a bad thing?"

He flinches. Looks away. "I just think...maybe too ambitious."

She thinks about the dad in the photograph. What happened? When did he stop indulging his daughter's dreams?

When she joined the force.

Their first argument.

Not a job for a young woman.

"I'm a good officer." Speaking to the memory of that argument more than her dad in the here and now. "I can be a great detective, too. It's what I want."

"I'm just worried. About your future. About your *happiness*." The emphasis on that word says everything.

She holds back a laugh. "My happiness? What would make me happy, Dad?"

A crash from the kitchen. Mum dropping something.

"I know you have this idea about what will make you happy, but you have to trust me ... everyone in this world, they want the same thing ..."

"Aye," Burnet says. "Love, kids, marriage."

"Security."

The laugh comes out now, sharp and short. Vicious. "Would you be like this if I was a teacher? You know, something safe? Something that women are *supposed* to do."

"Your mum was happy as a teacher."

"And then she had me. She never went back to it. Couldn't have loved it that much, could she?"

The door opens again. Mum lays down the dinner plates. "I was happy with looking after you. And your dad brought in the money." Words upbeat, eyes distance.

Burnet shakes her head. "Marriage and kids?" Another bitter bark of a laugh. "You saw me when we met Janice, remember?"

"Aye, and her lovely wee bairn," Mum says, heading back into the kitchen.

Doesn't matter. Not talking to her. Talking to her dad. Tone steady, hold back the anger, keep it cool and clear. "You saw what happened when she tried to make me hold that wee girl."

Keep those fists clenched below the table. Don't show the anger.

"All babies cry," her dad says.

"You're not listening. I was the one who wanted to cry. It was crying because it knew I didn't want to hold it."

Mum's back, ladling out the meat and gravy onto the plates. "It's different when it's your own," she says, in a sing-song tone, like this is all just going to blow over.

"When you meet someone," her dad says, "you know that they'll be intimidated by what you do? I mean, it's a man's job, really, isn't it? Do you really want to wind up a spinster? Who'll carry on the family?"

"The only girls who don't have children," Mum says, "are lesbians. And no daughter of mine is a lesbian."

Burnet can't help herself. She stands, scraping back her chair. "I'm going out." She stops at the door. "Leave some if you want. I'll heat it up when I get back."

11

KELLEY PULLS THE MURPHY BED DOWN from the wall. Unmade, the mattress sagging from years of use.

He's only been here fifteen months, but knows Mrs Marsh hasn't changed the room in decades, other than putting in the TV. Even then, it's an old set from the fifties, before Kelley was even born.

Outside, on Union Street, punters pour into pubs.

Kelley grew up across the water – in Newport, on the edge of Fife. Night-time noises relegated to the rustle of animals, rain rattling against the window.

Now, the near-constant noise of the town is soothing. Even raucous raised voices and passionate arguments punctuating chuck-out time.

Kelley turns on the TV. It takes a moment to warm up. The picture's fuzzy at best. On BBC2, he sees the third episode of *Law and Order* is due later – this one from the point of view of the barrister.

A whole show dedicated to the corruption in British policing?

Watching the first episode, Kelley had choked with anger. He'd expected anger. Outcry. What he got was a sanitised corruption. There were things not even the BBC could get away with showing, it seemed.

After, he lies on the bed, arms behind his head, listening to the noise of the city.

Later, he dreams about his father. But there's rain battering against the windows of the room they're sitting in, and the noise drowns out the other man's words, no matter how hard Kelley strains to hear.

* * *

He wakes at six. Checks his watch by the moonlight.

Sweaty and damp. Nightmares? The details fade.

Change of clothes. Downstairs. Outside. Fresh air.

The city is still, holding its breath in anticipation. But of what, Kelley can't say for sure.

He walks past the Overgate, round near the McManus building. Women wait in some of the doorways. One or two step forward. But then they seem to realise something about him, and step away again.

Pound the pavements. Count the steps. Keep the beat.

Blood throbs through his skull. His brain shakes with each pulse.

Swallow hard. Keep walking.

Past the McManus, now up towards Meadowside.

No destination in mind.

Walking the arteries of the city as it comes awake, stretches.

All he needs to do is keep moving. For now, that will be enough.

A distraction. A purpose.

Until he can figure out what to do next.

12

TWO MORE WEEKS PASS.

Burnet folds her uniform the night after she gets the news, carefully placing it in a box under her bed. Thinking, *this is a mistake*. Sooner or later she'll have to pull the skirt out once more and smooth down the hat as they put her back on the bloody beat.

Sorry, doll ... Bad communication ... No place for a pretty thing like you ...

But in the meantime ...

CID.

Plainclothes.

Some confusion over what that means. The guidelines seem arbitrary, as though no one's really thought about what a plainclothes woman detective should wear. The men have a choice: any old suit and tie they want.

The first discussion after Redman told her she'd got the post had been about whether she could wear trousers.

Women who'd previously worked CID, usually in traffic and filing, had remained in uniform during their stint. But as Burnet was working cases alongside Dow – at the senior detective's insistence, apparently – it seemed only right she should be in plainclothes as well.

After the brief, one-sided decision – skirt, white blouse, good shoes – he'd hurried her to a meeting room where the Chief Constable was waiting for her. He beamed, offered a hand. Shook strong and brief. "It's good for the department. Having a woman work cases in capacity alongside the male detectives. It shows Dundee as a forward-thinking force."

Burnet tried to look grateful. She liked the Chief. He took pride in the history of Dundee and Tayside. Kept reminding everyone in the room how female officers had been 'the backbone of the force since even the early 1900s. He'd written a piece for the Police Yearbook in 1974 that had made an impression on Burnet. It was one of the reasons she had decided to apply for the force.

More: he was a hero. In late '77, he'd allowed himself to be swapped for a hostage during a bungled effort to rob a post office. They'd held a shotgun to his head, forced him into a car, resulting in a tense car chase.

In the end, the Chief had managed to resolve the situation. The man who'd taken him hostage got fifteen years. The woman who'd been with him got six months.

And the Chief Constable got to be a hero. A man seen as taking real responsibility for law and order, and the safety of the public.

"It looks even better," the Chief Constable had said, talking to Redman specifically, "when our first plainclothes detective is also a Friday Girl. So make sure you take good care of her."

That part rankled her.

She isn't a publicity opportunity.

She doesn't want to be one.

On her vanity: a frame with the cutting staring out. Mum had insisted she put it on display – to "remind herself how the world sees you".

Burnet turns the frame round every day when she comes home. Every day, while she's out, Mum turns it back round again. A passive-aggressive war of attrition. No words spoken – continuous and without end.

Now she looks at the photo, and a girl she doesn't quite recognise stares back. She remembers putting on full makeup, letting them tell her that maybe she should do something a little more with her hair. *Go on, love, give us a smile!* The eyes are trying for bright and cheery, but with something hidden there between the tiny pricks of ink that replicate her face.

Tayside Police's Friday Girl!

Bubbly Elizabeth Burnet, 21, wants to make a difference by walking the beat.

All the right words, but not necessarily with the right meaning.

She just wants to be polis.

To be good at her job.

The papers don't matter. Being bubbly doesn't matter. Being the "face" of the force is of no interest to her.

But these are sacrifices she must make.

This is what it means to be a girl – she wishes she could think, *woman* – in a world where the default is always a man.

* * *

First shift.

Renate on reception grins. "Looking sharp."

Take a breath. Walk through the double doors.

A few stares as she heads up to CID. The WPCs nod in greeting. The men appear embarrassed, as though she has the power to cut off their balls if they dare look at her the wrong way.

Not a bad feeling. Better than them stuck between wanting her to shag or mother them.

In some cases, thinking, *both*.

In CID, she half-expects a spaghetti western scene – where the stranger walks into the bar and everyone stops what they're doing. The last notes of the piano fade into silence, and someone spits out a challenge.

Instead: only three detectives on duty.

Garner prods one-fingered at a typewriter. Extreme concentration. Whether it's the technology or basic grammar that's causing him trouble, Burnet can't tell.

Garner's a big man. Broad shoulders. At the typewriter, at the desk, he looks like a giant playing with a child's toy. Hemmed in by the paperwork, forced into a space that's too confined for his frame.

Peck. Peck. Peck.

At another desk, a young DC – Ernie Bright – stubs out a cigarette.

There's a third Burnet recognises but can't name, screwing up paper balls and throwing them into a bin.

Her assigned desk is opposite Dow. He's not here yet. She takes a seat. Paperwork waits.

She fills in the forms with a pen.

The *peck-peck-peck* of Garner's typing goes silent. She doesn't look up. His chair scrapes across the floor. Footsteps. She still doesn't look up.

"This is the future, aye?"

She puts her pen down with deliberate slowness. He looms over her, making sure he uses his full size. A big man, even if he is out of shape. Best thing you can say about his features is that you wouldn't want to meet him down a dark alley.

Polis or thug? Someone like Garner, it's hard to tell.

"So you're serious?" Pushing for a response.

"About the job? Aye."

"No job for a girl."

"I'm not a girl."

"Sorry." Not meaning it. "*Woman*." His lips curl when he says the word. "Aye, well, got to say it's a bloody sight better looking across at you than it was that streak of piss, Kelley."

She returns to the paperwork. Scribbles as she speaks. "I heard he had you on the ground. That other officers had to interfere before, you know, he actually hurt you."

She knows what she's doing – poking a very angry bear. If she wants to make an impression, she has to give as good as she's going to get. The first punch must belong to her.

She waits for his response.

The only sound is her pen skritching across the paper.

Then: "Should be careful who you listen to round here. Believing that kind of shite could get you in trouble. And you don't want to get into trouble, right? Our wee poster girl. Teacher's pet or whatever."

He walks away. She keeps pen to paper.

Focus on the questions and answers. Throw up a silent prayer that he's done for now.

Garner raises his voice. "Think about what happened to that wee shite who used to sit there. Believing his own press, thinking he was better than the rest of us. Don't think I don't know what he was doing, and don't think I don't know you two are friends, or whatever it is. So just think about what happened to him when he stepped out of line. And he's the son of a fucking hero. Remember that. Who're you? Some wee lass whose face gets us good press?"

She scribbles faster.

No one else says a word.

Peck-peck-peck resumes again.

Hitting the keys just to remind her that he's there. That he'll always be there.

13

ONE WEEK LATER, AND BURNET'S LATE for the morning briefing. Problems with the bus. Not that it matters. This isn't school: if you're late, you catch up.

Dow fills her in: "I volunteered us for this one. Because something about it made me think of you."

"What?"

They're walking down from CID to the ground floor. Burnet hasn't even had time to remove her coat.

"Remember that dead cat last month? The official line was animal attack?"

"Aye," she says. "Although, officially, it was more like, let's just write anything down so the crazy old biddy stops calling."

"You tried to talk to me about it," he says. On the ground now, out the back entrance to the car park. "Me and the boy – back when he was still in favour. In the canteen. You said it wasn't an animal attack."

"Human teeth," she says. "The bite marks." She takes a breath. Forcing down anger. "They passed it on to Garner. He typed some shite, filed a report, and that was the end."

"Except for the woman's calls."

Mrs McDiarmid calling several times in the days following the death of Fluffs. Soon enough there was a codeword so Garner could pretend he was out of the office.

"She didn't feel like Garner treated her with respect," Burnet says as they head out of the building.

"Surprised she didn't go the papers."

"She did." Into Dow's car, now. Leather seat cracks as she slides in the passenger's side. "They told her to get knotted. Which was when she started calling me. She thought maybe I'd be able to do something." Seatbelt on. Sudden memory: early days in uniform, talking to primary schools about road and car safety. The kids asking if she knew Kevin Keegan or Alvin Stardust since they did road safety adverts on the telly. "You know, being the Friday Girl and all."

"I forgot I was working with a celebrity," Dow turns the key. Two attempts, then he remembers the choke. "That didn't make any difference?"

"All I could do was tell her that it had been given to a senior detective and that he had made his report. I wasn't a detective. Pretty soon, she gave up."

"But you believed her? That it wasn't an animal?"

"Unless there's a lion out by Tentsmuir no one knows about."

It would make for real headlines if they found one.

She settles back as they hit the streets. Dow reaches down and turns on the radio. The BBC's Radio 4 Scotland service. She's heard they're planning to replace it with a dedicated Scottish radio station sometime later in the year. Maybe something to do with all the talk of devolution that had been in the news. Rumours of a referendum, a vote on Scotland's future sometime in '79.

The idea doesn't sit well. Burnet's proud to be Scottish, but she's no dyed-in-the-wool Nationalist. The SNP? They strike her as troublemakers more than anything. And she has a feeling that this referendum won't make any difference anyway.

As they hit the Kingsway, she asks, "So why are we going back out? Has she started calling again?"

Dow looks at her. "I'm sorry," he says. "I ... I should have been clearer ... There was a call this morning, and I thought I recognised the name. When they mentioned the cat, I made the connection. Specifically, the complainant, Mrs McDiarmid. She's been murdered."

Burnet gets a sinking feeling. Nothing to do with Dow's driving.

Now she knows why Dow wants her on this call. More than giving her a chance.

The dead cat, the dead woman.

There's a connection. Maybe she's the only one he can trust is going to see it.

* * *

Burnet gets out of the car. The air turns thick. Like she's wading through mud, pushing against it.

Dreamlike.

The house doesn't seem real.

Something half-remembered.

Maybe it's the light? Last call-out, the air was crisp and the sky cloudless. Now, it's a dark day, with a storm threatening.

The uniforms are outside the main gate. Ramrod straight. They'd rather be lounging against the wall, sparking up. But the neighbours are watching, their net curtains twitching.

Both constables are men. They greet her with odd expressions.

Maybe surprise?

Or suspicion?

Or resentment?

Does it matter? Burnet's been met with all three during her few weeks as a detective.

"Someone's inside?"

When they don't respond, she presses: "With the deceased?"

Still nothing.

"Well?" Dow. Standing behind her.

The uniform closest, speaking over her head: "Sorry, sir. Didn't realise it was you."

"You were told CID were on the way."

"Yes, sir. I just didn't—"

"Expect a woman?" An acid edge to Dow's question.

Well intentioned, but Burnet gets this fleeting irritation that she tries to ignore.

"It's the future, constable," Dow says. "We'd better all get used to it."

The constable keeps his attention on Dow. "We received a call." Fastidiously careful about not directly addressing either detective. "Concerned neighbour hasn't seen the victim in two days. We were closest, so we came round to check on her."

"Did you enter the premises?" Burnet asks.

The constable finally grants her a direct answer. "Not through the front door, as it was securely locked. But we decided to take a check round the back, just in case. You know, a wee keek through the kitchen window. And that's when we saw her. My colleague here tried the back door, and it opened on contact."

Dow asks, "What condition was she in when you found her?"

"Face down on the floor. We could see blood, but all the same, you have to check, don't you? I tried to roll her over, and that's when ..." His face pales. "When we knew that we had to call in CID." Hesitation. "It's why ... when I saw you, ma'am" – looking at Burnet sheepishly – "I wasn't sure what to say. That kind of scene, I'm not sure it's one that a woman should have to—"

"I worked the beat," she says. "You can try your best, but one day you'll see something and you'll know it's something no one should ever see." Her tone is even, and she maintains eye contact the whole time. "So don't think you need to protect me."

His face contorts. Burnet doesn't wait for him to work it out, and walks past, up to the front door.

Dow follows. Leans down by her ear: "You know what he's going to be saying about you later, right?"

"I'd rather be called a bitch and get respect, I suppose."

She doesn't have to look round to know he's smiling.

Outside the kitchen when the smell hits.

They stop short, like they've come up against a wall. Burnet swallows to stop from gagging.

Dow says, "They could have warned us."

Burnet keeps a hand over her face as they enter the kitchen. Hiding her expression of disgust.

The smell is so strong, it has a physical presence.

Flies buzz in a cacophony of excitement.

Mrs McDiarmid on the kitchen floor. Blood-slick trails where her body's been turned over. Her face is intact, although her eyes have sunk back into their sockets and her skin seems stretched. Artificial, like a plastic replica of the person they'd seen not so long ago.

Her blouse and pinny have been ripped open. And then her stomach.

Entrails spill.

Burnet blinks and swallows, unable equate the woman she met with the meat and blood on the floor in front of her. Fully expects Mrs McDiarmid to bustle into the kitchen asking who would have the gall to make such a mess inside her house.

Dow murmurs, "Saints preserve us."

Burnet leans against one of the counter tops. Trying to look casual. Holding herself up.

Dow says, "Just the blouse. He only ripped her blouse."

"Didn't touch her dress. He didn't rape her."

"Doesn't look like it. Doesn't mean it's not sexual though."

More silence. Neither of them in a hurry to get too close.

Burnet says, "You mentioned the cat."

"And?"

"This is what happened to the cat. Same wounds. Torso. Ripped open. The entrails."

"We'll find bite marks, then." Dow opens the door onto the back garden, and air comes rushing in. The smell doesn't dissipate. An unwelcome presence.

Burnet looks out at the back garden.

At the woods. The trees.

Dow says, back over his shoulder, "I don't think this was an animal attack."

Burnet doesn't say *I told you so*. She focuses on not being sick. Tries to block out the sound of the flies.

14

FRANK GRAY SITS UP. FOR A MOMENT, he's in hell, in the dark, demons in the shadows around him. He's sweating. Must be the flames.

Beside him Jeannie stirs, but doesn't wake.

The air cools.

Frank's sheets are soaked through with sweat.

The dream fades.

Was he dreaming about hell? Or was that just how it felt when he woke up?

Fuck if he can remember. He thinks, *get the heart rate down*.

Slowly, his breathing returns to normal.

Frank's old man died of a heart attack. Pale and wheezing in front of his son.

Frank watched him die.

Is that what's happened? Is Frank having a heart attack?

Frank swore he wouldn't be his old man. He wouldn't be weak. He wouldn't be—

He stops the thought there. Best memory of his old man is the way he died.

He's still shaking. The world feels like it's spinning too fast.

He spirals with worry.

The fights. All those punches to the head. Double vision the least of his worries.

You're fine, you fucking fanny.

There it is, the voice of his father.

He swings his legs out of bed. In his underwear, he pads downstairs to the kitchen. Passes his son's room. The light is still on, shining under the closed door of his bedroom. When he was little, the boy used to turn on the lights after Frank had turned them off. Said he couldn't sleep in the dark, that when the lights were out he heard things whispering to him in the dark.

Monsters.

Frank wasn't having any son of his afraid of the dark. He'd sorted it sharpish by removing the bulbs every night, locking the door. Add in a few good skelps, and job's a good'un.

The kind of solution his old man might have had. But then his old man would have followed through with a real beating for good measure. The fucking *tawse*. The smack of leather on skin. The sting of tears.

Don't fucking cry, boy. Go worse for you if you cry.

In the kitchen, Frank pours a glass of water. Strange taste at the back of his throat. Metallic. Rusty. He pours the glass back out after a couple of sips.

Thinks about the light coming from under his son's door. The lad seventeen, now. Too old to still be scared of the dark.

So what're you going to do?

He doesn't have an answer.

What can he do?

He made Jeannie promises. About their son. About how he wouldn't turn out like them. About how they were going to make things better for the boy.

When she'd heard about the bulbs and the skelps, she'd threatened to leave.

What was he supposed to do? How was he supposed to prepare his son for the world?

Two glasses. Still dry as a bone.

Something scrapes the kitchen window.

The back of the house. Facing the Templeton Woods.

An animal?

He hears it again.

Thinks about something his son said recently. About how anything could be hiding out in the woods, in the trees, in the dark. Frank had told the lad to quit talking shite, but now Frank has to wonder if maybe there really is something out there.

What was he dreaming about?

He tries to remember specifics.

Realises he's afraid.

Frank Gray frightened of something in the shadows.

The man they called the Beast of Balgay.

He looks at the window.

Another scrape.

And he barks out something that he hopes is a laugh.

Branches of a tree. The small thing close to the house, like a skeleton rising from the earth. The one Jeannie planted when they moved in. Told him at the time it was an apple tree – a mark of the start of their new life. It never took, not really. Never produced fruit.

He pours what's left of the second glass down the sink.

Throbbing now, on the right side of his head. Just below the skin.

He goes back upstairs.

Again, the light under his son's bedroom door.
The lad should be sleeping.
The throbbing increases.
He puts his hand on the bedroom door.
Stops.
Turns back.
The throbbing continues.
He knows what he has to do.

15

KELLEY WAKES UP MOST MORNINGS WITH a hangover now.

What else is there to do? The days fritter away. The nights get worse.

No purpose. No sense.

Waiting.

All he can do. The waiting kills him. So he drinks.

Kills brain cells. Kills time.

No bottles under the bed. Standards are maintained. Always the pub. Different place each night. Stops people talking.

The drinking helps. Up at the bar, order a few pints. Chase with whisky or two.

This pub's round the back of the new Wellgate Centre. Where no one wants to know your name.

Three pints in, someone taps him on the shoulder. "Haw, do I know you?"

Old man. Mutton chops. Once black, now grey. Breath that shouldn't be allowed near open flame. A nose so red, Santa could guide his sleigh by night.

"Don't think so." Kelley goes back to his drink.

"Naw, I do. I mean ... like ... naw, not you! Your father? I mean, you're the spit!"

Maybe he'll just fuck off if Kelley keeps his back turned and his nose in his drink. But this bugger's one of the insistent ones.

The old soak's not wrong, though. The older Kelley gets, the more he looks like his old man. In youth: favouring his mother, with dark, wavy hair and long, elegant limbs. Older: stockier, chest more barrel-like. Even his face has changed.

Looking in the mirror now, he sees someone he doesn't want to recognise.

Mutton Chops says, "He was a copper. Aye, so he was."

Kelley turns now to face the man. "And let me guess? You worked with him?"

"Aye, well, you could say—"

Except he doesn't get a chance.

Kelley doesn't even think about it. He just gets off the stool, grabs the guy by the neck and walks him across the room.

Other drinkers turn their heads. But just for a moment. Better not to get involved. Even the bartender tries his best to pretend that nothing's happening.

"Whoa there, chief!" Mutton Chops says. "Come on, now! I was just—"

"Just what?"

"Took me back was all. I mean, your da, he was good people, aye?"

Mutton Chops folds backwards over a table. Kelley holds him there.

Keeps the eye contact.

Mutton Chops says, "I just wanted to say he was a hero was all. I mean, seeing you— brought it all back, like!"

"What were you to him?"

"We were mates."

"What were you to him?"

"Jesus fuck, what do you want?"

Kelley lets go. The man collapses to the floor.

Kelley pulls out his folding ID, holds it up. "Same as my old man," he says. "CID."

"Except you're an arsehole."

"Look in the fucking mirror."

As Kelley leaves, he says to the bartender, "If you think I'm paying for that pisswater, you're sorely fucking mistaken."

* * *

Outside, fresh air hits like a cricket bat to the face.

Kelley blinks. The world turns too fast.

Flashbacks:

Grabbing Mutton Chops by the throat.

Stepping back as the old soak drops to the floor, slides off the table.

It wasn't that Mutton Chops said he looked like his old man.

It wasn't that Mutton Chops said anything about his old man.

It was that Mutton Chops *could have* said something.

Kelley strides down the street as fast as he can without falling. Veers left, right. Almost falls onto the road.

Thinking about what he expected.

What he thought he would hear.

Time off giving him time to think.

Not even the drink can stop him doing that. Might allow him to pretend he doesn't, but the truth is that underneath the fog, the wheels are still turning.

Union Street, he reaches to grab a wall for support.

Misses.

On his knees.

Shock up his legs. His spine.

On his hands and knees now.

Pissed.

He sits with his back against the wall. Raises his head to look up at the sky.

Clarity rushes. Not sobriety, exactly – but something that leads to it.

Memories of an uncle. Big man. Big drinker. Always a smile and a joke. Kelley looking forward to his visits, never sure why his parents weren't so convinced. Like there was something they knew, and he didn't.

Kelley got old enough, and he saw it. Late at night, his uncle passing through merry and out the other side. Breath stinking like he just suddenly downed a pitcher of gutrot. Kelley making excuses soon after for not being there when the man came to visit.

A few years later, after his dad's funeral, Kelley comes out a pub with his mates, seeing this pathetic tramp on his hands and knees on the pavement. Takes a moment to realise who it is. Crosses the road to avoid him. His uncle doesn't recognise Kelley. Calls out for help and assistance and any change these handsome young lads could spare for a poor bastard down on his luck.

Kelley was consumed: anger. Shame. Humiliation.

He'd heard that heavy drinking runs in families. He'd always believed it to be an excuse, something weak people tell themselves. Everyone knows someone who's a drinker, right?

He closes his eyes. Still not ready to stand.

Cold spots on his face.

Rain.

It gets heavier.

Soaks through his skin.

He sits on the corner. A pathetic drunk.

Thinks:

He could go back to being a copper. Go with the fucking flow.

But he knows that when his review comes up, they'll sling him out on his arse.

How could he think any different?

His father's son?

How could he be when he never even knew his father?

16

BURNET TRIES NOT TO SHIVER.

Beside her, Dow rubs his hands together for warmth.

Metal hatches line the walls. They're beside a table covered with a white sheet.

Underneath the sheet?

Burnet tries not to think about it.

The doctor – when he emerges – doesn't seem to feel the temperature. His scrubs are thin, and there's a light sheen of sweat across his forehead. He takes off his glasses and pinches the bridge of his nose. "There are times when I regret ever agreeing to this." The man's paid well for his expertise. He's grousing just because he can. "I can give you the basics. That is, I mean, you don't have to see—"

"We do," Burnet says.

Dow nods his agreement.

The doctor's eyebrows raise. "Don't say I didn't warn you." He looks directly at Burnet.

Underneath the sheet, Mrs McDiarmid's corpse is like a prop from a film; real and yet not real.

"So..." The doctor sounds hesitant to start speaking. "There's a lot about this one that's strange."

"Apart from the disembowelling?" Burnet asks.

She doesn't intend sarcasm, and yet he looks at her, as though about to rebuke. Then, he gives her a thin smile instead. *Bloodless*, she thinks.

"Her stomach was ripped open. Some ... thing chewed on her organs."

"Something?" Burnet knows he's holding back.

"Some*thing*," he says. "Aye. The bite marks are large enough to be human, but there's something ... the shape of the incisors ..." He stops, as though trying to consider what he's saying. "When I was growing up, I used to go the Forest Park cinema and watch the X-rated movies, you know? The horror films. All those Hammer films that give bairns nightmares. But you know what this one made me think of? The Wolf Man."

Dow says, "The Wolf Man?", trying to hide the laughter in his question.

"Aye," the doctor says, deadly serious. "The bloody Wolf Man. The shape of the teeth, they correspond closely to that of a wolf, although the bite pattern's definitely human."

Burnet gets a shiver. Tries to hide it.

Dow, blowing on his hands like a child in the snow, asks, "Anything else?"

"Saliva. Human."

"Jesus." Burnet can't help herself. She's seen dead bodies and met killers. But something like this feels otherworldly. Never mind the Wolf Man, she's thinking of Christopher Lee snarling, going for the jugular.

"Cause of death was not the bite, however. Blood loss occurred from a stab wound to the stomach."

Sharp intake of breath. Pale and uncomfortable.

"Was she alive when this bastard started eating her?" Anger overrides Burnet's sensation of horror.

The doctor hesitates.

Dow says, "She's not a woman. She's polis. Like me. So just say it."

The doctor takes a breath. "I believe she was, yes."

Burnet clenches her fists hard enough to draw blood from her palms.

Dow says, "Is this based on your re-examination?"

The doctor hesitates.

Dow says, "That's as much an answer as anything."

The doctor drops the sheet back over Mrs McDiarmid with a gentle reverence.

Burnet reminds herself he's a volunteer. Taking time out from his patients to do this. No one in their right mind would *want* to be around death like this.

Dow says, "Your report on the death of this woman's cat concluded that it was due to an animal attack. A fox or similar."

"It was politely recommended that I reach that conclusion."

Burnet jumps in. "Recommended? You mean, you knew that it was a human who chewed at her cat's insides?"

The doctor can't look at her.

Bloody right, too. He should be ashamed.

"Why'd you say different on the report?" Dow asks.

If the doctor answers, he'll name names. He doesn't want to. Whoever requested the omission on the original report, he's scared of them.

Burnet tries a different tack. "And why tell us?"

"Because whoever this is ... if they're killing people ... I mean, even one person ..."

"That's why the lead detective asked you to omit your findings?" Dow looks like he wants to laugh. "Because they felt there was nothing could be done? That it wasn't serious?"

"I was told it would cause panic. *Unnecessary* panic."

Burnet runs fingers through her hair, pulling tight.

Dow presses further: "And the lead detective told you that?"

"Not exactly."

Burnet had expected Garner to bury this one because it was too much effort for him to track down an unknown killer with a weird fetish.

But if he wasn't alone, then was there some other reason?

Dow walks over to a tray where medical equipment is carefully laid out. Scalpels. Saws. Burnet thinks of *The Texas Chainsaw Massacre*.

Dow runs his fingers along the contours of the tray.

The doctor doesn't take his eyes off him.

Dow says, "What do you mean 'not exactly'?"

The doctor swallows.

Dow waits.

* * *

Later, in Dow's car – neither of them saying a word.

Burnet thinking about teeth ripping into flesh.

The doctor had hypothesised:

Some kind of metal dentures fitted over the killer's own teeth. Not something you could easily buy. You'd have to make them. Know what you were doing.

Hairs on both corpses. Human hairs that did not belong to Mrs McDiarmid.

But that told them nothing. What use was hair to anyone at a crime scene?

Dow turns on the radio.

They listen to the patter for a while.

Finally: "This is serious. You know that?"

Murder is always serious, but Dow has a point: this is unusual in execution and ferocity. The metal dentures adding an element of the gruesome that neither of them has encountered before.

Dow clears his throat. "This sort of thing, they should want to be all over it. The Chief Constable, the newspapers ... a major bloody investigation."

Burnet steels herself. Expects this to mean she'll be taken off the case. "Which is why Garner and his ... wee pal ... didn't want anyone to know."

The doctor hadn't named names. But he'd given them enough of a description of the second man accompanying Garner.

Dow nods. "Dashing fucking Davie. The Socialist Shithead."

Burnet allows herself a smile. "It makes sense, him wanting it kept quiet. Panic on the streets, and a local election coming up."

"Would have thought it would make a good case for his party," Dow says. "Get out of the Conservative stranglehold and all."

Burnet nods. "Maybe. But again, who would want to go into a local election pledging to protect us from a cannibal?"

"Either way, a counsellor has no right to decide what the police do or don't investigate. And why was he even here with Garner? I didn't think that prick had friends in high places. He'd get vertigo in the gutter."

"I also thought he voted Tory," Burnet adds.

David Darling – Dashing Davie, as the papers called him – was one of the youngest councillors in the city's history.

And, on paper at least, no friend to the police.

Barely two weeks would pass without a story in the local papers from Davie claiming that the police were bugging the phones or reading the mail of those on the political left. *A jackboot conspiracy* was how he described these actions in one of his more colourful letters.

So what would he be doing coming to the morgue with a police detective? Why would such a man ask the on-call doctor to adjust his autopsy report?

Is he involved?

There's no connection, though. Mrs McDiarmid's not in his catchment area.

"This was your catch," Dow says. "I can back you, say that we spotted something the initial investigation missed. But I think you need to be working this with me. You can do it. I know you can. We just pretend like no one told us there's a cover-up. Plead ignorance."

She looks at him. His eyes are calm, and reassuring.

Dow keeps the eye contact. Letting her know he's serious. "Know what they said to me when I suggested working with you? They said that I was a horny old bastard. That all I wanted was to have a Friday Girl on my arm when I went to a crime scene. Here's the truth: me and the missus always wanted a daughter. We got a son, and he's a good lad. But we wanted a girl. Her, because she thought having a girl, we could make the world better for her, give her what the missus never had. Me, because I was the only boy with five sisters, and I suppose I got used to it growing up. I know how tough girls can be, and I know you're great polis. But something like this, the scrutiny's going to be intense." He looks away again. There's something troubling him.

"You're thinking about Mone, aren't you?"

He nods.

Before her time, but only just. Made all the papers.

1976. Young lad takes a class of girls hostage at his old school. Shoots their teacher. He's been in the army, come out with problems and something to prove. His demands are incoherent. There's a siege. When the police finally storm the classroom, he doesn't resist arrest. But the damage is already done. The teacher has died trying to protect the girls in her class.

His name is Robert Mone.

Dow had been one of the first officers into the classroom. He refused to speak to reporters about what he saw.

"I can handle the attention," she tells him.

"I'm sure you can. But you need to know. Because the worst thing you can do is let it go to your head. One minute, you're the conquering fucking hero, the next you're a bloody pariah; a joke to them. They – the public, the newspapers – want immediate bloody results. Things wrapped up in a neat little bow."

Burnet had followed the case in the papers. The speculation, the talk about Mone's motivations, the mention of police bravery. But also – months later – a follow-up in the *Dundee Herald*, where someone asked Dow about what he'd seen when he went into the classroom. After giving the official line about Mone just sitting there, shotgun at his feet, the reporter had asked if he had any idea why Mone had done it.

Dow's response was off script: "He's crazy. And there's no point trying to rationalise that, is there?"

There had been fallout, of course. These days, Dow shied away from cases that required publicity. He was a solid polis, but even if his work was respected in the department, he was considered a loose cannon. Why they were happy for him to work with the misfits and troublemakers like Burnet and Kelley – kept him out of the way.

Burnet says, "An old woman's dead. No one deserves to die like that."

"I need you to be sure."

"I am sure," she says. "I can handle this." She wonders if this is why Garner tried to hide the truth behind Mrs McDiarmid's death – avoiding the shitstorm that would come from having to tell the public someone out there was eating human flesh and killing vulnerable pensioners.

Dow nods. "Right," he says. "Let's bloody well do this, then."

17

WORKERS SURGE PAST FRANK'S STOOL. Midday shift change. The lobby switching up from deadly quiet to a sudden surge of activity.

Even after layoffs a year or so back, the place is still busy.

The Cash, they call it. Where people in Dundee come for good, reliable work. NCR is one of the city's biggest employers alongside Timex. Cash machines or watches. That's where the money is now. Gone are the days of "jam, jute and journalism", when Dundee had been one of the richest cities in the world. Of course, the "jam" was a bit of a joke. It was marmalade, really. Keiller's had been the last bastion of the trade in the city.

Frank used to wonder whether everything really had been better once. People talked like they remembered, but Frank couldn't. His whole life had been graft. No jam or jute for him. And journalism? Aye – the DC Thompson mob wouldn't look sideways at someone from Frank's part of town.

There are worse gigs. Frank's done most of them, too, during his days down the docks. Between the bare-knuckle fights that made his name, he hauled crates and collected debts for Joe

Kennedy. All the same, it feels harder, some days, sitting on this stool, counting down the clock until the end of the shift, taking home cash that's already been eaten into by the taxman by the time it reaches his envelope. Thinking of how much the bosses are earning, and how little those on the factory floor really earn.

Somehow all that is more exhausting than physical labour. He can't say why.

"Frank?"

Mr Birrell. A small man with a round face and hawkish eyes. Always wired, ready to explode with tension – as though he's privy to secrets no one else knows.

"Mr Birrell." A tiny moment of inferiority sparks in Frank's brain. Like he's doffing his bunnet to his betters.

That little voice inside him – an echo of the old Frank – laughs.

"Think I can have a word?" Birrell says.

The stream of workers has slowed now. Frank follows Birrell through to the man's office.

"Take a seat."

Frank takes the seat. Grips the armrests. Tries to relax.

Fails.

Birrell moves to the other side of the desk. His chair has a higher back. Makes him appear bigger, somehow. He leans forward; elbows on the desk, hands clasped. As if he's about to pray.

"You know how things are at the moment," Birrell says.

"Stretched."

"That's one word for it. Look at this city, eh? The pride of Scotland, but sometimes it feels like the rest of the country's grinding us down under their heels."

Birrell's not Dundonian. Check the near-English vowels dropping plummily from his mouth. So why does he keep talking like he's from here?

Frank thinks about reaching over the desk, grabbing the bastard and pounding his face to mince.

Birrell says, "We're a national company. We've got a good record. We like to think we treat our employees well across the board."

Frank waits for the gunshot.

"But these are tough times. Not just here, you understand? And the people at the top, they make tough decisions."

They call this place the Cash for good reason. You need money, you can always ask at the Cash and see what's going. They'll see you right. Give you a job for life. *No more worries, you'll be set for life. Honest work.* Good pension, too. The works. Made Frank a real solid citizen.

Birrell clears his throat.

Get to the point, Frank thinks.

Birrell says, "To that end, some positions at this factory are currently under consideration. Not on the line yet, but supplementary positions—"

"Positions such as mine," Frank says, pulling the trigger himself. Quicker. More merciful.

Birrell goes red. His hands clasp tighter. The knuckles go white. "Yes."

Frank's old life, what he liked was that people said what they meant. If they didn't, you beat the shite out of them until they did. But in this world, people seemed to hesitate in saying what they needed. As though they could mitigate the fallout of their actions by hedging their bets.

Birrell says, "There will be a final payout, but I'm afraid ... we need to let you by the end of this week, Frank."

Frank nods.

"I put in a good word on your behalf, and of course we'll give you a reference. You'll find—"

Frank's lips go tight. He breathes through his nose.

Birrell tries to compose himself. "I understand if—"

Frank stands up.

Fuck this.

Birrell unclasps his hands, sits back. As though trying to escape through his chair.

Frank turns, not a word, and leaves the room.

18

RICHARD CARAWAY WALKS INTO THE ROOM – trailing the scent of booze and fags. Half-shaven, gaunt features. Passably handsome in a bad light. A smile that reeks of undeserved confidence.

It's just past two in the afternoon – he's just come off a liquid lunch.

Reporters.

He looks Burnet up and down, and smiles.

No – not the right word. He *leers*. "I always expect female detectives to be kind of hacket, you know?"

As opening gambits go, she's heard worse.

He says, "Hard in your own way, though? Aye, guess you'd have to be."

Caraway works the crime beat for the *Dundee Herald*. Word is, give him a big enough bottle of whisky, he'd keep schtum if you caught Jack the Ripper.

Those are the rules for the boys, of course.

Burnet's relearning a lesson she realises she should have absorbed by now – *it's different for girls.*

Caraway takes a seat. Casual. Louche.

Burnet stands.

He pulls out a pack of cigs, offers one.

She refuses.

He lights up.

"You know they're linked to cancer, right?"

"Aye," he says, "But we all have to die of something. In your line of work, you'll have to know there's worse ways to go."

Memory: her granny in hospital, lungs mutating, lumps inside her, face drawn and eyes rheumy. The sound of her breathing more painful than a scream.

Caraway says, "You know there's going to be interest in whatever you do as a DC, right?"

She nods.

"I mean, you started it. Agreeing to do the Friday Girl slot in the first place."

"I didn't have much choice," she says.

It's just a picture in the papers. Makes us look good in the department. Makes you look good. Besides, today's paper is tomorrow's chip wrapper, right?

If only.

Most Daily Girls were shop assistants and secretaries – nice young girls doing nice feminine jobs that they could easily give up when they finally met the right man.

But she'd been a WPC. A woman in uniform. WPCs have been around for decades, but there's still an element of titillation to the idea of a girl with access to her own handcuffs.

Burnet can't conceive of a less sexy feeling than cold metal wrapping her wrists.

Caraway waves his hands through cigarette smoke. "There's always a choice. In the modern world, we all get to choose, right? That's what women burned their bras for."

She swallows down her response.

Caraway says, "And now you're CID, well, I suppose it's a good decision. Put a pretty face onto dirty work. Although I'm surprised they let you near murders." He leans forward. "I mean, how do you cope? How can you look at all that and still," he gestures expansively, taking in everything about her, unable to articulate what he means specifically, "be you?"

"You're the crime reporter," she says. "How do you cope and still be—" mirroring his gesture, "you."

His lips hint towards a smile. He takes a long drag of his cig. The scent of the smoke is oppressive.

"The 'Friday Girl Becomes Detective' story, that's got to be old by now. I've smiled for the cameras again, I've done my hair up nice, and I've said all the things I was supposed to say."

"Then why am I here?"

"The woman whose cat was killed."

He blinks a few times as if that might shake the name to the front of his brain. "McDiarmid. That's it, right? She wrote to us."

"Yes," she says. "A citizen did report the death of her cat."

"And the official judgement was that an animal attacked poor kitty? I mean, hardly front-page news, right?"

Burnet says nothing.

Caraway breaks first. "Okay. Aye, you've got me. I know that the same woman was killed the other day."

"A possible break in," she says.

"And you've been keeping it hush hush."

"How much do you know?"

Caraway skips the next few steps of the dance. Maybe he's impatient. Maybe she's stepping on his toes. "So my famous charm's only going to get me so far? Or maybe you're a dyke." Pause. Leer. "Or maybe I'm just losing it in my old age. But you need to give me something. Because I have other sources, and what they're telling me is that the way this woman died, it was the same way that little kitty corked it. Am I right?"

She leans against the far wall.

He persists: "My source, he's never steered me wrong before."

"So it is a man."

"Good luck narrowing that down, darling." Nonchalant. Hiding panic that flutters behind his eyes.

She has the upper hand now. She stays against the wall. "What keeps you from going to press with the story, then? Name your price. An official comment?"

"From one of the officers in charge of the investigation." He allows his grin to grow wide. "Jesus! And you've only been in CID how long? A month?"

"As I'm sure you've worked out," she says. "I'm no daftie."

"No, love," he says. "A woman with brains. Maybe I should report on that one, aye?" Making a show of considering the idea. "Nah. No one'd believe me."

"Keep it up," she says. "And you'll get out of here with hee-fucking-haw."

"The power of the press," Caraway says, "is that we shape how people think and feel."

"Getting a bit ahead of yourself." Burnet folds her arms. "Wee local paper and all."

"Okay," he says. "But the word of the *Herald* carries a lot of weight in Tayside. Just remember that."

Why he's here. They need him to work to their schedule.

"If your source is as good as you claim, you'll know that there's something wrong with this death."

"That the person who killed the cat, and the person who killed its owner ... that they ... I mean, if it's true ...?"

No point lying. "They ate the cat's flesh. They ate the owner's flesh."

"Fuck." Then: "Like, a nibble? Or are we talking a three-course banquet?"

"This isn't going to be a wee local story." Not flirting, but he adjusts his position like she is, so she leans into it. Giving herself control. "This is going to be national. This is going to be the biggest story of your career."

"The cannibal killer," he says.

"If you want to get all tabloid about it."

He lifts his left hand, rubs finger and thumb together. "Go where the money is."

She has an urge to leave the room and take a shower.

"Do we have a deal?" she says. "No supposition, no second guessing, you wait until we come to you. And you get access."

"Are we talking access to the investigation or ..."

"The investigation."

"Can't blame a man for trying."

She keeps her expression as neutral as she can. No anger. No disgust. All he wants is a reaction. Rattle the wee girl, try and find her weakness.

He stands up. "If that's all," he says. "Then I'll go write up something else about muggings down Lochee way."

"Any in particular?"

"I'll throw a rock," he says. "Or just resubmit an old report, see if anyone fucking notices."

19

FRANK KNOCKS BACK THE WHISKY, then turns to the half pint, downing that, too. He slams his hand on the bar.

On the other side, Tumshie gives him the eyeball. "Come on," he says. "This isnae like you, Frank."

"You have no idea, son," Frank says. He motions for the drink again.

Tumshie sighs, sets up another round. Stick-thin, with deep-set eyes that seem permanently half-shut. A waster. Nineteen, maybe twenty. Nothing wrong with working in a pub, but to have no ambition beyond pulling pints …

Frank despairs. This kid, he runs with one of the local gangs, spends his weekends looking for fights. Makes money off the side paying protection to a crooked CID officer. What the fuck kind of life has he got to look forward to?

The old Frank – *the Beast of Balgay* – whispers: *Still better than your own flesh and blood.*

Frank can't argue with that. Lad's a waste of space. Fucking up his job, acting like a space-cadet.

Jesus fuck.

Hannigan says the boy has talent at shop work. Claims he sometimes works on his own projects using the machines. Secretive, though, telling no one.

So, what the fuck happened that his own son – his flesh and blood – became this ... this *fucking thing*?

It can't have anything to do with Frank.

No fucking way.

And look at Jeannie: her genes are straight up hard work and good values.

So what the fuck happened to their son?

It's society. The way things are changing.

Disrespect and swearing in the pictures. And the fucking Sex Shotguns or whatever they called themselves saying "bollocks" on television.

The youth are being corrupted. The rot has set into society. His son's a fucking victim.

Too fucking right – and victims have no one to blame but themselves.

"There you go." The drinks land on the bar in front of him. "But I think I should be cutting you off."

Frank looks at Tumshie, managing to catch those lidded eyes, hold them with his own. "You'll cut me off when I *say* you cut me off."

"It's not just the drink ... there's your tab."

"What of it? My money's good here."

"Aye, Frank, always has been. But there's a limit for everyone, you know?"

"Thomas," Frank says, using the lad's given name, giving it weight. "I'm not everyone. I mean, surely you're not so fucking young you don't know that?"

Tumshie hesitates.

Fury fizzes in Frank's head. Like the tide coming back into shore without warning.

Old memories.

Old sensations.

Old fucking anger.

The old Frank whispers that in the old days, Tumshie would show respect and *pour him a bastard drink*.

It would be automatic. Fucking *instinct*.

Maybe Tumshie needs reminding?

A hand lands on the bar. "Tumshie, lad, just give the man his drink."

"Aye, Mr Kennedy, sir ..."

Frank looks up.

Joe Kennedy smiles down at him. Grabs an empty stool. "Fancy seeing you here."

"No really," Frank says. "It's my local, Joe."

Kennedy smiles, nodding. Looking halfway to sad, but it could be the light. "Joe," he says, as though hearing the name for the first time. Like he's trying it on for size. "Been a while since anyone called me Joe."

"I should call you Mr Kennedy?"

"Like all the other arselickers? No bloody danger." Smiling now.

It's been years. Kennedy's got old. Hair's thinner. Face is lined.

Frank wonders what Kennedy sees when he looks at his old pal.

"What're you here for, anyway?"

"It's my pub."

"Any in this city that aren't?"

"None that matter."

Then: the silence of old friends.

Kennedy and Frank were at school together. At fifteen, they left together to find work down at the docks. Kennedy was the smaller of the pair, but he had brains and a knack for getting other people to do what he asked. Frank was the muscle. But the muscle was important, too. Without the Beast of Balgay, Joe Kennedy would just be another wee nyaff with ambition.

Joe Kennedy owes Frank.

As long as he remembers that, nothing else matters.

Kennedy says, "Your boy, he's almost a man now?"

Frank nods.

"I never really understood it back in the day," Kennedy says. "I always was a late starter. But ... since my two were born ... Maybe I understand why you wanted out." He smiles, looking at something only he can see. "Of course, too late for me, right? In too deep by the time they came around. Too many enemies. There comes a point, you've been fighting so long, you can't stop or you'll lose everything."

Frank feels the urge to knock back the round before him. But he resists. To give in would be to show weakness.

Kennedy says, "But what I have now, I keep it for them. They're my boys. I want the best for them. I want them to see a father they can look up to. The same as you."

Frank gets this tight feeling across his chest. Starts breathing faster.

Fucking stop it.

He grits his teeth.

Tumshie pops a couple of glasses in front of Kennedy.

Kennedy knocks back the whisky first. "A man in my position hears things. Rumours. Sometimes even truths. And what I heard was that the council has fucked up worse than ever before.

All this shite about the new Wellgate Centre, this idea that there's a bright shiny tomorrow just over the hill . . . it's all crap. This city has been stomped into the ground. All the great things that belonged to the people have been taken away by councillors and politicians who don't give a toss about the wee man. Who think that jobs happen because they say they will. We've been here before, right? You and me. In the old days."

Frank nods.

"Our fathers, they had it good. And then we had a taste. But it's all an illusion. I hear things, like I say. They say NCR is fucked, sorry to tell you. Layoffs coming in the year that'll cut those bastards to the bone. People out of work. Good people, Frank. And where do they go?"

Frank shrugs. "Timex always has something, right?" He can't say that the cuts are already starting. Can't admit being fucked over like that.

Of course, Joe Kennedy already knows. Never starts a conversation he doesn't know how to finish.

"Aye," Kennedy says. "The fucking Cash. And who's to say that one won't be up the swanny next? Greedy bastards, all of them."

Frank's hand moves to his drink.

Kennedy touches his hand, as though to stop him.

"The business isn't the same without the old guard." He lets go of Frank, sits straight. "The kids today, they don't know what we had to go through, men like you and me. They're soft. No sense of the real world."

"What're you saying?"

"I'm saying I came here because I know who you are, Frank. You and me, in the old days, we knew each other. Had each other's backs. I still have yours. If you'll let me."

Frank looks at his empty whisky glass.

Kennedy says, "Nothing goes on I don't hear about. It's not right, them letting you go. A man with a family. A fucking family. A man who's good at his job. You were a good soldier, Frank. A good fucking soldier. You still are. I know it, just looking at you. This drinking and whinging isn't you."

Frank's dizzy. How a spider feels being swept down the plughole.

"The Beast of Balgay," Kennedy says. "Young lads like Tumshie don't remember. But you can remind them. You can remind them. And you can take care of your family, too. Isn't that what you want? I'm offering you a chance, Frank. A chance to be who you always were, and a chance to still take care of them."

Frank hates his son, and yet he has to take care of the lad. He resents Jeannie most days, and yet he chose to marry her.

He has *responsibility*.

A man takes care of his responsibilities.

Kennedy smiles. "You know what you want."

Frank knows.

Kennedy gestures at Tumshie. "Two more pints," he says. "And you can close this bastard's tab down, too. Starting now, he drinks on me."

20

"I SAW YOU," THE OLD DUFFER SAYS, "in the papers." Peeping at Burnet through bottletop glasses. "A nice young lass like you shouldn't be doing such a dirty job."

"No one should have to," Burnet says. "But I can't just stand by while people are hurt."

The old fella nods. Looks towards the kitchen. About to ask again if they want a cup of tea.

People think they're being polite. She just wants to do her job.

Dow breaks in quickly: "We really don't want to take up your time."

Déjà vu for hours now. Knocking on doors. Asking people if they have a few moments. This part of the city – middle class, mainly – not many doors slammed in their faces. But a lot of indifference. Or desperation to air grievances on any topic *except* the death of Mrs McDiarmid.

Bread and butter investigative work.

Off their arses, knocking on doors.

Burnet's aware that this man doesn't see her as real polis – just a wee girl playing at this job until she meets a husband. He might let something slip if Burnet does the talking.

Sometimes, being a woman has its advantages.

"Did you know Mrs McDiarmid well?"

"Well enough. We'd chat in the street, you know? Kept herself to herself, like any decent woman should. Don't think she had children. None that came to visit, anyway. Think she was a widow, ken? Such a shame, the way some people treat their parents these days. My lot, they know well enough to look after me. Every Sunday, here without fail. Andrew fixing a roast, and—"

Burnet pulls the man's attention back. "So she had no family? What about friends? Anyone who came to see her at all?"

"Och, not that I can recall. She lived for that wee cat, though. Every night, just before dark, she'd be out calling for it to come inside to her. I think she was afraid that something would get it." He thinks about this for a moment. "I suppose she was right." His shoulders hunch, as though struck by a sudden cold. "I've locked my doors every night since, you know. Never had to do that in all my years. Always lived in a good neighbourhood, decent people. What's the world coming to? They still havenae said anything in the papers, but I heard there was an animal on the loose. Another of they black cats."

Burnet answers the question: "We can't really say at the moment."

"You know about the black cats, don't you? My niece, Dorothy, she lives in Fife, near Auchtermuchty. She saw one in the fields. Huge muckle thing. Like a real beast. Panther or something. They say it was rich people brought them over, then let them out in the wild. You know, when the law changed."

Burnet's heard stories like this for years. The first panic was in 1975, the tabloids filled with nonsense stories. In the last few years, there've been reports of a puma out by Loch Ness. Unproven, naturally.

The man's still talking. "I mean, no person would ... surely? Naw, it's one of they beasts. Got bold, came out of the country and into the city." He looks towards Camperdown. "Or escaped from yon park there. They've got wolves and other beasts. I can hear them at night, in the woods. I think they've escaped and they're trying to cover it up." Attention back on Dow, now: squinting through the bottletops. "Is that what this is? A cover story. They're paying you money to—"

Dow says sharply, "At the moment, we're investigating all possibilities. We need to know as much about this woman as we can. Her friends, family, anyone she talked to."

"If it really was an animal, then you catch them," the old duffer says. "That's your job, isn't it? She may have been an old busybody, but no one deserves to be murdered. I hope you catch the bairns who did this, and I hope you hang them!"

Burnet resists the urge to tell him that no one has been sentenced to death by hanging since 1963.

"If you think of anything else," Burnet says, as they leave. "Please call the station."

* * *

Two more houses. Two more conversations about nothing.

Waste of a day. The only people at home are OAPs starved of daytime conversation.

Walking to the next house, Burnet says, "This is a waste of time."

"Is there anything else we could be doing?" Dow says.

"There's the computer system back at West Bell Street. Databases. They can cross check what we have with records far faster and more accurately than just digging through the archives."

"Cross check for what?"

"I don't know ... people whose crimes might lead to ..." She gestures, not quite having the words. "I mean, you don't do something like this for your first kill, do you?"

"Most killers," Dow says, "act on impulse. They don't walk around with their mother's corpses in their basements or killing because the little voices tell them they can. And if they do, then they get locked up the first time they step out of line. Besides, a computer file isn't as useful as talking to people."

"You know Norman Bates was based on a real killer?" she says.

Dow stops dead. Sudden intense expression. "That fella back there – said something about this job not being right for a girl like you."

All this time they've been working together, and only now does he question her effectiveness as polis because of her gender?

He raises a hand. "Wait, just wait a second. That's not what I mean. I mean, not entirely. But it's unusual, I mean. You really want this, don't you? I mean, it's not just about making a stand for women in the police force, but you really have a feel for it?"

She shrugs. "When I was young, our neighbour was murdered. By her husband. Lovely woman, lived next door, used to give me sweets when she saw me playing outside. Always said not to tell Mum. At night, I'd hear her and her husband yell at each other through the walls. I mean, I could hear other couples, too, but their arguments are the ones I remember."

"Because they were louder? More violent?"

"Maybe. But mostly I think it's because of what happened in the end. One day, they were arguing. Don't ask me what it was about. Mostly it was raised voices and banging, and I never really made out the specifics. I didn't want to. Mum used to pretend it wasn't happening, and I did the same. You know, when you're young, all you can do is copy your parents because they're the best role models you have. But this one, what I really remember is he just stopped yelling. I didn't know until later, but he walked into the kitchen, came back with a knife and slit her throat."

"You heard that?"

Burnet shakes her head. "All I knew was that it went quiet. And that was it for a while. Maybe three hours later – I don't know who called the police or even why; if they did it that night, why not any of the hundred other times? – I saw the police cars screaming and stopping outside our block. I was outside by then with some of the other girls I knew. We all stopped playing. Went to see what was happening. All of us wondering whose daddy had been nicked for stealing from the local shops, or whose mum was being pulled in for the work she did at nights. And then we saw them bringing the body out. She was covered, but still, you knew..."

"Jesus," Dow says. "How old were—"

"Nine or ten. I watched the policemen as they sealed off the crime scene. Even after we went inside, I watched from my bedroom window. One of them, the one who came to our house, he didn't blink when I asked him what had happened. He told me the truth. My mum was horrified, but I heard him telling her later that he found it was best to be honest with children."

"You admired him?"

"Aye, in the way only a ten-year-old can. And I suppose at the time, it didn't even occur to me that he was a police*man*.

All I knew was that he was catching people who hurt other people. All I knew was that it seemed like a good thing to do with your life." They stop outside the gate of the next house. "And when I told Mum, she patted me on the head and told me it was a good idea."

"Really?"

"She thought it was a tomboy phase – something I'd grow out of. When I actually applied to join up, she went mental."

Dow lets loose a half-laugh. "But what you were saying there, about murderers ... you know these things ... you ..."

"I read a lot. I wanted to be polis, and I took it seriously. Because that was the thing about that day, when our neighbour was killed ... I wondered ... why would you do that? I mean, what does it take to walk out of the room, get a knife and stab someone to death because you're having an argument? The idea freaked me out. I was a bookish kid. Best present ever was a library card. And I was a good reader, so they used to let me into the adult section. As long as I took books that didn't have heaving bosoms on the covers, they didn't mind what I checked out. I think they were just happy to see a girl taking an interest in books."

"Well? Did you ever get an answer?"

"I thought I would. I mean, the books gave me something, but the police ... Thing is, the more I see ..." She stops talking, unable to finish the thought.

Dow looks up and down the street. "This kind of place," he says, "is where we're supposed to be safe. These neat little houses in their neat little rows with their neat little gardens out front. But that's the thing, isn't it?"

She nods. "Nowhere's safe."

"You said Bates was based on someone real?"

She nods. "American killer. Loosely based, I should say. But the guy who wrote the book said Bates was inspired by this guy called Ed Gein. They changed some of that for the film, but it was still there."

"Of course. But that's America. This is Dundee, you know…"

"Americans are people, too. We have this idea, like somehow their killers are alien to us. But I sometimes think … it's the culture that makes the difference. The way we look at them. We have killers, too. People who take lives for no real reason, or because it gives them a thrill."

"Not in Dundee," Dow says, firm. "At least not like this bastard."

She raises both eyebrows.

"Come on," he says. "We should get off our arses, right?"

21

FRANK WALKS INTO THE GARAGE. Hunkers down next to the green MG. "Hey, you seen my boy?"

The guy underneath slides out. His face is streaked with oil. He raises his goggles. The skin around his eyes is dazzlingly white. "Frank? How you doing, pal?"

Frank shrugs. "Aye. You?"

The guy – Jesus, Frank can barely remember his name – shrugs, then gestures at the back office. "Think he's on a break."

"He's always on a break," Frank says. Might be a joke, except he means it.

He knocks on the office door, walks in. Like he owns the place.

He very nearly did, once. Different life. Maybe, if he'd gone all in.

But Frank's not one for reflection. At least, he tries not to be.

The boy's drinking a mug of tea. Seventeen, now. Lanky. Awkward. Folk used to joke how he didn't look anything like Frank. They didn't joke for long.

Now look at him: dead eyes. Slumped shoulders. Frank wonders when his bright-eyed lad became a shambling sack of flesh.

Jesus wept.

For a second, Frank thinks about what Jeannie suggested: that he apologise for what he did with the lad's tapes. That he explains – calmly, clearly – how he only wants what's best for his son.

Do things different to his own father.

What he said he would do when the boy was born.

But just looking at his son, Frank burns in his chest. An old loathing he remembers from his days as the Beast of Balgay. This person before him is a waster. Not worth anyone's time.

He's your son.

And he's still a waste of human skin.

The door opens.

"Frank, what're you doing here?"

Old Man Hannigan.

Old Man, and he's only three years older than Frank. But that's what they always called him for reasons lost in the haze of the bad old days.

"Just in to see my son's here, that he's pulling his weight."

Hannigan says, "Aye, he's on his tea break, like – but he's doing fine, right enough."

Hannigan turns to Martin. "Two minutes, on the floor. Think Benny's got something for you. Show you how to work the lathe."

Frank says to Hannigan, "Maybe you and me could have a wee chat?"

Martin keeps staring at his father with those eyes. Does he even see Frank?

Frank and Hannigan walk out. Round the side of the garage, across the road and through the estate.

Frank asks: "He's really doing okay?"

"Aye, he'll be fine. Quiet, like. But no trouble."

"He knows what happens if he is."

Hannigan chuckles. "If he could have seen you back in the day, he'd know what you could really do with that right hook of yours."

Frank looks down at his feet. Thinks about the nights he wakes up sweating, ribcage aching, limbs trembling. The old sensations returning when he least expects.

"That was the old me."

Two Franks.

The Beast of Balgay belongs to the past. The new Frank is a solid citizen. A father.

Who should listen to his wife and try to make his son understand with words, not fists.

"Right enough. So ..."

"Spit it out."

The two men stop on the corner. No one else around.

"You have any contact, still? With the old man, I mean?"

"Kennedy?" Frank shakes his head. "I'm not part of that anymore. Family man. You know that."

"I ... it's just I still can't believe you could just walk away. After everything you did, everything you knew ... that he would let you ... that you would want to—"

"Family changes you," Frank says. "You know, when you have something to protect and all that?" Twinge of discomfort twisting in his gut; he changes the subject. "Why were you asking, anyway? If I still had contact."

"Times are tough," Hannigan says, like it's no big deal. His eyes say different. "If the old man still ran games, maybe ... you know?"

Frank's gut tightens further. "Aye," he says. "Times are hard all over, but . . . you remember the speech I used to give? Like, how I'd look people right in the eye and tell them that if they borrowed from the big man or owed him money after a game, there was a price to that. You can't pay, you shouldn't play."

"I remember."

"Just wanted to be sure," Frank says. "I don't know anything, but I know someone you could call. When we get back, I'll give you the number." He thinks it over. "But look, if it's something I could help with . . . ?"

"Nah, nah." Hannigan holds up his hands. "All I want is to get in there, get a little cash to cover myself. I can do it. You know I can."

"You were a demon, right enough. King of bluffs." Frank scratches behind his ear. Cards aren't the best choice. The best player in the world can still fuck up with a bad hand. The worst player in the world can still accidentally do something right. Frank knows that the odds are always in the house's favour. Especially when that house belongs to Joe Kennedy.

Hannigan has to know this, too. They're from the same estate. Hannigan started his business with a cash injection from local businessman and philanthropist Joseph Kennedy. Under the table, naturally, and all paid up now. So there's no harm giving the number. The man gets in trouble, you can't say he didn't expect it. He wants to play cards, let him play cards.

No skin off Frank's nose. None at all.

They walk back the way they came, Frank stumbles slightly. His gut strains even tighter. Trying to alert him to something urgent.

22

KELLEY AT HIS FATHER'S GRAVE. Bottle in a bag. Half-afraid, half-stupid.

Is this what it's come to?

He takes a breath. Clears his throat.

"Am I supposed to say something?" Steam rises with his words. It's cold out, his scarf wrapped tight around his neck.

A sip of the hard stuff.

Sensation between warmth and pain at the back of his throat.

"I suppose that's why I'm here. Because I'm dreaming about you. About the times you were disappointed. About the times you looked at me, and I wondered if maybe you thought I was a mistake, wished Mum had gone to see some back-alley doctor. I mean, I know it's not exactly of the faith, but it was too late for a rubber, and look at what the fuck you brought into the world."

He stops talking. Thinks about how he sounds.

Harsh. Angry.

Petulant.

That's the word, isn't it?

Coming to your old man's grave, having a go at him about things he probably never even did.

He clears his throat. "You'd be right to think that. You and me, we were two different people. And that's how you wanted it, aye? Always telling me how police wasn't for me. Thinking you were doing me a favour." He shakes his head. "Jesus, you prick, why couldn't you just come out and say it? That to get by you did things you didn't think you'd have to do, that didn't sit right with you. That I'd have to do the bloody same."

Another swig.

He's not drunk. But he's lightheaded, suddenly. Off-balance. Shifts from foot to foot, then gives in and sits with his back to his dad's headstone. Knows how it looks – doesn't care.

Another hit.

Closes his eyes. Places his head against the cool roughness of his stone.

When he opens them again, there's a man standing there: white hair, gaunt features, boilersuit, toolbelt.

"No drinking here, son. This isn't a public house."

"Sorry, pal." Kelley gets to his feet, feeling the old man's eyes on him as he walks off. Probably thinking Kelley's just another jakey looking for someplace quiet to get smashed out his head.

Almost enough to make Kelley laugh.

Almost.

* * *

Kelley gets off the bus. Unsteady. Holding the rail. Like he's afraid he'll fall.

Worst part of being drunk: the moment you realise what's happening.

Onto the pavement. The cold hits fast. As the bus pulls away, Kelley considers running after it: *I made a mistake, please take me back.*

Too late.

Across the road, a pebbledash semi on a street of identical buildings.

It's a quiet little neighbourhood. Not moneyed, but not poor. Most of their neighbours had been happy with a copper living close by – it made their little community feel safer. Maybe that was true. But there are so many lies that people tell themselves, Kelley's no longer sure that he can trust anything.

He stops outside the house, looks at it. The building's smaller than his memories – a bungalow with low ceilings. There's a window above, his old bedroom, in what would have been attic space. But still, he marvels how three people – even if one of them was a child – could ever have lived with any sense of privacy.

His dad used to talk about how he'd grown up in a one-bed flat with two sisters. At one point, they'd installed a mattress and taken in a lodger. Six people. One-bedroom flat.

Kelley takes a deep breath, walks up the path to the main door. Sober, now. Agitation in his stomach; like whatever's in there's starting to boil.

He pauses.

Fresh paint.

He knocks.

Waits.

He almost doesn't recognise the woman who answers.

She's aged. Hair gone white, face sallow, eyes sunk a little deeper. Her lips – always thin – are a painful slash of cruelty.

She barely reacts when she sees him, merely looking up and nodding. Then, she steps back, and into the house, the open door the only sign that she's inviting him inside.

In the front room, she sits down. He sits opposite her, on the sofa.

Plastic covers crinkle.

A clock ticks on the blocked-up mantlepiece. An electric heater has been installed where hearth would have been.

Two of three bars glow bright orange.

Kelley says, "How have you been?"

His mother nods, as though considering the question. "Your sisters say you got a promotion."

"I did."

"The papers say you fucked that up."

Always the same; the one-two sucker punch. She'd been easier when his father was alive. After his death she became crueller around Kelley, as though she blamed him for what happened.

"I did." Voice flat and neutral.

"Is that why you're here?"

At least when Dad was alive, he'd softened her harsh edges.

He says, "I came to talk about Dad."

"What about him?"

"The months before he died."

"I need a tea," his mother says, shuffling out of the room. She's taken to walking like an old woman; play-acting the role, getting all the little signs in so that people will understand how hard her life is, how tough it is to grow old.

He follows her through to the kitchen. Leans against the jamb of the door until she's done rattling through the cupboards. She pointedly doesn't hand him a cup. Small aggressions are her specialty.

"Everyone said he was a hero," Kelley says. "I just ..."

"It was in the papers." Making the point: the papers tell the truth, not his sisters. Which is why she's disappointed with him.

He doesn't give her a chance to say anything else, and dives in, trying to act like a detective, not a son. "Do you remember a man Dad might have worked with? Big fella by the name of Garner?"

She turns away too fast. Her hands shake as she reaches for the mug on the Formica worktop. "So many people your dad worked with," she says. "At the funeral ... so many faces ... people who thought they'd met me, I didn't remember."

"Mum," he says. Addressing her directly. "This is important."

She turns back to him, sharp again, that momentary display of weakness gone. "You've disgraced his memory! He knew you weren't cut out for the police, but you didn't want to listen. He knew it would end badly for you, and now ... what? You're here to denigrate his memory? You want me to say he was as bad, as weak, as you?"

"I want you to tell me the truth!" His blood courses. He lifts his hands, fists forming.

His mother cowers.

The feeling of power fades, and he unfolds his fists, palms out. *I didn't mean to.*

"Get out," she says.

"Please," Kelley says. "You must remember something. There are things ... people have said things. That maybe Dad wasn't—"

She steps forward. He retreats on instinct, suddenly feeling like he's a boy again, about to get the back of her hand. They stand, frozen for a moment, in some odd tableau. She moves back first.

"Go upstairs, if you must. In your old room. There's boxes there. His files, he said. His *memoirs*. I've never looked. But maybe they'll tell you what you need to know, and you can let me live in peace. Your own mother, on her own, just as she has been since your father died. Since you abandoned her."

Kelley doesn't bristle at the accusation. He turns to head for the stairs, feeling her eyes on his back as he does so.

23

THE RINGTONE ECHOES.

Frank's ready to hang up when Hannigan answers: "What can I do for you, Frank?"

"Looking for Martin."

"What?"

"My boy."

"I know who he is, Frank." A pause. Hannigan'll be double checking the clock. "But he's my employee and—"

"He finished at five. His mother has dinner out on the table."

A few seconds of silence. "Well, he left like normal. Or he signed out, anyway. And you know I wouldn't let him work on without phoning home first. Jeannie'd have my guts for garters if he missed his mealtime."

"He's been showing up, though?" Twisting the cord of the phone between his fingers. Squeezing tight. "I mean, he's not skipping shifts, nothing like that?"

"Oh, aye. He's a good lad."

Hannigan's always been a soft touch. One of the reasons when Frank asked about whether he'd consider taking on Martin, he knew Hannigan would agree.

That soft touch gives Frank doubts. "You're sure he's not still there?" Twisting. Twisting.

"Maybe a problem with the bus?"

Frank grunts and hangs up.

Hannigan won't mess him around. Hannigan's known Frank a long time. Long enough to know what happens when people lie to Frank.

He left that life behind, sure, but it's still part of him. His history. His reputation – however dim and distant.

Why he likes his job. Security at the Cash is easy money. No one causes any real trouble. Only once or twice has Frank had to get physical – always a threat more than anything real.

The job has allowed him to leave his old self behind.

All the same, Frank knows that there's an animal hibernating inside, waiting to wake up.

In the kitchen, Jeannie's at the oven, forehead creased in concentration.

"You've turned it down?" Frank says.

She looks at him, like he's just asked the stupidest question in the world. Maybe he has.

But dinner won't wait forever. He says, "He left work on time."

"Should we start without him?"

"He said he would be here. A man's word is his bond, right?"

"He's not a man."

"He's seventeen."

"And still acts like a bairn."

She looks at the oven again.

Frank gets this restlessness in his gut. Fingers flex again, but there's no cord to wrap round them, and he looks like he's strangling the Invisible Man.

Jeannie doesn't say anything. But he knows she saw.

"We should just start," Jeannie says. "Talk to him when he comes in. He might have—"

Frank walks to the door. Jeannie reacts like there's been a gunshot. He's never laid hands on her, yet he knows she worries about the day he will.

There's no doubt that he will lose control.

She loves him and she's afraid of him. Would have been a kindness to walk out on her years ago.

But a man's a man for aw that. And sticks by his responsibilities.

Frank grabs his coat off the hook.

"You don't even know where he is."

"I'll find the wee shite," he says.

"And do what?"

No answer. He just walks out the door, into the night.

* * *

Frank gets in the car, turns the key three times to start the engine. Cold out, so the car's having a sulk.

Feeling calm.

More frightening than the anger.

The old Frank was always calm.

The old Frank was a brutal bastard.

Why he went into hibernation. The responsibility of fatherhood. Frank knew what it was to grow up in violence. He never intended to become a father, but when it happened, he made a conscious decision to turn his back on the violence that kept a roof over his head.

Joe Kennedy had approved, even if he'd left Frank with an open offer: *some men can't change who they are. You ever find that's you, you just come back.*

Frank pushes memories of the past where they belong.

Focus on the here and now.

His son.

The lanky wanker.

Sometimes, when the beast inside him mumbles in its sleep, it says: *how can that be your son? Are you sure the bitch didn't sleep with the fucking milkman?*

Frank loves Jeannie. He trusts Jeannie. The only woman he was ever faithful to. The only woman he ever wanted to be faithful to.

She wouldn't.

She just—

Focus on the boy.

Where would he go?

He has no friends. Maybe once, at school, but when he saw his son with other kids, they treated the lad like a ghost. He was with them and not with them at the same time.

The embarrassment of thinking *that's my son* had made Frank's gut churn: actual, physical pain.

Where would he go?

Frank thinks about when he was last in his son's room.

The posters on the walls.

The music and the tapes strewn around.

One of the tape covers reads: *Anarchy in the UK.*

What the fuck is his son listening to?

And that book open on the bed, full of clippings.

A stamp album. But filled with pages torn from the papers about the wolves in Camperdown and others from textbooks about animals and predators.

A grown man doesn't collect clippings and paste them in books. Not without a purpose. Not without it being like a record of something important.

Frank still has a collection of articles about his fights – the legit ones, of course – and even a few scraps about some of the beatings he handed out that made the papers. Not that he was named in many of those, but they were his just the same. A man owns his actions. He kept all of these in a box at the back of a wardrobe. He hasn't looked at them in years.

Frank thinks about the wolves. Remembers one night at the dinner table, the lad unusually talkative. Animated, even.

Which was unusual – his son usually the very definition of sullen. But that night he wouldn't stop talking about the majesty of the beasts, about the loyalty of the pack, about how it must feel to be part of something like that.

And then, something about how some wolves were destined to be alone.

This had been shortly before that business with the cat; that old woman's pet killed by wild animals.

Like wolves.

There were no wolves in the wilds, were there? Not near Dundee. Go the Highlands, maybe. But here?

Wolves in captivity.

The lad had talked about them that night.

Frank had tuned out.

But now he remembers.

Maybe it's nothing, but at least it gives him a place to go. A starting point.

Try the engine again.

This time it kicks right in.

* * *

The car park's near empty.

Camperdown's been closed for a few hours now.

Out of the car, Frank shivers. He's vulnerable out here.

What the fuck kind of thinking is that?

Getting old. Getting soft.

Aye, wasn't that the idea?

The old Frank had been lean, mean and feared. The old Frank always had to be on his guard.

Now?

The new Frank: soft tissue and beer belly.

The new Frank: vulnerable.

But the new Frank still sometimes thinks like the old one.

Things have changed in the city. There are new gangs out there. Kids with no real aim in life except to beat the shite out of anyone not from their territory. Frank hasn't kept up. Only knows what he reads in the papers.

But he's sure that there's gang territory somewhere round here. They see him – middle-aged man with a beer belly, alone at night, looking for his son – they won't give a toss that his name once made men piss their breeks in fright.

Maybe the lad's got in with one of the gangs. Jeannie would be horrified. But, to Frank, the idea's oddly comforting.

Frank walks to where they keep the animals. Closed off at night, gates locked. But Frank knows a padlock doesn't stop anyone with determination.

Frank's still thinking about his son.

Maybe the reason he hopes that his son's joined a gang is he half-expects to find the lad wanking over the wolf enclosure.

That is, if he's even here. Frank's not a detective. He's uglier than Bogart with nowhere near the smarts of Mitchum; just an ageing thug looking for his son.

And when he finds him, he'll beat the crap out of him.

* * *

Frank almost doesn't make it over the fence.

You're an old man. Why don't you fucking remember that?

The wolves are kept at the centre of the park, locked up for their own – and everyone else's – safety. Quiet, tonight. No howling at the moon. Like in the *Wolf Man* films a boyish Frank had snuck into when he wasn't supposed to.

The Wolf Man.

He'd been, what? Nine? Ten? Even then, knowing what he had the capacity to be, identifying with the man as he became the monster. Thinking that it spoke to something he could never put into words but felt almost constantly.

He'd worked it out sooner or later. He wasn't a wolf man. He was just a bastard.

That rage inside was all human, all him.

Look at the sky: not a full moon. Not even half.

Accounts for the quiet in the enclosure. Maybe it's just a full moon that sends these bastards into a frenzy.

But then he thinks he's heard them before, their howls carrying on the wind all the way over to Frank's house. More and more lately, too, their howls becoming background like passing traffic in the city centre.

So why are they so quiet tonight?

As he approaches the wolves' enclosure, he sees Martin.

The lad's alone. Just him and the animals. No rammie, no hi-jinks. Just some lad, lonely shite breaking into a zoo so he could ...

So he could what?

Frank cuts the thought dead. Keeps walking. His feet echo on the concrete. But Martin doesn't seem to hear. Or he doesn't care.

He's right up at the bars, hands up, fingers through the netting. There's a wolf watching him, cautiously. Direct eye contact.

Images from that old movie play through his mind. The transformation. If he watched them now, he'd laugh, but back then the effects had seemed so real. In his memory, there's ripping clothes and flesh and a kind of horrific terror to the scene. A bloody, visceral terror. The monster ripping its way out of prison.

You're not a wee boy anymore. No such thing as the fuckin' Wolf Man.

He walks to his son, grabs the boy by his shoulders and spins him round.

The cages rattle.

Now the wolves start to howl, that one that had been watching Martin leaping forward to the cage bars, snapping and scratching.

"What the fuck're you doing?"

Martin stares at his father with wide eyes. Like he's not really there.

Frank gets flashbacks to when Martin was just a bairn:

Sleepwalking. A phase. Something that happens. *He'll grow out of it.*

But it looks like he hasn't.

You should never wake a sleepwalker. It's dangerous.

The wolves are mental now. Yowling and howling and screaming.

Still no sign of that full moon.

So what—?

Martin blinks once, twice. His forehead creases with anger. The eyes are alive again. In a way that Frank's never seen before.

"What the fuck?" Pushing at his father's chest.

Frank's reaction is automatic. Anyone else, he'd punch them right out. But this is his son, so it's a cuff round the ear to leave bells ringing in the boy's head. Martin slams back the enclosure. The wire rattles.

The wolves back away, eyes watching the whole time.

"You were supposed to be home hours ago. I called the garage, they told me you left when you should ..."

"I'm seventeen," Martin says, sounding uncertain. "I'm seventeen. I don't have to—"

Frank grabs Martin by the collar. He hauls the boy up. The lad's legs kick out, uselessly, like he's trying to run on air, as Frank pulls him close. "You're a man, then," he says. "Seventeen and you're a man." He throws Martin down again, stands over him. "Men make promises and keep them. They don't keep fucking scrapbooks about wolves or break into zoos because they want to look at the fucking animals like some wee fucking bairn. They don't let their mother sweat over a fucking stove for nothing."

The wolves are howling, now.

The sound seems to wake something inside Frank. Like there's electricity running through his body.

The old Frank wants to come out.

Wants to run with the wolves.

Frank lets go of his son. Expects Martin to crumple. The boy stays on his feet. Shaking, but upright.

Even under the poor light of the moon, and the weak reflection of bulbs shining into the enclosures, Frank notices tears on Martin's face.

Frank clenches his fists.

How he can be this disappointment's father?

24

MORNING.

The next day.

Déjà vu redux:

Near the end of the last street, finally. So many houses. Faces. Names.

Same story each time:

She was a good woman.

If I saw something, I would have said.

Why can't you find this sicko instead of harassing people?

On and on. Older people continuing to show deference to the fact they're coppers, while younger folks show suspicion.

Not a surprise, maybe, given the state of cinema the last few years – all these films showing up the police force as corrupt, even inept. Even on telly, you have *The Sweeney* – people have to question if the police aren't closer to the criminal fraternity than to *Dixon of Dock Green*.

"Come on," Dow says. "Only a few more to go."

The man who answers this next door is tired – bags under his eyes, red-raw roadmaps around his pupils. Clean shaven at least. There's a scar – only just visible – beneath his left eye.

Burnet would place bets on him having spent time inside.

Before they speak, he says, "Polis?"

Dow leads: "How'd you know?"

"What d'you want?"

Maybe he'll react better to the soft approach. Burnet hates doing it, but it's better than turning a simple inquiry into a confrontation.

"You're aware of an incident that occurred in this area a few nights ago?" She tilts her head back to where Mrs McDiarmid's street is. "Just that way."

"You mean the old woman got murdered? McDiarmid, wasn't it?"

"That's right."

He shrugs. "Why ask me?" Defensive. But not overly. He has the look of a man who'd rather be left alone.

Dow steps back in. Playing the authority role. "We're asking everyone. Looking for anyone who might have seen or heard something. No matter how small. Who might know of any enemies the woman had—"

"She was an old woman who loved her cat too much," the man says. "That kind of woman doesn't have enemies. Doesn't have friends, either."

Burnet says, "All the same, we need to ask. So that we can say we've asked. So, maybe, if we can have your name?"

The man looks at Burnet. "Do I know you?"

She shrugs. "Maybe. Have you had dealings with the law before?"

"That's not it," he says. Then: "No sense hiding it, is there? This bugger knows." Looking at Dow.

"Frank Gray," Dow says. "Of course. You retired, right?"

"Out of the life," he says. "Going on fifteen years now."

"Had a bairn, didn't you? Must be doing okay if you're living out here."

"Security work," he says. Then, before Dow can open his mouth: "I know what you're thinking, but my past was a bonus."

"Set a thug." Dow leaves the rest unsaid.

Frank Gray's still staring at Burnet. Finally: "Fuck. I mean, pardon my French and all. But now I know. Where I've seen you. In the papers. You're the Friday Girl. First woman CID assigned to lead a case, or some shite."

Of course that's why he knows her. Why he remembers her face.

She'd hoped that CID might mitigate the Friday Girl effect; that people would see only the rank and not the face.

Some bloody hope.

Not with the way the papers touted the transfer at the insistence of the Chief Constable.

"DS Dow's the lead," she says.

"Aye," he says. "We knew each other back in the old days. Like a fucking terrier, this one." Then, to Dow: "No need to worry about me anymore, pal. Christ, you probably work alongside worse, am I right?"

Baiting the older detective.

Burnet attempts to defuse: "So you've left all that behind?"

"Swear on my bairn," he says.

"Can we come in, then?" Dow asks. "Like she says, just so we can tell the brass we've talked to you is all."

Frank Gray weighs up his options. "Aye, might as well. Get this over with, eh?"

* * *

Frank Gray's front room is small. Black and white TV in one corner, record player on top of what looks like an old sideboard. The couches are well-used, but not overly worn.

Dow sits without asking. Frank's left eye twitches. Controlling himself. Maybe he was telling the truth about being reformed.

Burnet looks out the window to the back garden – clean and maintained. Past the back fence, the trees of Templeton Woods. The woods from here run past the back of Mrs McDiarmid's place, too.

Burnet wonders what's out there in the trees. Whether it was just watching Mrs McDiarmid's place, or if it knows everyone here.

Dow forces politeness with his opening gambit. "Having a child changes you, I hear."

"That's right."

"Not always for the best?"

"In my case ..."

"Aye." Playing it cool.

"Back then, you had more hair."

"And you were a hard bastard."

"You said about how bairns change you ... guess they make you soft, right?"

"You've really gone straight?"

"You said this was about the dead woman."

"What DS Dow is getting at," Burnet says, light and breezy, "is that if you're really no longer part of that life, then there's no need to hide anything from us. We're not here to trip you up. Frankly, we don't care how you know anything. All that matters is getting the sick bastard that killed this woman."

"And what would I know? I mean, she was attacked by an animal, right?"

"We can't comment at this stage." Dow gets in quick, before Burnet can say anything.

"I haven't seen any animals round here." A pause. A thought. "Unless you count hearing the bastards. Like the wolves."

"The wolves?"

"At Camperdown. But they're in captivity. Can still hear them, though, even here. Their fucking howls travel at night."

"Then you haven't seen anything connected to this case, Mr Gray?"

"No."

"Your wife, then? Or your—"

"Son." An edge. One Burnet recognises from the way her own father talks about her. Disappointment trying to hide itself. "And, no. He hasn't said anything, and neither has she. Not that the lad says much to me. He's seventeen. You know how that is."

Burnet nods like she does. "Is he home?"

"At work." Nervous, now. Clear in the way his hands start to clench on the arms of his seat. Scratching at the fabric. Clawing, maybe.

Burnet thinks of Mrs McDiarmid. The killer putting his hands inside her, pulling at her intestines. Clamping his jaws around them.

Frank says, "He works at a garage."

"What garage?" Dow asks, tone insistent.

Burnet adds, "In case he's seen anything."

Frank looks at her. Only for a moment. Difficult to see what he's thinking. "He didn't see anything."

"All the same," Burnet says, "we have to ask."

25

THE GARAGE – HANNIGAN'S – IS FIVE OR SIX MINUTES' drive away.

In the car, Burnet says, "You and Gray have history, then?"

"He was Joe Kennedy's biggest bruiser. For years. The Beast of Balgay."

"Aye? That one?"

"He's older now, and he's got a paunch and all, but, aye, that was him. Used to be a champion bare-knuckle fighter down the docks, back when that kind of thing still went on."

"And he was also an enforcer?"

"They went to school together. From what I can tell, Frank was the troublemaker, but Joe kept his nose clean, even if he was usually the one instigating shit. Safe to say, Joe hasn't fucking changed."

"So is what he said true? I mean, about leaving Kennedy's gang?"

"Apparently. Like, no one really believed it – but he's kept his head down this whole time. Now, he's just a memory to men like me, and like a legend of half-forgotten bogeyman to the new lads on the block."

"Kennedy just let him walk away?"

Burnet has never met Joe Kennedy in person, but she knows his reputation. Not someone who gives up leverage on anyone for any reason.

"I mean, they were friends, so it's not impossible ..." A frown. A reconsideration. "Nah, that prick doesn't do friends. Just the appearance."

They pull over, opposite the garage. Standard lockup, hand-painted sign over the main doors: HANNIGAN'S AUTOS. Below that, the promise of CHEAPEST MOT IN DUNDEE. Couple of guys out front on smoke breaks. Grease-stained overalls. Big shoulders.

Bouncers or mechanics – hard to tell at first glance.

Burnet puts a hand on Dow's shoulder before he can open the door. "There's something personal," she says, "between you and Kennedy."

"You could say that."

"It's why some of the other detectives don't like you?"

"It's why I get saddled with the newbies and the ones no one else wants to deal with."

"Like me?"

"I didn't mean it like that."

"You did."

He turns back to face her. "The papers like to talk about Kennedy. How the polis are always breathing down his neck. The Chief likes to set up task forces with the goal of bringing the bugger down. But ... most cops don't want him gone."

"They work for him?"

"Some, aye. But that's not the only reason. Some of them think he does a better job of policing violence in the city than they ever could."

She presses: "But others are on his payroll?" Pulling a name out of the air: "Garner?"

"I never really had names. I took my concerns to a few people, though. Nothing you can do about coppers who don't care, but being on the take's another matter. And then I had a few visits." He closes his eyes. "No, *I* didn't have a visit. My wife and son had a visit. I was on a night shift. They were home. Cookies and milk in front of *Opportunity Knocks*. And then: men in masks, like the fucking IRA or some shite. That kind of frightener. Came in through the back window, knocked them around. They didn't ... but they could have."

Burnet's throat is suddenly dry. He won't say, but she knows. The threat men always use against women when they get the chance.

But something else in his hesitancy, too:

"The men in masks ... they were polis?"

"I'm saying someone knew. My reports were filed away somewhere. The bin, maybe. And when I learned about what had happened ..."

She nods. Understanding. The personal violation. The implication of what could happen.

"We're supposed to be the good guys," she says.

Dow nods. "We're only as good as the worst of us," he says. Then he reaches out for the handle again. This time, Burnet doesn't stop him.

26

MARTIN GRAY LOOKS NOTHING LIKE HIS FATHER. Where his father's big, he's small: small shoulders, small eyes, small hands. Arms like pipe cleaners. A habit of chewing the right side of his bottom lip. Skin pock-marked where he's battled acne.

He hunches into himself, doesn't look them in the eye.

They're sitting in the cash office at the garage: the two polis and the skinny, awkward boy.

If Dow takes the lead – authority figure, age same as his father – the chances are that Martin Gray will clam up.

Looking at the lad, though, Burnet's not sure he won't if a girl says two words to him, either.

"Did you know Mrs McDiarmid?"

"Aye. Like, you know ... I'd seen her about."

"Did you talk to her?"

More lip-chewing. Then scratching at the back of his right hand.

"Martin?" Burnet says, keeping him in the moment.

"Aye, like, I knew her. In the street and that, she'd say hello. When I was young, I was in the Cubs ... she'd get us to do garden work for bob-a-job week and that. When I got older, though, more often she'd tell me off."

"For what?"

"Hanging about."

"You often hang about?"

"I like to walk."

"You don't hang about with friends?"

Silence.

Burnet remembers lads like Martin Gray from school. No one talked to them unless they had to. Jesus, given this kid's father, you'd expect him to have some level of confidence. Instead he acts like a dog who's been beaten too often.

Burnet *wants* him to talk. Just a few words. She's certain he knows something. "We're just trying to find out why someone would hurt her."

"She was a bat, but she was all right. Anyway, it was an animal who killed her."

"Aye?"

"People don't eat other people."

That gets Dow interested. "Want to tell me what that means?"

Martin withdraws into himself again. Gaze down on the tabletop, the middle finger of his right hand tapping involuntarily.

"Please, Martin, this is important," Burnet says.

"People say things, don't they? Maybe Dad. Maybe he read it in the papers." Mumbling. A sulky toddler.

Dow shakes his head. That detail hasn't made the papers. Not explicitly.

Neighbourhood gossip? Possible. Someone overhearing the police at the scene, or just putting two and two together.

"We don't think it was animals," Burnet says. "None from round here anyway."

"You read about it," Martin says, looking up now, a sudden confidence in his manner. "Animals, that is – ones you don't expect. Like the black cats."

Again – not the first time they've been mentioned.

But Mrs McDiarmid wasn't eaten by an urban legend.

Dow says, "You sound like you know what you're talking about."

"I read. A lot."

"Aye?"

"It's true."

Burnet looks at Dow. He's shaking his head. Clear what he thinks: the lad's just a wee nyaff.

"Well," Burnet says. "If you think of anything else ..."

"I hope you find who did this." Martin's speaking clearly again, looking directly at Burnet. She gets this odd chill, and he says, "I hope you find them. And I hope you kill them."

27

THREE BUSES. OUT TO DOUGLAS, then onto Charleston, then Lochee. Frank needs to be sure he's not followed. He's meeting Joe Kennedy at a pub called the Crow and Claw.

The visit from the cops was little more than coincidence. No way they'd know he's talking to the big man again.

Just a little cash in hand. A little to tide him over. Nothing major. The old Frank isn't making a comeback. He's too fucking old.

Bag drops, collections, light work. Talk to a few people, pick up a package here, deliver it there. Don't look inside. If you don't know, you can't tell.

The polis never give a fuck about the messengers – they want the big prize. Way it's always worked: you don't make a loud noise, they'll leave well enough alone.

All the same:

A pricking back of his neck. A child-like fear of something waiting for him in the shadows.

Kennedy's taken a table near the back of the room.

Frank sits across from his old friend. Takes a long draught from a pint already poured.

"You seem agitated?"

Frank tells him about the polis.

"Crying shame what happened," Kennedy says. "An old woman, too."

"An old bat," Frank says, reflexively. Then regrets it.

Kennedy chuckles. "As may be, but still an old woman. And old women deserve respect. She's someone's mother. Tell you what – if you hear anything about the sick bastard that did this, you come to me, aye? These cowards – men who attack defenceless old women, who rape, kill them – they deserve the worst that can be thrown at them. The good old days, when you could hang for that kind of thing." He looks at Frank. "It was bad enough they made executions private. Some people could benefit seeing a coward's final moments. Now? Jesus, soft pricks they are, letting them live on in their cells. Too fucking good for the likes, aye? I ever get my hands on the prick; he'll be wishing the polis had been there to clap him in irons."

Frank thinks that there's a chance both he and Joe Kennedy would hang for things they had done together decades earlier.

"Not feeling chatty, Frank?"

Frank takes another long, slow drink from his pint. "The visit rattled me is all. The lead polis, he remembered me from the old days."

"No need to worry about that," Kennedy says. "Times have changed. I have reached ... an understanding with CID." He grins. "You might say they even support some of my practices these days."

"Oh, aye?"

"There's only so much they can do to combat human nature. And anyone with a practical mind knows that laws are all about signalling intent more than actually having any real say on what's right or wrong. Laws change. Look at those bastards, the ones lobbying parliament about sex with children ..."

"Sick fucks," Frank says.

"Perhaps. But that they can even lobby parliament about changing laws ... does that not tell you something?"

"That politicians are pervs, too?"

Kennedy shakes his head. "I don't doubt it." A wink. "In fact, I know it. But what I'm talking about is the fact that there's a difference between the law and what's right and wrong, do you know what I mean?"

Frank nods.

"And what I'm saying is that the polis get it, too. At least the ones with their heads screwed on the right way. So trust me when I tell you that whatever that pair of cunts wanted, it wasn't you and it wasn't me. And if it was" – he shrugs – "then there's others can set them right."

Frank finishes his pint.

"Good man," Kennedy says. He hasn't touched his own drink. "Now, let's get down to it, shall we?"

* * *

The job is simple: lads on one of the estates are muscling in on Kennedy's action. Frank is to deliver a message.

"And it needs to be clear, you know what I'm saying?"

Frank's hesitant. "Told you that wasn't me anymore. I've been out of it too long."

"You're still a big man."

"Aye, but I'm out of shape."

Kennedy locks eyes with Frank. His eyes are black. Holding Frank in place. "You were my number one guy. You still fucking are. These are kids, Frank. Am I going to send kids to deal with it? The young lads, they're still learning. You know how it goes. You can be a fucking example. Those were the days, eh? When you put the fucking fear of God into anyone. A beast, that's what you were. A fucking beast. And maybe we need to remind people, aye? Show them you still have teeth?"

Frank tells himself he isn't going to be sucked in. That he has limits now.

Kennedy claps a hand on Frank's shoulder. Friendly. "I wouldn't ask. I know you said you just wanted to do a few favours, but ... Look, I hesitate to say it, but we're short-handed."

"Aye?"

"The fucking World Cup, can you believe it? Not even the end of May, and some pricks have already pissed off to Argentina."

Frank's been worrying about whether he can afford a pint out to see the match, never mind jetting off to Argentina.

"Fucking bampots, spending all their savings to get out on the march with Ally's Army, all that bollocks. Not a thought spared for what it means for their jobs."

Frank knows what it means. They won't have jobs when they come back. *If* they come back. Some of them would have to be smart enough to know how Joe Kennedy would react.

"It's a one-time thing," Kennedy says. "Just to help out."

A one-time thing.

Aye. Right.

A sick feeling in Frank's stomach. Bad pint? Nah, he's too smart to lie to himself like that.

Kennedy's waiting for an answer.

Frank takes a breath.

He needs the money.

Kennedy knows.

Kennedy knew when he bought Frank that first pint. All this bag-handling shite was just about getting Frank back in the game.

Joe Kennedy never does anything without a reason.

"Okay," Frank says. And then, as futile a gesture as it is, adds: "One-time only, like."

"One time only," Kennedy says, smiling.

When Frank leaves the pub, he catches a glimpse of himself in the window of a parked car. Doesn't see the Beast of Balgay. Sees what he told Kennedy he was: an old man, out of shape. Still big – but fat or muscle? He can't say for sure.

In the window, the reflection's colour is faded out.

A ghost of the man he believes himself to be.

* * *

Frank's got company on the job. Guy waiting down the street in a Morris Minor, listening to the radio. Tapping his fingers on the steering wheel in time to the Bee Gees. "Stayin' Alive."

Jesus, if only they knew.

Frank gets in the passenger side. The guy starts the engine. Frank introduces himself.

"Heard a lot about you," the guy says. Then, as he pulls out, he says, "Davey Burns."

Burns is maybe twenty years old. Broad shoulders, thick dark hair, and the attitude of someone who thinks they're walking through a movie. One of those American gangster flicks: all attitude.

Frank thinks about his son – stick-thin, acne-ridden. Only a few years younger than this one.

Burns says, "You're something of a legend."

"That so?"

"Oh, aye. The big man there, speaks like you walk on fucking water."

"He's exaggerating."

"Better not be," Burns says. "I'm just yer driver the day. The heavy stuff's up to you." He slows down for a junction. "Know what I've been told? Watch and learn. Watch and fucking learn."

Frank looks at his reflection in the rear-view. He thinks that his eyes look tired, that the skin underneath them is too puffed up.

"So tell me about the boys," he says. "Joe – Mr Kennedy – says it's one of the gangs?"

"The Huns, I think," Burns says. "Does it make a difference?"

"How old are you?"

"What's that to do with anything?"

"You can't be much older than some of these lads."

"Aye, but I've got my head screwed on straight. Like, getting into scraps, fighting over territory, that shite, it's all fine. But it's not enough, you know what I mean?"

"You want more."

"I want what your generation had."

"My generation? I'm not your fucking grandad."

Burns laughs. "No offence intended. But, fucking hell, you lot had it sorted. You and the big man, ruling this fucking city like you did. Like he still does. The balls it took, doing what you did."

"Different time," Frank says.

"Aye," Eddie says, nodding like Frank's made a good point. "There's that, right enough. So, what then?"

"You're in charge?"

"I'm talking to you."

"Right. Good enough. I'm here to deliver a message."

"Aye?"

"On behalf of a man whose business you're fucking with."

"Free market," Eddie says. "We're ... entertainers ... nah, that's not it ..."

Jesus fuck ...

"Entrepreneurs."

"Aye, that's the one. Uniquely British, that. Being one of them. They say even the French haven't got a word means the same."

Frank takes a breath. There's brains, then there's brains. Lad's seen Maggie Thatcher talk once on the telly, thinks half-remembering what she said makes him smart.

A talker, too. He's still going. "New economics, old man. We have the product, so does your boss, and so whoever wins is the one who gets the sales, right?"

"This is Dundee," Frank says. "So fuck your free market."

Eddie shrugs. "You gonnae do something about it?"

"You know who my boss is, right?"

"The old bastard, Mr Kennedy? Oh, aye. He's sent other cunts. Think they're in the hospital, like." He looks past Frank, towards the Morris Minor, and Burns behind the wheel. "Like, the ones who had the balls to actually do anything. Fucking hell, this one's sending his grandad in to do his dirty work? Aye, fucking scary right enough." A pause. A slow look back to Frank.

"You have two choices. Quit dealing on Mr Kennedy's turf. Or kick the profits up the line. Simple enough, isn't it?"

Eddie smirks.

There's your answer.

Frank can't say he didn't try.

Eddie can handle himself – clear in his stance and in his build. He's also fast. Soon as Frank shifts his weight, he's on the defensive.

But – he's too big.

Frank ducks in under Eddie's arms and slams a punch to the lad's kidneys.

Eddie staggers, breath knocked out of him in one go. Tries to readjust and whirl a haymaker at Frank.

Frank's operating on muscle memory now.

He moves while Eddie's still winding up.

Under the fists, in at the other side. Two strikes to the kidneys.

As Eddie staggers, Frank grabs his head, pulling him down and into Frank's knee.

The wet noise of a nose breaking is louder than a gunshot.

Eddie drops.

"You got blood on my trousers," Frank says. He lashes out with his boots. Stomps Eddie's face in further.

Eddie groans, rolls away, and then stops moving.

Frank adds, "And you fight like a poof."

Eddie's alive, but he's not going to be any more trouble. If he's smart, he'll never be trouble again.

Frank says, "You know what's uniquely fucking *Scottish*? Knowing your place."

Message delivered. The lads choose to ignore it, that's their look out.

Walking away, Frank feels different. Taller. Younger.

This is who I am. What the fuck was the point even trying to deny it?

The old Frank resurgent.

28

GRAEME WHYTE – OVER SIX FEET TALL – has to stoop to go through doors as he leads Burnet and Dow into his office. Gestures for them to grab a bucket seat. They have to remove books from them to do so.

Whyte leans against his desk. Sandy beard, and long hair. Like a taller, skinnier Richard Dreyfuss from the movie, *Jaws*. She remembers the opening of the movie in '77, at the Royal Victoria Cinema. A true blockbuster – queues snaking through the street. They had to turn away over eight hundred people. The police were called in when riots kicked off. She was glad not to have been on duty that day.

"Something like you're suggesting," Whyte says, "it wouldn't happen with a lone wolf escaping the enclosure. Besides ... as you've just seen ..." He shrugs, clearly believing what he thinks is self-evident.

Burnet almost apologises for wasting his time. But they have to ask. Three people they talked to have mentioned hearing wolves howling near Templeton Woods, including Frank Gray. Even at their loudest, the sound wouldn't travel that far.

Whyte's adamant that they have to be mistaken. "I mean, could there be a wolf out there? Aye, maybe. But he'd be lost if he was. Wolves tend to hunt in packs. A lone wolf would stay away from centres of civilisation. A wildcat's more likely. But then ... I mean, they say don't believe everything you read in the papers ... but I've never heard of a wildcat killing anyone, not in their own home, and not like—"

Whyte shrugs. So confident, he doesn't even need to finish.

Burnet scratches at the back of her neck. "Is there anything that people might mistake for the sound?"

"Not much. And definitely not a wildcat." Whyte looks at the two detectives for a moment, as though trying to make up his mind about something. "The papers keep implying it was an animal attack. You're here asking about wolves. But I don't think you're convinced, are you?"

Burnet feels Dow's eyes on her, imploring her not to say anything.

But she has to be sure. "The teeth marks appear consistent with those of a wolf," she says. "But the bite pattern ..." She hesitates, not quite knowing what to say.

"Her killer was human?" Whyte says, sharp enough to fill in the blanks "And they made it look like an animal attack?"

"We believe they were wearing dentures designed to mimic the shape of wolf's teeth."

"Jesus," Whyte says. His eyes go left.

On top of a set of filing cabinets: a cast of an animal's jawbone with teeth, wired together. She tries not to imagine them ripping through human flesh.

"The shape of a wolf's jaw is different to that of a person," Whyte says. "Anyone wearing dentures, there would be clear differences in the pattern of the wounds. But if they attacked her in the manner of a wolf... the tearing, the ripping... It might throw someone who didn't know any better."

Burnet nods.

Whyte breathes out long and slow. "Fuck."

"Perhaps," Burnet says, "if anyone comes asking unusual questions or showing an unnatural interest in the animals, you could ring the station; ask for either DC Burnet or DS Dow?"

"What would 'unusual' mean?"

Burnet gets a sudden spark at the base of her spine. She straightens. Catches her breath. "Why do you ask?"

Whyte draws in a breath. "I don't know. There's this lad keeps coming round, asking about the wolves, how they feel being kept behind bars, that kind of thing."

"How old?" Burnet says. If he's talking about a child, he's barking up the wrong tree. But Whyte doesn't seem like an idiot. If he's asking the question, she thinks he has a reason.

"Maybe sixteen, seventeen?"

Burnet gets that spark again. Thinks about the kid at the garage. "Could he be a little older?"

"Maybe. Hard to tell, isn't it?"

"Skinny? Pale?"

"You have a—"

Dow's hand is on her shoulder. "It's a lead," Dow says. "Someone fitting that description may have more information, but they aren't currently a suspect."

"Of course," Whyte says. "All the same, if he comes back, I should call you?"

Dow says, "Just keep an eye out. Anything suspicious, just call us. That's all."

"I hope you catch the bastard," Whyte says. "I'll not have anyone giving these wolves a bad name."

* * *

Back at the station:
　Paperwork. Incident reports.
　No further leads.
　Interviews conducted.
　No further leads.
　Animal attack still marked as cause of death for the pet.
　No further leads.
　Mrs McDiarmid marked as "pending".
　No further leads.
　Burnet wanting scrap the form, file a new one.
　No further leads.
　But she knows.
　She knows.
　That kid in the garage:
　Tall, skinny, quiet. The pictures in his room. His family history.
　Violence does not make a killer.
　Behaviour isn't inherited.
　Nature/nurture.
　Burnet keeps going back over the forms:
　Cause of death.
At the other side of the room, Garner holds court: his thoughts on the Scotland lineup for the cup. There's a list downstairs of volunteers to provide security when the team leave from Hampden. They're calling in assistance from forces across Scotland. It's going to be big. The kind of celebration as though they've already won.

But football is a distraction. Burnet has other things on her mind.

Dow walks into the room, gives the others a passing nod. Stops in front of Burnet's desk. "Just heard the word. We've been summoned."

"Good or bad?"

If it's not good, then it must be bad.

She follows Dow up to the top floor.

That morning's *Dundee Herald* is spread out across DCI Redman's desk.

He's red around the cheeks. A vein in his forehead *thrums*.

"What the fuck are you two playing at?"

"Sir?" asks Dow.

Burnet stands a little straighter, wondering if by trying to hide how she feels, she's overcompensating.

"This shite!" Redman stabs a finger at the newspaper. At the headline:

SICK KILLER IN TEMPLETON WOODS?
Exclusive report by Richard Caraway

Burnet blinks. Reads it again. The back of her neck goes cold.

Focus.

She will not show weakness.

She will hold onto her anger.

Caraway.

That fucking dick reporter.

Their arrangement.

Of course he fucking broke it. The lure of the headline, the readership, the possible syndication – too big to ignore.

Redman says, "Which one of youse blabbed?"

"Aye, maybe. So let's see if you can show these wee shites how they do it old school, aye?"

* * *

Old school.

Jesus.

But the lad's young and willing to learn. Ambitious, too. Wants to get ahead. Davey Burns has a future; his head's screwed on straight.

Burns directs him to a bus stop – always at least two or three of them there, wearing the colours, stuck halfway between boredom and expectancy.

Their territory. No one'll move them on. Not their elders, and definitely not the coppers.

Time was, these lads would have had jobs. But something's in the air – Frank can't deny it any longer. Since the end of the sixties, maybe even earlier than that.

Reminds him of when he was young, too – there were no jobs, then, for people like him. But you still went out and got a gig of some kind. You didn't just hang around.

Joe Kennedy's the same generation. They didn't just give in. They went ahead and took what there was to take. Built something.

These gangs, in Frank's eyes, are just boys playing at hard men. Not a clue, not a single fucking one of them, what anything really means.

What did his granny used to say?

The price of everything and the value of nothing.

But Frank's not here to set their lives straight. Leave that to whoever the fuck can be arsed to pick up the slack the parents forgot to take hold of.

Frank's just the messenger.

"Ho!" one of them says as he approaches. "Grandad!"

Five of them at the stop. Blue and red jerseys.

One of them spits on the ground. Hangs back, leaning against the bus stop. Bigger than the others. Might have an idea how to handle himself. Maybe the leader. Certainly thinks he is.

The mouthy one approaches Frank. Cock-walk. "You fucking lost or something?"

"You're holding?" Frank asks.

One of the others laughs.

"You got the cash?" the mouth says.

Enough for Frank – these are the right lads.

He punches big mouth in the face. Hard. Fast.

The others are slow to react. Frank lamps the one with the quickest reactions. The other two dance back, behind the big fella.

The big fella steps forward. Slow. Smarter than the others. Hard to tell with big guys. One of the things Frank's always been proud of – he's smart as well as tough. Helped when he was boxing on the docks, and certainly made it easier on the streets.

"Get him, Eddie," one of the cowards says.

The big lad – Eddie – nods. Still taking it slow. Assessing. Says, "You got a fucking problem?"

"You lads are dealing, right?"

"You're just gonna take the gear, then? That what you're thinking?"

"If I wanted to do that, you'd be on the ground, now. Like your mates there."

Dow isn't daft. She follows his lead.

Dow says, "If you think this isn't a leaky ship, then you need to get a better handle on your department." He waits a moment, and then adds a pointed, "Sir."

Burnet wants to hug him.

She keeps her hands locked behind her. Standing at attention. Looking just over the top of DCI Redman's head. Fixing to a spot on the far wall. No eye contact.

Redman takes a deep breath. "Someone in the station's been talking. This prick, Caraway, he's written about some maniac killer on the loose. Like this city has enough troubles without reporters deliberately trying to induce panic." He looks first at Burnet, then at Dow. Burnet keeps her gaze focused on that spot on the wall. "Do you even have any leads?"

"We've been following them up, sir."

"Hence your visit to the bloody wildlife park this morning?"

Dow clears his throat. "There's someone," he says. "A young lad we talked to. Bad home life. Lives near the woods. Has a bit of a thing for ... wolves."

"Has a thing for wolves?"

"Yes, sir."

"A young lad. Who has a thing for wolves?"

Silence.

Redman says, "I know you're two of my more educated officers. I know that most of the lads – at best they read the local papers and maybe the *Sun* if they're feeling adventurous. They might even read a police manual or two if they're in an especially intellectual frame of mind – although I suspect they skip words of more than one syllable." He leans forward again. "But you two ... Dow: you know they call you a fucking bookworm, right? Because every break, there you are, with a book in your hand. And when you do read the papers, it's the fucking *Manchester Guardian*."

The bait's too much for Dow: "I believe it hasn't been the *Manchester Guardian* since '59, sir."

Redman twitches ever so slightly. But refuses to be thrown off his point. "But see, what I know, that the others don't, is that what you're also reading are novels... Raymond Chandler, isn't that his name? These *Americans* writing about crime, the worst their country has to offer. But this is *Dundee*. What we have here is real fucking life. There are no killers who can't be caught. No geniuses, or masterminds, and no one who kills people because he thinks he's a fucking animal. This lad you mention – is he the one in your report from earlier?"

"Yes, sir," Dow says.

Redman chuckles. Like air expelling from a balloon. "I'm not a bloody eejit," he says. "The name rang a bell. I thought you were smarter than that."

Dow takes a breath.

Burnet says, "I've no history with his father, and I felt—"

Redman holds up a hand. "Here's the thing," he says. "Dow has a history of leading young officers up the garden path, of making them think that they're doing all their own thinking, when what they're really doing is parroting his shite. It happened with Kelley, and I don't want it to happen with you. I mean, how would that look? A high-profile recruit like yourself – leading the charge for feminism in the force – and you're parroting the prejudices of a bitter old man who wants revenge on some retired thug?"

"It's not about his father."

"It's all about his father," Redman says. He looks directly at Burnet. "Maybe you should ask him what happened between him and Frank Gray. I mean, the real story. Find out that this liberal duffer act is exactly that: an act. He was old school, this man. Him and Kelley senior, the two of them cracking heads and not giving a toss about the rules." Now, his attention back on Dow. "I mean, did you ever tell the lad the truth about his father?"

Dow's standing straight, shaking slightly, like there's a tension in his spine, a tautness like the pulled string on a bow.

Redman says, his lips starting to twist, almost like a smile: "Get the fuck out of my office. Both of you."

* * *

The *clang* echoes into the corridor. Dow doesn't seem to care. He kicks again. And again.

Burnet remains in the door. Hesitant to enter a space she thinks of as belonging to the male members of the squad.

But Dow's kicking hell out of the locker.

This isn't the man she knows: placid, controlled. No anger. No violence.

This is ... someone at the end of his tether.

"You need to tell me whether he was winding you up, or if there's anything I need to know."

He stops kicking. The only noise now is from the strip lights overhead; a perpetual buzzing, only ever audible in dead silence.

"I've always been honest with you," Dow says. "And when I say that my feelings about that lad are genuine, I mean it."

"I believe you," she says. "But there's a reason you didn't want me to say anything to Whyte earlier, isn't there? You knew this would happen."

Dow nods. "Joe Kennedy." As though that explains everything.

"What about him?"

"You ever wonder why he's never faced jail time?"

"I can make a few informed guesses."

Dow smiles at that. They sit on the benches, look at the lockers as they speak.

"I ... I never did, but I also refused to call him out on it. Or anyone. I was tempted more than once to just take the money, keep my mouth shut. But when push came to shove, I couldn't take anything from anyone. They made it sound harmless – just turning a blind eye to small crimes here and there. You know, for the sake of peace in the city? But it's the old slippery slope."

"And that's why no one works with you except the newbies and rejects?"

He points his finger at her like a gun. "Bingo," he says. "In one. And I didn't help my cause any by doing whatever I could to dent Joe Kennedy's dealings. Making a point of it, I suppose." He grins, but there's a sadness in his face. "Arrogance of youth," he says. "Pretty soon I learned that keeping your head down is the best policy. But not before I had a few run-ins with your man there, Mr Frank Gray. And more than a few with some lads higher up the chain. You know, telling me that maybe I wanted to reconsider my attitude."

She remembers what he said before about what happened to his family, how it scared him into silence. All of this confirming what he left out then.

"Tell me about Frank Gray," Burnet says.

Dow goes to a bench and sits down. Burnet joins him.

It's the first time she's thought of him as being actually old. The way he sits, deflated, the weight of years pressing down heavy on him.

"Frank came up along with Kennedy. The big man was the brains, but Frank was the muscle." He tells her about Frank's fighting years, his reputation on the docks. "After a while, just the mention of his name was enough. Knowing that he was coming round would make anyone find the spare change down the back of their sofa. His own mother probably gave him a packet every time he popped over for tea. He was on the hook for a number of assaults, but no one ever confronted him."

She lets him continue at his own pace.

"So I was the only one who tried. Hauled him in every time, even though I knew it didn't matter. The idea being to wear him down, because sooner or later he'd make a mistake."

"And?"

"And of course the cu—the bollocks... filed charges. Official complaint lodged with the DCI in charge of CID."

"It wasn't Redman?"

"He was rank and file, then. Like the rest of us. Nah, back then the prick in charge of CID was definitely thick with Kennedy. Redman... Aye, well... I always suspected he just doesn't want the hassle of rocking the boat. So, the old DCI, he told me that if I hauled Frank Gray in one more time without provable charges, my career was up the spout. Not just here, but across the force. Some people, they have one thing in life they're good at, and mine was always being polis. The moment I put on my first uniform, I felt it, the pride and the absolute certainty, you know, that *this*, this is who I am." He shakes his head. "Sounds like nonsense, I know. But there you have it. Polis through and through, that's me. Always have been, always will be. So I made the choice. I found the line, and decided it was better to keep my head down, wait for things to change." He leans back, stretches, as though suddenly tired. "I thought maybe they were, when Kelley came through. And you, too. Young minds. Young ideas. A different kind of polis, you know?"

She laughs, despite herself. "That's what I thought. I mean, there's always been women police officers, but I always felt ... that we could do more, that there was ... it was like a token position, something to appease us, you know?"

"My wife was a copper," he says. "On the beat and everything. Traffic, mainly, but still."

"She *was* a copper?"

"When we married, she stayed home, looked after the bairns."

She tries not to react, but maybe something crosses her face, because he raises his hands.

"Look, not my idea," he says. "No one's idea, when I think about it. We just kind of did it because ... it seemed the thing to do."

"My parents think I'm here to find a husband."

"And?"

"And even if I do ... I like the job. You know what you said about your uniform? I felt the same way."

"Maybe there's hope, then."

"If they don't force me out," she says.

"That's the bind," he says. "Working with someone like me, and not siding with them. Look at what happened to Kelley."

"He brought that on himself."

"I can't help wondering, though – if I maybe encouraged him in some way. The way I talked to him, the advice I—"

"I like to think I have a feel for people," Burnet says. "I think you can look at someone and you can see who they are. In the eyes, maybe, the way they carry themselves. Kelley's a good man, or at least he means to be. But he's also violent. He's got a temper. If he didn't lose it at Garner, it would have been something else." She shrugs. "And besides, he's not gone yet. Still the hearing, still a chance for them to say he's learned his lesson, welcome him back into the fold."

Dow lets loose a short snort that might be a laugh. "Some hope," he says. "Once they bet the house against you ..." He trails off.

Burnet senses another story. One he won't tell her.

"I believe the lad knows something," she says. "Did he do it himself? Hard to say, wee skinny thing he is. But you saw what I saw. When we talked to him. The way he was. The way his father talked about him. Something's wrong. And it's definitely connected to Mrs McDiarmid's death."

"What do you do when no one wants to touch a case?" Dow says.

Burnet allows herself a smile. "You do what's right."

He looks at her. "Like I said ... there's hope for the future right there."

29

LOCK THE DOOR. UNPLUG THE PHONE.

Who's going to call, anyway?

Kelley's stone-cold sober. A little shaky, but it doesn't matter.

Box on the Murphy bed.

Take a breath. Look at the box. Watch it closely.

What are you expecting?

Something he heard once about a scientist who puts a cat in a box. While the box is unopened, the cat is both alive and dead.

So . . .

What's in the box?

Kelley goes to the sink, douses himself in water then towels down hard. Fabric rasps; rough, cheap, synthetic.

He can't put this off.

Open the box. Pull out the papers.

Space cleared on the floor. Lay them out. Sort by type.

Bills. Banks.

Boring.

Kelley's mind is sharp. Thoughts becoming short, focused.

Find the truth.

What does a policeman do, son?

Finds the truth.

Only in stories. In real life, he just tries to help people as best he can.

Kelley shakes memories away. These files are not his father's life.

What are they? Pieces of a puzzle. Leading to the truth.

He's not polis anymore. They made damn sure of that. The axe will fall sooner or later. They're dangling him now. Teasing him. Letting him suffer in limbo a while.

Fuckers.

He sorts further.

Notebooks. Filled with lines and dates and names.

Ledgers. Numbers and letters – initials at best, scribbles at worst.

Look at the ledgers.

They're not accounts. Not in any way Kelley understands them.

His dad was never poor, but never rich.

What are these sums? Where are these amounts going? Why keep track?

Open the notebooks.

Diaries?

His father wasn't one for writing, for reading. He read books every once in a while, but most of the time, Kelley noticed his dad never reached the end. So many old scraps of paper abandoning texts:

At the beginning, near the end, somewhere in the middle.

His father was not a man of words.

And yet:

Tiny, cramped handwriting. Pages and pages of thoughts and ideas.

Kelley doesn't know where to start. No dates, no markers, no sense of context.

What is he looking for?

His father tidied these notes away. Evidence of something intended to be found. Kelley's sure of that.

But found by who?

Not his mother. She wanted nothing to do with her husband's effects. His death was the closing of a door. Shutting herself alone and away.

Kelley thinks about what he's heard over the last couple of years. The innuendos. The implications.

He can't believe what they say about his father. He doesn't want to believe it.

But these documents say something before he even looks at them.

Check the ledgers first.

Don't think of him as your father.

Look at the names, dates, amounts.

No full names used – initials. Look for something familiar…

SG.

Stephen Garner?

A long shot? A wish? Maybe. Amounts go from a regular payee labelled WO to SG and others.

Kelley checks the initials. Most of them are the same as detectives his father works for. All the same payouts. And in there:

AK

Alexander Kelley?

Check the bank books. Check the dates. Check the amounts.

Nothing going in. But if it's under the table ...

Kelley closes the ledgers. His eyes swim with numbers and letters he doesn't understand.

Chest tight, breathing rough. Dizzy sensation. Breathing hard and loud. The only sound he hears now, aside from a dull rush like a waterfall.

Kelley grips his fists, bangs them on the floor. Forces the world back into view. Breathes out slow and angry. But keeps his cool.

All he has is supposition.

Evidence is key.

Solicitors mention it in court all the time: *chain of evidence*.

The one thing that will sink a case before it even starts in the courts. If you can't chart a path from intent to action by evidence then no matter if you know the truth, you're fucked in the courtroom.

Kelley learned this early on, giving evidence against a serial B&E rapist: guilty as sin, but never saying it – smiling the whole time like he knew a secret he'd just love to share with the rest of the world.

That kind of look, it's a guilty look. Not as in feeling guilty, but as in the guy knowing he did it. Wanting the polis to know he did it. But still getting away with it.

On the stand: Kelley's evidence being taken apart by the solicitors, the Procurator Fiscal looking on with this pitying expression, the guy in the dock with that smile twitching, those eyes never blinking.

Chain of evidence.

Not Kelley's fault. His fellow officers. Their errors – their *sloppiness* – made him more determined to get it right. Watching the guy walk out the court after the trial, a free man, winking at Kelley, making this little gun with his index finger was something that would never happen again.

Chain of evidence.

Make it airtight. Don't make assumptions. Don't trust others to do their job.

You are the one responsible.

Look at the notebooks.

The scribbling. Find the last entry:

They know. They know I'm having doubts. They know there's a line. They've already crossed it. They think I will, too.

Kelley doesn't need more. The chain of evidence is there. In the damn notebooks. The ones his father kept and filed like they were just so much day-to-day necessities, hidden among bank statements, chequebooks, mortgage agreements.

His father knew something was rotten in the force.

How deep was he?

Was he involved?

Ask Garner – he'd say, *yes*.

What line did he refuse to cross?

One thing to think you know. Another to prove it.

Kelley needs more than initials, more than cramped handwriting and money that doesn't even exist.

He needs answers. Proof. Witnesses.

And he knows that the chances are he won't get anything close.

* * *

A memory:

His father's funeral.

Pomp and ceremony. Dress uniforms for the police. The Chief Constable himself out, shaking hands, commiserating.

Kelley should cry. He should also be stoic. His father's dead. Crying is a sign of weakness, and he has to be strong.

What a man does, right?

The wake is at the Queen's Hotel in the city centre. The Chief Constable comes round to Kelley after about half an hour. They shake hands. The Chief Constable's palms seem warm.

He says, "Your father was a good man."

"I was going to follow in his footsteps." Not what he intended to say. The words just tumble out of his mouth.

The world stops for a moment.

The Chief Constable nods. "If you're serious, we could always use new officers. Dedicated officers."

He's gone after that, as though his duties have been seen to.

Kelley stands, his hand still held out.

An older detective who no one else seems to talk to comes over. His name is ...

What is his name? *Dow*. That's it.

He's got a shock of white hair and features that seem hewn into his face. His eyes are a sharp and piercing blue, although right now they seem a little clouded. He's been drinking at the bar since the wake started. "Be careful what you wish for."

"Why?"

Dow seems about to say something before thinking better of it. "Your old man was born to be polis."

"And I wasn't?"

"Not saying that. Just that there's some realities he needed to confront, that you'll need to face as well."

Kelley's about to respond when a big man puts his hand on Dow's shoulder. "At the booze again?"

Dow shrugs the hand off his shoulder.

The bigger officer's named Garner. He's got a cruel face coloured in hues of red that range from angry to furious. Kelley's met him in passing, but they've barely spoken.

Garner looks at Kelley for a moment, before deciding what to say: "I'm sorry about your old man."

Everybody's sorry.

That's the pain of funerals. Everyone saying the same thing, no one actually able to do anything. Mourning is impotence. What does it achieve?

Kelley wants to take action. He wants to talk to the prick who killed his dad.

Except the prick killed himself first. According to the arrest reports.

Kelley looks at the two detectives. Physically and mentally polar opposites.

Garner: big, gregarious.

Dow: smaller, withdrawn.

Garner says, "Least the prick who killed him got what he deserved."

No. He didn't.

Garner says, "Your dad died a bloody hero."

Did he, though? Wrong place, wrong time. Not exactly heroic. What Garner means is Kelley's father died doing his job and doing it properly.

But he seems insincere. Something in his tone that Kelley doesn't quite believe.

Kelley thinks he needs to corner Dow later, get him to say what he was trying to before Garner waded in with his size twelves. But he never gets to ask the question, at least not in a way that Dow ever seems willing to answer it.

* * *

Now:

Kelley stares at the paperwork on the floor. His father's handwriting everywhere – a glimpse into the old man's life that still doesn't tell Kelley what he needs to know.

The ledgers, the notes, suggest that Kelley Snr was aware of corruption. More, they imply that he was *involved*.

The initials in the ledgers: all of them could connect to officers that Kelley knows on the force. Those initials he doesn't know? He has a feeling that if he looks back over men who've retired, he'll make the connection.

There are some names missing.

Dow: a pariah in the CID for reasons no one ever talks about.

His initials aren't in the ledger.

Why not?

Kelley asked Dow over the years what he'd been trying to say at the funeral. Always the same excuse: *I was drunk, emotional. Not thinking straight.*

Not good enough.

Kelley still has Dow's home number. While they worked together, he never called, despite invitations from the other detective.

But now?

Kelley checks his wallet. Enough smash for a call. He heads out to the street, down to the nearest phone box.

Sun's going down. Getting dark.

Kelley leans against one wall of the box and makes his call. Puts in the coins, dials the number, waits.

"Dow residence."

Dow's wife.

"Mrs Dow, it's Detective Constable Kelley—"

"Oh, how are you? It's been an age—"

"I know, I know. But I need to talk to your husband. It's a matter of some urgency."

"Police business? I'm afraid he's . . . he's out."

That hesitation is noticeable. She doesn't know Kelley's *persona non grata*, asking if he's calling on police business. And she'll be wondering why Kelley would call her husband at home if he's on duty.

"It's okay," Kelley says. "I wasn't sure he'd be back yet. Look, could you just ask him to call me when he gets in?"

"Of course."

Kelley gives her the number of the phone box. Reckons he'll wait an hour, then head back inside. He sparks up a cigarette, waits at the box, hopes he has cancer sticks to last.

30

JEANNIE LOOKS UP FROM THE KITCHEN TABLE as Frank walks in the back door.

"Where were you?"

He doesn't say a word. What can he tell her?

"Frank..." A warning in her voice. Also, a hesitation.

They don't fight, not really. Not anymore.

Thing is, he's afraid...

Aye, admit it: *afraid*.

He made her a promise. But things have changed – the pendulum swinging backwards. Frank can't keep his promise and keep food on the table now.

Bite the bullet.

He pulls the envelope from his jacket, puts it on the table.

"Frank?" Hard to tell what she's thinking.

"Open it."

She picks up the envelope. She looks inside. Then looks at Frank.

He walks past her, upstairs, to the bedroom.

* * *

Later, he rolls off her, sweating lightly. She stays where she is, breathing short and sharp.

"Not done that for a while."

He doesn't say anything.

"Frank?" In the dark, her voice sounds small. "Frank? Are you sure about this?"

Lots of people, back when he quit the life, thought it was Jeannie made him do it. Rumours flew – the woman bullied the Beast of Balgay into domestic bliss.

But it had been his choice.

She'd asked the same question when he told her was quitting. *You're sure about this?*

Of course he was sure. That was why he made the promise. Because he wanted the best for her, and for their son.

He'd been toying with the idea since she first got pregnant, but after Martin was born, he'd really taken it seriously, thinking about what it means to be a father. An *example*.

Aye, well, look how it turned out? And they can't even talk about that, both of them aware that there's something wrong with the lanky lad, but unable to articulate it.

Hadn't always been like that. When he was a bairn, Martin had been Frank's reason for making and keeping the promise.

And now?

If Frank wasn't the lad's father, he'd cross the street to avoid him.

Frank never says this to Jeannie; wonders if she feels it, too.

"Frank—?"

"I'm sure," he says. "World's not what we thought it was."

"You could get another job."

"No," he says. "A man like me? They'd laugh me out the building. This city … it's not what it was, you know? The industries dying, the money bleeding out. Joe was always ahead of the curve, knew that there was only one kind of work that people would always need."

"I love you," Jeannie says.

He lets her words echo lonely in the darkness.

31

EARLY MORNING. BURNET AT A BOOTH NEAR the rear of the Washington on Union Street when she sees the *Dundee Herald* on the newspaper rack.

Front page:

OVERACTIVE IMAGINATION?
Police Chief casts doubt on "wolf" murder victim

Burnet grabs the paper. Spreads it across the Formica. Near knocks her tea over.

People look up at the sound.

She ignores them.

Skims the article, picking out the important bits:

Last night, the Chief Constable cast doubt on the earlier reported story, where police sources had told the Herald that the killer of Mrs McDiarmid (76) of Birkhill had left "unusual" wounds and bite marks on the victim's body.

"This appears to be a case of young, excitable officers leaping to over-imaginative conclusions," he told the Herald. "This murder

was a particularly vicious crime, but little about the details of this particular death can be deemed as sensational as those recently recorded in newspaper reports."

Burnet breathes through her nose. Her jaw clamps tight.

The most likely explanation, according to Head of CID, Jonathan Redman, is that Mrs McDiarmid was killed during a burglary gone wrong. "It is likely that she disturbed the suspects, who then panicked and attacked her." *DCI Redman continued to attribute the claims that the killer had left unusual wounds on the body of the pensioner to* "the point of view of a young officer who was lucky to have never witnessed such brutality before".

Burnet skims for any mention of her name. There is none. But anyone reading this – anyone with half a brain – can put two and two together.

Burnet's name was attached to Mrs McDiarmid's murder from the beginning. The curse of the Friday Girl – giving the story undue attention in the media.

Early on, her being assigned the case had been a positive. A cheap move to get the public on side: *look, the police are people, just like you! We're moving with the times! Women detectives are the future! They'll keep your grannies safe!*

"You okay, love?" asks the woman behind the counter.

"What?" A sudden flush of heat, as though she's been caught doing something she shouldn't.

"You're white as a sheet reading that. Bad news?"

Burnet shakes her head. "I should go."

"What about your tea?"

"Give it to someone else," she says, walking out.

* * *

"I can't let you in." The girl on reception has blonde hair in curls, a little too much blusher and makeup, thick accent, and dead eyes. "I mean, unless you have a warranty."

Burnet takes a breath. Doesn't bother correcting the girl. "Then call up and tell him I need to have a word."

The girl sneers dismissively, then picks up the phone.

Burnet stalks the reception of the *Dundee Herald* offices like a caged animal.

The girl's voice is monotone. "Is Cameron there? There's a WPC down here wants a word. No, she's not got a warranty."

Burnet balls fists.

The girl listens to the person on the other end, then looks right at Burnet. "Oh, aye," she says. "Like, on the rag, you know?"

Burnet grabs the receiver out of the girl's hand. "I don't want this to be official," she says into the line, "but I need to speak to him right now. Detective Constable Burnet. He knows why. And he'd better not fucking try and avoid me. I'm sure he's got at least one parking ticket I can harass him over."

She hands the receiver back to the girl, who stares at Burnet as though she's insane.

The girl listens down the line for a moment. "Aye, aye," she says. Then she hangs up. "Someone will be here in a moment." As an afterthought: "You can have a seat, I suppose."

Burnet would rather stand than use the faded sofas.

Maybe thirty seconds later, someone comes down. She doesn't know him. Verging on overweight, slicked brown hair with streaks of grey. Ruddy cheeks. Broken capillaries in his nose. Sniffs before he speaks. "Donny Bartlett," he says.

She knows the name, even if she's never met him. "I'm here to speak to the monkey, not the organ grinder."

"I should take your number," he says. "So I can report your attitude to a senior officer."

"I'll leave it for you," she says.

He licks his lips. Maybe he expects his position to carry some weight. Or maybe there's another reason he thinks he can lord it over a young woman in his office looking to speak to a reporter who has just royally fucked her all over the front pages.

"I understand you're the officer mentioned in Caraway's article?"

"The *detective*."

He nods. "Freedom of the press," he says. "Are you denying the doubt raised regarding the veracity of your claims?"

Oh, aye – dig the snoot: talk down to the wee girl in the uniform.

Burnet takes a breath. "Nothing has been determined. This is an ongoing investigation and—"

"And the Chief Constable spoke out on the issue. Publicly. On the record. Now, if you have an issue, I suggest that you take it up with your superiors. We are, after all, just doing our job and publishing reports that are in the public interest."

She considers punching Mr Bartlett in the nose. Give him a gusher, if she times it right.

The kind of thing Kelley might do. Maybe even Dow.

But not her.

She chooses her battles.

Maybe this is the wrong one.

* * *

FHQ. Front desk. Burnet seething, but at least no one's going to file assault charges.

Renate waves her over. "DCI Redman's looking for you."

Burnet trudges flights of stairs. Other officers stop talking when they pass her. The building feels like it's shrinking, walls closing in.

Why won't anyone look at her?

Redman's office, she thinks:

Maybe the best defence is offence.

"Let me explain—"

He looks up at her. Something in his face makes her stop talking.

She clears her throat, tries again. "Reading the papers this morning, it got to me. I understand that you could believe we're getting hung up on the lad because of Dow's personal connection to his father, but—"

She realises: his face is set hard, but there's no anger.

"Sit." His tone neutral.

Disappointment? She'd rather take a bollocking.

"When was the last time you spoke to DS Dow?"

The question throws her.

Why is Redman asking her about Dow?

"I don't know," she says. "Yesterday, maybe. End of shift."

She deflates. The defiance gone.

"What time?"

"Five-ish, I suppose."

"And you haven't heard from him since?"

"Sir ... what's—?"

"DS Dow was found earlier this morning out near the site of the McDiarmid murder." Redman speaks in a rush. Maybe thinks it's easier to say it like that.

"What do you mean, 'found'?"

"He's dead, DC Burnet. And given what the Chief Constable said yesterday about your theory, the facts of his death are ... disturbing."

The room is so small now; she can feel the walls pressing against her, crushing the air out her lungs.

"His stomach was opened. His intestines showed signs of something ... some*one* ... having chewed on them."

She sits down. Her chest is tight. Her lungs can't inflate.

"I'm sorry," Redman says, his voice echoing as though he's speaking to her from the bottom of a well. "I know you were close."

After that, Burnet is barely aware of anything that Redman says.

All she can do is look at a spot just behind his head. Think about how, suddenly, her own breathing is louder than his voice.

JUNE–OCTOBER 1978

32

BURNET STANDS NEXT TO DOW'S WIFE, Aislyn. Irish by birth, moved over with her parents, met Dow when at secondary.

A real love story.

A romance for the decades.

Aislyn hasn't cried the whole morning. Dignified. Refusing to play the weeping widow.

Burnet respects that.

It's a strength that their children have, too. They support their mother. All of them watching out for each other.

How he would want it.

Watch Aislyn down front during the sermon: back straight, head high. Listen to her when she speaks to the assembled of the man she loved, words measured.

Dundee creates strong women. In the old days, they were the ones who worked in the mills; the real breadwinners. Gender politics in Dundee is a little different to anywhere else because of it.

Now: graveside. Burnet isn't sure how she ended up standing next to the widow, a woman she'd heard so much about but never actually met. Even today, they've barely exchanged two words. They looked into each other's eyes, and that was enough.

The coffin is hoisted past by a group of colleagues and friends. Burnet gets dizzy. Like standing on the edge of a cliff.

Should have been with him.

The recurring thought she's had for weeks now.

They were working the case together.

She should have been with him.

She tries to look at Aislyn. Burnet has tried not to blame herself and failed. But she wonders: what does Aislyn believe?

Was there something she could have done?

Something she *should* have done.

The coffin is lowered into the ground.

Aislyn does not cry. Not through lack of emotion. You can see it, straining in her face. Muscles twitch as she watches her husband's coffin.

Closed casket.

A *closed casket* funeral.

Nothing the undertakers could do for him.

Burnet clenches her fists. Tries not to scream.

She turns her head slightly, looks at the others gathered. Sees familiar faces. Polis, mostly, with family dispersed among them.

One face absent.

Kelley.

He'd worked so closely with Dow, and he doesn't even show up to the funeral?

The clouds burst. Rain falls. Umbrellas open.

Burnet and Aislyn Dow do not shelter. They stand side by side in the rain, and watch the coffin sink slowly into the ground.

* * *

The detective on call that morning had been DS Garner.

The call came in just past eight. A dog walker whose mutt had run off the lead and into the undergrowth. Old story, really. Most corpses are found by dog walkers. In fiction, you'd call it a cliché. In police work, you call it a fact of life. Just one of those things you come to accept.

Garner didn't recognise Dow's body. The victim's face was hidden under a clump of leaves. His stomach had been ripped open. Intestines on display. Clear signs of a struggle.

Later, when Burnet forced herself to look at the crime scene photos, she thought about her childhood cat.

When she was young, her parents had a little cat that they let sleep outside. He would come in when it was raining, curl up next to Burnet, purring away as he did so. A big ball of fluff. A *cuddle-monster* her mum called him.

Burnet couldn't have been more than seven or eight.

Because her abiding memory wasn't the purring or the feel of her hand running through his thick fur. It was the day he came into her room and started to vomit

Not unusual. She'd seen it before. But this time, what came out of the cat's stomach was dark red, almost brown. A collection of hard, strange shapes, and something that she had initially believed to be a Chinese takeaway scarfed from a neighbour's bin. But then she'd looked closely.

The dark sauce was blood.

Not her cat's blood.

Semi-digested entrails. Small bones. Feathers.

A small bird. A pigeon maybe.

She never snuggled into the cat after that day. She'd throw him out the room when he tried.

Because she realised for the first time that he was a killer. With no emotion, no thought. Couldn't even digest the bird, and still killed it.

That memory of that dark mess resurfaced when she looked at the crime scene photos – her friend with his torso ripped open. *Violated* by a monster with no remorse and no hesitation.

The monster, she knew, would be someone's child, someone's loved one.

She had loved the cat.

Someone, somewhere, always loves the monster.

When Garner had put the photographs onto the board, Burnet had felt sick looking.

But she didn't show it.

She listened to the briefing.

Blocked out the chatter in the room.

Focused on the narrative of Dow's death.

It had been Dow's suit that Garner recognised first. Dark grey, wool-blend. People joked that Dow only had one suit, or else a full wardrobe of identical ones.

The suit was the first clue.

Holding his nose, Garner had reached into the pockets to retrieve Dow's ID. In the room, he denied reports that he had vomited on the corpse.

A later forensic examination confirmed that the injuries matched those found on Mrs McDiarmid.

The same killer.

The same set of metal teeth. The same bite radius.

The day after the Chief Constable's denial.

As Garner reached this part, he looked directly at Burnet.

And everyone else in the room followed suit.

Perfect bloody timing.

* * *

The day of the funeral.

Later, there's a wake at the Queen's Hotel. Burnet stands at the bar on her own. She nurses a glass of wine.

Aislyn Dow comes over. "My husband loved you like a daughter."

Burnet tries not to cry. She wonders if Aislyn is aware of some of the rumours that had been running around FHQ. "Like a daughter" wasn't the phrase on anyone's lips.

Aislyn – they've never even met, but here she is, talking like they've known each other forever; maybe they have in some sense – puts her hand on Burnet's elbow. "With that in mind, I want you to tell me something. And I want the truth."

Burnet breathes in sharp. Holds it. Maybe this is about something else, something darker.

"I want to know what happened. I know what they've told me, but there's more to this, isn't there? This case he was working on . . . you know he was becoming obsessed?"

"Obsessed, how?" It's not a word she associated with Dow. He was cool and calm. Even his conflict with Kennedy had been something he always couched in rational thought.

"Gordon always made an effort to split his life between the force and home. He promised, the first day he joined up, and every time he got a promotion or a reassignment, that he would never bring anything back with him. Not just paperwork. The burdens of the job."

Burnet nods. She understands.

"Secret to a happy marriage," Aislyn says. "He could be someone else at home. He could let it all go. Pretend it didn't exist."

Burnet wonders how healthy this could have been in the long term.

Everyone has secrets – emotions and thoughts that they keep to themselves.

But they have a way of coming out.

It's not human nature to compartmentalise.

"This case – *this* wolf thing – was different. He denied it, but at night, he would toss and turn and moan in his sleep. He would get up and walk around the house. He thought I was asleep when he did it, but I knew. He had notebooks – maybe you'd like to see them – he had notebooks, and he kept drawing pictures. Of wolves, of ... of this film we both went to see once, when we were first together ... Lon Chaney, the *Wolf Man*."

Burnet wonders about why Aislyn didn't confront her husband.

Maybe the question shows in her face. Aislyn says, "I know what you're thinking. I wanted to talk to him, but Gordon was insistent, all the time. He didn't want me to become involved with that other part of his life. I suppose in some ways, I became his safety net." She takes a breath. Her eyes are wet, but she's not crying. "I always knew when something was wrong. This case ... this dead woman ... he was bringing her home with him." She reaches up and delicately wipes at the corner of her eye with a fingertip. "The last few nights ... before ... well, before. He would leave the house in the car. I didn't know where he was going."

The murderer had struck from the woods. At night.

Dow had been told to leave it alone.

But if he could catch the suspect in the act, then ...

Burnet gets a flash in her mind. Dow raising his hands against an onslaught of long, loose limbs. Of metal teeth.

He wasn't a weak man, but the attacker had the element of surprise.

The cat and the pigeon.

Wolves and their prey.

Wolves.

She had come to think of the killer as a wolf – and, clearly, Dow had, too – but who had put that idea in their mind first?

It wasn't Whyte, the expert at Camperdown. No, they'd already been thinking wolves when they went to talk to him.

So ... who?

Frank Gray. He'd mentioned them first. Why? Just the idea of wild animals? Or something more specific?

Dow had been the one who made them go to Camperdown.

He'd known something. Suspected something.

Burnet's thoughts jumble into each other.

Aislyn says, "Are you okay?"

Burnet feels a burst of intense shame in her chest. Draws back. "I have to go." She runs from the building.

* * *

Doctor Michael Samuels looks up when Burnet pushes into the room. "Detective Constable," he says, formal, neutral, "how can I help?" As he speaks, he drops a blanket over the body on the table.

"You examined DS Dow's body? And Mrs McDiarmid's?"

"The wounds were similar, and—"

"The bite marks," she says. "They didn't look human at first. But then you decided ..." She doesn't know what to say. Not exactly. Something at the edge of her thoughts she can't articulate.

"You want to talk about the dentures?"

"Yes."

"This isn't your case."

"I know."

"So why—"

"Because you and I both know Garner was the one who initially dismissed the idea. Back when it was just an old lady who cared about her cat. But this time ... it's one of our own, so he can't ignore it ..."

"But you think he'll just pull a solution out of his arse to put it away as fast as possible?"

She nods.

"I'm inclined to agree. But, like I say, this isn't your case anymore, and—"

"And two people are dead."

He doesn't have a response to that.

"Look, I'm just doing due diligence, okay? How's that sound? This is just us talking, aye? You're not writing an official report or anything."

"If you say I told you anything, I'll deny it."

"I don't doubt it."

Samuels takes a deep breath. "They'd have to be constructed to be strong. My grandfather had dentures. Couldn't eat anything harder than a banana. I'd hazard a guess that these ones were overlaid with metal, perhaps. Sharpened to cut through the flesh. The perpetrator would still need to be strong, especially as it looks like at least some of the bite wounds were peri-mortem."

Burnet thinks of the latest James Bond movie – the mute killer with the steel teeth.

"The cat – Mrs McDiarmid's cat – was killed by someone or something with the same bite pattern."

"The cat was practice," she says.

"Which you already knew."

She doesn't say anything.

"The look on your face." Samuels answering a question she didn't ask. "I think you knew from the moment you saw the old woman's corpse."

"That kind of thing doesn't happen in Dundee," she says, remembering what Dow had said to her.

"The Black Dahlia," Samuels says, "is the greatest unsolved murder case in history. I have a feeling no one will ever know the truth about what happened to Betty Short. But it doesn't mean it could never happen here."

Burnet knows about the Dahlia. A crime so distant it feels almost like fiction. Dundee crime was: beatings and murders. Some of them shocking. But none of them so dramatic and particular as the Dahlia murders. That kind of thing could never happen here.

Right?

And yet, here she is considering the idea that someone could be trying to kill like a wild animal – creating dentures to make their fantasy more real, sinking deeper and deeper into their own twisted world.

It feels like the stuff of fiction.

But so does ex-soldiers taking classes of schoolgirls hostage. And witches being burned at the stake, like Grissell Jaffray, the last women to be executed for the crime in 1669.

Look hard enough anywhere, you'll find the worst that human beings are capable of. And then deny they could ever happen.

And then there were crimes across the country – the World's End murders in Edinburgh, for example. Again, far away and yet disturbingly close at the same time.

And for all the intrigue, Burnet knew that in the end, the killer would turn out to be some sad nobody. The reality of the murders would never match the juicy fictions people created in the newspapers.

Burnet says, "Aside from the possibility of these dentures, is there anything else unusual?"

"Everything."

"Something that stands out. Maybe something ... maybe Dow came to you with an idea? Maybe you told him something."

"Something that would account for the way in which he got himself killed, you mean?" He looks at her, head cocked to one side. "Do you smoke?"

* * *

The wind is cold. Biting. She bums a cigarette from Samuels. She's not a smoker. But whatever he's about to tell her, she'll need something to do with her hands. To stop from shaking.

They're sheltered from the main road – traffic rushes past the thick bushes that hide the entrance to the morgue.

Burnet takes a deep drag. A cough threatens.

Hold it.

Her lungs relax. The smoke coats the back of her throat.

"How old are you?" Samuels asks.

She says, "You should never ask a lady." A reflex reaction; a phrase she picked up from her mum.

"You're young enough to be my daughter. I'm not asking to get in your uniform."

She takes another drag. Trusting him a little. Something in his face, his voice, making her think of Dow. "Twenty-five."

He shakes his head. "Twenty-five. And you talk about death without batting an eyelid."

"I'm a police officer."

"You're a young woman."

"This is 1978," she says. "You know that Margaret Thatcher's tipped to be the PM? I know she's a Tory and all, but she's still a woman."

He blows out a long plume. "Only just." Another drag. Giving himself time to think. "The world is changing, you're right. But even Thatcher wouldn't want to know about someone ripping another person's guts out with a set of false teeth."

"She's not me."

Samuels says, "I liked Dow. He was a good man. A pain in the balls, but a good man."

"That's why I'm asking about this."

"No," Samuels says. "That's only part of it."

Burnet shakes her head. Loses her restraint, takes a second drag.

This one's smoother. Smoking and riding a bike, two things that come back to you.

"You're not someone who takes the easy option," Samuels says. "If you were a man, that would be an admirable trait."

A flash inside her head. Like lightning. White-hot anger.

Men could be complex and contradictory and varied, where women had to fit into neat little slots by which they were defined. But Burnet never felt like someone who fitted neatly.

She swallows the worst of the anger. "If I were a man, people might have listened."

"You asked about anything unusual," he says, changing topic suddenly, like she hadn't said a word. "I keep my eyes and ears open. I'm not officially polis, just someone who lends their expertise. So I'm not really supposed to be privy to gossip or whatever." He drops his cigarette, crushes it with the toes of his black leather shoes. Through this whole conversation, he hasn't looked directly at Burnet once. "But you hear things. And you notice things. And you learn when to stick your oar in and when to just sit back."

She lets him talk. He'll get to what he has to say in his own time.

Another drag on the cigarette.

"So what I noticed on my examination of both the late Detective Sergeant, and the old woman, was that their injuries were consistent. No surprise there. And then there's the tools used to kill them – those crafted teeth. Whoever did this, they thought they were some kind of fucking beast."

"But what haven't you said?" A gentle prod.

"I heard you were laughed out of the room for suggesting that the killer could be a teenager."

"Dow's theory. Son of some thug he had a personal issue with. The lad's definitely . . . weird."

Samuels wraps his arms across his chest. Takes a deep breath: "I'm guessing about eighteen or nineteen, overly skinny?"

"Close."

"Fits with what I'm seeing here."

Burnet frowns. "Really? I mean, I could see him taking on Mrs McDiarmid. Maybe the cat. But Dow? You said the attacker would have to be strong."

"Size and strength aren't always related," Samuels said. "Particularly in moments of extreme emotion." He thinks for a moment. "Did you catch that new American TV show? *The Incredible Hulk*?"

"The guy who turns green?"

"That's it."

"I saw some ads, but ... you know, it's for kids, right?"

He smiles at that. "I have two," he says. "It's about a man who, when he gets angry, turns into this monster. He grows in strength, becomes capable of tremendous feats of violence. A big part of why it happens is he's researching what happens to people when they have extremes of emotion. And it's nonsense, I know, but the show does mention real cases where mothers have been able to lift cars to save their children. Superhuman feats that people have been capable of in times of stress."

"You're saying—?"

"I'm saying that if this lad was angry enough, fast enough and intent enough, he could have killed Dow. I can show you what I—"

Burnet shakes her head. "I'll take your word," she says.

"Except I don't think anyone else will."

She came here to ask him a specific question. Now seems a good time to broach it. "You've had this conversation before." Framing it as a statement.

"Some of it, yes."

"We were thinking ... the killer was obsessed with wolves."

"He asked me about the teeth."

Answering the question she was talking around:

Yes, Dow had come to see him.

Determined to prove that the lad, Martin, was the killer.

"And?"

"And how someone could do what he believed this person had done."

"Do you think it's possible," she says, "that someone could believe they were a wolf?"

"That's why they kill like one?"

"They admire the creature so much, they ..."

"Wolves don't kill for pleasure."

"I've had the lecture before."

"He asked about the accuracy of the kill, yes. If a human could replicate the hunting style of a wolf."

"Wolves hunt in packs." Remembering what they'd been told by Whyte at the enclosure.

"Told him the same thing. Except, you know, most people ... they believe in the lone wolf – the one predator too tough to even hang around with its own. It's not real, but it feels like it should be."

"So that's what he came to ask you?"

"That ... and how he might make a set of metal dentures."

"That's all he asked?"

"He mentioned the kid, too. Said he was afraid that he was the reason they laughed you out of the room."

"He had prior with the lad's father."

"Look, Dow was definitely onto something. Like you are, now. He said he thought he might be able to find the evidence he needed. And then ..."

"And then he died."

Samuels shrugs again.

Two possibilities.

First: Dow had been killed by the kid.

Second: His murderer was a copycat.

Dow had previous with the father. Maybe it had seemed like poetic justice for Frank Gray to kill him this way after he insinuated the man's son might be involved.

Fucking beast.

The Beast of Balgay. That was what they used to call Frank, before he claimed to have retired and become a citizen.

Aislyn had said her husband had never got so close to a case before. Maybe he went too far. Maybe whoever killed him did it to send a message.

Burnet drops her cigarette. Crushes it out on the tarmac.

"Look," Samuels says, "I believed him. I believe you. But there are other factors at play here. From the word go, people have been trying very hard to ignore this one."

Not saying: *Garner.*

"Someone knows the truth?"

"Or they suspect that it won't turn out good for them, aye."

"This kind of thing has happened before?" Not a question. She sees it in his body language. He's been trying to tell her without telling her.

Samuels doesn't say anything.

"It's not right," Burnet says.

"Maybe," Samuels says. "But it's the way things are. Sometimes, the resolution you want isn't the one you're going to get."

33

FRANK STANDS IN THE DOORWAY OF HIS SON'S ROOM.

Unmade bed, tapes, wires trailing, discarded books and magazines. A few childhood memories linger – old toys lined up as though on display.

Frank reminds himself: the lad's still young. Maybe afraid to let go of these things and become an adult.

Frank became a man at fifteen or sixteen. No real choice.

Kids these days. Staying younger longer.

Is that such a good thing?

He wanted his son to have a better life than he did. Was that a mistake?

Can you ruin a child by doing the right thing?

Frank looks around the room.

No sign of the lad.

Window open.

Frank has to clamber over the bed, crushed against the wall, to close it. The sheets are cold to the touch. The lad hasn't slept here.

Which raises questions:

Why is the window open?

Where has he gone?

It's past midnight.

Frank's been unable to sleep. Staring at the ceiling, memories pushing to the front of his mind.

Thinking about this boy who owed Kennedy some money. Just a few days earlier. Another job Frank had said he wouldn't do, then accepted anyway. Frank and the other guy, Burns, putting the frighteners on, demanding the cash. Knowing he couldn't pay, and taking out the collateral in pain. They shattered the boy's right hand.

Burns took it one step further, threatening to chop off his dick.

I would have the money, but my lass, she's pregnant.

There was the violence Frank remembers, and the violence of the now.

Has he changed or has the world changed?

The moment had seemed more visceral than anything the old Frank whispered about. There was no righteousness, no sense that this had to be done.

The lad couldn't pay.

They knew he couldn't pay.

And they still asked him like he could. Made a show of it. Taunting him.

It wasn't simply business. It was something else.

The lad hadn't been much older than Martin. Same lanky build, too.

Which was why Frank had opened Martin's door when he got up for a drink of water. Thinking that just seeing his son asleep would be a reassurance of sorts.

Ever since the police came round asking about the dead woman, Frank's been filled with a sense of disquiet. Some of the things they told him ... Frank got this chill that ran from his balls all the way up to his brain.

Didn't know why at the time.

Still can't put it into words.

But knows it has something to do with his son.

Fear *for* Martin?

Fear *of* Martin?

Why?

The answer's there, hiding something in the back of his brain. As though it, too, is afraid.

Out of the window, Frank looks at the Templeton Woods. When he was a bairn, Martin would play out among the nearest copse.

Frank had always thought of it like a luxury. He'd come of age in schemes that were all concrete with no green spaces. Living out here on the edge of the city always felt like a luxury; a step up in the world. It had been a sign that Frank had made the right decisions in life.

So why?

How?

A memory. The incident with the tramp – Martin was maybe five, playing out in the trees, out of sight. And then, suddenly, screaming: howling like a stuck cat.

Frank remembers:

Hearing him from the kitchen, running outside. Then: Martin crawling back over the fence. Thumping on the ground, trousers halfway down his arse.

Behind the fence: a figure shambling back into the undergrowth.

Frank remembers:

Shouting at Martin to go inside.

Not bothering to take care of his son. Focusing on retribution.

Instinct for a man like Frank.

Protection is violence. Hit first before you get hit.

Frank shakes the memories. Back to the present; his son's bedroom, wondering where the lad has gone.

The tramp was somewhere in the Tay now. Long gone, long forgotten. Eyes eaten by fish.

Frank had always believed that Martin would forget what happened. Kids that age, he thought, were resilient.

If Frank had stopped to take care of his son instead of giving in to his instincts, maybe he wouldn't be thinking that—

No.

He pulls himself away from the window.

An itch in his brain. A half-formed idea, fighting to be fully born.

Ignore it.

He can't.

Picture on the wall. Cut out from a magazine. A wolf looking at the camera. Challenge in the animal's eyes.

Frank's thinks about Martin out by the wolf enclosure.

They haven't talked about that night.

Why?

The police told him that the attacks on the old woman and her pet were consistent with an animal attack, but that they were convinced the perpetrator was human.

Frank thinks about the wolves he's heard howling in the night.

The last few months. Starting just before the cat was killed. Growing in intensity and—

Could he really hear them all the way out here?

If wolves didn't make the noise, then …?

Stop it. This is fucking paranoia. This is—

Frank needs to know for sure.

He opens the chest of drawers.

Top drawer: underwear. Below that, tops and jeans.

Bottom drawer: t-shirts and shirts.

And: something hidden.

A box.

Small. Wooden. Smooth surface. Simple catch keeping it closed.

Frank pulls it out. Opens it.

A set of dentures.

They gleam. Coated in metal.

Not entirely human. Sharp, long incisors, front teeth at points.

He places the lid back on the box. Throws it back in the drawer.

And he's downstairs.

Toilet. Lock the door.

Drop in front of the toilet.

And vomit.

34

KELLEY'S CONSCIOUS OF THE CREASES IN HIS SUIT. He stands outside the door – third floor, One Courthouse Square – trying to flatten them out. A little late. But he still does it.

Like the Fat Man will care.

The Fat Man.

Private detective. Pain in the arse. Insurance fraud and divorce proceedings.

Kelley's sat across from him in court a few times, usually domestics. He's been friend and foe, depending on who's pressing charges.

The way he looks does him no favours. He lives up to his name. Breaks a sweat walking across the room. Sorts his ties by food stains.

So why is Kelley trying to press the creases out of his suit?

Because he still might need to make an impression?

"Come on in." The Fat Man's voice booming from behind the door. "If you're going to."

The Fat Man is at a desk with chipped legs and a faded leather top. Could be aiming for antique, but hits charity-store chic.

"Mr—"

The Fat Man waves a hand. "I know you," he says. "And I know what you call me."

"Not exactly professional."

"Who ever said the polis were professionals?"

Kelley can't argue with that. "Is this how you always start interviews?"

"Never needed to interview anyone before."

"Lone wolf?" Kelley asks.

The Fat Man shrugs. Mountains moving; slow and powerful. "Maybe I need someone for the physical side."

"Is that what it is?"

"Or maybe I just hate making my own fucking tea in the morning."

"I'm a little old to be a tea boy."

"Aye. Youngest detective in CID, right? And how'd that work out for you?"

Kelley's stuck between wanting to punch the fucker and liking him.

"I knew your dad," the Fat Man says. Not trying to ingratiate. Merely stating facts.

"You were polis, too?"

"For five minutes."

"Why'd you leave?"

"Reasons. Some would say I'm better suited to muckraking. And you? I hear things."

Pushing Kelley's buttons. Old game. You want to see who someone really is, then make them angry. Early lesson Kelley learned from his dad. One of the better ones.

"I'm not one of them." Almost true. Almost but not quite.

"No? I remember you giving me the stink-eye in the witness box."

"You were there to defend a shitebag."

"I was there to stop a man going away for something he didn't do."

"You believe he was innocent?"

"Of killing his wife? Yes."

"The chain of evidence—"

"Was weak at best. You wanted him to go away. Everyone in that room did. But just because someone's an odious little prick doesn't make them a murderer."

"He beat her."

"I never denied that. If he was up for beating his wife, I'd have let you throw away the key. But you hauled him in for murder."

"Who did it then?"

"Who knows? Not him. That was all my evidence needed to say, right? Finding the guilty party? That's down to our former colleagues?"

Kelley shakes his head.

The Fat Man drops the sparring tone. "Here's the thing, *Mr* Kelley. You're here because you're out of options. You saw the advert, called up, thought maybe you could make something out of this job. What I do and what you did in CID, maybe you think they're not too far apart. The difference is, I suppose, that I don't decide someone's guilty and then hang them out to dry."

"You said you knew my father."

"For a while."

"Was he part of why you left?"

The Fat Man tilts his head. "Interesting question to ask. He was a hero copper, your dad. Said so in all the papers."

Kelley stays quiet for a moment.

"Why d'you want to be an investigator?"

"I have the skills."

"Not what I asked."

Kelley holds his breath. Shoulders taut. *Give nothing away.*

The Fat Man grins, suddenly. "Had a couple of other lads in asking about the advert. Chatty bastards, all of them. In this business ... well, you need to be the kind of man who likes to talk to men who don't like to talk, you know what I mean?" He opens a drawer in the desk, pulls out a sheet of paper. "Trial period. Work a couple of cases for me. I'll see what you have about you. Maybe you'll even tell me why you're so angry at your father."

He slides the paper over to Kelley's side. Puts a pen down next to it.

Kelley takes the pen. Doesn't hesitate.

* * *

Kelley starts that afternoon.

Simple job: find someone who's skipped out on a bank loan. Not exactly challenging.

The Fat Man already knows where the man is. He doesn't say this, but Kelley's no idiot. The Fat Man wants to see what Kelley can do. This isn't like Garner sending a message – *watch your back* – with that little stunt at the high rises. This is about observation. The Fat Man genuinely wants to know if Kelley can do the work.

A little leg work. Check records for known aliases. They come up blank. So: take it to the public records office. Quick chat with the girl at the desk. Come away with mother's maiden name. Use that to make calls around addresses near where the bank had his previous.

Three hits. First name the same, last name the mother's.

No such thing as a criminal mastermind. Most people just do whatever comes into their head, go with that and think it's a plan.

In this case: False name, and a new set of rooms. Pay cash in hand to avoid a trail.

He had any sense, he'd have moved to another part of the city. Or, better, out of Dundee altogether.

People are creatures of habit. Why criminals get caught: repeating the same patterns over and over with an almost dreary sense of predictability.

Once a wife beater, always a wife beater. Once a B&E man, always a B&E man. On and on.

Telling themselves: getting caught the last time was just bad luck. This time is different.

It's never different.

Hit the lodging houses in a three-street radius. Show a picture. Ask some questions.

Lucky in three strikes. The landlord nodding, saying, "Knew he was a piece of work."

"Why'd you rent the room, then?"

"Cash in hand."

People say and think differently when they don't see Polis. Had Kelley shown up at the front step holding a warrant, the landlord would have clammed up. But now he's admitting to tax evasion like he's admitting he drinks water to live.

Second floor. No name on the door.

Kelley knocks.

No response.

He knocks again. "Got a delivery."

"Post's been."

Kelley suppresses a smile. "Needs a signature, doesn't it?"

"Aye?"

"Oh, aye."

The door opens. Kelley sees the man he's looking for. Presses papers into his hand.

Technically speaking, he didn't tell a lie.

The man bristles.

Kelley says, "This time, it's a reminder. Forty-eight hours, you'll pay what you owe?"

"And if I don't?"

Kelley doesn't say anything. Stares the man out.

The man backs down.

Kelley goes to the nearest payphone, and calls the bank who hired the Fat Man. Tells them they'll have payment in forty-eight hours.

35

BURNET SWEET-TALKS ONE OF THE TECHIES into pulling a file for her.

The force is embracing the future – bearded men with glasses in an airless room in the basement. Computers humming. Black screens with green text.

Like someone took the set of Star Trek and wiped all the optimism from it.

A smile and a pretence at ignorance gets her what she wants.

"Don't worry about the paperwork, doll," the guy says, handing her a printout. "I'd forget my own head if it wasn't screwed on. You just bring it down when you remember, I'll file it like it was always there." Smile. Yellow teeth. Nicotine stains. Crumbs in his beard.

Upstairs, at her desk, she sits down and reads.

Across the other side of the room, Garner's with his groupies – the detectives and uniforms who hang on his every word – loudly telling a story about how he made a suspect tell Professional Standards that he'd beaten himself up; Detective Sergeant Garner never touched him: no way, sir.

Burnet shakes her head. There's the public face of the force, and then there's the private one.

Burnet represents one.

Garner the other.

Which is why she's been relegated to shit-work since Dow's death: a few interviews with the local press where she's not allowed to talk active investigations, and where no one prints what she says anyway. Mostly, what happens is "smile-for-the-birdie", followed by half-remembered phrases about how the department's embracing women more than ever before.

The cases she lands now are the ones no one else can be arsed with: the lunatic who says he saw a UFO out near the Ferry; the woman convinced that her elderly neighbour is Elvis. Closest she comes to any kind of actual crime is the man whose pension cheque got snatched from an open window by person or persons unknown.

One upside: she has plenty of time to work on her own cases – the ones no one else knows about.

The identity of the Werewolf Killer.

There's an official explanation that sweeps the Werewolf Killer under the carpet, says that Dow was a wrong place, wrong time death.

Stranger danger – or the police equivalent.

In the weeks following Dow's murder, the Chief Constable stepped up patrols around key areas of gang activity. Detectives rousted the usual suspects, made them swear they never attacked nobody.

An exercise in futility, form-filling, excuse-making.

Dow's death downgraded to "natural causes" for an officer in the line of duty. In other words: wrong place, wrong time.

No one wanting to discuss what really happened.

As though they were all afraid of something.

Not even Dow's own notes provide evidence.

But they're all Burnet has.

Conjecture.

Circumstantial evidence.

All aiming towards the son of one man:

Frank Gray.

Hardman. Reformed.

Burnet intends to try and fill in the blanks. Create a real chain of evidence. Honour his memory in her own way.

Because she believes he was right.

Because she knows that someone in the department is creating a smokescreen.

Why?

Any number of answers. They don't want the embarrassment of one of their own following up a lead that had been denied at the highest level.

Or ...

Dow told her as much: some people had close connections to Kennedy. And Kennedy was an old friend of Gray's.

Back scratching?

Maybe.

At the expense of a dead polis?

Dow wasn't exactly popular in the department. He was tolerated as long as he kept quiet.

Burnet peruses Gray's sheet: arrest convictions – mostly bodily harm.

In the early days, these bust-ups are pub related. A stint for racketeering when illegal fights down the docks got busted up.

Later: intimidation and violence on behalf of organised crime. Most investigations dropped: lack of evidence and witnesses experiencing sudden changes of heart.

As she reads, across the other side of the squad room, Garner continues holding court. Off suspects now – telling stories about grateful victims. Most young and female.

Jesus.

Burnet tries to shut it out.

Back to Gray.

His association with Kennedy means he's practically royalty.

So why has she never heard of him?

Flip to the end of his arrest record. Stops maybe fourteen or fifteen years ago. Long before she signed up.

Burnet does the maths. Gray's son would have been a toddler.

Why did the arrests stop?

Why did Gray stop?

Timing tells her:

Becoming a father.

He stopped for his son.

The monster has a conscience, after all.

Burnet dives into details of his arrests.

Finds: a man unafraid of violence. Not a murderer – at least, not according to his files – but he's got a vicious temper and a habit of handing out long-term hospital visits the way old people hand out humbugs.

A thug, not a killer. Not someone who could escalate to something so unusual and dramatic as the werewolf killings.

But Dow had been focused on the son.

Who has no record.

But what if the boy has his father's capacity for violence?

You wouldn't know it to look at him.

But all the same—

"Burnet!"

Across the room, Garner's waving at her. "One for you." He has a phone receiver in one hand. "Burglary. Pub over in Douglas."

She nods. "Anyone free to help?" she says.

"You can do this on your own," Garner says. "We've got other things to take care of, you know? This one'll open and shut. Just make an appearance, take the report and the insurance company'll do the rest. Unless you see something everyone else has missed." He gives her this little smirk. "Feminine intuition, and all. Hear it works in mysterious ways."

Burnet fights the urge to give him the middle finger.

* * *

The Twa Sporrans is little more than a shack hastily erected at the end of a long row of tenements. As permanent structures go, it's clearly temporary.

The front door sticks. Only by shoving her shoulder against it does she get any traction.

Inside, she wonders if the thieves broke the meter, too: the place is in darkness. But she realises quickly that's likely deliberate; a way to hide all the dust and dirt. Stop the drinkers seeing scum floating in their pints.

At the bar, she presents her warrant card.

The man behind the bar looks her up and down. Licks his lips. Thick lips, Combine them with the wet eyes and shiny skin, she thinks he might be part fish. "I'm the owner. Meant to be my day off, aye?"

"But you were called in this morning due to a break-in overnight." Not a question.

The landlord looks at her for a moment. She expects the glance to be sexual, but it's more like disappointment. "I'm guessing there's not much hope they'll find whoever did this?"

"Why?"

He smiles without humour. "They sent you, love. Only time WPCs come out is when the polis want to send a message, like ... *nothing's getting done*." He looks her up and down again. "But at least they send along someone attractive to make up for it." A pause, and then – a little lamely, as though realising he might have offended her, "Or some hacket bird, you know, if they want to say we're wasting their time. But you ... you're familiar?"

Of course she is. Bloody Friday Girl.

Stay cool.

"Show me where the break-in occurred."

He presses those thick lips tight. Gestures for her to follow.

At the end of the bar, a small door leads into a back room. Cramped. Damp. Burnet forces herself not to breathe too deep.

A shattered window looks out onto a back alley. A safe lies open and empty, locks clearly forced. Not that it would take much effort. More a box than a safe.

A face appears on the other side of the broken window. "Detective Constable!"

Lincoln. Her old partner on the beat. Still in uniform. They haven't spoken since she transferred.

"Wondered who they'd be sending down."

"This your patch now?" she asks.

"Just go where I'm told."

"B&E?" Burnet skips the small talk.

Lincoln nods. "Before you ask, I checked: all the glass is on the inside." He taps at the side of his head. "No flies on me."

Burnet turns to the owner. He never introduced himself, but she remembers his name is Finn Gaske.

"Mr Gaske," she says, "can you tell me how much was taken?"

"Yesterday's takings. I do a trip to the post office every morning." He seems to think about this for a moment. "Except weekends. Ken, when they're closed?"

She turns back to Lincoln. "This is your patch, then? Any known burglars? Someone you think might do this?" A tried and tested method: *round up the usual suspects*.

"Aye, it's my patch for now," Lincoln says. "But I've only been here, what, two weeks?" Looking past Burnet, at Gaske, as though seeking confirmation.

"Aye, that's it," Gaske says. "Two weeks since the other lad moved on."

"Promotion?" Burnet says. "Or—?"

Gaske says, "What's that have to do with the price of fucking cheese?"

Burnet fixes him with a hard look. "If I know who the previous beat officer round here was, he might be able to tell me something that Officer New Bollocks here can't."

Gaske steps away, eyes wide. Her tone, or the words? Gaske probably believes women shouldn't swear.

Lincoln says, "I'll ask around."

Gaske steps in close to Burnet. "Look, lass," he says, voice low, "I'm sorry. I mean, I wasn't thinking, when they sent you ... Look, I suppose you're with them, right? And I know ... I mean, I know I'm late."

She doesn't know what he's talking about. Not right away. But what she's learned is that sometimes if you say nothing, other people will make up your half of the conversation. More so if there's something they really need to get off their chest.

"I can get the money," he says. "No need for this shite."

She just nods. Looks at the safe.

Thinks, whoever did this, they knew what they were doing.

36

A BLACK AND WHITE TV IS BALANCED on Garner's desk. One of the uniforms hauled it up from the lockup earlier that day, the evidence tag still hanging off the aerial. The detectives on duty spent twenty minutes finding just the right location, and now they're all gathered round, watching the game between bursts of static, all hoping that the phones will stay quiet for at least the length of the match.

Burnet sees the man she's looking for. Young, thin face, pencil-moustache. Part of the recent intake. Clear from the way he and Garner talk how he got the transfer.

An air of anticipation in the room. The conversation will have to wait.

Burnet thinks about all she hears on the streets these days are people chanting about being on the march wi' Ally's Army. That, and

Fitba' crazy . . .

Fitba' mad . . .

The match closes in on half time. Maybe a chance for her to catch the new detective. Halliday, that's his name. The uniform Lincoln replaced on the beat.

She's done her research – his approach to the beat was heavy handed. Lessons from his mentor, no doubt, and didn't do any harm on his application to CID.

"Haw, Burnet! You no watching the game?" It's Halliday himself. Sounding merry. Pre-match courage on his breath. "Come on, this isn't about football – it's national pride!"

A cheer goes up. Rattles the windows.

Burnet opens her folder.

She wants to join in. The whole country's watching this match. No one's doing any actual work today.

Except her.

But she can't do it. She can't let go. Can't stop thinking about what she knows. Or what she thinks she knows.

Garner sits on the edge of her desk. He leans in close. "What're you looking at anyway? You're telling me it matters more than this?"

She shrugs. "Football or break-ins," she says. "Tough call. I have no idea why I think this could be more important."

"We're here, aren't we? Half the fucking nation's skiving off – and that includes the fucking bampots and arseholes we'd be out arresting any other day. But we're here, so give us that. Fucksakes. You don't want to watch, then fine. So ... mebbe to make up for your grumpy fucking puss, you could give us a wee peck?" He lowers his cheek down to her. "For luck?"

She ignores him.

"Or one on the lips, you know? That's real luck." Real close now, so only she can hear him whisper, "And, like, a bit of tongue—"

A roar comes up from the other side of the room. None of Garner's groupies are paying attention anymore. That roar's more primal than watching one of their own get knocked back.

Garner's off the desk, back over the other side of the room. "The fuck?"

"They just equalised"

"Get to piss!" Garner shouts back to Burnet. "One kiss! Jesus, one lucky fucking kiss! They would have missed!"

"God's sake," she says. "Grow up."

"If we lose," he says, "it's your fucking fault." Giving her the finger.

Burnet tugs at her hair a little harder than usual. No point grabbing Halliday. Not when she's the bloody Jonah for the national team.

Focus on the reports. The work.

Read the files.

Break-ins over the last few months: business premises. Pubs.

Look for a pattern.

The officers on the beat. The detail is in the reports.

Look to be a bloody detective. Maybe the only real one in the room.

* * *

The last month and a half – an increase in unsolved break-ins. Much of them focused around establishments in Douglas and Charleston. No witnesses. The owners often forgetful or uncertain about how much cash might have been taken: statements incomplete or incoherent.

Burnet thinks:

Read between the lines.

She recalls the reaction Finn Gaske had when he realised she was CID – like she was there to collect dues.

Think about that prick, Halliday: one of Garner's groupies.

Several of the pubs are/were on his beat. Including the Twa Sporrans.

A further eight in areas under the protection of Joe Kennedy.

Witnesses who won't talk. A wall of silence.

Interview transcripts: no one pushing too hard.

Half time, now. The squad room quiet. The lads out having a fag, mostly.

Leaving:

Just her and Garner.

"Garner?"

Lacking an audience, he doesn't play up. Keeps his distance. "What?"

"You know something about the open investigations into Kennedy, right?"

He smirks. "You catch something from Dow? Fucker was obsessed."

"I just wanted to know if the official investigation was still open."

"Until we catch him in the act of doing something – you, me, all of us treat it as closed. Do you know how many times he's tried to sue the force? Besides, I'd rather have someone like him out there than some of the twisted fuckers I've met. Or those Kray boys down in London? Jesus, the shite they try and pull. Kennedy's an old-fashioned man, and we're better with the devil we know. Besides, it's not your job to try and bring him in if that's what you're thinking."

"Maybe," she says. "But I can't stop thinking about something ... when I went down to the Twa Sporrans break in."

His face sets tight and grim. Panic in his eyes? Maybe. But he's trying to hide it.

She says, "I mean … It's probably nothing, but one of the punters said they heard someone threatening the owner. Like, a few days before the break-in. Said they thought it was a copper. Plainclothes, too."

He doesn't respond.

"I mean, probably shite, right? Someone pretending to be polis, thinking they can pull a fast one?"

When he doesn't say anything, she reaches up and scratches the back of her neck – jumps in with both feet: "I was hoping to have a word with Halliday. The break-ins are focused around his old patch, and I wondered if he—"

"You know you're not a real fucking detective, right?" He stands, walks over to her now. "I mean, this is all about making us look good. We had poster boy for a while. With his good looks and hero dad, and that didn't work out. So now we have you, and we can say we have a woman in CID."

"You've had women working here before."

"Aye, but you're special, aren't you? The Friday Girl, all that shite?"

"I'm a detective the same as you. I'm here because—"

"Because that old foosty fuck Dow had a soft spot for you. The only reason you're still here is because it looks good. They asked us, you know? How we felt about you staying on after his death? We all agreed it was fine, because – well, let's be honest – it's nice to have a pretty face around. And it keeps the feminists from crawling up our arses about equality and all that. But don't go thinking you're a fucking detective like me, like the lads, even Daddy fucking Dow. Put the case away. Go and work what we want you to work. Do what you're told."

Halliday, who's just come back from his smoke break, jumps in: "And make us a cup of tea while you're at it!"

"Milk," Garner says. "Two sugars."

* * *

End of shift.

The game finished. Near silence from the squad room.

Three–one to Peru.

Ally's Tartan Army. More Ally's Red-Faced Army.

Burnet had heard the pre-match banter. Scotland were not just going to win the game – all they really had to do was turn up and it was theirs for the taking. Then, all that was left was lifting the World Cup. Payback for all the years of England crowing about '66.

But now?

Fat. Bloody. Chance.

"Fucking Peru? Seriously?" Halliday says before leaving the room.

Burnet sticks it out at her desk, doing what she needs to do. Fighting the distraction of the football result, her moody colleagues. They'll get over it.

Thinking about what the owner of the Twa Sporrans said to her.

It was Halliday.

He was the one taking the money. Who knew when the place was empty. Could have cased the joint easy.

Garner knows it as well as she does.

And she thinks:

The pair of them are in it together.

There are supposed to be lines. There needs to be lines. Even a copper taking the occasional bung wouldn't be so daft as to commit a B&E on his own patch, right?

She can't prove it.

Smug bastards.

She walks to the bus station, jacket tight against the cold. Wind picks up. A car passes her. Slows down. She's the only pedestrian on the street. The driver's turning his head, looking at her.

The windows are steamed up just enough she can't be sure who it is. But she can make a good guess.

They want her to look.

To be unnerved.

Burnet keeps her eyes ahead.

The car speeds up, drives on.

Burnet pulls her coat even tighter.

37

"BEEN A WHILE SINCE WE SAW YOU." Dr Hughes looms over Frank, facemask pulled up, light shining from his headtorch. Dr Frankenstein looming over the monster.

Frank says, "You know how people feel about dentists."

Dr Hughes ignores the remark. "Have you been experiencing any discomfort?"

Frank shrugs as best he can, lying in the chair. Gripping the armrests tighter than he should. He's never enjoyed this. Since the introduction of the NHS, he's been one for going to see the dentist when he can – but he still has childhood nightmares of being forced to go – *for his own good* – to a man who was little more than a sadistic torturer.

"In my experience, when someone shows up months after their last appointment – close to a year – it's because they have something that needs dealing with."

Frank pushes Hughes away and sits up. "It's my son."

"Then why didn't you make an appointment for him? Or why didn't he make his own? He's been doing that for the past few years. Good teeth. And a good lad, of course. He was here three months—"

"He has a set of ... dentures." Frank being careful. Knowing how he might sound.

"Yes. I made them for him. Well, the cast at any rate. He didn't steal anything from me."

Frank doesn't know what to say. Dr Hughes made that ... monstrosity?

"Your son has an interest in dental hygiene."

"What?"

"Last time he was here, he was asking how it works – creating dentures. I don't know if he'll get into college, but ... I thought what was the harm in showing him? So we made a cast of his teeth."

Frank wishes it was as simple as his son having ambition or an interest in dentistry.

But Frank knows enough about his son. Sure, Hannigan said he was a decent enough worker, but Hannigan had always been a soft touch. The truth was he'd be letting Martin away with—

The word *murder* sticks in his mind.

He tries to push it away.

Wonders if he knows his son at all.

"I didn't want to be a dentist when I was younger." Dr Hughes removes the facemask and headtorch. "I'm sure you didn't want to be a security guard. But we don't know always know when we'll find the path that's right for us, do we? Is there a reason you're so concerned about this?"

Frank thinks about the dentures in Martin's room. The shape of the teeth.

"You used his teeth for the cast?"

"Of course."

"No animal teeth?"

He's thinking of what he found in his son's drawer.

Hannigan talking about how he'd find Martin using the lathe in the workshop for "personal projects" he wouldn't talk about. Hannigan not saying whether he put a stop to it or not.

Dr Hughes creases his brow, shakes his head. "Human dentures. His own. Designed for his mouth. Based on his own teeth."

"Could he ... I mean, is it possible he could have adjusted them somehow?"

"I don't know what you mean, Mr Gray."

Frank gets up.

"Mr Gray, I have to say I'm a little concerned—"

"Don't be," Frank says. "Just a stupid moment, that's all. Just—" He leaves the room quickly, slamming the door behind him.

Downstairs, outside the main door of the building, he stops and leans against the jamb. Takes deep breaths. Chest tight. Mind racing.

Closes his eyes.

Sees the teeth.

The metal.

He has to be wrong.

He has to be.

The alternative ... he can't think about it.

He won't.

38

BURNET AT HER DESK.

Another day.

Another day of her dream job sinking into a nightmare.

Just get on with the job.

Someone's behind her. They don't make a noise, but she's aware of their presence. Before she turns, she can smell the aftershave.

Jesus fuck.

Hai Karate.

She knows before she looks up.

Garner.

"You busy?"

"Well?"

When she looks at him, she tries her best to hide her reaction. Garner looks like Jack Nicholson in *Chinatown* – nose bandaged, eye blackened.

"Got this thing I need a hand with." Acting like everything's normal. "Just came in. Look, I know you're a fucking bra burner, but I need a woman."

She almost flinches before realising that it isn't a come-on or an attempt to make her feel uncomfortable. He's serious.

"Domestic. Missing girl. The mother's ... I just think rather than two big bastards turning up, maybe, you know ... A woman's touch?"

"Are you sure the filing can survive without me here?"

He waves a hand at her. "Aye, go on then," he says. "You try and—"

"Fine," she says. She doesn't want to go anywhere alone with him, but she's still polis and she has a duty.

And maybe it's a chance to come out from under the shadow of the werewolf killer.

Maybe this is her way to make her voice heard again.

* * *

Photographs on the mantlepiece. Happy families, for the most part. The girl growing over time. Becoming a woman.

Burnet says, "When was the last time you saw your daughter?"

Mrs Talbot – forty going on sixty-five, nicotine-stained fingernails – thinks about this. Like she's taking a test. "Three weeks ago."

"You only called this morning." Not an accusation. Just trying to establish a timeline.

Mrs Talbot chews the inside of her cheeks for a moment.

"Thing is ... Tessie could be a little ... impetuous." The word is chosen carefully, but pronounced uncertainly. Intended as a demonstration to this police detective that Mrs Talbot is a good mother and an educated woman. Mrs Talbot lives in a small house, rented from the council, but she still has her pride and she's as good as anyone else.

Burnet pushes down her empathy. Keeps looking at the pictures on the mantle.

"Did she have a boyfriend?" Asking as casually as she can.

"No. I mean, I think there was this lad at her school was interested ... shy, like ... but not her type."

"Okay – an ex?"

Mrs Talbot hesitates.

"Anything you can tell us ..."

"There was this other lad ... Dickie ..."

"Dickie has a surname?"

"Borer. Dickie Borer. Lives out near the Hilltown."

"With his parents?"

"Naw. One of the reasons I didn't like him. One of those lads, liked to act like he was king of the world."

"A bad influence?"

"My daughter wa—is her own woman."

The trip of the tongue seems to echo round the room, making the atmosphere heavy with dread possibility. Mrs Talbot scrunches at the hem of her dress. It's off-yellow, heavy wool. She wears tights underneath. She's a woman who dresses old before her time. Burnet thinks they could be closer in age than you might think at first glance.

"But they split up? You daughter, and this Dickie lad?"

"Oh, aye."

"Her or him?"

Mrs Talbot does the scrunching thing again. "I don't know."

"She didn't talk about it?"

"When she told me, she said I wasn't to say anything. You know how it is at that age."

Burnet makes a mental note. A few possibilities present themselves.

"Would you say Dickie was a violent person?"

Mrs Talbot's face scrunches like she's trying to add up too many numbers at once.

"Mrs Talbot?"

"I never saw any sign."

"But you suspected?"

"Has he done something to her? D'you think—"

"We don't think anything yet," Burnet says. "She's nineteen years old, so she can go her own way if she wants to. She doesn't have to tell you where she is or with who."

"But she's not like that. We got on."

Except, Burnet thinks, *for the part where she didn't tell you anything about her boyfriend or why they broke up*. Every daughter has their secrets. Some are bigger than others.

Burnet thinks about her own mother's belief that her daughter's nearly thirty years old, and yet somehow never been kissed. It's almost enough to bring a smile to her face that she has to fight back down.

The door to the living room opens. Garner walks in – size twelves, two cups of tea. As requested.

His usual bravado is closed down. The atmosphere in the room freezes over. Not just the expression on his face – imagine, a male detective making the tea! – but there's also the fact that Mrs Talbot clearly doesn't want to talk to him. Now he's come back, all of the progress Burnet has made evaporates.

The fact he still looks like he's come fresh from a fight doesn't help matters either.

Burnet wonders what happened to give him that shiner.

"Youse have a productive wee natter?" Garner talks to Burnet like Mrs Talbot's not even in the room.

"We were getting to know each other." Then, because he's going to ask: "There was a boyfriend."

"Case solved." Garner sits down across from Mrs Talbot, and puts his hand on his thighs: position of authority. "Your daughter will be down this lad's house, probably thinking that whatever they're doing is tantamount to getting married. I know I'm being blunt, but that's the reality these days." He turns to Burnet, fully expecting support. "Isn't that right?"

Burnet swallows down her instinctual response. "My colleague here is trying to say that we think your daughter will be all right. When I was her age, I had a thing for bad boys, too. What's most likely is that he's come back to her, and she's decided to believe he's really sorry. Did you fight about him, this Dickie?"

"Aye, all the time."

"Okay," Burnet says, keeping her tone soft, trying her best to back up Garner's preposterous theory for the sake of appearances. "At that age, girls like to rebel against our mothers. I'm sure you did, too, in your way?"

Mrs Talbot's lips twist. It takes a moment for Burnet to realise the woman's trying to smile. "We used to have awful barneys if I went out to the dancing," she says. "I'd sneak out through the bedroom window, come back in late at night. I was always afraid she'd know I was gone." She talks faster, thinking about her daughter again. "But I was always back the same night! I'd never *step out* with a boy!"

Burnet hunkers down in front of the woman, who picks her hands away from the hem of the dress – holding them up and squeezing them. "The world is different today. But it's all the same, too. You have to trust me. Everything you've told me about your daughter says she's a sensible young woman, and what we're going to do is we're going to find her and bring her home."

"You mean it?" Mrs Talbot says, pulling Burnet's hands closer in towards her. Now that Garner's back in the room, she acts like she really does have hope that because a woman's here, the police might *understand*.

"Aye," Burnet says, fighting down a sick feeling in her stomach. "We'll have Tessie home before you know it."

* * *

Outside, she stops Garner on the front steps. "I asked you to leave the room for a reason."

"A wee girly chat?" Dismissive prick. He was the one asked her along.

"She was worried, and she wasn't telling us everything. Because you came in like a bull in the china shop."

"You said it yourself: the lassie's shacked up with some ex-boyfriend. We go down, we drag her out and we bring her home, job done."

Burnet walks away. Playing it casual. No point poking the bear.

"Jesus," Garner says, jogging to catch up, "you really are determined to fucking show me up. Is this a feminist thing? Setting little traps to make men feel like arseholes?"

Can't help herself: "You do a good job being an arsehole without my help."

Keep it under control. Save it.

"Listen," he says. "You're right. I asked you out here because, aye, I needed a woman to deal with the old bird in there."

"Old bird? She's not much older than me."

"Having bairns ages a woman faster."

She almost laughs at that. "Is that a fact?"

He nods, not a trace of irony. "Biological. Anyway, sometimes you need a feminine touch. And she gave us the boyfriend. That's something. Chances are, the girl's with him. So we go and find him, we bring her back."

No control: she laughs.

He looks at her. "Seriously? What, is it the time of the month or something?"

Keep it together. "Is this all I'm good for to you? Keeping the women calm and doing paperwork?"

"Like I said: biology. Not sexism. You're a woman, right? You're different to men. You have different fucking strengths. And they can be useful. Happy? Fucksakes." He steps away from her, fists clenching.

Burnet can't help but notice his hands. Big. Like fucking spades. Everything about Garner is big. He's a walking threat.

"This is why I never settled down with anyone," he says. "Women ... you know how fucking infuriating you can be?"

She says nothing.

"Look, what I'm saying is that maybe you're good at doing the sensitive shite. Maybe it's good to have you along, to talk to people like the fucking mother there. But most of the time, the people we deal with, we need ... we need to do things that you're physically incapable of."

She knows what he's saying. Let him keep digging. Here, in the daylight, on the job, all his threat is gone.

Which makes her wonder what happens when he's in front of his audience again.

"What I'm saying," Garner says, "is that we go find this Dickie cunt, you take the daughter out of the room and tell her whatever home truths the mum told you, while I give him a good kicking. And, you know, maybe she could see him after …"

"Why the fuck would you—"

"Good life lesson," Garner says. "For her to see what happens to cunts who make bad life decisions. Maybe make her think better about the kind of lads she's going with, you know?"

39

KELLEY SHOWS UP TO WORK EVERY MORNING, clean, freshly shaved and outwardly sober.

The Fat Man told him, "Start every day like you're calling on one million quid." Meaning: *give an air of giving a shite, and the clients will trust you.*

Kelley'd figured when he found work again, he'd drink less. Truth?

Drink helps him sleep at night.

If he doesn't sleep, he looks at his dad's notes. Names, dates, numbers.

The choice is:

Come in hungover, or come in sober but sleepless with all those thoughts running inside his skull.

But he does his job well enough that the Fat Man doesn't have any complaints. Maybe the best he can do.

Nine sharp, at his desk: same as every morning.

The Fat Man comes through the door that divides their office. "You and me need to talk."

Kelley wonders if he's been slipping. Is there alcohol on his breath?

The Fat Man comes to his desk. "Mind when you came to work for me, you mentioned you had some person work you might want to do. Your dad's death and all that?"

Kelley says nothing.

The Fat Man stands, blocking all light from the window. "Do you still want to know what really happened? With your old man?"

Kelley says, "All I have are notes. They could mean anything." Wishing he'd never mentioned what he found.

The last few months, he'd got too comfortable. Thinking of the Fat Man like an equal maybe. A colleague.

Not a friend.

Never a friend.

The Fat Man doesn't do friendship.

Why Kelley never thinks of him by name. Even if the words "Fat Man" never cross his lips.

"What you're afraid of is that these notes could implicate him," the Fat Man says.

Yes.

Kelley's father died a hero.

Is he willing to risk his old man's memory?

"What do you know?"

"You're a good detective," the Fat Man says. "As in a private one. A good cop? I doubt it. Most polis are at their best when they don't *invest* in the job. Emotionally speaking. Your old man knew it."

Kelley tries not to smile.

The Fat Man makes a clucking sound with his tongue. "Check you, in all your masculine fucking glory. The strong, silent type. Gary fucking Cooper – all action and few words." A sudden intake of breath. He does this sometimes, like he's forgotten to breathe while he talks. "Mind if I take a seat?"

Kelley waves his hand, as if to say, *be my guest*.

The Fat Man sits.

"Do you know what it is to feel guilt? Real guilt, I mean. The kind that fucking stabs in the heart every day because you know you can never do quite enough to atone for it."

Kelley can't help himself. "Are you giving me the noble hero speech?"

"Are you giving me cheek?"

Kelley raises both his hands; *I surrender*. The Fat Man's expression is *serious*.

The Fat Man takes another breath. A slight rattle from his lungs. "I've done things I'm not proud of. Everyone has. But when I was on the force ... There were things I saw ..."

Kelley's done the maths and the background. Knows enough. "You joined up at the same time as my old man."

"Aye."

"You weren't friends."

"No, we weren't friends. Not exactly."

"So why hire me?"

"You had the courage to do what he couldn't."

"Which was?"

"Walk the fuck away."

* * *

The Fat Man tells his story in his own time.

Kelley listens.

The Fat Man believed in the polis. The ideals. Joining for reasons he said were "personal", never expecting to look back.

He walked the beat for a while.

And then people started asking him questions. Older, more experienced cops.

Questions like: what do you do when someone asks you to look the other way?

What if someone fucking *deserves* a beating?

The Fat Man was no innocent. He'd known that the job might involve a degree of moral uncertainty.

Kelley knows what the man's talking about. Part of the job was always going to be about walking a fucking line. Doing what was *right*, not always what was procedure.

But Kelley believed: change the procedure, you make things better.

The Fat Man and his father had joined up in a different time. No one thought you could change the procedure. And, so, you either accepted or you became disillusioned.

"Your old man was back from the war around then."

"He never talked about his time abroad."

"Of course he fucking didn't."

"You didn't serve?"

The Fat Man looks away. "There were reasons. Outside my control."

Kelley doesn't ask. Maybe the man had been a conscientious objector. Maybe his weight had something to do with it. Maybe there was something else there he wasn't willing to talk about.

"Most of the others at that time, they all had shared experiences. Made me an outsider. Your old man, he wasn't so bad, but others – Garner – treated me with suspicion. Maybe that's why it took me so long to cotton on."

"To what?"

"To the Veteran's Fund. That's what they called it. *The Veteran's Fund*. The idea was pretty simple. Take a cut from any monies recovered from illegal activities. Note it down wrong in the official reports, take the difference and put it into the fund. Most of the men were into it. I think Garner was the one in charge. Some of the younger officers looked up to him."

"My father included?"

The Fat Man nods. "I didn't see too much, but like I said, I didn't serve and so I was an outsider; not to be trusted. For all they knew, I'd been a conchie. I learned about the fund when I caught your father skimming a bit of cash. We'd arrested a couple of hoors who'd got into some kind of turf war. While I called for the van, your dad went into the bedroom to catalogue evidence. I went to inform him about when backup would be arriving, found him with the money, and noticed how it seemed off, what he was doing. He told me the truth. One thing I can say is that he was one for honesty."

"In some cases."

The Fat Man shakes his head. "You have to understand how things worked back then."

"I think I have an idea."

"If you were polis, you had power. But only so much. The guy above you had more power, so even if you thought what he asked you to do was wrong, you still did it. Maybe it was a forces thing. You know, you do what the senior officer tells you. But I think your old man just didn't have a problem taking money off those who had obtained it illegally. A little Robin Hood thing."

"For the veterans."

"Precisely."

Kelley doesn't want to hear this.

He remembers: his dad had tried to warn him, about all of this. Without saying anything, of course. How could he have gone into detail if half of this is true?

Lightning pulses through Kelley's brain. Not anger. Something else – roiling and boiling inside his skull.

Making it hard to focus.

But he has to.

You start something, you finish it.

One of his dad's lessons. One of the few Kelley thinks might not be tainted by any of what he's about to hear.

The Fat Man tells him more about the Veteran's Fund. How they divided the spoils, distributing it to men who had served and gone to war, and keeping some aside for those who might be injured in the line of duty.

Kelley thinks about his father: quiet, reserved, intense. Intent on teaching his son about living the right kind of life.

Why would he have accepted this?

Because he was only one man?

The Fat Man seemed to think that Kelley's father got in over his head. "Your father was a reasonable man. He understood that the Veteran's Fund wasn't above board. But he thought it was a higher cause, maybe. Don't know if you remember back in '72, the Chief Constable of the Met calling out his own CID as the most 'corrupt organisation in London'? Aye, well, he was right about that in most places, wasn't he? But not the kind of corruption you're thinking of. Most cops, they look the other way, or they skim off the top because they think they're serving a higher cause. That was your old man, I think."

Garner had different ideas. The Fat Man started asking questions after Kelley's father told him what was going on. He looked deeper into what some of his fellow officers were up to. The uniforms were mostly just taking advantage of grey areas, but CID had started to develop some more questionable practices in the name of keeping the peace.

"Garner used to drink at pubs owned by Kennedy. Had a few tabs. Not evidence in itself, but—"

Kelley knows what the Fat Man means.

Gut instinct.

All detectives – all good detectives – have good guts. The Fat Man prided himself on his. The trouble was, back then, his gut was good enough he worried it might get spilled.

"I was young. I was fucking stupid."

"So you decided to follow up on what you knew."

"The DCI in charge put on a good act. He knew how to play to the Chief Constable. Said all the right things, made it look like he gave a damn how his department was perceived."

"But then you went to him? To the Chief?"

"With evidence."

"And?"

"And ... I got told to leave it alone. That maybe CID might have reasons for forming contacts with certain undesirable elements, and I was too green to understand."

The Fat Man talks low and slow. Keeps his voice even. But the anger is clear. Just beneath the surface.

Roiling and boiling.

After all this time.

Kelley wonders if it ever stops. Ever ceases.

Knows the answer. Doesn't want to admit it.

40

THE FAT MAN'S STORY RINGS TRUE, even if Kelley wants to deny his own father's part in these events. But he knows the truth.

The idea that men like Garner could hold influence over those with higher ranks. That the chiefs might cover up schemes and dodges in the name of the thin blue line – if all of that is true, then why not the detail of his own father's involvement?

Why else would he spend so much time discouraging his son from joining?

It took his old man's murder for Kelley to finally break through.

Accept it.

Accept the sins of the father.

And that everything leads back to Joseph Kennedy.

That everything you ever believed about your father was a lie.

"Your dad wasn't a bad sort. He told me to keep quiet, but didn't threaten me."

"And what did you do?"

"What he asked. But I said there was a line. He understood that. He had his own lines, too."

Kelley wonders: *what were those lines? How deep was my dad's involvement?*

"He got promoted," Kelley says. "And you got fired."

"That was later. I mean, the Veteran's Fund was only the start, like I said. Your father, he told me just to leave it alone. But I couldn't. Garner was dirty. Not just taking the skim like your old man – which, let's face it, is almost a victimless crime – but he was moonlighting for Kennedy. As a bag man. Disguising pick-ups and drop-offs as responses, that kind of thing. He had a close cabal who were willing to ask no questions and tell no lies."

"My father wasn't involved, though?"

"The Veteran's Fund was as far as he went."

The pressure in the room lifts.

Kelley lets loose a breath he didn't realise he was holding.

"Did you have proof for any of this?"

"Why do you think I specialise in tracking down people who don't want to be found? Nothing like some on the job training, right? The fucker's good, and it took me a while, but – when I realised he was delivering packages for Kennedy – I thought, there's a point you can't turn a blind eye any longer."

Kelley can pretty much write the rest of the story:

The Fat Man taking the evidence to the top brass, getting reassurances followed by silence.

Then:

Frozen out by other uniforms. Overlooked for promotion.

And then:

"Maybe I should have seen it coming."

One of the reasons that newer officers look down on the Fat Man: he left the force in disgrace. Stash found in his lockers during a routine inspection. Dealers willing to say that he let them get away with their business in exchange for product.

"You were fitted up?"

"Course I was. But I don't think your father knew. Or rather, I don't think he was involved. He was turning a blind eye because he knew there wasn't anything he could do."

His old man already had one toe in the sewage pipe. Garner would have enough to destroy not only his career and reputation, but likely his life.

Kelley had attended a training course about corruption. White-haired lecturer on the stage in the university lecture theatre, telling them that corruption doesn't start out as something all-encompassing. It creeps in slowly. One small favour here. A blind eye there.

The snowball effect.

Kelley's waiting for the bombshell.

Why would the Fat Man wait this long to tell his story?

He knew about the papers.

He knew what Kelley now knows.

So what's the final twist?

Kelley fights the urge to grab the big bastard by the collar, yell in his face: *Get the fuck on with it.*

Hands twitch.

Jaw clenches.

The Fat Man says, "I'm telling you all this so that you understand."

"Understand what?"

"Understand why I couldn't tell you the truth before. I had to know. Not just that you were his son. But that you would believe me."

Kelley gets the fizz in his brain.

Anger bubbling.

Keep it down.

Listen to what he has to say.

"I think I know what really happened to your old man. I don't think it was an accident."

Kelley's freefalling. Drowning in the fizz of his brain.

He focuses on the Fat Man.

Listen to him.

"See . . . he came here a few weeks before he died. I thought maybe it was about a case I was working on, something like that. You know, coming here to tell me to butt out, or maybe even do a wee trade of information. But he needed my help."

The Veteran's Fund was still active. But Garner's extracurricular work, according to what Kelley's dad told the Fat Man, was getting to the point it could no longer be ignored.

"Everyone has a line, right?" the Fat Man says. "That's why you walked. That's why I should have walked before I was pushed. That's why your old man came to me. Garner was getting greedy. His work for Kennedy paid better than solving cases. He was getting worried that someone in CID might develop a spine. So his solution was to make sure that everyone was dirty. And he'd told your old man if he wanted to keep benefitting from the Veteran's Fund, he'd need to do more than just take an envelope and keep his mouth shut. Told him it was necessary to prove he was part of the team."

Kelley's fingers clench.

A fist.

The snowball effect.

Kelley's father had been in freefall after that conversation.

"He told me about you, how you'd wanted to be polis, how he'd tried to discourage you. What frightened him most was not even you finding out the truth. It was you turning out like him. Or, worse, like Garner."

"He could have told me."

"Really?"

Kelley wants to say *yes*. But he knows the truth. So he asks, "Why did he come to you?"

"He came to me because I wasn't part of the system, because he thought I could help him get evidence on Garner. Make what he had public. Kind of a scorched earth policy, maybe."

"And did you agree?"

The Fat Man intertwines his finger across his stomach. Clears his throat. Can't look Kelley in the eye.

Kelley presses: "Did you agree?"

"I said I'd think about it. I was scared. Of course I was fucking scared. I'd seen what Garner could do to people, the kind of power he had. Your father knew, too."

"But he wanted to stand up."

"And he died."

Kelley bites his lower lip. Tastes blood.

Repeats the words: "And he died."

41

FRANK KNOCKS ON MARTIN'S DOOR. Walks in without waiting.

Martin on his bed, headphones on. Looks up as his dad enters.

Frank rips the headphones from his son's head. Noise explodes.

Anarchiiist!

Frank throws them away. The music continues, tinny and distant.

Frank says, "You're coming out with your old man."

"What?"

How could Frank ever believe this pathetic pishbag capable of murder?

"Got a job tonight. Figured you might as well learn what I do to keep you here – keep you fed."

"You sit on your arse all day at the Cash. And I've got a job already. At the garage."

"Hannigan's too soft for his own good. I know he lets you skive off on your own time. Think he has this idea you might be simple, lets you away with—" The word *murder* sticks in his throat. "—All kinds of shite. But you can't be a fucking apprentice forever, and God knows you'll never be a fucking grease monkey for real. So maybe you need to see some of life. Understand about pulling your socks up and getting to real work."

Martin's eyes are blank. No hint of emotion.

Frank gets a chill that starts at the base of his spine, then travels up to his neck.

Ignore it.

"Come on," he says. "I'll show you what it takes to be a man."

* * *

The multis loom. Frank pulls up. They get out the car.

Martin looks around. "Fuckin' dump," he says before looking over at his dad, eyes wide for a moment as though he's afraid of something. A good skelp coming his way, maybe. The way Frank used to punish him.

But if Frank wants the boy to become a man, he's going to have to let go of certain habits.

Want him to be a man?

Treat him like one.

Frank says, "We're here to talk to a wanker who's in over his head."

"How?"

"He borrowed some money. Didn't pay it back."

Martin twists up his face. He doesn't believe that's the full story. But Frank's his father – the one in charge. The boy's not proved himself capable of being treated as an equal. If he does, maybe they'll talk more.

At the back of Frank's brain, a voice tells him he's making a mistake.

He ignores it.

* * *

Fifth floor of the multi. Frank knocks.

Martin leans against a wall, hands in pockets.

The door opens. Frank smiles. "Awright, Ferret?"

And then:

Pushing Ferret into the flat. Fucking eejit he is, just opening the door like that. Place like this, could be all kinds of nasty fuckers outside.

"Close the fucking door." Frank tries not to add that old favourite, *were you born in a fucking barn?*

Living room. Martin following at a distance. More awake, suddenly. Interested in what's happening.

Frank throws Ferret into an armchair.

Ferret's face is white and sheened with sweat. "Jesus, I heard you were back in the game."

"Fuckin' right."

"Look, I'm good for it. I already told Davie Burns that—"

"I hear that a lot."

Ferret keeps trying to glance round Frank, work out who the new lad is.

"Don't look at him. Look at me. He's not here, okay? It's just you and me."

"I don't have the money. I mean—"

"You've been avoiding your debtors."

"Aye, aye, that's right . . ." Ferret blinks fast as he talks.

"Thing is," Frank says, "that you knew what would happen if you didn't pay on time. And maybe, maybe if you'd come forward and told the truth we coulda worked something out. But you've been avoiding people, and now here we are."

"Jesus ..."

"I mean, you had to know what would happen."

"Jesus ..."

"I'm surprised you answered the fucking door.

"Jesus ..."

"How much do you have?"

Crying, now. Big tears. Snot in his nose. The whole works. Big, bubbly bairn. Pathetic.

Frank glances over at Martin.

The lad's watching.

Intensely.

Frank says again, "How much do you have?"

Ferret sniffs, wiping his nose with the back of his hand. "Nothing, okay? I've got fucking nothing. I ... I tried ..."

"You tried? How hard?"

"Jesus, just a little more *time* ..."

"Too fucking late for that. I've been in this business a long time, and you know what I've found? That most pathetic wee shites, they always have something ... hidden under the mattress, in their granny's house, whatever ... it's just that they don't want to part with it until someone can persuade them it's a good idea."

"I don't have a fucking granny," Ferret says.

Frank backhands the prick across the face. Ferret rocks backwards. Clutches at his face.

Frank waits for a moment.

Turns to Martin. "Think he's telling the truth?"

Martin's approaches Ferret and walks around him.

Something has changed. Frank can see it.

Martin's not looking at Frank anymore. Focused on Ferret. His head is bowed slightly, and his long limbs move with purpose. A predator stalking prey.

After he's circled the snivelling man a few times, Martin says, "How do we make him pay?"

"We show him it's worse for him if he doesn't," Frank says.

Martin walks towards a sliding door to the rear of the room. A small kitchen. Little more than a cupboard.

Frank waits where he is.

Intrigued.

Drawers slide open. Cutlery clinks. Martin comes back with a long knife.

Frank steps back. This is the moment, then.

Martin hunkers down in front of Ferret.

Silence for a few moments.

Then: Martin asks, "Have you ever tried to kill yourself?"

Ferret's puzzled. Looks past Martin at Frank.

Martin gently cups Ferret's chin with one hand, pulling his attention back.

Frank watches, a chill spreading through him.

Whoever this person is, they look and sound like Martin, but it's as though the son Frank's known for all these years isn't present.

Frank remembers:

The police visiting his house.

The dead woman.

The dead copper.

He didn't think it was possible.

No, he *convinced* himself it wasn't possible.

The boy's never been right. Frank always thought it was because he was weak.

But was it always something else?

"Answer his question," Frank says to Ferret.

"Have you ever tried to kill yourself?" Martin says, again, his tone utterly calm.

"What the fuck kindae question is—"

"I have," Martin says.

Frank swallows nausea. Lightheaded.

This is a dream.

It has to be.

Martin says, "The mistake people make is simple." He lifts up one arm, and then runs the knife across his sleeve in a cutting motion. "They cut across the wrist. Think that'll be enough." He lowers his arm again. "But all it does is, it hurts." His left hand, holding the knife, moves quickly. He slashes the upper part of Ferret's arm, creates a red slit through Ferret's shirt.

Ferret squeals. Pushes back as though trying to escape out the back of his chair.

"Stay still," Martin says. "Stay still."

He's utterly calm. Not how Frank expected him to be at all.

Franks forces himself to stay still.

Martin's still speaking. "The way to do it is to cut down the wrist." He grabs Ferret's arm, pulls it forward, the wrist up. He places the point of the knife down on the skin, ready to pierce Ferret's pulse. "It hurts, you know. It hurts and it stings, and the blood drains slowly. You die, but in pain."

Ferret's shaking, now.

Martin says, "I could kill you easily. I could kill you and make you suffer."

Frank decides enough is enough. Steps forward. "Your choice," he says to Ferret.

Is there a tremble in his tone?

"Fuck," Ferret says. "I don't have the money here. I don't. But I can get it. I can get it. In the morning, I fucking swear."

Martin presses the point of the knife into Ferret's wrist. The skin breaks. But he's not in deep yet.

Frank places a hand on his son's shoulder. "That's it," he says.

Martin tightens his grip on Ferret's arm. Increases the pressure.

Ferret closes his eyes. Shaking real hard now.

Frank says. "That's enough."

Martin's not listening.

Frank pulls the lad up, spins him round.

"Enough!" Getting in Martin's face.

Martin presses forward, his teeth bared, his eyes wide. Makes a sound that sets Frank's teeth on edge – a low, angry growl. More animal than human.

And then, suddenly, he pulls back, dropping the knife. He turns and walks out the flat.

Who the fuck was that?

Frank's brain floods with fear.

Like someone else was in the room. The Martin that Frank knew had vanished, replaced by someone – *something* – else.

Does Frank even know his son?

"Fuck," Ferret says. "You were bad enough. Where d'you think they breed cunts like that?"

42

RICHARD "DICKIE" BORER'S ABODE is a one-bedroom flat above a Hilltown pub. Burnet and Garner pull up at half-two in the afternoon. Half-cut oldies are already staggering on the street.

One of them nods at Garner as they get out of the car.

Garner looks away. Makes straight for the front door.

Burnet follows.

The old duffer doesn't give her a second glance.

Second floor, Garner takes the door. Polis knock. Loud. Staccato. Unmistakable.

No answer.

Again.

Down to the letterbox. "Come on, Dickie! Open up!"

Burnet stands back. Observes.

What happens next could be testimony. Direct, eye-witness testimony.

Corruption, violence, overstepping boundaries.

His defence: that's how the police do their fucking job. How the coppers before him did it. How he was *taught* to do it.

Arrest him, you'll have to arrest half the force. Maybe more. Can she stand by? Knowing what he'll do to Dickie?

She has to.

She has to be ready to testify.

Act *when the time is right.*

Wee skinny guy, naked from the waist up, answers the door. Has to be Dickie. Thick, shaggy, dark hair. Big brown eyes that Burnet can understand a girl getting lost in. A rough-around-the-edges Donny Osmond. The long-haired lover from the Logie estate.

"Come on, man," Dickie says. "I'm keeping the bloody music down. Those pricks're just—"

Garner pushes Dickie into the flat with practised, violent ease.

Burnet follows.

Garner and Dickie push through to the living room.

Let the lads have their little talk, then.

Burnet clocks another door – closed.

Inside the bedroom, it smells of sleep and sex, and something a little sweeter. A girl – maybe seventeen, a little older or a little younger – naked, hides her modesty with a sheet. Not afraid or startled. Her eyes are hard, and she greets Burnet with a stare.

Burnet says, "You'll be Tessie, then?"

"No." She looks almost right. Same hair, face shape. But it's not Tessie. She's a little harder than the girl on the mantlepiece. "That wee bitch kicked Dickie to the kerb weeks back." A smile. "Didn't know what she had, silly wee cow."

Burnet nods. She steps into the room. Closes the door a little behind her, enough to dampen the sounds of Garner having his *quiet little chat* with Dickie in the front room.

"What's your name?" Burnet says, perching on the end of the bed.

"Don't have to tell you anything."

"You really do," Burnet says. "I mean, unless you fancy a night in the cells."

She's not angry with the girl. She's angry because she's here with Garner. She's angry because this isn't the way they should be doing things.

Deep breath. "We're looking for Tessie. She took off. Her mum's worried about her. Thought she might be with Dickie."

"Not my problem."

"She's not been here since they broke up?"

"I'd have scratched the bitch's eyes out."

"He's a catch. Nice eyes." Enough truth there that Burnet sounds genuine. That Donny Osmond vibe probably gets him a lot of luck.

"Not all that nice." The girl's all front, but there's something else, too, in the way she's holding up those sheets.

Burnet says, cautious, "Like, he treats you well?"

"Any girl'd be lucky to—"

Burnet takes the chance. Reaches out, yanks the sheet. When it falls away, she does her best not to gasp. The girl's body is black and blue round her sides, her ribs and midriff. There's other marks, too, and Burnet wishes she didn't recognise them as cigarette burns.

The girl pulls the sheet back.

"Name," Burnet says – full authority. "Now."

The girl hesitates.

"Give me your name."

"Lis Devon," the girl says, softly. "I'm eighteen next month. I—"

"You're putting your clothes on and going home."

The girl nods.

Burnet says, "But first I want you to tell me all about Dickie."

"What about him?"

Burnet just raises an eyebrow. The girl knows exactly what they're going to discuss.

* * *

In the living room, Dickie's on the sofa, nursing a black eye and a swollen lip. Blood trickles from the side of his mouth.

Burnet looks at Garnet, who shrugs and says, "He got lippy."

Dickie's a streak of piss compared to Garner. An easy target. Burnet thinks: the man needed a punching bag.

Burnet says, "The girl in the bedroom isn't Tessie."

"No," Garner says. "Lis, right?" Clearly the boys had a chat between the beatings.

Garner would say his methods get results.

He's not wrong.

Not right either.

Burnet looks at Dickie. He's willing to talk. She can see it in his eyes.

He's willing to talk because an officer of the law beat the shite out of him.

Can she let that slide?

Play the long game.

"You're a piece of work." She looks at Dickie, but could mean Garner, too. "Telling her that this is how other girls like it."

Maybe he deserves it. Maybe it's the only way you get through to arseholes like this.

Dickie lifts his head to give her a wink with his good eye. "You don't know till you try it."

"What I do know is you get your kicks hurting girls. Not even women . . . girls. What, you were going to throw Lis away like you did with Tessie, when she turned seventeen?"

"She's almost eightee—"

"Don't piss me about." Burnet keeps her voice even. "She's sixteen, but you told her she might as well be eighteen."

"Sixteen's still leg—"

This time, it's Garner who stops him talking. Walking up behind the sofa, slapping the back of his head.

Burnet says, "Do you think anyone with a daughter is going to care?"

Easy to get into the rhythm. Let the anger take over.

There's the law, and then there's justice.

You make your decision about which side you fall on.

She tells herself she's just playing a role for now.

That's all.

Is inaction the same as action?

Just a matter of choice.

Intent.

"Maybe you just need a little yourself, doll?" Dickie says, raising his head again. Trying for the hard man routine, thinking the wee police lady won't hurt him. All it gets him is another smack across the back of the skull from Garner. Harder this time.

Burnet shakes her head. "Hit him any harder, you'll concuss the wee bastard." Trying to keep this on the right side of deniability without pissing Garner off.

"Brain damage might be what he needs."

Burnet hunkers down on a level with Dickie. "My colleague here's something of an impetuous man. Know what that means? Impetuous? Sure you do, smart lad that you are. But just in case ... I mean that he can't always control himself. And, like I said, someone who has a daughter themselves, they're going to get angry with you even if sleeping with girls over sixteen is legal. I mean, beating them black and blue isn't exactly—"

"She consented! She loved it."

Another slap from Garner. Harder again.

"See, I can maybe stop him hurting you – or least hurting you worse – but only if you show willing to cooperate."

Dickie blinks a few times as though to stop his vision spinning. "Aye, like how?"

"You know why we're here?"

"Because you're nosy bastards?"

No slap this time, but he flinches.

Garner still looming over the lad.

Burnet keeps her gaze locked on Dickie's face. "Because we wanted to talk to you about Tessie."

"Why? I haven't seen her in months, moaning cow that she is."

Garner leans in close to Dickie from behind, talking into his ear: "Show some fucking respect."

That flinch again. His eyes a little damp.

Burnet says, "You broke up with her?"

"Aye."

"Why?"

"Because she was dragging me down."

"Because she wasn't putting out," Garner says. "I know lads like you."

Burnet resists the urge to ask whether he *was* a lad like Dickie.

"Aye, well," Dickie says. "So I told her I'd rather see Lis there, and she threw a strop."

"When was this?" Burnet asks.

"Like I remember? Maybe two weeks past Wednesday?"

"And you haven't seen her since?"

Dickie turns his head to look at Garner.

Burnet says, "Don't look at him. Look at me."

He does as she asks. "I think so. Look, she was a frigid wee cow, and it wasn't worth the effort."

Burnet stands up. He could be lying, but she gets the impression that he really doesn't know where Tessie is. She says, "Pity you don't have much luck with girls. Like Lis through there – she's going home to her mum and dad, and you're never going to see her again."

Dickie's about to speak when Garner jumps in. "And I know you're going to ask about how we can stop you. Well, the answer's simple, son. You know how it is with polis – someone somewhere always owes us a favour. So, you know, if I asked people to keep their ears to the ground, I'd know the second you were in the same room with that girl. And what would happen then, is that I'd pay you a little visit, and we'd have a little chat. You know, man to man. No ladies present."

Dickie's breathing hard now. His face is tense. He's shaking with what could be anger or fear. Maybe it's both.

Burnet leaves the room.

Garner follows maybe five minutes later, when Lis is dressed and ready to be escorted out the door.

43

BURNET PULLS THE FORM OUT OF the typewriter, crunches it, throws it in the bin under her desk.

More crap. Glorified secretary. Clearing other officers' paperwork.

Because the men can't be arsed doing their damn jobs.

They want her to know her place.

She thought that when she grew up, left school, she'd escape bullies and petty digs at her sex.

Some fucking chance.

The Friday Girl.

Do the typing.

Look pretty.

All you're good for.

The typewriter clatters.

Another mistake. Another wasted form.

One of the detectives across from her smiles over his desk. "Not going well?"

Maybe he's empathising a little.

Surely someone in here's on her side?

And then: "Time of the month? My girlfriend's the same."

She tries not to wince. Carefully inserts a new sheet into the typewriter.

Types carefully. Ignoring him, as he waits for a response.

Finally, only just above a whisper, she hears, "Frigid bitch."

* * *

The phone on her desk rings.

She stops typing.

"Detective Constable Burnet."

"It's me."

Kelley. Ex-Detective Constable Kelley.

"Can I help you?" Trying to keep her voice neutral. Wanting to ask why he wasn't at Dow's funeral.

"I need your help."

"Aye? You know that's going to get me in trouble."

"I thought you liked trouble."

"I like having a job."

Silence on the other end of the line. Then: "How'd you like to take the fuckers down?"

She doesn't respond.

"I'm serious. All of them."

"What do you mean?"

"Garner. His cronies. The whole rotten lot."

"What do you want?"

"Ten minutes of your time."

She checks the clock on the wall. "I'll give you five."

* * *

They meet at a bar across from the bus station. The place has been in the news for running "European hours", selling alcohol early in the day. Apparently, this continental approach will lead to rack and ruin, making Dundee as bad as France. Or Glasgow. The papers don't specify which would be worse.

Burnet knows that people are looking at her when she walks in. She's the only woman in here. Reckons that wouldn't be too different no matter what time of day they met.

Kelley's at a table in the far corner. Half pint and a glass of water. She knows which one's hers.

"You're working, right?"

She shrugs. "If you're not messing me about, then I'll need something harder."

He starts to stand. She waves him back down.

"You think you have evidence against Garner? Can you be specific?"

A sip of the half. A deep breath. "He's been involved in a scam for years. Skimming money from evidence, sharing it out among other officers."

"You have proof?"

"There's more. We all know that for Kennedy to keep his hold on the city, he needs someone on the force. I think Garner's that man." A pause. "I *know* he's that man."

"You've been here before. People are going to say this looks personal. Because you blame him for what happened in the high rise. And now, again because you blame him for your having to leave the force."

"I know." Another sip. White knuckles. Any more pressure, the glass will shatter. "But this is different."

"Aye?"

"There are people willing to go on record. I have evidence. Documents. Names. Places. Times."

"Think that's really enough?"

Kelley takes a breath. "You know who my dad was?"

"I know. The bloody hero."

"After he died, I joined up to show that I could be as good as him. He'd always discouraged me. I thought it was because he thought I wasn't good enough. So my application was rushed through because of the name. But the more I learn, the more I realise that he was discouraging me because he didn't want to disavow me of this notion that being polis was something honourable."

Burnet wants to tell him that it *is* honourable, despite men like Garner. But she needs to hear this, and lets him talk.

He tells her about what happened when he joined up: the insinuations from Garner, DCI Redman implying there were some truths Kelley's old man had kept from him.

"Jesus," she says. "I'm sorry. He was supposed to be a hero, and he was ..." She can't finish the thought out loud.

"They all were," Kelley says, and stops to take another sip of the half. "The Veteran's Fund. I mean, it was low level, but that's how it starts, isn't it? An opportunity, and then suddenly things are out of control. I don't think anyone thought they were corrupt. It was just ... things, the way they used to be, you know? The working man taking a little for himself. Not really hurting anyone. Especially when the only people who lost out were people who were going to lose anyway. Dealers, pimps ... *criminals*. What did it matter if some of the sums didn't add up?"

It's not easy to admit your parents' failings. It had been hard for Burnet to realise her parents never wanted her to be in the police, that they pictured a life for her she never wanted, even when she was a little girl. But their flaws were in their character, in their beliefs.

Their actions? They'd tried to dissuade her, but never stood in her way.

Kelley's father had been a criminal. There was no getting away from that. Whether intentional or accidental, small or large scale, he was as guilty as anyone else that his notes and records implicated.

He tells her about the Fat Man. She's heard other detectives talk about how he used to be one of theirs and then became a bottom feeder, undermining investigations and throwing trials in the name of lining his pocket. She's met him once or twice; he's done nothing to dissuade her of these ideas. Overweight, with a handshake that was both firm and slippery. His skin blotched in patches of pale red. A tomato ketchup stain on his shirt. How could a man who looked like that not be an arsehole?

"So," Burnet says, when Kelley's done. "He's willing to testify?"

"No," Kelley says. "But he knows enough that he can point someone in the right direction. Someone willing to do what's needed to get to the truth."

He downs what's left of his drink. His eyes – sharp, electric blue – are more alive than she's ever seen them before. Challenging her. Calling her out. Asking if she's really willing to walk away from this. If she's willing to sacrifice her beliefs for her job.

She knows the answer.

Knows the risks.

44

TESTIMONY IS KEY.

Testimony and evidence: what you need for any investigation.

Except in this case, they don't have the resources of the force. They're working blind. In secret. Alone.

Kelley returns to his rooms on Union Street. Sits in the dark. Listens to the city outside; the traffic, the people. Rides the rhythms.

Feeling clear for the first time since leaving the force.

Purposeful.

No longer angry.

Anger had made him sloppy.

But now ... he can do something. Make a difference.

And he has help.

Burnet is the future. Polis through and through. Natural born. Kelley knows that he got into the job because of his father, and his father's father and on and on, but Burnet is someone who has real instincts, not just some sense handed down by family.

She's the future.

Someone who does the job, who *believes* in the job.

Is he risking all of that by asking for her help?

If all of this goes wrong, then her potential will be thrown away. Wasted.

But who else could he ask?

The only other copper he ever trusted – admired – had been Dow. The old man's death had been a blow. Kelley had this kind of fantasy that they'd be able to work together – the old hand and the young buck – to clean up the town. Like an old western, maybe. *The new law's in town, folks, and we're gonna clean it up.*

A stupid idea. Childish.

Projecting onto Dow something he wished for in his father.

And now?

Burnet is different. Burnet's willing to help. Burnet *believes*. And if they can do this, then the future will belong to police who don't just trust in the old ways, the acquired habits, the prejudices and the little lies that every copper learns to tell themselves.

The 1980s are just around the corner.

The future is coming.

* * *

Kelley and the Fat Man come to an arrangement. Kelley works cases, but keeps the load low.

The Fat Man gives him names. Everything he has.

Ex-coppers who might talk. People in Kennedy's organisation who might know something if they're asked the right way.

But the Fat Man won't come forward himself.

"There's a reason I quit. They'd have ruined me. And what did I have? Hearsay."

"Corroborating—"

The Fat Man raises a hand. "I'm too old and tired. If you can't make a case from what I've given you, what's the point?"

"They're going to ask where it came from."

"This is big enough that the brass – the real brass, I mean; the Chief Constable and all those boys who play politics over policing – won't care. It'd be a fucking disaster for their image, right? That's what they care about more than anything."

Kelley worries about provenance. This couldn't become a war of words. Evidence. Dates, times, credible witnesses – they need it all.

Kelley can work on the Fat Man later. For now, there's work to do.

Start with the names.

Ex-cops, ex-recipients of the Veteran's Fund.

A few snitches.

Men who used to work for Kennedy.

Kelley needs someone who can connect the dots.

The name he finds is a name: Donald "Donnie" Brunton.

Ex-fence, ex-stick-up man.

A grass for Kelley's old man. Also an occasional clean-up guy at illegal games organised by Kennedy.

That was in his better days.

Now? He robs liquor stores, does his time, gets back out and fucks up again.

Strictly independent.

A middle-aged, alcoholic, two-bit thief who's no good at his job.

Great fucking witness for the prosecution.

Read between the lines: he has a habit. Maybe not drugs, but drink at the least.

But if Donnie Brunton can confirm a few facts, maybe that gives more leverage to help build the case.

They need to get him to talk.

But do it the right way.

No strong-arm tactics.

They do that, then what happens is they fall into the same trap as his old man: *the slippery slope.*

This can't win – not properly – unless they take the high ground.

Kelley looks at the list of names. Looks at the files on his desk.

Thinks about what it means to take that high ground.

Wishes he was like a private eye in the American novels. With a belt of whiskey in the drawer.

* * *

Burnet meets him at a car park at the bottom of the Hilltown. She waves when she sees him, breaks into a jog for the last few metres. Anyone watching might think they were meeting for a date.

In civvies, she looks different – jeans, hair down, bag on her shoulder.

"So what have you got?" she asks. Still all business.

He passes her an envelope.

She rifles the contents. "Where do we start?"

"You know the polis won't talk. Even the ex-polis."

"Thick blue line." She keeps reading what he's given her.

"Name on there I thought we might start with – Donald Brunton. See what he has. What he's willing to give us." He starts the engine, pulls out onto the street.

As he drives, she flicks through the files. "B&E man."

"My old man's informant. Worked both sides. The polis, Kennedy's people. He might be able to point us in the right direction."

"And why would he want to do that?"

"Good question." Kelley stops at a red. Daylight's dying across the city. Headlights click on. "I know the temptations to go for the higher hanging fruit, but—"

"But that's more difficult."

"Like you said: thick blue line. Why do you think no one's gone public about anything? The public are either happy or scared, and the police don't want to fuck up a good thing going."

The lights change.

Kelley says, "No one said this was going to be easy."

"No," she says.

"It's not too late," he says.

"If I'm going to help you," she says, "I need you to tell me something."

"What?" He's checking junctions as he drives.

"Why weren't you at the funeral?"

He stays silent for a moment, keeps looking ahead.

"You don't have to tell me," she says. "But if you're hiding something, you can stop the car right now and let me out."

"Okay," he says. "I wasn't there. Me and Dow, we were ... we were friends. And I wanted to be there ..."

"But?"

"I was in a bad place. When they put me off-duty, I started a wee habit of heading out in the evenings. Grabbing a few pints. Just to get me over to sleep, you know?"

"And a few became a few more?"

"Something like that." He pauses, taking a turn to the left. Once they're on the move again, he continues: "I didn't think I could trust myself. I mean, Garner, all of them, they'd be there too and..."

She nods, understanding.

He takes that as an invitation to keep driving.

* * *

The far end of Pitkerro Road. A tenement building that's seen better days.

The front door's been kicked in more than once. The scent in the stairwell makes Kelley think of decay. The building's dying, or already dead.

Second floor: flat with a flimsy door, chipped and battered. Scrawls on the walls. Gang slogans, and other – more personal – insults.

Kelley looks at Burnet. She shrugs. Bangs on the door.

It opens maybe an inch. The man who peeks out is small, with greasy black hair, and a half-arsed attempt at a beard. His skin is pock-marked, his eyes are the kind of milky blue that makes him look permanently unwell.

"Come on, open the door," Burnet says, flashing her ID.

Donnie relents. Burnet enters first. Kelley follows.

Donnie goes into the front room. Grabs a cigarette from an open pack on top of a glass coffee table. "They've relaxed the fucking dress codes, then."

Kelley says, "We're here unofficially."

"Hoy," Donnie says. "So where's your badge, then? Could be any old sod, couldn't you?"

Kelley keeps silent.

Donnie gets the hint. Sparks up the cigarette.

Making a point by not offering them anything?

Or too rattled for social niceties?

Donnie takes a long drag before blowing smoke out the open window. "The fuck d'you even want, then? I've been here all fucking day. I've been a good boy, you know."

"Come on," Burnet says. "Man with your record?"

"I'm getting old, you know."

"And careless. How many times this last year have you been before the Sherriff?"

"Maths was never my strong point. So, what? Someone's done something and you decide to come here and—"

Kelley blindsides. "You used to be a grass, right?"

"The fuck?"

"Detective by the name of Kelley."

"Even if I was, I couldnae tell you, could I? That kind of thing, it's inconsequential. Like talking to a priest."

Confidential. Kelley nearly corrects. But holds back.

"Besides," Donnie says. "Fucker's dead, isn't he."

Burnet takes the lead again. Fast, like she thinks Kelley might take offence. "So you're working for someone else?"

Donnie blinks. Goes pale. "Like ... I mean ..."

"Because looking at your arrest record ... nothing ever seems to stick."

"Aye?" Donnie looks anywhere but at Burnet. Shaking and trying to hide it.

Fear or withdrawal?

"So someone is looking out for you?" Burnet says, keeping in his line of sight.

"What the *fuck* do you want?"

"What do you think we want?"

"Fuck!" Donnie looks at the ceiling. Like he'll find any help there.

Kelley says, "How deep are you?"

"I may have got in over my head with some less than legitimate lenders."

"Loan sharks?" Kelley says.

Donnie shrugs so that his neck disappears. "Ehhh," he says, like there's maybe a grey area in there somewhere. "You could say that. I got in on one of Kennedy's games. You know, cards and shite? Figured maybe there was some skill, you know – which makes a better bet than the horses."

"And?"

"If there's a skill, I didn't have it. Maybe I should have twigged earlier. But, aye, I got deeper in the hole. You know how it is?"

Neither Kelley nor Burnet say a word.

"So I wind up with a choice. Broken legs, like, or do a spot of a job." Donnie clears his throat, suddenly looking a little embarrassed at something. "Post office job out on the Clep."

Cleppington Road. Kelley doesn't remember anything on Donnie's file about that one.

"And you did it?"

"Oh, aye. Like you can guess, Mr Kennedy doesn't give you much choice."

"He told you *directly* to do this?"

"Naw – that's the point, right? What you want to know? The boys running the game ... They were fucking polis, okay? Like you. Plainclothes and all. But they werenae shy about it, know what I mean?"

"They actually *said* they were polis?" Burnet keeping him focused.

Kelley keeps in the background. A variation on good cop/bad cop. The more he stays silent, the more unsettled Donnie's going to become. He's going to fucking sing for them.

"Oh, aye. That was part of it, you know? Saying how if I didn't agree to the work, they'd fit me up for something else. So, like, I agreed."

"Why the Clep Road job?"

"Like I know why? All I know is the fucker who got me on board was a copper. And that the bastard leading the raid was one, too. In cahoots."

"You could identify them, both?"

"Aye, aye. Sure, whatever you want." Panicking for a moment. Then: "But I need something myself, like. You know? I mean, you cunts—" he stops short looks right at Burnet as though just realising what he said. "I mean, you know what I mean?" Trying to pull himself back together. "Youse need to realise that if they know it was me giving them up, they'd batter seven kinds of shite out of me. So, you know, like ... I need a wee something too. Like immunisation." He looks from Burnet to Kelley and back again. Then adds, to clarify: "From any further arrests."

Kelley takes a second to realise what he's asking.

Burnet says, "We'll do what we can. But what we need you to do, Donnie, is just to identify some people for us. That's all. If we can, we'll keep your name out of it."

Donnie nods. "And you'll make sure these bastards serve some time? I mean, they're fucking polis, right?"

Kelley steps forward. "Just one more thing," he says. "An incidental matter."

Donnie flinches. It's good that he's afraid.

Kelley says, "The copper you used to grass for. Is he one of these men?"

"I mean ... he never ... I don't know, man. He asked me to do him some favours, like. I mean, I used to hold packages, all that, as well as letting him know about any action he needed to know. But ... fuckit, I don't know, man."

Burnet's hand is on Kelley's elbow, restraining him. Kelley knows that he's pushing this. That he wants evidence to contradict what the Fat Man told him. But they have to focus for now. No use thinking about the dead. Think about the here and the now. And the future.

45

FRANK LEANS AGAINST THE WALL, drags on his cigarette. His contact is late.

When the fucker does arrive, he walks nonchalantly down the alley, past the bins out back of the Trades House pub.

No offer of a handshake. Not even a polite greeting. Just: "I don't fucking appreciate this shite."

Frank's spoiling for a fight. Ever since he took Martin out with him to Ferret's place, he's felt uneasy. He keeps remembering the look in Martin's eyes when he hurt that junkie fuck.

Keep it under control. No need to throw any punches. Just make it clear he's in no mood for this deluded prick to throw his weight about. "I look like I give a toss? I'm just the fucking messenger."

"And I'm on duty."

"Boo-fucking-hoo." Frank takes a long drag.

The crooked DS puts his hands in his pockets. Knows the rules of the game. Fucker thinks that gives him power.

Frank remembers this fuck from the old days – always liked to throw his weight about. He was a dick then, and age has done nothing to mellow him.

Truth is, he was always a waste of space.

He can give it the old Billy Big Bollocks all he wants, but Frank represents Joe Kennedy. And Joe Kennedy owns this fucking prick. Wholesale. No matter what the arsehole might tell other people.

"Your patch was light this month," Frank says.

"I know. You've heard about the fucking break-ins, right? Some of the bastards were coming up light and—"

"So?"

"So, I'm dealing with it. Fucksakes, this is a mutually beneficial relationship, right? Your boss needs to fucking remember that. Who's keeping him out of jail, aye? Who turns a blind fucking eye to his shite?" The DS reaches inside his coat, pulls out an envelope. "This is most of what you want. The rest—"

Frank doesn't even shift his weight. Punches low and hard. The DS drops, clutching his stomach.

Frank stands over him. "That's where a prick like you belongs," he says. "On his fucking knees before his betters."

The DS coughs and splutters, his breath ragged.

Frank says, "Get this into your head. I don't know who the fuck's been dealing with you until now, but there's a reason Mr Kennedy asked me to come deal with you. See, what you just said, it tells me that you're getting ideas above your fucking station. Like, somehow, this is an equal partnership? *Mutually beneficial?* Aye, just keep telling yourself that one."

"Jesus," the DS says. "You're a real hard cunt, you know that? Aye, big fucking man here – just because you're back in the game, working for His Highness once more?"

Frank lets the man vent.

"While I'm down here, you want me to suck your dick?" the DS says, getting his breath back. "That what this—"

Enough. Frank knees the prick in the face. He goes down proper this time. Blood gushes from his nose.

Frank pockets the envelope. "Tomorrow." Even tone. No anger. Keep this shit on an even keel, and they'll really shit their breeks. "Same time. Same place. You don't show up, you're fucked. You show up light, you're fucked. Because, here's the thing, I can beat fuck out of you and all that, same as anyone else. But you know what happens if the big man decides you're of no use to him anymore. He has records. He has evidence. He wants it, you're exposed. A dirty fucking polis. Right to the jail, and fuck knows what'll happen to you in there, aye?"

Frank walks past the fallen DS, who's spitting blood on the ground and slowly pushing himself up off the concrete. "Aye, go on, you cunt," the DS yells. "You're an old man now. You know that, right? Fuck the Beast of Balgay. You don't know how the world's fucking changed since you went to sleep. You're under his protection now, but you'll get yours soon enough, you fuck!"

Frank keeps walking. "Tomorrow, Detective Sergeant Garner," he says. "Tomorrow, or you're the one who'll get yours."

* * *

He drops the envelope at a solicitor's office on Commercial Street. The girl on the front desk smiles when he walks in. If he wasn't married, he'd take the chance. Since the death of the old woman, and the police coming round claiming Martin was responsible, he and Jeannie haven't been close. Secrets between them.

His fault? He can't be sure.

Jeannie thinks so. Why she's taken to sleeping with her back to him, bunching the sheets around herself like a cocoon.

He doesn't want to lose her.

"You can go through."

"Huh?" Frank's back in the room. The girl behind the desk is smiling, her poloneck sitting just tight enough to feel like a promise of some kind.

No, no. He's imagining it.

You're old enough to be her father.

Rough patch is all. Everything changing in his life. Can't let that get to him. He's still the same man Jeannie said she loved. He just has to remind her.

And forget about looking at girls in tight sweaters.

"You can go through." The girl gestures to the door. "He's ready to see you."

"Oh, aye," Frank says. "Thank you."

"You look like you could do with some sleep," the girl says. "Burning the candle at both ends?"

He doesn't say anything. Walks through the door, to the far end of the corridor.

The solicitor looks up from his desk. Wide-eyed, like he's been caught doing something he shouldn't. "Most people knock."

Frank's not most people.

He places the envelope on the desk.

"What the fuck happened to your nose?"

"Nothing as bad as what'll happen to you if you ask that again."

The solicitor holds up his hands. "Usual funds, then?"

"Charity donations," Frank says. "Big-hearted man, Mr Kennedy."

"That he is." The solicitor smiles at Frank. "Anything else I can help you with?"

Frank shakes his head. As he leaves, he says, "You shouldn't snort on the desk. Anyone could walk in here."

46

IN THE PASSENGER SEAT, DONNIE TRIES to sink into the footwell. He's wearing a hat that he's pulled down low.

And he couldn't look any more suspicious if he tried.

Kelley says, "Would you just relax?"

Donnie shakes his head. "How the fuck can I relax? Coppers to the left of me, hard bastards to the right . . ."

Kelley keeps his eye on the street. "And here I am, stuck in this motor with you."

"That's him," Donnie says, when a man comes out of the pub across the way. "That's your man."

Kelley recognises him. One of Garner's groupies: Detective Constable Halliday. Mid-forties. Sandy hair. Side parting. Moustache. Glasses. Wears this tan leather jacket like he thinks he's Dave Starsky.

Check the swagger, too.

Donnie's ID confirms Burnet's suspicions. But Kelley needs to be sure.

"He's the one provided the muscle at the games?"

"Aye."

"The one they sent to collect the debts?"

"Aye."

"The one you said broke your wrist?"

"How many fucking times?"

"I need you to be sure. I need you not to be lying to me."

Halliday crosses the street just ahead of them. Donnie sinks further into the footwell. "Fucking hell, it's him. Okay? I'm not shitting you. I wouldn't fucking dare."

"You need to be sure. You need to know you can say it in a court."

"Aye, aye. I can fucking say it. I know the cunt. Burned on my fucking brain, his face. His fucking attitude. Can even remember how he fucking smelled. Doused in fucking aftershave, so much it actually hurt to breathe next to him."

Kelley watches Halliday climb into a beat-up red Ford Cortina.

So far, Donnie's information seems on the level. Halliday doing the rounds of local businesses, collecting "contributions", presumably for the Veteran's Fund, or whatever the current iteration was known as. Halliday wouldn't have been part of the original crew – he's too young to have served in the war – but he's part of it now.

Kelley wonders how many of them got into it with their eyes open. Is it possible that some of them genuinely believed that this was just how things worked?

Like your own father?

Kelley follows at a discrete distance. They drive to the city centre, to Albert Square. Some of the working girls are already out and waiting for early clients.

Halliday's car parks up nearby. Kelley drives past, slowing a little, watching as Halliday gets out. Kelley keeps an eye on the rearview as he slows to a crawl. The DC crosses and waves to the girls. Not a friendly wave. Letting them know he's there. He's not busting them, either.

Kelley realises, Halliday's taking collections.

He thinks about letters to the papers concerning the girls: about how the city centre should be safer, should be family friendly. He thinks about the excuses from the top about resources and tackling the causes, and thinks that it's all a load of nonsense.

This happens because certain people want it to happen. Because Joe Kennedy's offering a cut for it to keep happening.

Because Joe Kennedy's contributing to the Veteran's Fund.

Because DS Garner owes Kennedy a favour.

Because the whole fucking system is corrupt.

* * *

Kelley drops Donnie at his flat, tells him not to answer the door to anyone except him or Burnet.

Donnie protests and then agrees after Kelley gives him a pack of cigs to pass the time.

Kelley drives back to Albert Square.

Getting dark now.

Slow down at a set of lights.

One of the girls comes over. Dark hair, cut short. Dark eyes. Young. Maybe twenty, maybe a little less.

Nausea swirls in Kelley's stomach.

"Help you?" the girl says.

Kelley nods. He takes out a file photograph of DC Halliday from the glove compartment. "This man," he says. "You know him?"

She doesn't react. "Who are you?"

"Does it matter?"

"Of course it fucking matters."

"I'm not police."

"You know he is, though?"

"I just need you to tell me what he was doing here earlier today."

The girl raises her hands, backs off. "Don't know you from Adam," she says. "Get all kinds of fucking perverts in cars, you know."

"I know," he says.

The lights have changed. There's a car behind him. They blast their horn.

Kelley says, "I'll be back. If you want to talk. I'm serious. It'll be worth your time."

The car blasts again. The girl gives him the finger, and returns to the small group of women who're gathered nearby.

Kelley takes a breath, drives on.

47

HALLIDAY'S PHOTO IS ON THE DESK, FACE UP.

Burnet says, "You never worked with him?"

"Garner's crowd ... they were just a pack to me. Faces that blended in. Names that all sounded the same."

"You ever wonder what would have happened if you'd just sat back, like Garner warned you to do?"

Kelley shakes his head. "Can you sit back?"

"No."

"Same here. I get an idea in my head. You know what they say about dogs and bones?"

"Dogs and cars," she says. "Do you ever worry that even if we do get Garner ... what happens after that? It's all fine and well talking about change, but we're just two people. Garner's not the only one up to his neck in shite?"

Kelley doesn't have an answer for that. What they're doing, it seems simple. But she's right: catch one thief, there are still others out there. Catch one murderer, there'll be more. Same rule with corrupt coppers.

Back when he first joined the force, Kelley walked the beat for a while with an Irish copper by the name of Bruen. Older fella, said he stayed in uniform because he "felt he could do more good" that way. Ask him about CID, he'd say they were nothing but posers. A religious man, Bruen had once asked Kelley, "D'you know the patron saint of police?"

Kelley didn't know. But Bruen was all for telling him. The patron saint of police was St Michael. "He's also the one who'll lead the army of angels in the final battle against evil. Reckon he'll have all of us behind him then, too. Continuing the good work we do here." Bruen had laughed, then. "Thing is, that for all that, I always thought maybe we got the wrong saint. What I always thought, we should double up on St Jude. Because this job, most days, it feels like the most hopeless fucking cause. We're sticking our fingers in a dam. For all that we do, we can't really change anything. Not in the grand scheme."

Bruen had retired soon after that. Kelley had a few pints with him, promising to stay in touch. "No one ever does, lad."

Truer words never spoken.

But right now, Kelley understands what the man had meant, talking about St Jude.

He says to Burnet, "We have to try, though."

"Aye." She runs both hands through her hair. "I saw Garner in action today." She tells him about the missing girl, about Garner beating the boyfriend.

"Thing is," she says, "there was part of me thought if he hadn't done that, maybe we wouldn't have worked out that the girl in his bed wasn't the girl we were looking for. You know, go in all polite, he sends us on our way, we have no idea anyone's in there ..."

"That's how he justifies it."

"I know."

"There are better ways."

"I know."

He looks at her. She's tired.

"It's a long game," he says. "We both knew that."

"And if I take a shortcut, I'm just like them. I know."

Kelley feels for her. They could cut corners. Plant evidence where it needs to be. Maybe ask Donnie to lie for them. But it would taint the end goal.

Actions matter as much as intent.

48

KENNEDY'S AT THE BAR WHEN FRANK walks through the door. Swings on his stool, smiles. "Come on. Get yourself a drink."

Frank sits. Behind the bar, Tumshie sets to pouring a pint.

Kennedy says, "You're looking well."

Frank shrugs.

"You missed it, didn't you?"

Frank shrugs again.

Did he?

When he was young, violence came easy. But now he feels hesitation.

Hesitation can get you killed.

Out of practice?

Or...

He tries not to think about Martin, about what happened in the high rise.

"That's the Frank I used to know," Kennedy says. "None of the gallus shite. Just a walking slab of mean. When you walk into a room, everyone pisses themselves." Kennedy claps a hand around Frank's shoulders, pulling him in. "Except me, of course."

Frank gets the hint of booze on Kennedy's breath. Waits just the right amount of time, before pulling back.

Frank says, "Our friend . . . you talked to him?"

"Aye." An itch in Frank's brain. Conscience? Fine time to develop one.

"And?"

"And he said he'd sort it." A pause. "I made sure he had incentive."

"I'm beginning to think," Kennedy says, "when it comes right down to it, there's no one more untrustworthy than the polis. Wouldn't you agree?"

"Wouldn't trust any of them," Frank says. "Dishonest bunch of bastards that they are."

"Getting ideas above their station," Kennedy says. "You know that I'm hearing rumours they've opened another investigation into me?"

"Jesus."

"I'm a public-spirited citizen," Kennedy says. "Holding this fucking city together. I'm the one who lets the polis get away with their shite. Who deals with the real problems. Even the top brass, much as they deny it, know they can't live without me." He takes a long draught of his pint. "So maybe we need to send a message. A wee reminder."

"Such as?"

"I've been hearing things, about an ex-cop and a wee lassie who've been asking questions. The kind of questions that could cause an embarrassment to certain people. Maybe this pair . . . maybe they could do with a hand finding the arseholes in their midst. Our mutual friend . . . he's got to be near retirement age. It's not like he'll be around forever. And besides, he's got his proceeds from the Veteran's Fund to take care of him in his old age."

Frank takes a sharp breath between clenched teeth. "You're sure this is a good idea? How d'you know that's not going to bring the heat down even more?"

Kennedy smiles at that. "Human nature," he says. "Men like our friend are ten-a-fucking-penny. There's always someone else who thinks they can get away with murder, or can be leaned on just the right way so they'll commit it for you. Besides, even without the police, I still have an ace in the hole."

"The councillor?"

"Aye, the handsome one. The fucking Young Turk of British politics." He raises his glass. "To the future," he says.

Reluctantly, Frank raises his own glass. "The future."

49

KELLEY'S READ HIS FATHER'S JOURNALS OVER and over. Now, when he closes his eyes, all he sees is the tight, closely spaced scrawl on the lined pages.

But it's not enough. Every time Kelley thinks he's come across a direct confession, it seems like his father can never quite find the courage to write it down.

Some things cannot live up to their own promise. Some people can never be the person they pretend to be.

Kelley talks the talk. He wants to be better. He wants to be good polis, to *make a difference*. But his temper – his nature – was always going to be his downfall.

Punching Garner out in the interrogation room.

Refusing to face up to the consequences of his own actions.

Kelley's not polis in the way he wants to be.

But he believes such people exist.

He *knows* they exist.

Burnet. The purest polis he's ever known. Embodies everything the force needs to be.

She's willing to fight for the principles of the job. And do it right.

But to do it right will take time.

And for all he's said to her, he knows that at least one of them needs to cross a line.

It can't be her.

Not if they want things to change.

Her victory cannot be hollow.

There's a phrase Kelley read once in a thriller about the CIA: *Plausible Deniability*.

What you don't know, you can't be responsible for.

Which is why Kelley's still not told her everything about Halliday. Which is why he's told her to *wait*.

"We need something we can use against him. Let me do what me and the Fat Man do best. Let me make sure that what you have is airtight."

Halliday's been on night shifts for a week. Which means at this time of day, he's home alone. The wife's out picking up the kids from school. And Halliday's upstairs, sleeping.

Suburban bliss.

Kelley makes sure the street's quiet. He walks up the garden path, slipping on the balaclava as he does so. A brief glimpse of his reflection in the windows, looking for all the world like a member of the IRA.

He thinks briefly about adopting an accent.

No.

The mask is enough.

Halliday won't recognise his voice. Not if he does this right.

Kelley hammers the front door.

Waits.

The handle turns.

Kelley pushes in.

Full on frightener.

Keep the fucker off-balance.

Halliday crashes on his arse.

The door slams.

Silence.

"What the fuck?" Halliday crab-crawls away from the man in the mask.

Kelley slams his heel down between Halliday's legs.

Halliday bawls, quits the retreat, folds in on himself.

Foetal.

In the background, the lunchtime news. Something about the French testing nuclear bombs on some island.

Halliday clearly wishes he was on that island. He'd be safer there.

He's sobbing now, holding his balls, cradling them for comfort and relief.

Kelley says, "We need to talk."

"Fuck you," Halliday says, lifting his head, trying for defiant and managing petulant. "Who sent you here, huh? We told you the money was fucking coming. We're fucking sorting it. You just have to—"

Kelley steps forward. Halliday yelps and crawls back again, desperate to avoid another heel coming down.

Beneath the balaclava, Kelley's trying not to smile. Halliday doesn't hear his voice. Only the words. All his attention taken by the mask. His fear of whoever he thinks Kelley might be.

Better than Kelley could have hoped.

Of course he doesn't think Kelley's IRA or anything close. They don't target Scotland. No point, is there? Not when England only cares about itself.

"Then tell me," Kelley says, "what you're doing to get it?"

* * *

Half an hour later, Halliday has some reserves left. Unconvincingly playing at Billy Big Balls. His nose is bloodied, his face blackened and bruised.

He says, "You're not one of Kennedy's lads, are you?", voice thick with blood and snot. Slowly, painfully, he raises his head. "So who the fuck are you?"

Kelley says, "You're going to get a visit from another police detective. You'll know who when they arrive. You're not going to tell them about any of this, but what you are going to do is tell them everything that we talked about. Is that clear?"

"And if I don't?"

"Do you really want to know how far I'm willing to go here?"

"Fuck off."

Kelley figured this would happen. He's not an idiot.

He reaches into his jacket, pulls out an envelope.

"You own this house," Kelley says. "Except *you* don't. It's your wife's. Her money. Inherited. In the case of divorce or separation, I would guess that means you're out on your arse."

Halliday starts to shake. Rage or upset?

Kelley waits.

Halliday opens the envelope. His eyes go wide.

"Come on," Kelley says. "You had to know this would happen one day."

Except his expression makes it clear Halliday didn't know. Of course he didn't. People don't think about consequences, except as idle thoughts. Kelley learned that during his time on the force – talking to career criminals, habitual reoffenders, people who knew exactly what they were risking and went ahead anyway.

The bad things only ever happen to other people. You deserve the good life. You deserve to get away with whatever you do. Because you're doing it for the right reasons, or because you're smarter than other people.

You get away with something once, some small thing, you believe you'll get away with it forever.

Kelley had gone back to Albert Square. Talked to the girls, asked them about Halliday. He was a bag man, sure, but did he ever try and take advantage?

Aye, of course he did.

The Fat Man's speciality is divorce cases. What that means is that he can take photos other people might consider to be impossible.

Like the ones in the envelope.

"Jesus." Halliday puts his head in his hands.

Kelley says, "When you get the visit, you know what to do." He gathers up the photographs, puts them back into his jacket.

As Kelley's leaving, Halliday says, "I know you, don't I?"

Kelley walks out. Gets to the end of the street, turns a corner, takes off his mask. Leans back against a wall, wipes the sweat from his forehead, takes gulping gasps of air; a man who's just come up from drowning.

50

BURNET'S AT HER DESK WHEN THE PHONE RINGS.

"Our friend is willing to talk."

She looks around the room. Suddenly paranoid.

Do they know what she's been doing?

Jesus, don't be stupid.

She's barely slept the last few nights. Can't stop thinking What they're doing. The names, locations, implications. At least six CID officers working muscle at Kennedy's bookie joints on the regular. The same men – maybe others – running as bag men, all of them handing the proceeds up to a DS who then passed a cut back to Kennedy.

There are others. Some of them, Burnet knows. But she couldn't afford to tip their hand yet. So while she's been carrying on as usual, Kelley's been doing the legwork. Going places she can't now that he's no longer polis.

But there are lines.

She's been worried about them.

She thinks she can trust him not to cross them. As much as she can trust anyone.

And that's the problem. She can't trust anyone.

The paranoia is closing her throat.

Garner stands with two uniforms she doesn't recognise. All three of them deep in conversation. No one's looking at her.

She says, quiet, into the receiver, "We were supposed to confront him together."

"I did it my way."

She keeps her voice low, hard. "I can't work with you if—"

"He's expecting you. He'll cooperate."

"What did you do?" Sinking sensation in her stomach. Kelley was supposed to be a man of principle.

But she's seen the look in his eyes. He's more like Garner than he'd care to admit.

"What I had to. What's important is that he's willing to talk."

No point in fighting among themselves. If they do, Garner's already won, before he even knows he's fighting a war. All Burnet can do is hope she's wrong and that nothing's going to bite her in the arse. "He'll come to see me? Voluntarily?"

"Expect the call," Kelley says, and hangs up.

Burnet holds the receiver a few more moments.

Garner's finished his story. As she hangs up, he comes over. "You follow up on what that lad told us?"

The "lad". Meaning Dickie Borer.

Burnet sees his split lip and black eye when she closes her eyes.

Garner had been holding back for her benefit.

At the time, part of her wished he hadn't.

If Kelley isn't so different from Garner, is she?

Are they embarking on a moral crusade that will achieve precisely nothing?

"I'm still phoning some of the girls on the list." Dickie had given them contact details for some of Tessie's friends. The threat of a further beating had made him more than willing to cooperate. "Hopefully one of them will know where she is."

"I still say she met some other sleazeball. That's the thing, once a girl's been damaged ..." He lets the thought linger for a moment, then smiles at her. "I know you're an optimist, though. Even working the beat as long as you did didn't seem to cure that." Then, as an afterthought: "Thought we worked well together. In the end, you have to realise, the way we do things works. I'm not against change. But it needs to be effective."

She says nothing. He seems to take that as agreement.

She closes her eyes, sees Dickie's face, battered and bruised. Gets a twist in her stomach that makes her want to vomit.

* * *

The call comes through that afternoon.

She meets Halliday at the riverside, near the old stanchions of the Tay Rail Bridge, the one that collapsed. He's leaning against the dyke, looking out at the water, and turns as she approaches.

She almost recoils when she sees his face. Broken lip, one eye half-closed, bruises purpling and swelling on his cheek.

"Your friend," he says.

Meaning Kelley.

Kelley did this to him.

What was he thinking?

She leans against the stone. Keeps calm. "Tell me why I'm here."

"I'm part of a small group of officers who ... do favours for people. DS Garner's the one in charge." He swallows hard. "We have a private fund. We share it equally among the officers. Mostly, the revenue comes from money skimmed from raids, that kind of thing. Used to be known as the Veteran's Fund, you know, for officers who served in the war? Now, it's just ... the fund."

"But there's more?"

"Some of the money that Garner brings down comes from Kennedy. It's an arrangement we have. He keeps the peace and helps us out, and sometimes we do favours for him."

"Define favours?"

"We watch out for places that he owns. We collect envelopes from them sometimes."

"What places?"

"Pubs, clubs, you know? Also, sometimes, he'll have us collect money from girls on the street. The price of protection."

"From who?"

"From anyone looking to cause them trouble. And, I suppose, from arrest. That's the deal – they pay, we let them ply their trade. Keeps everyone sweet."

Not exactly news, but he's admitting it to her. More than she'd expected.

The question is, can he do the same in court? Will he commit to going on the record?

A lot can change between an unofficial chat and a date in the dock.

"How long has this been going on for?"

This time, he snaps back at her: "Is this an official interview, Detective *Constable*?" Emphasis on her rank. Same as his. Being a detective is a sideways transfer, not an automatic route to seniority. Plainclothes can act like they're in charge, but they're no different to any other office in practice.

"Not yet," she says. "But it will be."

He nods, suddenly reticent. His mood swings tell her more than she wants to know about how Kelley got him to come forward. "You're making these statements of your own free will? You're cooperating with no duress?"

"No duress," he says, softly.

Lying. Does it matter?

She ignores the voice at the back of her head.

"Then tell me," she says, "how long has this been going on for?"

51

FRANK KNOCKS ON HIS SON'S DOOR.

No answer.

They haven't talked in days.

Martin's keeping himself to himself ever since Frank took him out on the job.

Frank's been happy for it to stay that way. But sooner or later they'll need to talk about what happened.

Frank's been thinking about it a lot. The change he saw in his son. Like a switch flipping. Like his son became something – *something* – else.

More than just Frank's influence. More than an inherited capacity for violence.

Martin came *alive* when he threatened that fucker.

If Frank hadn't been there ...

But there's only so far that Frank can take that thought.

This is his son. The baby he held after he was born. The lad he walked to his first day at school.

Frank the family man.

That's who raised Martin.

Trying to save the lad from becoming like the old Frank.

So what happened?

Frank did everything he was supposed to. He was a good father.

Wasn't he?

Jesus fuck, now's not the time to doubt yourself.

He raps on the door again.

But Martin's not in.

Frank walks inside. This is his house. His son's room, but *his* house.

The room's a mess. Clothes everywhere. Tapes on the floor.

The Sex Pistols.

Christ, the lad lives like a bloody animal.

Was it the music? *The Sex Pistols* – would anyone with a shred of decency listen to a band called *The Sex Pistols*? This fucking world. A cesspool.

Has Frank been wilfully blind? Ignoring all the things that could send a boy – a *sensitive* boy, as Jeannie used to say – over the edge?

Is Frank looking for excuses?

Frank picks things up. Like he's tidying the place. Gives him something to do.

Some of these things should be thrown out – the tapes, the music. Everything that's pulling Martin away from the real world.

A pile of clothes. Jeans, t-shirts, pants.

The books on wolves. Lying open and discarded. Pen marks on the pages. Images circled.

Other books from the library: metalwork and more.

In his son's junk, he finds a girl's top. Frank can't help himself. He smiles. Maybe his son's normal after all.

Then, closer inspection:

Rip at the neck. Smatter of blood on the side.

What have you been up to, son?

Frank hides the top in a shoebox at the back of the cupboard. He'll talk to Martin later.

Maybe things aren't what they look like.

Maybe he had a girl back in his room, and Frank and Jeannie were just too stupid to realise.

Aye, maybe that's it. A normal fucking teenager. The kind of stupid shite that Frank understands. Maybe they need to have a talk about it. Aye, like a normal father and son.

Normal.

Everything's normal.

The idea relaxes Frank. He goes downstairs, grabs his coat, heads out the door. Worried about his son as he is, he still has work to do.

And his employer isn't one for granting family time.

* * *

He takes the bus to town. Same alley, same time.

Waits.

Garner shows up. Two minutes late. Hands Frank an envelope. "Told you we'd make it up," he says. Not a word of apology.

Frank takes the envelope. Puts it in his pocket.

Grabs Garner by the collar, shoves him against a wall.

In his face: "This does not fucking happen again. Do you understand me?"

"I fucking understand." Trying to play it cool. But his eyes give him away.

Frank throws the cop to the ground. "You're walking around at the big man's pleasure, you know that?"

"Aye, I fucking know." Playing it humble. But Frank thinks he's just taking the piss.

What? He's not afraid of Frank? Not afraid of the fucking Beast of Balgay? Garner's old enough to remember.

Or old enough to forget.

Make the point. Make it clear. Remind the prick. "Just because you're polis doesn't mean you get special treatment. You showed up light, and that means we add interest."

"How much?"

Frank gives him the number. With 10 per cent on top. Fuck Garner, he deserves the extra weight.

Garner climbs to his feet. Eyes fixed tight on Frank. "You're fucking kidding me?"

Frank shakes his head. "Price you pay. No more excuses."

"Or what happens? You can't do anything without his say so. You're a fucking monkey, and Joe Kennedy's the organ grinder. You've been gone a long time, and you don't seem to understand how things are between me and the old fella. I'm the one who allows him to operate in this city. I'm the fucking organ grinder's organ grinder."

Frank nods. "You're right," he says. He stays his ground, keeps eye contact with Garner. "I don't do anything without his say so."

He moves fast on Garner's blind side. A low punch. To the kidneys. Tight and powerful.

Garner goes down.

"He told me: if you got out of hand, I was to do what I do best."

Frank grabs the man's hand, hauls it up hard. There's resistance. Garner makes a noise that sounds like an animal in a trap. Frank holds Garner's wrist tight with one hand, grabs his middle and index fingers with the other.

"What the fuck're you—"

Frank answers the question without words.

Bones snap.

Garner screams.

Frank steps back.

Sweat on his forehead. Cold. Hopes Garner doesn't look at him too closely.

Garner remains on his knees, cradling broken fingers. Whimpering.

Pathetic.

A fucking baby.

Frank gives him a moment. "I want you to remember this. Remember what I tell you. Because I'm the one who saved your fucking bacon. The big man, he wanted to make an example of you. He wanted to throw you to the wolves. I was the one who told him maybe you'd listen to reason."

"This is your idea of reason?" Garner says, still cradling his hand.

Frank feels twenty years younger. Cock-of-the-fucking-walk.

Garner starts to shiver.

Shock setting in.

Good.

"Remember your place," Frank says. He steps past the detective. "And pay the fucking interest or next time, I'll snap off more than your fucking fingers."

52

BURNET KNOCKS ON DSI REDMAN'S DOOR.

"Come in."

Redman has a visitor perched on the edge of the desk.

Davie Darling. The politician's not unattractive, but there's a look in his eyes that's always unsettled Burnet. A predatory gleam. The cocky confidence of someone who doesn't understand the meaning of "no".

She thinks again about him being present when the autopsy report got changed. What is his relationship to this?

What is his relationship to Redman?

Is it coincidence?

Does he know something?

"Don't mind me." Darling stands, flashing a smile. "Just having a wee catch up with your boss, here." He looks her up and down.

A mental undressing.

Burnet says nothing. It's all she has.

Wait it out.

Don't rock the boat.

Too many complaints, and they'll call her unstable. *Hysterical.* Pick the fucking battles.

Not like there's a shortage.

Darling brushes past her on his way out. The back of his hand lightly lingers against the side of her legs. A little too much contact.

Aye, he's a predator.

But her instinct says he's not a killer.

There's something else going on with him and the department.

Politics and policing. They go hand in hand behind closed doors. She'd be foolish to believe otherwise.

Redman stays where he is, behind the desk, and folds his arms.

Darling closes the door behind him.

Redman waits for Burnet to speak. He has a granite expression.

Does he know why she's here?

"We need to talk," she says, "about DS Garner."

Thinking she wouldn't get the words out. Forcing herself to hide surprise when she does.

Redman shakes his head. "I know the young are meant to be ambitious, but why you're taking against a man with as many years' service to the department as—"

"Due respect, sir, I've seen his casework up close. I know for a fact that his records don't tell the full story."

"It's not the police officer's job to be perfect."

"That *is* the job—"

"No, the job is to be authoritative in the eyes of the public. Which means getting results. And DS Garner gets results. His arrest record speaks for itself."

"His arrest record doesn't tell the whole story." She tries to keep her voice level.

Hysterical woman.

No job for a girl.

Must be her time of the month.

Ignore the thoughts.

Stand up.

"DS Garner's approach to interviews may result in arrest records, but you have to wonder if he always gets the right man."

"An innocent person wouldn't—"

"An innocent person scared for their life would," she says. "Besides, isn't the job of the police to be *better* than those they arrest?"

"Your little friend, Kelley, already tried this. He came to me with similar concerns and—"

"And you ignored them." Is she overstepping the line? "I know, sir."

"So why do you think I'll listen to you?"

"Because I'm not just here about his treatment of suspects. I think you're willing to overlook that, and maybe there's nothing I can do about that. But you can't ignore that one of your senior officers has been running a protection scheme for local businesses, possibly with the support of a known local gangster. And that some of the officers in his circle may be responsible for the recent B&Es that have taken place at businesses related to this protection business."

Redman remains still.

"I know you think you can turn a blind eye to some behaviours, but this is something you need to hear. Something you need to know."

Redman nods. He indicates for her to sit down. "Show me the evidence," he says. "Because if you can't do that, Detective Constable Burnet, I'll ask you to hand in your warrant card here and now."

53

THREE WEEKS FOR THE DUST TO SETTLE.

Burnet takes extended leave. The detectives in the pool are told that she's taking "personal time". None of them ask any further questions.

Kelley and Burnet meet once a week. Always somewhere different. Paranoia? Maybe. She keeps him up to date.

No one knows what's happening until everything's in place.

Kelley meets with the Chief Constable. He walks into the room, sees Redman first, the DCI's expression unreadable.

He tells them everything he knows.

Testimony comes from:

Kelley.

Burnet.

Halliday.

Kelley's father's journal is submitted as evidence.

One of the business owners agrees to come forward. A shopkeeper. The Chief Constable himself guarantees that there will be protection for all witnesses who are willing to talk.

But everything is quiet.

A duck on the surface of calm water. The legs kicking away where no one can see.

And then:

Three weeks later.

Kelley buys a copy of that morning's *Courier*, and sees the headline:

POLICE DETECTIVE ACCUSED OF CORRUPTION, BREAKING AND ENTERING

He reads the paper in a corner booth at the Washington Café. His coffee gets cold as he reads the same page over and over again.

Twelve policemen involved, including one "senior detective". Garner protests his innocence, but not in the papers. He doesn't grant interviews and his name is not printed until the day of the trial.

The paper gives the facts of the first day's proceedings. Little more than attesting to the litany of charges, with Garner and eleven of his cohorts proclaiming their innocence. The twelfth, unnamed officer is a witness for the Procurator Fiscal's side. No mention of the deal he's cut.

The waitress passes, glances over his shoulder to see what's got him so engrossed he hasn't touched his drink. "Terrible business," she says.

Kelley looks up.

"Terrible," she says again. "You used to be polis, didn't you?"

He doesn't say anything.

"Can see why you left. Useless bunch of bastards. No wonder they never solve anything. Too busy doing the crimes themselves."

"Not all of them."

"Aye, but enough, right? If one's at it, there's others."

Kelley tries not to nod in agreement.

"Better out of it," she says. Then, "Refill? That's got to taste like ice now, you've left it so long."

He nods, and when she moves off to get the coffee, he looks back at the paper.

He reads through it again, noting the details.

Gets a sick feeling in his stomach where he expects joy.

Realises this isn't the end of something so much as it might be a beginning.

* * *

The Fat Man says, "You've done it now."

Kelley grabs mail from the desk. "If they call me, it'll be good publicity for us."

"Aye, but hardly discreet."

"Discretion's your middle name, right?" The Fat Man chuckles gently.

Kelley opens an envelope to check its contents. A cheque from a client, along with a hastily scrawled note telling the agency to "fuck off".

Some people say they want the truth, but aren't happy when it comes knocking on their door.

The Fat Man says, "You'll need to shave."

"What?"

"If they have you in court, you need to be even more presentable than when you were polis."

Kelley keeps opening the mail.

"I'm serious. You've no friends left there. I know you think you know, but the truth's going to hit you when you walk into the court for the first time. People like you and me, we're not just low on the totem; I think they all believe we're worse than criminals. Which means that you're going to be in there testifying against a long-serving officer—"

"One with whom I have a known grudge."

"Aye, there's that, too. So there you are, in the witness stand, with all that shite over your head – and then everyone has this idea of you sitting in cars, taking pictures of men having sex with their mistresses and—"

"To be fair, I have done that."

"Aye, and it's a living. But the normal Joe on the street doesn't understand. And to the police, what we are is a pain in the arse. Then the PFs all think that we're going to trip up their case at any moment, because we're not bound by procedure or whatever ... what I'm saying is, when you go in you need to look your best. Tell them all you're fucking *respectable*."

"I've seen you go into court," he says, "and that's your best?"

"What God gave me," the Fat Man says. "But I have an advantage over you, my friend."

"And what's that?"

"My winning fucking smile," the Fat Man says.

Kelley doesn't respond. How can he? Even after several months, he's no idea if the Fat Man's crazy or some kind of genius. Maybe even a little of both. He's a talented detective – the kind of smart that would do Sherlock Holmes proud – but also a cynical prick. Doesn't believe in much of anything except the power of the pound. Cross his palm with silver, and anything's possible.

The Fat Man reaches up to massage the top of his head with his fingers. Like an aggressive Stan Laurel in Oliver Hardy's body. "All I'm saying, is that you represent me in there.

You represent my business. And there's two ways something like this is going to go. You're either going to paint a fucking target on this office that the polis will take shots at ..."

"Or?"

"Or you're going to drum up more business than anyone could dream possible." The Fat Man grins. "I'm not saying your continued employment rests on the outcome ..."

Kelley takes the mail into his room. He needs to be alone. To gather his thoughts. Maybe work out once and for all whether the Fat Man's a professional wind-up merchant.

54

A NOTE WAITING ON HER DESK.

"RAT."

Simple. Clear.

No pictures or props. Nothing to illustrate the author's meaning. Not like when they were sticking Friday Girl pictures round the place.

This is something else.

Doesn't matter that she's a woman, not now.

She's worse than that.

She's a RAT.

No gender discrimination for a RAT.

Fuck.

People in the room look at her. Sly and subtle, their faces turned away as far as possible.

But they're looking at her.

Everyone might be in on it.

Who knows? Her identity was supposed to be kept a secret.

She makes a show of balling up the paper, throwing it in the trash.

Redman walks into the room, looks around. "Everyone here?" he says. "Good. Get your fucking arses in gear. We've got a very fucking special briefing today."

He doesn't look in her direction.

She knows it's no accident.

* * *

Only one seat left. Right down the front. Isolated, on the right-hand side.

She takes it. People stare at the back of her head. She's heard the phrase "looking daggers", and now she knows what it means. The sharpness penetrates her skull, her brain.

Ignore it.

After the charges were made public, eight detectives were suspended off rotation. A mix of new recruits and transfers from other forces now take up the slack.

All of them aware who's responsible.

Redman takes up position at the front of the room.

Someone else walks in.

No murmurs.

Surprised silence.

The Chief Constable.

Redman glances about the room, catching eyes. Everyone except Burnet.

Making it clear where she stands in the new order.

She'd known this was coming. He couldn't ignore what she showed him, but that didn't mean he had to like it.

"Okay," he says. "I'm sure most of you have seen the papers this morning. The rumour mill's been working overtime since DS Garner took voluntary leave following serious accusations made against him and other members of this department. Let's be honest, this is not the first time he's been in the hot seat. But if—"

"Stick it up yer arse!" someone shouts from the back of the room.

A mix of jeers and cheers.

Redman gives his best glare. Everyone goes quiet fast.

The Chief Constable steps up. "I'm aware that emotions are running high," he says. "But these are, as your DCI has said, serious accusations."

"Aye? Made by who?"

If Burnet turns round, maybe she can see who it was shouting out.

Is it the person who left the note?

But she can't – won't – turn round.

The Chief Constable keeps talking. Expression fixed. Words carefully measured. "It can be a shock when you learn that a colleague has been bending or even breaking the rules and standards that we expect of all officers in Tayside Police. It has happened before, to people that I have worked with, and people I even liked and trusted. But we cannot allow our emotions to get in the way of the pursuit of the highest of standards. The CID in Tayside has a long and proud history, and should our colleague be vindicated – and I hope that he will – of all charges, then we can all breathe a sigh of relief. But we cannot simply assume—"

"Innocent till proven guilty!"

A minor flinch. But he keeps talking like there was nothing to react to. "... cannot assume that he is guilty simply because he is one of us. Now that these accusations are in the public domain, we must all do our best to reassure the public that the standards of this department are beyond reproach. We must continue to work cases. We must continue to do our jobs. And we must always remember that should the DS be found guilty of the acts of which he has been accused—"

"Free the Dundee one!"

The Chief Constable stops speaking.

Redman steps forward. "Constable Breen," he says. "You'll be in my office after this, where we will discuss how a detective acts with decorum at all times." A sweep of the room. Detectives flinch and look away. "Anyone else have something they want to get off their chest? Now is the time. Because I need you all to remember that cheeking a senior officer is a *disciplinary offence*."

The Chief Constable clears his throat. He's been in this job a long time. He should have their respect. He *does* have their respect.

As long as he lets them do their job.

Right now, he's wondering how far that respect really goes.

Burnet thinks that he's not looking at her deliberately. As though that might stop anyone from realising she's the one who dobbed in a colleague.

Too late for that.

RAT.

She keeps her hands clasped on her lap. Her neck hurts, and she wants to reach back and crick it into comfort. But she can't move. Anything she does to bring attention to herself could make things more tense than they already are. Everyone knows who landed Garner in the shite. Everyone knows that she's in the right, and yet they don't want to admit it.

Why?

Because they might have to look at themselves in the mirror. Even men like Redman, who might not condone such behaviour, but do their best to excuse it.

A boy's club problem?

Or something else?

"The watchword," the Chief Constable says, finding his voice again, "is professionalism. Business as usual. We will work our shifts. We will clear cases. The bobbies will be on the beat. Nothing will change. No matter what the outcome of this investigation, we will show that Tayside Constabulary is stronger than the actions of a few rotten apples. And we will not allow them to spoil the barrel." Another pause, as he gauges the room. "But let me also be clear that if these accusations are shown to be false, or the result of malicious intent, then we will swiftly react against those responsible. We stand together with a common purpose."

If they were in Hollywood, captured on film, maybe his speech would be followed by a slow build of rapturous applause; the fearless orator bringing the reluctant crowd to his side.

But this is Dundee. 1978. A city that has been through hard times, and still can't be sure if it will recover.

So the speech ends with silence.

The Chief leaves the room.

People start to move again. Low rumblings. Officers leaning into their neighbours.

Burnet sits alone.

No one speaks to her.

Finally, she gets up and leaves. She goes to the toilets. Locks herself in a cubicle.

Sits down.

Starts to shake.

But she doesn't cry.

She doesn't fucking cry.

55

SHERIFF MACDUFF-DUNCAN IS A BIG MAN in every sense of the word. He sits at the front of the court and looks around at the jury, at the press in the public galleries, at the solicitors gathered before them.

The silence lasts maybe half a minute.

Feels longer.

"Before the accused enter the room," he says, "I want to make it perfectly clear that this is not a circus. It is not a place for mudslinging or for making tribal defences of the thin blue line. This matter is one of the most serious I have encountered in my career. More so than any murder. Because this case involves a betrayal of trust that runs deep in the fabric of our society. Should these accusations be proven within the court, then there will be a very public – possibly even national – fallout. But I fear the same for any verdict reached."

Kelley's at the back of the galleries. He won't be called for a few days. He shouldn't be here, showing his face in the public galleries, but he can't stay away.

When the trial starts properly, there's a great deal of pre-amble. The charges against Garner and his co-conspirators have been focused on the B&Es. It's been recommended that no one makes a direct connection to Kennedy. The case will focus on Garner himself, his formation of a local protection racket, and his retaliation against those businesses he deemed to have come up short.

The case proceeds at the kind of pace a snail would find tedious. Always the same, Kelley thinks. The public get the edited highlights on the news bulletins and in the papers, but sitting in court, waiting for the arguments, counterarguments, procedures and pleas, the drama becomes a blur of tedium.

But Kelley stays.

Because he knows what's at stake.

Wants to watch it happen.

To know it can be done.

The eleven men in the dock keep their heads high. Garner's right in the middle, and what Kelley notes is that all the other officers look to him for their cues. They don't blink without first glancing in his direction.

Kelley wonders what the jury see when they look at them.

Do they see eleven police officers who were only doing their damn jobs, and who got caught up in some attempt at payback by someone seeking to ruin their careers? Or do they see what Kelley sees? A group of men so self-absorbed that they pervert the very thing they claim to uphold.

* * *

Witnesses.

Evidence.

The jury asked to leave and come back.

On and on.

Star witness sequestered.

Burnet assuring Kelley that Halliday will be kept safe. That she has the assurances of the Chief Constable.

Burnet takes the stand, three days in.

At the back of the court, Kelley wears a hat and dresses down in jeans and t-shirt. He could be anyone. A lookie-loo. The courts have never been so busy in the public galleries.

She looks good, he thinks. Strong. Walks with confidence. Wears a trouser suit and draws a few looks for it. But that's a good thing. Keeps eyes on her.

Kelley thinks most of them expected her to show up in a skirt. Ten years ago, he remembers the fuss some of the papers made when the wife of someone on the honours list turned up to the ceremony in trousers.

Twentieth century right there.

On the floor: one real polis and eleven pretend ones.

They ask her what gave her cause to think the behaviour of DS Garner was in doubt. She answers succinctly and clearly. Cites dates. Talks about the aftermath of the flasher arrest.

The solicitor acting for the accused – a rat-faced fuck in a two-penny suit – lets her talk, then walks up to her. He doesn't get in her face, but what he does is get close enough that she might flinch. She doesn't. He asks whether it's possible that Garner was heated on her behalf; whether she might misinterpret chivalry for chauvinism.

He sees her lips twitch. A momentary expression of disbelief at the question.

Quick recovery.

Is it enough?

The jury is made up of eleven men and four women.

The men look to be an average age of fifty.

The women? Maybe the same age. Hard to tell. Buttoned up and prim and proper, their expressions tight and guarded.

What do they think of Burnet?

When they look at her, do they see what Kelley sees?

Burnet bats off the question. States that while Garner's past actions played into the reasons she came forward, what forced her into action was the evidence surrounding the recent burglaries. She tells him about the reaction of the pub owner who thought she was there to pick up the protection money and how that first raised her suspicions.

"Why did you not put this in your initial report?"

It's a fair question.

Kelley's nails bite in the palms of his hands. He's clenching.

She can hold it together. He knows she can.

And yet part of him must be having doubts. Not because the defence are good at their job, but because he doesn't know how people are going to react to her.

She's one woman.

Against eleven men.

She's a new detective. The accused have over sixty years' experience between them as police officers.

Who do you believe?

Listen to the way the rat-face fuck frames his questions and his statements. Walking the line of implying that Burnet just has a problem with male authority figures. He even asks her point blank at one stage if she's a *feminist* in the same tone that fifteen or twenty years ago, people might have asked, *are you a communist?*

He wants to knock her down.

But she fights back. Sticks to the facts. Doesn't react when she's needled. And doesn't once look at the men in the dock.

* * *

The wheels of justice grind slowly.

Cliché with a touch of truth.

Weeks pass.

The officers on trial flaunt their freedom. No holding in jail for them.

Evidence. Arguments.

The papers summarise daily.

The *Dundee Herald* falters a little in its pro-police stance.

The star witness waits in the wings.

Kelley's turn on the stand – the one he'd hoped to avoid – goes faster than he'd like. Later, he tries to remember what he said. Draws a blank. Hopes it was something close to the truth.

He checks for his name in the papers.

They call him a "hotheaded former DC" and note that his father's "testimony from beyond the grave" is "hearsay at best".

Letters come to the Fat Man's office addressed to him. Some praise, but most are written with the kind of hate that can kill. Some, perhaps, are cranks. Kelley suspects the majority originate from fellow officers.

There's a code, after all.

Kelley remembers something he learned at school about the armies in ancient Greece – the Spartans in particular – living by a code of equality. That is, no one really had seniority; these men would die for each other. The whole mattered more than the individual.

Something like being polis, he thinks.

The idea of the police is larger than the individual policeman. One person steps out of line, it affects everyone else.

The thin blue line.

But someone has to step over it when the majority make the wrong choice.

Someone has to take the plunge.

And if more than one person does it, it means something.

He's stepped over.

Burnet's stepped over.

But is that enough?

56

"WHAT DID YOU DO?"

Burnet's mother is crying at the kitchen table – head in her hands, forcing words between sobs.

Her father leans against the cooker, arms folded across his chest. His face is thunder; reminds Burnet of when she was a child, still testing what she could get away with.

The room is cold. Not just metaphorically. Wind gusts through the broken window. The shattered glass has been cleared up, but the brick is on the kitchen table. Waiting for her, along with her parents, when she arrived home.

Another note, of course.

This one from a poet:

"RATS GO SPLAT."

Hardly sophisticated. But clear.

One thing for it to happen in the station. Now it's followed her home.

"I'm sorry," Burnet says. Almost meaning it, too.

"Your mother was here," her father says. "Right here in the kitchen when that fucking thing came through the window. It could have hit her."

"I was trying to do the right thing," Burnet says. She thinks about all the lessons she learned in school about being a good person, a good citizen. All the times she listened to those stories in church about Jesus standing up and doing the right thing.

She'd believed.

She really had.

"You're acting like a spoiled madam," her dad says. "Because things haven't gone your way."

Burnet closes her eyes. He doesn't understand. Doesn't *want* to understand.

"You should have left it alone," her mother says. "We all know the polis are out for themselves. But getting wee girls like you mixed up in all that ... I thought you were just supposed to be making the tea."

"You always told me I could be what I wanted to be."

"Within reason," her dad says. "Jesus, this polis thing was supposed to be just a phase. A whim."

Her mum runs a hand through her hair, like she wants to tug it out by the roots. It's a gesture that Burnet associates with childhood and those times she would drive her mum to breaking point. "I thought maybe you'd meet someone nice there ... settle down."

"Isn't that why any young woman goes out to work?" her dad says. "To keep herself until she doesn't have to?"

Her mum looks right at her. A hard expression that Burnet's never seen before. "Unless there's something wrong with her."

"You were always a troublemaker," her dad says. "Even at school."

"Just another phase," Burnet says. Her head is hot. She's got a sharp pain behind her right eye. "That's all it was, right?

Your headstrong, tomboy daughter, just going through little phases until she grows up and becomes a woman. Settles down and knows her place."

Her mum looks at the brick on the table. The note spread out beside it. "Better that than this," she says. "You need to take it back. Say you made a mistake."

"You need to leave that job," her dad says.

"No."

He steps forward.

She's never seen him like this. This isn't the warning anger she remembers from childhood. It makes her think of the way that men have approached her on domestic calls, or the look in the eyes of that flasher when he realised she wasn't just some passing girl, but an undercover officer.

This isn't her dad.

Or is she just seeing him for the first time?

"What did you say, young lady?"

"I said, 'no'."

"You realise that you live here because we let you?"

"You're going to throw me out?" She manages to cut off her laughter just in time.

"If it means we don't have any more rocks through the window, then yes."

"Jesus Christ, Dad," she says. "Jesus fucking Christ."

That puts him on the back foot.

"I was doing the right thing," she says. "And I'll keep doing the right thing. Because you know the same as me, that even if the polis are corrupt, and even if that's how it's always been, that isn't how it *should* be. There are standards. And we need to stand up for them."

"But you don't need to," her mum says. "Let the men sort out—"

"This is 1978," Burnet says. "Nearly the 1980s. We've got a woman in charge of the Conservative Party—"

"Maggie's no ordinary woman," her dad says. "She's got steel in her spine."

"She's an exception, then? And I'm not?"

"Is this what they taught you at school?" he says. "In my day, girls just—"

"Listen to your father," her mum says, stepping in as peacemaker. "Please, listen to him."

"You have a choice," her dad says. "You can give up this foolishness and we'll support you. Or you can get out this house right now." He stands straight, now. Confident. Holding all the cards.

Where would she go? In his mind, she doesn't have a choice.

But she can't let him win.

She can't let *them* win.

* * *

He meets her on the street, just outside the Club Bar, near the railway station footbridge.

The pub's getting rowdy already, so she's glad when she sees him.

He looks tired. His skin is sallow, and he has a few days of stubble. Red in his eyes. Like he hasn't been sleeping.

Maybe he hasn't.

"I'm sorry," she says. "I just didn't know where—"

Kelley shakes his head. "There's not much space," he says, apologetically

They keep quiet on the stairs until they get inside his room. He's already hinted at what his landlady might think, knowing he had a girl up here who wasn't a family member.

But who else could she call?

Her old friends – the ones she knew before she joined up – have scattered, and she knows if she called them there's a chance they'd already have heard from her parents, wouldn't want to risk the hassle of her staying with them. And forget asking any of the other WPCs for help. Anyone in uniform's got it out for her – she's betrayed the cause.

So that leaves:

Kelley.

She can trust him. She's sure of that. He's not someone who'd misread or misunderstand. She has to believe that; it's just a feeling she gets around him. He has his faults, but she's sure he's a gentleman at heart.

When they get in, Burnet looks around. The room is small, cramped. There's a stove, a Murphy bed, a sofa. A TV in one corner.

"Like I said, it's not much."

"It doesn't need to be. Thank you."

"You can take the bed," he says. "The sofa's mine."

"You don't have to—"

"Please," he says. Then, "Tea?"

The question feels mundane and comforting. It breaks some of that tension, and she allows herself to laugh quickly, before saying, "Yes."

He puts the kettle on, gestures for her to sit.

She does so. Feels springs beneath the cushions.

"You don't have many guests."

"Not girls, anyway."

"Not anyone."

"Any reason?"

He finishes making the tea, brings her a cup, then sits on the edge of the bed. "I'm not a people person."

"No," she says. "You're not."

There's more silence. Then he says, "I'm sorry. About what's happening."

"I knew there'd be a price."

"All the same ..."

"Garner and his type, they need to know. Change is coming for them. School bully syndrome, right? They keep at it because they know that everyone's scared of them. But the second someone stands up to them ..." She shrugs. "Jesus, I always thought life would be different out of school."

"It's all the same. People get set in who they are, they don't really change. Not in the important ways."

"You really think that?"

"I do," Kelley says. "People can adjust their behaviour, maybe, try and present a face to the world, but underneath that, where it counts, they don't change. They can't."

They sit for a while, drinking their tea in silence.

"You were good," he says. "In court. I don't think I told you."

"Thank you."

They sit for a while longer, sipping at their tea.

Burnet looks round the room. Sees the bottles – ranging from half empty to empty – thinks to herself that drinking tea isn't what he'd usually be doing of an evening. She wants to ask if she can have a belt, but thinks better of it.

Those red-rimmed eyes. That slightly haunted look. A night off from the booze might do him good.

A clear head is what's needed. The trial's coming to a close. And they both know that there's worse to come.

57

FRANK SITS DOWN ON ONE OF THE HEADSTONES. Fights the urge to fold his arms against the cold.

He's at the curve of the hill in the Necropolis, looking down towards the Tay. The city falls away, and the water glitters as it breaks up the light of the moon.

This place could be peaceful if you didn't know what was lurking in the shadows.

The jakies weren't dumb, of course. They all knew that taking on a man like Frank would be more trouble than it was worth. All the same, he needed to make sure they remembered that. Hence why he couldn't show fear, discomfort, or anything close.

He's here to meet someone.

The figure comes from his left, wrapped up in a heavy coat and scarf. "Jesus. What the fuck is so important?"

"You know."

"You know that it's going to be okay," Garner says. "The big man has nothing to worry about."

"Open your fucking coat," Frank says.

"Oh come the fuck—"

"Do it."

Grudgingly, Garner holds open the coat. Long tails flap in the breeze.

Franks pats him down. The way he was taught earlier.

"Man in your position," Frank says, "might do something foolish to save his own skin."

"Heard a story," Garner says, "about a stoolie in the States who tried to record meetings with some drug dealers. They wired him up with those of those battery-driven recorders. You know what happened?"

"What?"

"He was sweating so hard, the fucking batteries got wet and leaked acid on him."

"That true? Sounds like something they'd put in a fucking film."

"Swear to God, it's true. No fucking way you'd get me wearing something like that."

"So you say."

Garrner raises his hands and turns away. Goes to the lip of the hill, looks at the water. Talking to himself, like he's forgotten Frank's even here. "Jesus fuck, you know I love this city? Born here, lived all my life here. Good and bad. Became polis because it seemed a good prospect. And what's a man to do when he comes out of service? You get institutionalised, you want to stay that way."

Frank thinks the same's true of some men and prisons.

"Why not remain with the army?"

"Had my reasons."

There were rumours. Things Frank had heard.

Dishonourable discharge.

Ask three different people what he did, you'd get three different answers. But whatever it was, it had been enough for him to leave.

Fuck it. They're not here to share secrets, talk about their feelings. The fuckstick might be feeling hard done by, but that's his own fault, and now he's got to own up to that and sort out his mess.

Garner keeps looking out at the water. "I'm not talking to anyone. If I have to fall, I fucking will. Tell the cunt he's safe with me."

Frank says, "And the other problem?"

"You mean the fucking turncoat?"

"Aye."

"He won't be a problem."

"How can you be sure?"

"I'm taking care of it, all right?"

Frank doesn't say anything. He just nods. Garner's aware of what will happen if he fucks up.

"But the big man's keeping his side of the deal?"

"The jury will do what they're told."

"That's all we need."

"But if that cunt's testimony makes the papers, there will be questions."

"I fucking *know*, all right? I fucking *know*."

"You said we could trust everyone you brought in."

"I don't know what happened. I ... It's standards, isn't it? The world's got no standards anymore."

Says the police detective who runs protection for a local gangster. Garner can dress it up all he likes, but that's the hard truth.

Frank wouldn't piss in Garner's ears if his brain was on fire. Man doesn't know it, he's the lowest of the fucking low.

Garner turns to look at Frank. Suddenly, he's looking old. Despite his large frame, he seems small as though the events of the last few days have made him shrink in on himself. "I've always been loyal. To the man. And his crew. For the sake of my fucking city."

Frank tries to look relaxed.

Garner keeps talking: "Turning a blind eye, you know, when I can? That's what I do. What I've always done. Arrest reports lost, witnesses changing statements ... evidence conveniently overlooked." He's trying to convince someone. But Frank can't be certain of what.

Frank's lungs freeze with each breath he takes. Not just the night air. Something more elemental.

Garner runs a hand down the back of his neck, like he's trying to calm himself. "I had a call out near the woods the other week," he says. "Someone found what they thought was a body."

"Not this again," Frank says. Images rise in his mind: his son's room. Finding that girl's bloodied top. "Didn't that detective – the one who's got you on the fucking ropes, I might add – get slapped back down over that? The papers said she thought it was a fucking werewolf, right?"

"Aye, but it was less about that than ... Well, her investigation was creating trouble internally. So maybe we should have this new shite coming, right? And this is fucking Dundee, right? All the deaths here, they're from fucking fights and stupidity. No one wants to admit there's a fucking psychopath on the loose? One who thinks he's fucking Dracula or whatever."

Frank knows he needs to get this over with.

"So why are you mentioning this girl? The fuck does it have to do with anything?"

"She was rotting," Garner says. "A couple of weeks old. Mutilated, of course."

"So you're saying that the detective ... she was right? There is a fuckin' werewolf killer or whatever the fuck she said it was?"

More flashes in his head: Martin with blood in his mouth, those fucking dentures. Martin in the back of a police car. Behind bars. No way they'd let him in a normal prison. He'd be hospitalised. Drugged.

Frank's son: a fucking loony.

Fucking stop it.

Stop thinking like that.

He can't let Garner see his fear.

Garner doesn't know anything.

So why is he mentioning this?

Garner lets loose what could be a cough. Takes Frank a moment to realise it's a laugh. Forced and hard. "Jesus, you tell me. Because this girl ... I found her purse which had enough to identify her. Tessie Talbot. An alleged fucking runaway. A case I was working with that bitch, Burnet."

"What's that have to do—"

"See, I'd already been covering up a few pieces of key fucking evidence from the nosy cow. Mostly that the last person Tessie Talbot was seen with, according to some of her girlfriends, was some lad she'd known at school. Creepy prick. The mother actually called him soft, you know? Too soft for her daughter. Lived out with his parents near the Templeton Woods. Now, him being soft didn't make him an obvious suspect, but I still got the name ... Martin ... Martin something ..."

Frank's stomach lurches.

He swallows back hard, gets a burning at the back of his throat and nose.

"It's fucking dark out here, but even I saw that." Smiling, now. Back in control. "When I heard the name, I thought I'd keep quiet because you work for the big man, and like I say, I keep him and his crew safe. Fucking loyal, you see. What I thought was, maybe your wee lad was seeing this bird, maybe they had some kind of arrangement, and what business was it of mine?"

Frank's shaking. Not the cold. Muscles are cramping. Slick sweat creeps cool on his forehead.

"And then she turns up dead," Garner says. "In those woods. Stomach opened, all that good stuff. Doesn't take much to put two and two together. I mean, fucking Dow did it already, didn't he? Wanted to go after you and your kid, and the brass said to go fuck himself because of your history. Good for you, good for him. And maybe there wasn't any proof, anyway, or not enough to justify hauling the wee shite out in irons. And then Dow winds up dead, victim of the same fucking killer? Fucking mental, right? Good job I'm the one they passed the case on to, isn't it? Because they wanted it to go away, and so I put the kibosh on all the rumour and speculation, and I fucking prayed the sick wee prick had had enough of killing. Which it sure looked like. Until this girl showed up."

Frank gets flashbacks.

Back in the room with the junkie and Martin. The look in his son's eyes. Frank telling himself that Martin had been acting – showing off for his old man, treating it like a fucking game. Easy to do when you don't see the other person as human, maybe. Frank had done it enough times himself.

But, no, the look in Martin's eyes had been something alien. Something terrifying.

Something Frank had done his best to deny, dismiss, fucking forget.

"I know why I'm here," Garner says. "And I wanted to remind you how useful it is to have someone on the inside. Someone whose loyalty has been proven over and over and the fuck again."

Frank takes his hands from his pockets.

Leaves the blade in there.

Garner nods. "You can guess that the moment anything happens to me, all of this gets leaked," he says. "The person who found the body, they've forgotten it ever happened. If little Tessie is found, it's a tragic accident, I'm afraid, that she took a tumble near the Henderston Quarry." He takes a moment as though thinking about something. "You've no idea how long it took to clean the bastarding car after moving her. The only good thing is that polis vehicles always smell of something, so as long as you scrub hard enough, no one's going to think anything's too much amiss. Blood, shite, puke, everything ends up back there, you know?"

Frank's stuck now. Feeling rooted like the gravestones. His feet are heavy, and his legs won't move. His breathing is slow and soft. This isn't panic. It's somewhere beyond that. A kind of mortified quiet that makes him think of how it must feel to be dead.

"So, here it is: if I'm around, Tessie's death is a tragic accident. If anything happens to me …" He lets that one hang, his intentions clear.

"What do you want?"

"Nothing has to change. Go back to the big man, tell him you trust me to sort this."

"And?"

"And then, later, when this is done, you and me will have a wee chat. You know, about how we conduct this relationship in the future."

* * *

Fuck.

Fucking fuck fuck FUCK!

Frank batters the steering wheel hard as he drives. He screams and roars, his voice echoing inside the car.

Inside his own fucking head.

What the fuck is he doing?

Pull over on Blackness Road, near the school. Sit in the car for a few moments. Deep breaths.

He should have fucking done what he was sent to do.

Should have knifed the cunt, left him to bleed out.

But what if the story Garner told is true? What if he tells the world, Frank Gray's son is a lunatic.

Howls at the moon.

Literally.

Frank calms down.

Think this through.

No use crying over what he should have done. It's what he does now that matters.

Keep a lid on everything.

Work out a plan.

Old hothead Frank would have sorted things out with his fists.

But he's older now. More mature. Right?

Or more afraid?

There has to be a better way. A cleverer way.

Aye? And once you deal with Garner, what do you do about Martin? What do you really do? Because you can't keep ignoring—

He pushes that voice to the back of his head.

One thing at a time.

He starts the engine again, drives to the pub, where Joe Kennedy is waiting for him.

Kennedy's taken over the manager's office. His name is nowhere on the licence, but everyone knows who owns in the place.

How it works in Dundee: there's the official, public-facing city, and then there's something like a shadow city where the real world happens. Where people pay fealty to men like Joe Kennedy.

Someone else just leaving the room as Frank arrives.

Frank recognises the beard, the face. Councillor Davie Darling himself. Champion of the people. In Kennedy's pocket like everyone else.

The old days were heady, but since Frank left, Kennedy's developed real influence through the city. He heard someone say once that a man like Kennedy sits at the centre of the city like a spider in a web. Waits for his prey to come to him.

And it's true.

Real power is not having to move.

Real power is knowing that other people will do the moving for you. And you don't even have to ask.

"Frank," Kennedy says, with a grin. "Come in and have a drink. I trust you dealt with our little problem."

"Aye and no," Frank says.

The grin vanishes. "And what the fuck is that supposed to mean? Come on, Frank, you're my number one guy, right?"

"You told me to use my initiative. And here's the thing – I think that Garner can still be useful."

"You really think he won't sing if the screws get tightened?"

"He's made of stern stuff."

"Every man has his limits. Garner's the kind of man who talks a big game, but I don't know if he can be trusted to—"

"Do you trust me?" Frank's voice starts to break. He can't be sure that Kennedy notices. He hopes the big man's not playing close attention.

"Aye," Kennedy says. "We go back, right enough."

"Then trust me when I tell you, Garner's going to come through this. And if he goes down, he's going alone."

Kennedy comes round the desk and places his hands heavy on Frank's shoulders. "We're old friends," he says, "but you know what happens if you get this wrong."

"I know."

"You came back for your family."

"I did."

"Then don't do anything to put them in danger."

"I won't."

Kennedy nods. Goes back round the desk. Opens a drawer. Holds up a bottle. "Then join me," he says. "Because I'm sure you saw the cunt who just walked out this little back room."

"That I did." Frank tries not to sound relieved that the crushing pain in his chest has abated.

"Him and me, we have an arrangement. One that'll pay off soon. For me, for the fucking city." He shakes his head. "The modern world, everyone thinks power goes top down, but the smart fucks, we know that it runs bottom up."

Frank keeps quiet. Joe Kennedy's always been like this, bursting to spill his secrets, but unwilling to really trust anyone, even those he calls friend.

"It's the pyramid principle," Kennedy says, pouring out two glasses. He passes one to Frank. "If you turn a pyramid on its point, it'll just collapse. It's the bottom where all the power is, all the strength that holds it up. The tip, the point, is just there to focus the eye."

Frank knocks back his drink. He doesn't really understand. He doesn't really care.

All he knows is that his heart is slowing again.

And that he wishes he'd never come back to this world.

* * *

Frank heads to another pub after he's done with Kennedy.

Where no one cares who he is.

Where the light is low, and the staff are deaf and dumb.

Whisky after whisky. Knocking them back hard and fast.

When the tab comes up, he pulls the guy over the bar and tells him that he's going to be lucky to end the night without a broken neck.

Outside, the blast of cold air near knocks him off his feet. He grabs at the doorframe to steady himself.

He walks it. Long way home, but he needs to. Taxis pass, and some slow down, maybe hoping for a fare. He waves them on, stumbling every time he stops focusing on the next step.

He walks through Lochee. Near enough to kicking-out time. People look to confront him, then recognise his face and back off.

He doesn't have to do anything.

Reputation enough.

He's the Beast of Balgay again.

But is he?

He's an imposter. A joke. Wearing the mask, but underneath he's a shadow of what he was. The conviction is no longer there.

Garner noticed it, back in the graveyard.

What happens when someone else realises?

A drunk staggers across his path, pissed up and uncertain. He places a hand on Frank's shoulder, as though to steady himself. He gets in close. "I know you, pal?"

"Naw." Frank pushes the guy away.

"I fucking do," the drunk says, coming back again for another close look. "Like, we went to school, right? You were at Craigie, right? Aye, I'm sure that's where—"

Frank blinks, and then he's straddling the fucker, hands around his throat, bashing the back of his skull against the pavement. Blood. The wet sound of skull cracking stone.

The guy's eyes are rolled back in his skull.

Frank lets go, gets to his feet.

The drunk isn't moving. Is he dead?

Frank can't be sure.

He should be ashamed of what he's done.

But he isn't.

Maybe the old Frank is still inside him, after all.

Or maybe it's something else. No, no room for doubt. He pushes memories of his son's face from his mind. Doesn't want to think about that. Not now. That's why he went out drinking, to forget. To find some kind of fucking peace.

People are looking at him.

"That's what you get." Talking to everyone. Making a show of it. The old Frank is back in town, fuckers! "That's what you get when you fuck with me."

No one's moving.

Frank continues to walk home.

The blood on his hands starts to dry.

58

BURNET WAKES UP. FOR A MOMENT, she can't remember where she is.

The room is barely decorated. The bed is cheap. Second-hand mattress. She can still feel the indent of the previous occupier.

Somehow, it's even worse than the Murphy at Kelley's.

At least it's clean.

The curtains are thin, cheap material. They let the light in.

Weeks of rent, but it's not where she intends to stay. It's a stopgap. A temporary solution to a problem she worries could be permanent.

She showers. The water's cold – close to freezing – but she doesn't mind.

She dresses carefully.

Today's the day. At long last.

Halliday's due to testify against his fellow officers. He's been kept in protective custody for the duration of the trial. His safety has been considered paramount. The Chief Constable has vouched for the men he has in charge of Halliday.

She trusts the Chief. His heart's in the right place.

He believes in the force.

That it needs to change.

The corruption is further down the chain. Just high enough to be effective, and just low enough to be invisible.

Until you shine a light on it.

She arrives at the courthouse by taxi. Back entrance. The press have already gathered round the front, awaiting the accused's arrival, creating as much drama as they report.

She's sent to a small room, and told to wait until they need her.

She smooths her skirt periodically, gets up and paces.

Wishes she smoked. Something to do

A book in her bag: *The Boys from Brazil* by Ira Levin. People keep talking to her about it.

She wants to read, but something stops her.

She should read.

Distract herself.

She just can't.

The trial's entering its last few days. She doesn't feel confident.

Was this a mistake?

She's been here before, sequestered and waiting to be called. Acting as a professional witness isn't something that police officers worry about for long. After the first few, a kind of routine sets in. Most hearings follow the same pattern. There's a relentless and relaxing kind of monotony.

But this is different.

This isn't a case against a housebreaker, thug or dealer. Not in the usual sense.

The defendants are fellow officers.

Burnet's a key witness. Since her turn on the stand, she's been dreaming she's back there every night.

Sod it.

There's a jug of water on a table. She fills and refills her glass, drinking not because she's thirsty, but because it keeps her moving.

She tries to read, to lose herself in the book. But she skips words, keeps looking up over the pages to watch the door.

Waiting.

Waiting.

She hates waiting.

* * *

When the door opens, the last person she expects to see is Kelley. Antsy, like he wants to break something.

"The sheriff cleared the court after their defence said he wanted to have a word in private."

This isn't good.

"Kennedy?" she says.

Kelley makes this face; his lips pressing tight, his eyes closing for a moment as though to give him the chance to think. "You mean looking after his wee pet detective? I don't know. If he gave a toss, do you think he'd have let it get to this stage?"

"What about Halliday?" The man's due to testify this afternoon.

Kelley pauses again. Pale. Uncertain. "He's the reason they had to clear the court."

* * *

Burnet wonders: did they push Halliday too far?

Kelley tells her what he knows. She fills in the gaps as best she can later on, checking official records, asking those who attended the scene. She even goes to visit Halliday's wife, but all she gets is a door slammed in her face. "I know exactly who you are."

She'd talked to Halliday only a day earlier. He'd told her that what he really wanted was to go for a pint. Not to have one brought in to him, but to sit in a pub somewhere and nurse a glass surrounded by other people. He told her that he knew he wouldn't be able to do it for several years, but when he got out, it would be the first thing he'd do.

He hadn't seemed sad or depressed. Not even angry.

No, he'd seemed ... *calm*.

Accepting, even.

She'd told him it might not be as long as he was thinking if he stuck to what he'd told her and the Fiscal during their meetings.

He'd smiled, said maybe she'd like to go with him when he got out.

She'd taken it for a joke and said nothing.

Twenty-four hours later, he was dead.

He hadn't been a suicide risk. So why – the moment someone's back was turned – did he decide to hang himself by his shoelaces?

The official verdict: an oversight, given that he had never been officially put through the system due to efforts to keep his identity secret. All it took was a moment of weakness on his part.

Burnet doesn't believe it.

How can she?

The man wasn't for killing himself. Maybe he'd been ashamed of what he'd done – the more she pressed him during their talks, the more he seemed to realise that what he thought of as misdemeanours were far more serious. But that didn't mean he'd take his own life.

No, his punishment was always going to be on earth.

And his redemption would come through telling the truth.

She and Kelley don't discuss it, but they both know that what happened to Halliday was likely not to have been suicide.

The Chief Constable trusted the men he put on to guard Halliday, but Burnet wasn't sure he understood how leaky his ship was.

Garner.

The man still worshipped like a hero by other officers. The same ones who sent her notes, who jostled her in the corridors, who walked out when she entered a room.

Garner.

He made men like Halliday do things in the name of the thin blue line. Beat suspects. Beat innocent people if they didn't have suspects. Skim from evidence and take money for protection.

Now she has to wonder . . .

Could he make them kill?

* * *

The Fiscal debriefs her later that afternoon, with a barely contained anger.

Blaming her for what's happened.

When she leaves his office, it's all she can do not to just lie down and die already.

She walks out of the courthouse, bruised by the events of the day. She's alone. No one else there.

Kelley is ...

She doesn't know where.

Pub, maybe. Drowning his sorrows as fast as possible.

He can go back to work at least.

Burnet can't say what the future holds for her.

She leaves the courthouse by the rear entrance. Raining outside, the wind heavy. The skies are dark.

Someone's waiting for her. Hood up against the wind and rain. Large shoulders. She has to squint to make them out.

Garner.

He comes towards her.

"What do you want?" Almost shouting above the rain.

"To see you were okay."

"To gloat."

"Not that your star witness would have made a difference – the man was a whoring, lying, drinking shitebag. But I'm sorry to see him go like that. Hanging's fucking nasty. It can take a long time, you know. Have you ever been underwater a little too long? That sensation of your chest trying to burst open, of not being able to fill your lungs? Jesus, I can only imagine how it feels. How desperate you'd have to be to do something like that to yourself." He pauses to wipe rain from his face. "I was there, at the last hanging in this country, back in '63. I went all the way up to Aberdeen just to watch the scumbag go."

"I suppose you'll be back on duty soon enough," she says. Keeping her distance. The only way to escape is past him.

"I don't have an issue," he says, "working with you. You were doing your job, right? Just let your emotions get in the way a wee bit."

"What?"

"What I'm saying is, all is forgiven." He looks ready to laugh. "I mean it. I hope they keep you on. Does morale good, doesn't it, having a wee piece like yourself around the place?"

She says nothing.

He gives her a little wave with his right hand. "I'll let you get on," he says. "Be seeing you soon, doll."

When he walks away, she leans back against the wall.

The brick is soaked through. She slumps to the ground. Her clothes are soaked through. The rain batters heavier. It's all she can do not to be sick.

59

FRANK SITS ON THE END OF HIS SON'S BED. He looks around the room. Thinking about the name of the girl that Garner found.

Tessie.

Tessie Talbot.

He doesn't know her name. Martin's never mentioned her, and yet ...

Frank can no longer escape the truth.

He knew. He knew even before her body was found.

He knew when he found the top.

He knew when he saw Martin with the wolves.

He knew.

He fucking *knew*.

He looks around the room. The posters. The music tapes. The books.

His son shouldn't be any different from anyone else.

Don't kid yourself, pal.

That look in his eyes. You've seen it before.

When he did his bit inside, Frank shared a cell with a psychopath called McKinley. Guy was a stone-cold animal.

Lived to hurt other people. Liked to hurt them in ways that seemed unnecessarily cruel. Most people stayed away from him.

The only reason McKinley left Frank alone was because of his reputation. He'd been excited to share a cell with Frank. Wanted to talk about the things he'd done.

McKinley had been caught after killing a man who walked in front of his car. He told Frank he had twenty other kills to his credit, but it was this one that got him. Because it had been spur of the moment; he'd lost control.

Frank thinks about his son.

This girl, left out in the open for anyone to find.

That had been careless.

No impulse control.

Like McKinley.

McKinley who'd been lucky until he killed the guy who walked in front of his car.

Had Martin been lucky so far?

You don't know that—

He does know.

And Garner knows.

Frank needs to protect his son. Doesn't matter what he's done. That's what fathers do: protect their children.

Unconditional fucking love.

His own mother once told him, *I have to love you, but I don't have to like you.*

Frank understands that, now.

He feels sorry for the girl.

But if he gives up on his son, then Frank will have been a failure as a man. As a father.

Fuckit.

Frank makes a decision.

Pulls out the drawers in the dresser. Finds the dentures shaped like wolves' teeth and throws them out into the hall.

He searches for anything that could connect his son to the werewolf killings.

The room is a maelstrom of chaos.

Frank doesn't bother to put anything back or hide what he's done. None of that matters. All that matters is finding the evidence, disposing of it.

* * *

Later, he stands on a patch of wasteland and watches the fire burn. He's done what he can.

Frank knows he should talk to someone. But what can he say? He can't say out loud that he suspects his son is a murderer.

He watches smoke rise and flames dance.

Tastes charcoal at the back of his throat.

It's still not enough. If he wants to protect his family, Frank knows what he needs to do.

The old Frank would fight back against a man like Garner.

Say, *go on, release what you have*, and then beat the cunt to a pulp.

The old Frank would have been reckless. The old Frank would have got the job done because he was willing to do things that no one else would.

But the old Frank is gone.

The new Frank has just been pretending.

Time to admit it: he's an old man. The world has passed him by.

He went to sleep seventeen years ago, and when he woke up again, he was no longer ready to face the world.

He should never have come back.

He knows that now.

And that he has to pay the price for thinking that he ever could.

* * *

Frank doesn't want to be here.

This is a bad idea.

Garner's manipulating him.

Children are weakness.

Love is weakness.

He has to do this. Or his son will be exposed.

And Frank will be forced to confront the truth.

Some things can't be burned.

And Frank, in spite of everything, isn't a killer. There are lines.

He's standing across the street when he sees her get off a bus.

Seeing her again, and knowing what he now knows, he isn't sure he can go through with this.

Just off Blackness Road. Not the smartest area of the city. Her tenement building doesn't have locks on the front door, and she's a woman living on her own. She's having a tough time making ends meet. She's not married, either. No sign of a man.

He's never had to hurt a woman before.

There's a code.

All the things he's done – his violence has always been against men.

Never punch a girl. That's the one, true sin. The first lesson he learned. And he's stuck to it throughout all the years.

He knew men who became wife beaters, who thought that the rules didn't apply in marriage. But Frank's never raised a hand to Jeannie.

There are degrees of violence and degrees of sin.

So what is he doing?

Why is he here?

Because that cunt Garner told him to put the frighteners on this girl. If Frank can do this, it's good for everyone in a way. It takes the pressure off Garner, which takes it off Kennedy, which relieves Frank of all his problems. At least for now.

Put the frighteners on her.

That's all.

He doesn't have to hurt her.

Except he knows that's what Garner meant.

Frank closes his eyes.

He knows what he should do. The *right thing*.

His son is a fucking monster. His son should be behind bars. Like that psycho, McKinley.

And yet Frank has to protect the lad. Call it paternal instinct. Call it fucking stupidity.

But he can't fail his son.

He's not a fucking failure. He's not his own father.

He will do anything for his flesh and blood.

Anything.

Frank takes a breath. Crosses the street.

60

A KNOCK AT THE DOOR.

Burnet gets chills at the back of her neck. Grabs the knife from the kitchen drawer, holds it behind her back, goes to the spyhole.

Thinking about the notes.

The threats.

Her fellow officers as dangerous as any psycho on the street.

Don't let it get to you.

But how could you not?

The person on the other side is just out of sight of the spyhole. "Got a delivery."

"From who?"

"I've only got your name here, doesn't say where it came from."

"You can leave it there."

"I need it to be signed for."

She knows the voice. She's spoken to this man before.

"I don't have all day." Impatient, forcing her to make a decision.

She's being paranoid. But she can't help herself.

Murder was not among the charges levelled in court at Garner and his crew.

But she can't be sure.

And she can't live in fear.

Make a choice.

Live your life. Or live in fear.

She opens the door.

The bastard's in, fast. He's got power. But she's ready. Steps back and away before he can touch her.

He slams the door behind him.

Big man. Older. Moves like a bruiser.

She knows the voice.

He comes forward.

She ducks, slices with the knife.

He springs back. A little too late. Grabs at his right forearm. Growls.

In her corridor, holding his arm, staring at her from behind the balaclava.

Only his eyes are visible. They look sad. Something about them is—

"Frank Gray," she says. "I interviewed you about the werewolf killer. Thought you said you were retired."

A flinch in those eyes. A moment of doubt. She doesn't know for sure if it's because she recognises him, or because she mentions the case.

"You know why I'm here?"

"I thought you'd gone straight."

"Don't believe everything you hear."

She knows why he's here. Who sent him.

"You worked for Kennedy," she says. "Is Garner really so important to him?"

"Does it matter?" Frank says.

"Maybe," she says. "Why send you here? To tell me to back off? To punish me for even trying to put that corrupt shitebag where he belongs. I can't believe Kennedy has any respect for Garner. A crooked polis would be lower on the rung than a bag of shite in the eyes of a man like him."

"But I'm here."

On whose orders? she wonders.

"So what happens now?"

He lets go of his arm. Blood drips.

"You were expecting someone, then?"

"I'm not an idiot."

"So why open the door?"

"Because I'm also not afraid."

"Maybe you should be."

"I'm the one with the knife."

He nods, thinking that one over. "The thing is, people with knives think they have an advantage. And sometimes they get lucky. But you're not used to wielding a blade. And I'm used to disarming people who think they are."

"I know that."

"And still ..."

"And still."

There's silence for a moment. "Why did you keep going? Why keep pushing? You knew who Garner was, what he did. Who he knew. And you're just a woman ..."

"Maybe that has something to do with it."

"You're a pretty lass," he says. "And being polis is ugly work."

"People keep saying that."

"Maybe there's a reason."

"I stood up to the school bully," she says. "Because no one else would."

Blood now soaks his jacket from where she sliced him.

"It took a woman," she says, "to do what any number of men couldn't or wouldn't."

"When you came round about the old woman," Frank says, "I remember you didn't seem upset talking about what happened to her."

"I was upset. Who wouldn't be? But I also had a job to do."

"Did you ever find the person responsible?"

"You read the papers, don't you?"

"They took it away from you."

"Not because I couldn't find them."

"No?"

"But because of you. Because of your boss, and because of his influence over men like Garner."

He licks at his lips. His skin has gone pale. Talking about the werewolf case, she realises that his reaction earlier was more about that than her knowing who he was.

She still thinks that he knows something.

But this isn't the time to push.

"They gave that case to Garner," she says. "And he buried it."

"Maybe there was a good reason. One you don't see."

She shakes her head. "I don't know what they told you, but even a thug like you has to know that this was an old woman who was murdered. Mutilated. An old woman who never did anyone any real harm. Who loved her cat. Loved her cat so much I couldn't help wondering for a while if that was what got her killed."

She lowers the knife, but keeps it in plain view. "I don't think you're a bad man. When we interviewed you, I believed what you said about being a family man, leaving this world behind you. So I don't know what's happened, but I know that you wouldn't want to wish harm on an old woman. And I know that you wouldn't want to protect someone who would do what that bastard did to her."

He seems to deflate.

She thinks: *he knows.*

He knows who did it.

But why protect them?

The son.

Dow had known it. Dow had suspected. But he had no proof. And somewhere along the line, the son's name had simply vanished, swallowed up by bigger concerns.

"Just leave it," Frank says, suddenly without conviction. "I'm asking you nicely because . . . because I'm a gentleman."

"And you don't hit girls?"

"Something like that."

"Come on," Burnet says. "Are you really here doing Garner's bidding? Does Joe Kennedy even know you're here?"

Two and two make four. She knows why. But she doesn't want to say. Right now, Frank's not a stable man. It's clear that he knows the truth about his son and doesn't want to accept it. Say the wrong thing, and this situation could go sideways in a moment.

Frank backs up and away. "Just leave it alone," he says. "Maybe find another line of work."

He opens the door and leaves. When he's gone, Burnet calmly goes to the door, pulls the chain across.

She collapses on the floor.

No tears.

But her body shakes.

OCTOBER 1978-DECEMBER 1978

61

BURNET WALKS OUT OF THE ROOM, and slams a fist against the wall so hard she worries for a moment she might break something. "They're monsters."

"Come on," Sergeant Wickes says. "It wasn't that bad. They're only children."

"Fucksakes!"

"Is that really the kind of language you should use in a school?" Wickes asks.

When she looks at him, he holds up his hands in surrender.

"Hey," he says, "I was just trying to ... Never mind."

This is what it's come to: forced back into uniform, out with old timers like Wickes – he should be in a retirement home, never mind simply retired – and talking to kids who didn't want to hear about how they should look both ways before crossing the road.

Four weeks, now.

Meaningless nonsense.

Constable in name only.

"Thought they would send out that Green Cross Code Man to do these things," she says. "Aren't actors always dying for work?"

"You know he's that Darth Vader," Wickes says. "From that Star Wars film."

"You're kidding?"

"No."

"Thought he was from Manchester?"

"Someone else did the voice."

"How do you know so much about it?"

"Have grandkids, don't I? Know how many times the old fella had to take them out to see Darth Vader and Luke Skincrawler duke it out this year?"

"I think it's Skywalker."

"Aye, whatever. The point is, I know these things. You have kids – or grandkids – you soak up some of that shite just so you can have a conversation with them. Thank fuck these things are fleeting. A couple of years, it'll be something else, and they'll have forgotten all about it."

The headmistress comes out into the hall. "Thank you," she says. "I know they're not the easiest bunch to deal with." She looks at Burnet. "You were very good with them, I thought. Do you have children of your own?"

Burnet's blood boils. She takes in a sharp breath.

The anger's like a lightning flash just behind her eyes.

Wickes sees it, and steps in between the two women, takes all the headmistress's attention. "They were just braw," he says. "Remind me of my own kids at that age, actually . . ."

Burnet takes a breath. Tries to keep a poker face. She's pretty sure that she fails.

* * *

Back at FHQ, Burnet tells Wickes she needs to file cold cases down in the basement. More of her new and "vital" duties, as assigned by Redman.

Wickes doesn't go down with her. Says the damp in the basement affects his bones. No one's ever questioned him on this.

Downstairs, the on-duty constable is picking his nose. There's a book on the desk – *The Stand*, by Stephen King – but the spine is intact. He's more interested in the contents of his nostrils, it seems. Maybe the sheer size of the book intimidates him.

"Back again?"

"Never ends," she says. "Sometimes I think they're just giving me busy work."

He nods. He knows she's nothing more than a glorified file clerk for CID; proofreading badly typed reports from the other detectives.

Sometimes they put in remarks that she has to delete.

No use complaining.

But it gives her some freedoms. Like saying she's down here to look into cold cases to help other detectives.

What she's really doing is looking for something specific.

She nods at the book on the desk. "What do you think?"

"Haven't started yet. Think it's about the end of the world."

"Aye," she says. "You could read that ... or maybe go to Cupar, see the real thing."

"What're you down here for this time?"

She gives him a case number she's been down to see before.

"You know where you're going?" He thumbs back to the stacks.

Oh, she does. And it's not where he thinks.

What she's really looking for:

Garner's case files.

Going back years, looking for anything she thinks might be suspicious, anything that might connect Garner to Kennedy.

An exercise in futility. Anything she does find will be waved away. But the urge to try is still there. She needs proof for her own sanity if nothing else.

And she's sure – more than ever – that the proof she needs is in one particular case. The one he took from her. The one that was buried.

A long shot? Or an obsessive inability to let go?

She tells herself it's about justice. Mrs McDiarmid has no immediate family chomping at the bit to find her killer – but she deserves justice like anyone else.

Real justice. *Closure*.

Not much chance of that after the department had done such a good job making sure the press made it clear there was no fire, despite the smoke that Burnet had raised with her initial inquiries.

She'd been hysterical and over-involved. These things happen. Especially with women.

Sometimes she wonders if they keep her around just to blame their own mistakes on her.

We're doing the equality thing, but look: everything that goes wrong is down to having a woman on board.

Which is why she's standing up and fighting back.

If she doesn't, she can't prove them wrong.

So what's she looking for in Garner's case files?

Garner works for Kennedy.

Frank Gray works Kennedy.

Frank Gray doesn't want to admit his son is a killer.

Garner took the damn case from her and buried it.

Why?

He's the kind of copper who would delight in finding some psychopath and beating seven bells out of them. Especially if said psychopath was a few stone lighter and looked like he couldn't punch his way out of a paper bag.

So why bury this?

Why pretend that there was *nothing to see here*?

There are several boxes related to the case, mixed in with the files on Dow's murder. Another forgotten case. Conveniently so.

There has to be *something*.

Next to the boxes – misfiled – another case. More recent.

Another case she worked on.

Another case Garner worked on.

The missing girl. Tessie Talbot. They never found her. It was only a few days after they'd talked to the boyfriend that the shit had hit the fan for Garner, meaning that a number of his cases were put to bed or conveniently forgotten.

She thinks about all the people she's let down over the last few months. She'd told Kelley that she wouldn't become like him; she wouldn't become so obsessed with Garner that she put her career in jeopardy.

But it still happened. Just in a different way.

Now she has become Kelley: sidelined and ridiculed.

Had he made the right decision when he left?

Why is she still here?

What does she hope to find?

She couldn't even find little Tessie Talbot. She couldn't find evidence as to who killed her best friend on the force.

But maybe there's something in why the girl's file ended up mixed in with the reports on Dow's death.

She pulls down the boxes. Skims the reports.

Absent-mindedly reads the dates.

Notices something.

An error. A date. Tipp-exed out.

No retype.

DATE SUBJECT FOUND.

She doubts herself. Possible Garner made a mistake and needed to correct. Possible.

Think about the way he types – bird-pecking with one finger.

All the same ...

She pulls down one of the werewolf boxes.

Because there was something else she saw a few days ago that appeared to be in the wrong place.

Once is a coincidence.

Twice—

"You okay back there? Can you find what you need?"

"Aye," she shouts back. "Just a wee misfiling."

"Okay, just as long as you're fine."

He's not coming. Lazy bastard. Lucky for her.

She smiles to herself, roots through the box.

The reports.

The evidence bags.

She looks for what she remembers. Pulls out the personal effects from Mrs McDiarmid, the cast of the bite marks, and then ...

She holds up the bag, thinking that it doesn't belong in this box.

A girl's purse. Too young to belong to Mrs McDiarmid. Not tagged, but it is bagged. Girly pink. Definitely not the possession of an older lady.

Burnet hesitates.

She needs to be careful. If she removes the purse from the bag, she contaminates evidence. If she doesn't, she can't prove or disprove her theory.

So:

Handbag. Tissues – the best she can do. Use them like a glove.

Take the purse out of the bag. Inside: some cash, a strip of images taken from a photobooth, and a receipt.

From a garage out near Templeton Woods. Not for services, but a few packs of cigarettes. Crumpled, but readable – a number, maybe a phone number. The date on the receipt is five days prior to when Tessie Talbot was first reported missing.

Burnet looks at the strip of photographs. A girl and a boy smiling together, goofing around. She recognises the boy: Richard "Dickie" Borer. His hair's slicked back, and he's wearing a purple shirt and leather jacket. He has his arm around the girl in most of the shots. They look good – a handsome young couple. They could be in a film.

The girl is easy to identify:

Tessie Talbot.

This was her purse.

What the hell is it doing in the box of evidence relating to the werewolf killer? Somewhere no one would even think to look for it.

It's not a mistake, she thinks. *It's not a mistake.*

62

KELLEY WAKES UP, SWEATING HARD.

The nightmares fade, leaving him with a feeling of empty nausea; a sense that there's something he's forgotten, or something that he needs to take care of. But he doesn't know what.

His sheets are on the floor. He rolls over in the Murphy bed, reaches over to the window and pushes it open for a cool breeze to slip in.

Kelley lies there, on his back, breathing in and out through his mouth.

Heart sputtering a beat that echoes in his ribcage.

Sweat cooling and drying on his skin.

Third time this week he's woken, convinced that his dreams mean something, but unable to remember the details.

He closes his eyes.

His dad had always intended for the diary to be found. Kelley's sure of that.

It was the only way the old man had of getting the truth out there and not putting himself or his family in danger.

But it hadn't helped.

The death of Halliday, and the suicide note he wrote about having been coerced into coming forward by *people with a deliberate and vengeful agenda against Tayside Police* had invalidated the trial. Even the Chief Constable had stepped back his rhetoric regarding corruption, seeming to admit that certain officers had been the target of some external conspiracy.

They'd aimed for the top, and all they'd done was get a man killed.

Somehow, Kelley knew this was his fault. He'd pushed too far and too fast. Same old problem.

When he threatened Halliday, he'd crossed a line.

He'd told himself it was fine, because he was no longer polis.

He'd been wrong.

He's supposed to be one of the good guys.

He sits up. Puts his feet on the floor. The boards are cold against his soles.

He's awake. No more dreaming.

Not until tonight.

He pads over to the sink in the corner of the room. Splashes his face. He looks at himself.

His face is gaunt, these days. His eyes seem sunken. He's lost weight since the trial ended. He feels like something's eating him from the inside.

He looks in the mirror.

Sees his father.

Kelley thinks about what people said about his father. He thinks about what Redman said, about how his father wasn't the hero he painted himself to be.

The apple doesn't fall far from the tree. Kelley's no hero either. Never was.

Just believed he could be.

* * *

In the office, a new client is waiting. They don't get many walk-ins, but those that bother tend to be of a type.

This one's late forties or early fifties. Once, he might have had a full head of dark hair, but now it's going grey; only small streaks of black left. Clean shaven, dressed in a grey suit and a shirt that looks tight around the collar. No eye contact. Seems almost ashamed to be here.

Kelley introduces himself, takes the man through to his room.

"Can I get you something?"

The man refuses. Gets straight to it: "My wife is missing."

"Have you been to the police?"

"I came to you. I've heard good things about this agency."

It doesn't directly answer Kelley's question, but tells him enough. The man has reasons for not wanting to go to the police. Either past experience, or fear of being discovered.

Kelley bears in mind the Fat Man's edicts about soliciting business:

Take the money and run.

"How long has she been missing?"

The man licks his lips. "Three weeks," he says. "She took the car to the garage and left it there for repairs."

"And?"

"And she never came home."

* * *

Kelley walks into Hannigan's garage. The hammering noise of drills and car engines is overwhelming. He tries not to put his hands over his ears. Waits for someone to notice him.

Finally, a man dressed in blue overalls walks over. He's losing his hair, keeping what he has gelled flat to his scalp as though to stop it from running off. "Can I help you?"

Kelley gives him a business card.

"A private detective? You don't have a funny hat like in the films."

"It's not compulsory."

"I used to love them films. Down the Forest Park Cinema House, aye? But I thought it was an American thing."

"You can be Scottish and a private investigator."

"Aye, well," the man says, as though suddenly realising this might be serious. "What do you want?"

"I want to ask about a woman who was here a few weeks ago." Kelley brings out the picture the client had left with him. "Have you ever seen her before?"

"Her husband came to pick up the car. He asked the same as you."

"Where she was?"

The man nods in affirmation.

"And?"

"And what would I know about it? She dropped off the car, paid in cash, said she was getting the bus home."

"Was it you who dealt with her?"

"I started the job, but I let our apprentice do the work. So she had a wee chat with him, too."

"Where is this apprentice?"

"You act like polis, you know that? Entitled." The man folds his arms across his chest.

Kelley knows he has a problem. People look at him and they see someone who moves like they should be in uniform. They can sense the polis on him, no matter how hard he tries to hide it.

"I used to be."

"Aye?"

"Not anymore."

Still not enough to ingratiate Kelley. He tries not to show his impatience. "They let me go. You know, because I actually tried to help people."

It's close enough to the truth.

"Aye, well ... you've got a stick up your arse, but you don't seem like a cunt." The man unfolds his arms, walks off, motioning for Kelley to follow. "Ask me, the wife was always going to run off. Just decided to do it that moment. Maybe she has a fancy man?"

"Maybe," Kelley says.

They walk deeper into the garage: a door at the rear leads to the back offices. "You married?"

"No."

"Best way to be." Kelley's already noted the man's wearing a wedding ring. But he still speaks with a weary conviction. "Sow your wild oats and all that. And don't get yourself trapped."

Kelley says nothing.

The back offices are something of a warren. Small, tight corridors, closed doors. They walk into what seems to be a coffee room, and the man in the overalls points to a lad hunched over a table, reading a dog-eared paperback. "Oy, Martin! This chap wants a word with you."

The lad – Martin – turns in his seat, but doesn't stand. Thin, with a sallow complexion, he has big eyes that retreat into his skull. He licks his lips, as though they're too dry.

"He's not polis," the man says. "Just wants to ask about a customer. Think it was you dealt with her."

Kelley steps forward and presents the photograph. "Do you remember this woman?"

Martin shakes his head, no, and turns away.

Kelley puts the photograph on the table. "I'm not accusing you of anything," he says, "but how are you going to remember if you don't even look at the picture?"

Slowly, Martin turns his head. He glances at the picture, and then turns away again. Kelley recognises the look on his face. He's afraid of something. He's afraid of the photo. "No," he says, quickly and quietly.

A hand on Kelley's shoulder. The man in the overalls. "Okay, he says he doesn't remember, and you know, he's a good lad, so he doesn't remember."

Kelley shrugs the man off. "He's avoiding the question."

"I never was a good judge of character," the man says. "You are actually a cunt, aren't you?" His left hand is on Kelley's shoulder again, tugging so that Kelley wheels to face him.

Kelley's ready for what's coming. Experience. Instinct.

The man's right hand is wound back, ready to swing for Kelley's face.

Kelley sidesteps. Slams a fist into the man's belly. The man drops, gripping his stomach. Lets loose a "fuck", like the air being let out of a tyre.

But Kelley's eye is off the ball.

Sudden weight on his back. Pipecleaner arms round his neck. Choking him.

The kid.

Looks a lightweight, but he's got some fucking strength.

Long legs wrap round Kelley's waist.

Tight.

Kelley tries to throw the kid off, but he can't. He runs backwards into the table, hoping to knock the kid off. No luck.

There's hot breath in his ear, on his neck.

And then a sharp pain.

"Fuck!"

The little shite biting. Hard and vicious. Not a nip, not an act of desperation. Like he's trying to get a grip, rip the flesh with his fucking *teeth*.

Kelley flips forward. The kid's grip slips.

The kid's on the floor.

Kelley steps back, touches where he got bit. Blood. More than there should be. Lucky the kid didn't nick a fucking vein.

A wild fucking animal.

On the floor, the kid's in a crouching position.

He bares his teeth. Blood on his chin.

He growls. Deep, guttural.

Kelley's instinct – fight or flight. Pure primality buzzing his brain.

The door opens.

Three men. All of them big. One clutching a tyre iron.

Kelley knows where this is going.

Readies himself.

But already knows the outcome.

63

JEANNIE'S AT WORK. EARLY SHIFT. CLEANER'S LOT.

They need some real income. A way of explaining the rent. Frank didn't like the idea, but she insisted. He thinks she just wants out of the house. Who can blame her?

Frank's in the kitchen, making a cup of tea – heavy on the milk, strong on the sugar – thinking how hard it's been for him to sleep lately.

Garner.

Sadistic fuck with his blackmail schemes, and his way of looking at everyone like they're insects to be stepped on. Like he doesn't realise how much of a cockroach he is himself.

Frank's son's a psycho? Garner should look in the mirror.

Frank needs to do something. But doesn't know what.

All he can do is make a cup of tea.

A cup of fucking tea.

Old man.

Fucking useless old man.

If he can get his head on right, he can figure out what to do.

About Garner.

About Martin.

About fucking everything.

The phone rings.

It'll be Garner again. The prick calling for another "favour". Every one "the last time", and every one followed by another.

Frank should have killed him. Called his bluff about someone else releasing the evidence on Martin.

Should have told Kennedy the truth. Or something close to it. Weren't they old friends?

Men like you don't have friends. Old, new, doesn't matter.

On the other end of the line: "It's Hannigan."

Frank thinks: *Martin.*

"We've got a problem at the garage."

Frank hangs up. Doesn't wait to hear anything else.

He knows. He fucking knows.

* * *

Not far past midday, and the garage is closed up.

Frank hammers the shutters. Hannigan lets him in to the workshop area. A few cars up on the lifts. Heavy scent of petrol and oil.

No one working.

The place shut down.

In the middle of the forecourt:

A man tied to a chair. Bleeding from a wound in his neck. Broken nose, too. Eyes swollen shut.

One fuck of a beating.

Frank recognises him.

The private investigator, the one who used to be a policeman. His face has been in the papers. First when he was hired – the son of a hero. Then when he was fired – under a cloud. And finally, when he brought charges of corruption – against Garner.

Pity. Frank liked the guy's style.

"What the fuck's going on?" More confused than angry. Hannigan's a solid citizen. The fuck is he doing with some nosy prick tied up in his place of business? And what does this have to do with Frank's son?

Sound of a door opening: Martin comes out from the toilets, wiping his face with a towel.

He looks at his father. Frank can see the monster in his son's expression.

Same as he saw in the junkie's flat.

More forcefully: "What the fuck's going on?"

Hannigan holds up his hand, trying to sound reasonable. "This prick came in, asking questions about some woman brought her husband's car in for a wee service. It was one of your lad's jobs, so, you know, I said he could ask. But he didn't ask nicely, so I told him to leave. As you can see, he didn't want to."

The private detective spits blood and phlegm on the floor.

Frank almost respects him.

"This woman you were asking about," Frank says, "how's she connected to my boy?"

The detective looks up at Frank. His lips twist like he might be about to laugh. "She's not. Or at least, if she is, I don't know much about it. All I know is, he could have been the last person to see her."

Frank thinks about what the woman polis told him in her flat. About what Garner said when they met at the Necropolis. About Martin's behaviour over the last few months. About the incident with the wolves. The dentures. The women's belongings mixed in with his son's clothes. They didn't just belong to this one girl, did they?

It adds up.

Frank doesn't want to do the maths.

He wants – *needs* – two and two to make five.

Frank looks at Hannigan. "Appreciate a wee minute alone with this one." Keeping everything calm.

New Frank, not old Frank.

But old Frank is in there. Growling and begging to be let free.

It's easier to sort your problems with fists. Act now, worry later.

Hannigan nods. "Tell him he's not welcome back here."

"He'll no be coming back," Frank says.

Hannigan puts an arm around Martin's shoulders and leads him out with the rest of the men.

Frank can't look directly at his own son.

After they're alone, the detective says, "So what's the plan? You finish what they started?"

"Why did you come here?"

"A client came into the office looking for his wife. The last place she was at was here."

"And my boy?"

"The wee psycho, you mean?"

Frank punches the detective straight in the face, knocking him back. The man manages to keep his chair upright, hawks up another gobbet of blood and spits it out on the floor. Something clatters on concrete. A tooth.

"Impulse control," the detective says, once he's got his breath back. "Same problem most thugs have. Encounter a problem, take the easiest route to solving it: break something or hurt someone. I know who you are. I didn't know that was your son. But I see it, now. He fucking tried to bite me. Like I tried to tell these fucking eejits, I was defending myself."

"Bite you?"

"Like a fucking animal. I didn't do anything. Asked him to look at a picture."

Frank believes the detective. His forehead starts to heat up. A prickling sensation starts somewhere just behind his ears.

"I can see you know what I'm talking about," the detective says. "I'm not a father, but it's got to be tough knowing your boy's a killer. Because I think you know what happened to that woman. You didn't witness it, but when I told you ... I'm a people person. Important in what I do. I don't like people, and people don't like me, but I can fucking read them. You think ... you *know* ... your lad did something."

Frank turns away.

The detective plays it smart and keeps quiet.

Some things in life, there's no escape from. Deny them all you want, they're not any less real.

Keeping his back to the detective, Frank says, "This woman's missing?"

"Aye."

"And she wouldn't have just run away, now?"

The detective shifts position in the chair, perhaps trying to get some life back into his limbs, get his blood circulating again. The feet of the chair scrape against the concrete floor.

"The husband and I had a long chat," the detective says. "I'm a good judge of people. As far as he knew, what they had together was solid. She wasn't running away with a fancy piece, nothing like that."

Frank wants to find something – a chink in this man's story to make him think this was some kind of coincidence.

"If I bring my son in here, and he denies everything in front of me, is that going to be enough for you to leave him alone?"

The detective nods. "I frightened him, okay. I get it. Maybe he over-reacted." Frank knows the detective doesn't believe it. But Frank's thinking the same thing: there's over-reaction, and then there's what happened between Martin and the detective.

Frank makes his decision. "I'll get him. But if you fuck with him or me, you know you'll regret it."

64

KELLEY CAN'T FEEL HIS LEGS.

He tries to flex his right thigh, get the blood flowing. The ropes pull tight. One wrong move will topple him.

Jesus, but he feels daft. Everything going sideways because he didn't know when to back away.

And now he's locked in a room with the man once known as the Beast of Balgay.

Frank fucking Gray.

And what does he do? Poke the bear? Tell Frank the truth about his son, even if Frank doesn't want to hear it?

This was supposed to be a simple missing persons case.

Bread and butter case for the Fat Man.

Now a monumental fuck-up for Kelley.

His vision blurs. Concussion, maybe. Hard to tell underneath the pain.

Three men lamping the shite out of him. And that fucking lad – Frank's *son* – doing his best impersonation of a wild animal; *trying* to rip out Kelley's throat with his teeth. Wee fucking psycho.

If he was Kelley's son, Kelley would have called the doctors on him.

It's a few minutes before the door opens again: Frank, his son beside him.

The lad's twitchy. The earlier anger is gone. What's left looks a lot like fear. His body seems smaller; those long limbs contracting in on themselves. He looks down at the floor as he walks.

Sullen teenager.

The transformation's unnerving.

Frank remembers Burnet mentioning that they had talked to Frank Gray when she was working the werewolf case. She and Dow had this suspicion the son knew more than he was letting on.

Kelley makes the connections.

The wife isn't missing. She's dead.

Her corpse bitten and scratched and left for dead.

Which meant:

Her. The cat. The old woman.

And how many others that they don't know about?

When Martin attacked Kelley, he'd bitten him, growling like an animal. A *predator*.

A wolf.

Frank *has* to know.

The son – Martin – raises his head. Another switch in stance and appearance. Looking at Kelley with eyes that seem almost black.

He sees, but also doesn't see.

Frank steps forward. Holding a knife. Big bastard blade.

Kelley tenses.

Frank cuts the rope.

Kelley drops off the chair. Blood starts flowing. His skin stings. He rubs at his legs and his forearms.

When he feels able, he supports himself with the chair and gets to his feet.

A dizzy sensation. Copper taste at the back of his mouth. He swallows thick, gagging gobbets.

Frank says, "Ask him again."

Kelley looks at Martin. Blank eyes, slack expression. Is the lad even listening? Is he in his own fucking head? "That woman I asked you about ... all I need to know is what happened after you agreed to fix her car."

Martin looks to Frank, as though asking what he should say. But Frank just shrugs. The boy needs to answer this himself.

Martin looks back at Kelley. His reply is monotone. "She left. To get a bus."

"She said that specifically?"

Martin bites at his upper lip, sucks it between his teeth. Puts pressure on it until it turns white.

"This is important, son," Frank says. "He's worried someone could have hurt this woman. And you know that you shouldn't hurt women. I taught you that, didn't I?"

Martin continues to bite at his lip. Now there's blood. A small trickle.

Frank lays hands on the lad's shoulders. "Come on," he says. "Please, because if this woman's been hurt by anyone—"

Martin looks up at his father. Roars in the man's face and pushes at his chest.

Frank stumbles, caught off guard.

Martin jogs backwards, baring his teeth as he does so. His expression changes. Slack-jawed to tight and angry. His eyes explode with anger. The dull emptiness becomes something else; something hateful.

Kelley can't quite believe what he's seeing; a transformation that seems not only mental, but also physical – Martin's body tensing, his loose limbs taking up positions with purpose. He hisses at the two other men in the room.

Frank stares at his son.

"Martin," he says. "Please—"

"Dad," Martin says. Again he's a young lad again, shoulders dropping, voice high-pitched and tremulous. "I'm sorry ... it made me ... it ..."

Frank steps forward.

Martin growls again and runs for the garage door.

Frank gives chase.

Martin's faster. At the door, he topples a rack of tools.

Frank awkwardly hurdles the obstacle.

But Martin's out the door.

Kelley stays where he is.

Frank reaches the door, then slows down. He leans against the garage shutters, then turns to look back at Kelley.

He looks old. Defeated, even. He can't control his breathing. His face is pale. His expression seems oddly slack.

The door at the back of the garage opens. The men who beat Kelley earlier walk out.

They look at the scene.

They look at Frank.

They look at Kelley.

No one says a word.

65

"BURNET? CALL FOR YOU."

Burnet's filing reports on traffic violations – more busy work from high up, more ways for her to count down the hours until the boredom forces her out of CID.

She's had a lot of calls recently. Same as when she was working the werewolf case. Except these are often malicious and threatening in intent.

Mostly heavy breathing, some sniggers, others just saying "Rat" through a handkerchief so that their voice is disguised.

Everyone's a suspect. Not just those loyal to Garner. This goes beyond his personal corruption. This is about her being a feminist out to cause trouble for men who're only trying to do their job.

All the same, she has to answer.

She takes the call at her desk, transferred through from the main switchboard.

The line clicks. She takes a breath. Steadies herself.

"It's Kelley."

They haven't talked since the verdict. She's tried, once or twice, but he's ignored her.

They were friends.

And then they weren't.

Leaving her even more isolated on the job.

But now he's calling her. His voice is thick like he's got a blocked nose.

"What do y—"

"I'm at Hannigan's garage. You know where it is?"

Of course she does.

Where Frank Gray's son works.

She's been sitting on the misfiled evidence. Even if she comes forward, she knows that any claims she makes will be dismissed.

Greek myth:

Cassandra.

Scream the truth as loud as you want, no one's going to listen.

"I'm working on a missing wife case," Kelley says, "for a client. Last place she was seen was here and—"

"I don't think I'm who you want," Burnet says. "Or haven't you heard? They've taken me off active investigations. I can transfer—"

"Listen to me!" An undertone of anxiety. "It's the werewolf killer. I know who it was. You know who it was. And now we have proof. I have got the fucking proof that he exists."

It can't be true. The case is dead. Garner made sure of it.

"Did you hear me?"

"I heard you."

"There's proof. We have a witness. One who wasn't willing to talk, but—"

Her heart skips for a moment. "What witness?" she asks.

When he gives her the name, she thinks she might pass out right there at her desk.

* * *

It takes her half an hour to get out to the garage. When she arrives, a group of men are smoking on the forecourt.

Kelley stands slightly apart from them. He walks over as she climbs out the car. Limping, his right arm at an awkward angle.

His face is bruised, dried blood caking his nostrils and upper lip.

No wonder he sounded strange on the phone.

"Frank Gray," she says. "Where is he?"

Their witness. Willing to testify.

So Kelley said.

"He's not here."

She wants to scream. The truth always dangling so close.

"You said he was—"

"He's afraid for his son."

Frank Gray's a thug. Someone who chose violence and criminality while trying to live like everyone else.

But he's also a father. Burnet knows he takes that seriously.

Of course he's going to have second thoughts about talking to the police. Especially if it implicates his son.

Doesn't matter.

He needs to talk.

If they can arrest Martin Gray, they can expose Garner as covering up Martin's crime – whatever his reasons for doing so. Show that evidence was deliberately misplaced that could have prevented any of this from happening.

If they do that, then they can bring Garner down. Maybe others, too.

Make a difference.

Change everything.

She says, "Where do you think he's gone?"

"He said he wanted to talk to Martin. He didn't say where he was going."

"You can guess, though?"

Kelley nods.

They both know.

Only one place father and son could go.

"Get in," Burnet says. "I'm driving."

66

THE FRONT DOOR IS OPEN.

Frank stops halfway up the path, sick sensation in his stomach.

Jeannie's on the early shift.

She'll be home by now.

If Martin's truly lost it, then—

No, Martin loves his mum. Loves her.

Right?

All the signs. There since Martin was a bairn. Frank had ignored them all.

Thump. Thump. Thump.

His heart. Ocean waves echo in his head.

The world tilts; a lurch.

Frank's sweating hard. He wipes his forehead with the back of his hand, looks at it. Expects to see blood.

But this isn't a nightmare.

This is real.

He's been in denial too long.

Time to stand up.

Face the truth about his fucked-up son.

If he can get his legs to work properly.

* * *

Upstairs.

Bedrooms.

Everywhere empty, like there's no one home.

Jeannie was on an early shift.

The woman operates like clockwork.

She always tells him where she'll be.

Both doors are closed.

Left or right?

Frank closes his eyes.

Man the fuck up.

Martin's door first. The place is always untidy, but this is different: a desperation to the chaos, with drawers on the floor, clothes and papers and books and tapes scattered.

Like a bomb went off.

He was looking for something.

But what?

Frank flashes on:

The girl's top.

The dentures.

Metal.

Wolf's teeth.

Frank burned the girl's top. Got rid of the cast of his son's teeth.

But not the metal fucking dentures. They hadn't been there.

Why didn't he fucking *think*?

Back at the garage, Hannigan had told Frank how Martin would always be working the lathe on a "special project" he didn't want to tell anyone about.

Frank had asked the dentist – Mr Hughes – about whether it was possible to create a cast that could replicate the teeth of an animal.

But he didn't listen to the answer.

Not really.

How has this happened?

How can this monster be his son?

Frank gets flashbacks:

His own mother telling him that he would go to hell if he did everything that Joe Kennedy asked of him.

Your best friend is a bad influence.

Frank had laughed it off. Whose friend wasn't a bad influence at that age?

The old battleaxe.

No such thing as God, he'd told her. How could there be in a life like this?

Not seeing the irony, even as life went on – getting married to Jeannie in the eyes of the Lord, taking Martin with them every Sunday, the church a habit more than a belief.

His mother had said – more than once, and even on her fucking deathbed – that he'd be damned.

Is this damnation? Realising that your own son is a sicko, a killer, a deviant?

Killing women and girls because ... because *why?*

That's the bit Frank doesn't get. He knows what it is to kick against those with power. To rage against people who have more than you.

But his son picks on the weak and helpless. An old woman who can't fight back. A young girl who probably thought she was meeting a nice young man.

A woman who thought he was a friendly assistant at the garage.

Frank doesn't understand what his son is.

But he knows that he is dangerous.

To everyone.

But especially women.

Jeannie should be home.

Frank drops to his knees.

The world starts trembling. An earthquake?

There's pain in his right temple. Sharp. Radiating out and down his face. His right arm gets this tingling sensation.

"Fuck it."

He forces himself to stand. The world goes blank at the edge of his right eye. He ignores it.

Just fucking panic. Get over it. Stop feeling sorry for yourself.

The window's open.

He shakes his head.

Martin was here. His son was here. He came, he took something from his room, and he left.

Frank's vision gets worse – a dark zone spreading in from his right peripheral.

Blink. Clear it. Ignore it.

Jeannie's day off.

Where is she? This time of day, she should be here.

Maybe she's with a friend. Or popped out to help one of the elderly neighbours. Following the death of Mrs McDiarmid, the neighbourhood's become more close-knit, more thoughtful about the older generation. Jeannie's taken to it big-time.

Aye, that's where she is.

All the same, Frank keeps looking at the closed door of their bedroom: the one place where he hasn't been yet.

As he gets to his feet, Frank feels like he's wading through treacle. His head feels like it's on fire, too, and he has to keep blinking that black spot away. But every time, it comes back with a vengeance.

He makes it to the door.

Hesitates.

Pushes it open.

67

BURNET PARKS THE CAR HALF ON THE PAVEMENT. Sloppy job. She remembers laughing at Lincoln, how he used to park the same way.

Less than a year ago.

Feels like a lifetime.

Kelley's out first, sliding over the bonnet to get to the house fast. Burnet almost laughs, thinking: *Starsky & Hutch*. The laugh dies when she remembers why they're here.

On the drive over, Kelley told her what happened at the garage.

Burnet's mind races, thinking about everything she's read about psychotic killers and what happens when they're cornered.

More, what the police find when they finally look into the private worlds of these men.

Frank Gray's a traditional villain; a man of violence, yes – but a straightforward, honest kind of violence.

His son is something different.

Kelley's in the door a few seconds ahead of her. Shouting out his presence.

As she walks inside the house, Burnet suddenly feels unprepared.

In America, the cops are always armed, ready to take on whatever they find.

But this is Scotland. And she's a woman, tolerated but sidelined in CID.

She has a baton.

That's it.

And she's damn lucky to have it.

Downstairs is clear.

Upstairs – the lad's room. Like a storm's ripped through it.

Then, the door to the parents' bedroom, left ajar.

Burnet looks inside.

The mother on the bed. Not where she was killed. She'd been placed there after her death. The blood streaks on the floor, on the sheets, tell the story of someone moving the corpse.

With old Mrs McDiarmid, the killer had taken his time. Even with Dow, there had been a level of care taken in disembowelling and displaying the body after death.

This is different. The violence is there, but slapdash and hurried. The ripped-open neck, the hands cut with defensive wounds, the torso ripped open from chest to stomach.

Burnet swallows down bile.

She thinks about what could have happened to Tessie Talbot, or the woman Martin met at the garage. Where are they now? What happened to them? Did they know what was happening in their last moments?

What did he do with the bodies?

But there's another reason that this crime scene feels different – more brutal – than what came before.

This is his mother.

She thinks about Dow. About what he told her he felt when he walked into the classroom when the Robert Mone siege was over. About how he couldn't understand this man, what drove him, what made him do the things he did.

Sometimes there is no narrative.

Sometimes people do things that seem incomprehensible.

That have no explanation.

Nature/nurture. An excuse to try and make sense of the unexplainable.

Kelley's in the room behind her. "There's no one else here."

She can't stop looking at the dead woman.

"He would have left by the window," Kelley says. "The woods. He thinks he's a wolf, right? An animal? That's why he kills his victims out there."

Focus on his voice. Focus on what you do next.

Stop looking at the dead woman.

Burnet nods. "I should call for backup," she says. "Armed backup." But she knows that by the time they get here, Martin could be long gone. Or someone else could be dead.

68

FRANK STOPS BY THE ROAD AT THE EDGE of the woods. Keeping himself balanced against a thick tree trunk. Ever since he saw Jeannie on the bed, he's been unable to keep himself properly upright. His right side is weak. He keeps listing, and his arm seems to lack power. His vision keeps blacking out at the edges, and occasionally it's like looking in the wing mirror of a car; objects closer than they appear.

Grief can do funny things to a man.

But he needs to stay calm.

When the car pulls up, Frank remains where he is, almost afraid to move. He can't show weakness, so he stays still. Hoping the other man will fall for the bluff.

Garner gets out of the car. Gun in his hand – an old service revolver from the war. Definitely not standard police issue.

Frank says, "You wanted to be the hero, right? You wanted your fucking redemption? You can put down the werewolf killer. Finish what you started." He's finding it hard to talk. Like his teeth and tongue are too big for his mouth.

"The werewolf killer who doesn't exist," Garner says. "You fucking—" He stops talking, looks at Frank with this odd expression. "What the fuck's wrong with you?"

"What?"

"Your fucking face. You've gone half-spastic."

Frank doesn't know what Garner's talking about, although he's aware of how numb his face feels. That whole side where the headache's at its worst feeling almost useless. His mouth feels strange, too, the lips weighted in some fashion he can't explain.

Garner shakes his head. "Never fucking mind," he says. "Where is the cunt? Jesus, I should have put him down when I found out. Too fucking kind, that's me."

Frank shrugs. "Here, somewhere," he says. "In the woods." He speaks slowly. The words seem to struggle.

"You're sure?"

"I'm sure. I know my son."

Garner looks about to say something, but then thinks better of it. He holds up the gun, so Frank can't miss it. "This is what we call a mercy killing," he says. "You understand that, don't you?"

Frank nods.

He's been running away from this for the past year. But sometimes a man has to step up and do what needs to be done.

* * *

The deeper they get into the trees, the more Frank feels like he's in a dream. The treacle is even thicker than before.

He can't discount the idea that he's dreaming.

Then he remembers a book that he once read to Martin as a child about children who walked through a wardrobe and into another world. One where a lion talked, and a queen ruled over eternal winter.

The woods belong to another world. One where the rules of reality no longer apply.

Deeper through the trees, snow starts falling. Gently at first, but getting heavier.

The neighbours are already putting their decorations out. Jeannie was beginning to hint to Frank that they should think about it, too. He used to think they only did it for Martin, and that when he got older, there would no longer be any need.

But now he knows it wasn't for him, but for her.

He'll never be able to think that again.

She's dead.

Killed by her own son.

Frank's fault. He ignored the signs. Didn't listen.

But was it more elemental? Something he'd passed down to his son? The anger that he had as a young man twisted, filtered and distorted into something unnatural.

All Frank wants to know is *why*.

But he's scared there might not be an answer.

Frank stops in a clearing. "Martin," he says, speaking to the trees. "Please. I just want to talk."

He waits.

Maybe he's wrong. Maybe Martin's gone somewhere else. The wolf enclosure at the park, maybe?

But Frank thinks that this is Martin's *territory*. This is where he has killed. If he thinks he's an animal, then he'll be thinking like one, too.

"Martin!"

A twig breaks.

Frank turns. Sees his son. At the edge of the clearing, crouched on all fours. Regarding his own father with a wariness that betrays the lack of recognition.

The boy's gone.

The animal's left.

Frank thinks about what happened in the garage. Martin saying something about "the wolf", like it was something separate and distinct from himself.

"Jesus," Frank says. He hunkers down to his son's level. "What happened to you? Did I do this? Was there something—"

He stops talking. Blood soaks Martin's clothes.

Frank saw what happened to Jeannie.

How can he forget?

This is his son, and yet—

How can he feel concern for the ... *thing* ... that killed his wife?

The headache returns. A thumping, buried in his right temple. Like the blood's gathering there, blocked just under the skin, trying to break free.

A fucking dam waiting to burst.

Martin looks at his father, eyes wide and black.

Same look Frank saw in the junkie's flat. Back when he should have done something.

Frank's almost crying.

The Butcher of Balgay's never fucking cried in his life. Never.

"Please," he says, voice soft and cracked.

The word feels too big for his mouth.

The world *tilts*.

Martin blinks.

His eyes aren't black anymore.

He approaches his father.

Frank realises he's down on his knees. The inside of his skull is on fire. The world has gone fuzzy. All he can see is his boy.

Frank pulls the boy close. There's no resistance.

Martin goes limp in his arms.

Frank sobs. Like holding a corpse.

Frank shakes, tries to grip tighter, but he has no strength.

"Let him go."

Over Martin's shoulder: Garner. His pistol aimed at the back of Martin's head.

"Let him go," Garner says again. "Unless you want to die with him."

That would be the easy option. Jeannie's dead. What else does Frank have to live for?

What does he have to live for?

Fear.

The question isn't what he has to live for – but what's waiting for him when he dies?

At the back of his mind, there's always been the fear that his mother was right. That little spark of doubt that remembers what he read in Sunday School about rivers of fire, that fears the wrath of a vengeful fucking God.

He no longer has the strength.

He lets go of his son, and collapses onto his back. His legs no longer work.

Martin looks at him, his eyes confused and uncertain.

Then he turns his head to see what his father sees.

Garner says, "Little fucking retard," and pulls the trigger.

69

Burnet runs in the direction of the gunshot. Leaves and twigs crackle underfoot. Branches sting at exposed skin and snag on the fabric of her uniform. A thorn scratches her cheek. She wipes it away and keeps moving.

A second gunshot. Closer, now.

Has anyone else heard the noise?

She doesn't know where Kelley is. They went in different directions when they left the house.

The plan: cover more ground.

Bad idea?

Running towards the sound of gunshots, she doubts herself.

What does she expect to do against someone who's armed?

What did she expect to do against some psychopath who murdered a senior officer in cold blood without a second thought?

Christ.

But she keeps running.

In the middle of a clearing, lying on his back, she sees Frank Gray. Clutching at his chest. He isn't moving.

He's staring up at the sky.

Dead.

No blood.

A heart attack?

The Beast of Balgay felled by a bad heart?

And, just a few metres away, there's Martin Gray.

Straddling a man, struggling, swiping with his hands like they're claws. The man's big, for all the good that does him. He's struggling against the sheer fury and speed of the smaller figure. Martin swipes with his hands, snaps with his teeth.

There's a clacking sound that echoes.

Burnet hesitates.

She looks for a branch, something she could use to knock Martin off the other man.

But she sees something better.

A revolver.

Maybe three feet from the two men struggling on the ground.

They haven't noticed her.

She moves forward. Cautious.

The man underneath Martin Gray has his hands pressed against the lad's forehead and chin – pushing the snapping jaws away.

Martin looks like he's trying to pull the man's face off.

She's almost there.

A twig snaps.

Everything stops.

The forest is silent.

Martin looks up at her.

She sees his mouth – metal dentures. Like fangs. Like wolf's teeth.

The world stops.

Dow was right.

Dow knew.

And she realises, *Martin Gray killed Dow.*

Martin springs off the bigger man with a lightness and anger she doesn't expect.

She's still too far from the gun.

Martin falls short.

The other man has his ankle, pulling him back.

"Fucking do it!"

Burnet grabs up the gun.

She's never fired a weapon in her life. Hopes it's as simple as it looks.

She remembers watching a John Wayne film where he teaches someone how to fire a gun. *Squeeze the trigger.*

She points the business end at Martin, who's now on his back, kicking at the other man, making a noise that sounds guttural and inhuman.

"Do it," the man yells.

Garner.

The man is Garner.

For a moment she thinks:

Maybe let Martin finish what he started.

It would be easier.

She pulls the trigger.

Blood, brains and bone explode from Martin's temple and onto the forest floor.

Burnet's down on her arse.

The gun's in the leaves.

Martin remains completely still.

Somewhere, a crow rasps.

70

A THIRD GUNSHOT.

Is Kelley too late?

He keeps running.

Calls Burnet's name.

No response.

He stumbles over a root and rolls down an incline. At the bottom, he tries to stand and his ankle gives way beneath him.

"Fuck!"

Then: "Kelley!"

He forces himself to his feet. She's close.

"Where are you?"

"Follow my voice. This way."

All he wants to do is lie down. He's tired now. But he forces himself forward, hopping and limping towards her voice.

In the clearing, two bodies: Frank Gray, dead on his back.

And Martin Gray: blood and brain on the forest floor.

Burnet's holding a revolver. Older model, Kelley thinks. He doesn't know where it came from. He sees a third man on the forest floor. This one on his knees, hands over his head.

Garner.

Burnet has the weapon trained on him.

He looks up, sees Kelley.

"Fuck you," he mouths.

Kelley does his best not to smile.

* * *

The next few weeks pass like a whirlwind.

The police search the Gray property, find Martin's diaries.

He writes about how the wolf speaks to him at night, and tells him of his hunger. How he first heard the wolf's whispers at thirteen or fourteen years old. How he learned to silence the wolf with music. It spoke to him at times of stress and worry.

He saw tensions between his parents, he heard people whisper things at school about his dad, and he became scared.

Frank's attitude to his son didn't help. Maybe he was trying to discipline the lad. But corporal punishments were regular and terrifying.

He doesn't describe his kills in any detail. In the diaries, he mentions the wolf "taking over", and how sometimes he would find himself naked out in the woods, and have to walk back home, shivering and limping because of the cuts on the soles of his feet.

His first kill happened shortly after the wolves came to Camperdown Park. He woke with the taste of flesh in his mouth, next to the body of a fox. He vomited and ran home.

But it wasn't the last.

The cat followed soon after.

And then the old woman.

And then ...

He writes about how the wolf speaks to him about how it feels to watch the prey. The break in his sanity becomes clearer.

The rest? Well, the rest is history.

Three dead women. One dead policeman. It still wasn't clear why he killed Dow, but he wrote about it in the diary.

Kelley learns about the diary through unofficial sources in Tayside Police. The diary is evidence and not for public consumption. But all the same, Kelley learns about it.

Which makes him one of the few.

* * *

The headlines read:

LIKE FATHER, LIKE SON: FAMILY FEUD ENDS IN MURDER

Which slightly betrays the story underneath.

Kelley reads with interest.

The thrust of the official narrative:

Martin Gray wanted to impress his own father, decided to show he had the balls to be a gangster. The women were practice. But Dow had been the real prize, the way to show his father he could be a hard man, too.

Three victims are mentioned:

Tessie Talbot, the woman from the garage, and Detective Inspector Dow.

No mention is made of the werewolf murders or Mrs McDiarmid. Details of the deaths are surprisingly light.

No mention is made of the diary.

No mention is made of Garner.

Kelley reads through once, then looks up.

On the other side of the table, Burnet sips her tea.

"Jesus," Kelley says.

Burnet says nothing.

"A cover-up of a cover-up," Kelley says, still trying to get a reaction.

But there's none to be had.

Burnet says, "Better than we could have hoped for."

"A half-truth."

"Better than a whole lie."

Kelley isn't so sure he agrees.

Their bacon rolls arrive.

"There's a trade-off, though?"

"There's always a trade-off."

"I thought the idea was you wouldn't play their game."

"It's this or don't play at all." Burnet's tired. Her skin seems tight on her face. "Look, Garner's off the force, on a suspended sentence. No one wants to admit they got his trial wrong. It's the only thing keeping him out of jail."

"You don't even get vindication for what they put you through about the werewolf killer shite."

"Trade-offs," she says. "And next time, I make sure it goes better."

"Now you're a DS?"

"Bravery in the line of duty and all that."

The article made specific mention of how Burnet uncovered evidence that Garner had doctored, went to confront him and wound up defending herself with a weapon that "belonged to Frank Gray". In this version, she was the one who killed Gray and the son, both in self-defence.

"You don't think Garner will argue with this?"

"You know," Burnet says, ignoring the question, "I could put in a word for you. We could try again. What we talked about. Reshaping the force from the inside. Now that Garner's out on his arse, everything that was used against you is—"

He holds up a hand. "Aye, you could do that. But I don't want you to. I thought I was polis, but maybe I'm as bad as Garner, all the rest of them."

"I know you bent some rules to—"

"I'm happier," he says. "Honestly. Working for the Fat Man isn't always pleasant, but it kind of works for me."

"If you ever change your mind . . ."

"I won't."

There's silence for a while as they eat.

Kelley wonders if the truth will ever come out. And he wonders if Burnet's as happy with her compromise as she claims.

MARCH 1979

71

IT'S NOT HER CASE.

But she has to be there.

She pulls up at the edge of the tape, gets out the car, nods to the uniforms on the line. She steps past and under the tape.

Redman's already on the scene. "You're working other assignments, Sergeant," he says. "We still don't know exactly what's happened here."

"All the same..."

He takes in a sharp breath through gritted teeth, puts a hand on her shoulder and takes her to one side.

When they're out of earshot, he says, "I know why you're here, but you're forgetting that what happened... didn't fucking happen."

"I just need to know... we found the bodies mentioned in the diary, the ones we know about. But—"

"But nothing."

"Come on, I have to know. Female victim. This location. Jesus, only, what four months after I blew the wee bugger's brains out?"

"The Chief Constable doesn't want you near this. You've got what you wanted, and you know the price."

"If there's another victim ..."

Redman shakes his head. "Come with me," he says.

He leads her to a small patch of ground that's been sealed off, waiting for the medical experts to arrive. The woman's body is there, exposed to the world.

Burnet doesn't feel anything as she looks at the corpse. She looks at it for maybe twenty seconds, before turning to Redman. "She's been dead, what, less than a day?"

"Looks that way. In this weather, I suppose she could be preserved a little longer than usual, but ..."

"So she can't be one of his."

"No."

Burnet walks away from the body. Redman follows her. "I hate to admit it, lass, but you've got good instincts. I mean, if we'd listened to you last time ... but we didn't, and maybe some of us were more at fault than we would have liked ... but what I'm saying is, sometimes a dead body is a dead body. Doesn't mean it's a serial. Doesn't mean we won't catch the killer or that he's some sick fucker like that lad."

She nods. "And meantime I've got my own cases."

"That you do," Redman says.

As she trudges back to her car, she overhears someone say they think they have a name for victim.

"I hope they find them," she mutters, "whoever did this to you."

As she climbs into the driver's seat, she thinks that for everything that's changing as the seventies end, some things will always be the same. And no matter how hard she fights, she wonders if change will ever come fast enough.

Acknowledgements

This book has been a long time in the writing. After finishing my "modern" J McNee quintet of detective novels set in the city, I knew I wanted to go back in time and look at the city during a very different period of its history (eagle-eyed readers will notice younger versions of certain characters from that series pop up in some scenes here).

Dundee in 1978 was a city on the verge of change. The old businesses were dead or dying, and there were concerns over new projects such as the "modern" Wellgate shopping centre. There was also the "Dundee dossier" scandal, involving corruption on the local council.

As is the case with any book that intersects with history, certain elements come with a degree of dramatic licence. While real-life crimes (the Templeton Woods killings of Carol Lannen and Elizabeth McCabe, or Robert Mone taking a class of girls hostage in 1976, for example) inform the background of the book, I stuck to reported elements of these incidents, giving my characters an incidental connection (such as Dow having walked into that classroom or mentioning the real-life story of Robert Little, Chief Constable of Dundee and Tayside, exchanging himself for a hostage during a dramatic post office raid that turned into a car pursuit).

In other cases, truth and fiction seemed to combine by happy coincidence. I had already written the sequence where Garner and his crew are arrested and put on trial when I discovered that in real life a crew of Dundee police officers were put on trial for a series of B&Es in the city at around the same time. The details are very different, but it served to make the book feel more real to me.

The near-riot when *Jaws* was shown at the cinema and there weren't enough seats is true, while the details around Keiller's closing and NCR being in trouble are more or less accurate to history (although specific details have been dramatised or adjusted to better fit the action and themes of this story).

The *Dundee Herald* is a made-up newspaper I've featured in my novels since *The Good Son* back in 2008. But in real life, the *Evening Telegraph* (known as the *Tele* or *Tully*, depending on who you ask) did run a series of snapshots of ordinary young women at their work with the rather brilliant title of "Sunny Smile" every Wednesday and Thursday. This became the Daily Girl in the fictional *Herald*, and instead of being two days a week, it was a daily thing. Originally, Elizabeth Burnet was the Monday Girl, but my publishers believed the Friday Girl scanned better as a title ...

I also want to acknowledge that while my fictional police department is fairly corrupt, this – forgiving the unfortunate coincidence mentioned earlier – is purely for dramatic purposes and isn't intended to represent any particular police officer or detective who served on the force during this period. And while Elizabeth is the first woman in plainclothes in the reality of the book, there were instances of Dundee having women in CID at this time, although even Robert Little admitted in a book he wrote on the history of Dundee's CID that they mostly did filing and traffic work!

The Friday Girl is a work of fiction. The city of Dundee as presented is intended to mirror certain aspects of reality, but in some cases won't quite reflect the lived experience of some people. I don't think any novel ever could, not really. But I hope that the way in which it twists and uses the history and character of the city is one that feels accurate and fair. I spent a decade living in Dundee, first as a student and then working in local bookstores, and it's a city I have such affection for.

I'd like to acknowledge, here, the assistance of Dundee City Libraries, and in particular the local history section in the Wellgate Centre – Erin Farley was of great help during my last few visits and found me a few unexpected sources I could reference in looking at crime in the city during this period. Mostly, I used primary sources such as newspapers and police reports, but I should also acknowledge former number-one bestselling Scottish book, *The Law Killers* by Alexander McGregor as having been a huge help as I learned about crime during this period of Dundee's history. Perhaps ironically, that book shares the same publishers as *The Friday Girl!*

This book would not have been been possible without help and assistance from so many people. Financially, the Royal Literary Fund and the Society of Authors have saved my bacon several times during the writing of this book – these two organisations offer vital help to authors, especially in an economy which seems to value them less and less, and where opportunities for artists in general are disappearing almost daily.

On the publishing side, Allan Guthrie at The North has been an absolute rock – he first saw this book at the beginning of the pandemic, and even when it got lost amidst the chaos, encouraged me to keep working at it and to keep believing in it. That paid off when my magnificent editor, Rachel Morrell at Black & White Publishing, decided to take a chance on this novel, and truly fought for it, while encouraging me to stick to my vision.

And thank you to Lisa Horton for the fantastic cover design. I'd also like to thank Lewis Wardrop at Restless Natives Studios, Lucy Fawcett at Sheil Land, and Don M and Susan M for all their encouragement over the last few years.

My former colleagues at Waterstones in Dundee (those who are left, and those who were there) deserve a shoutout – in particular, bookseller extraordinaire Kevin Breen, whose knowledge of and love for the city is almost unmatched. I'm slightly afraid for him to read this one. And the real-life Gordon Dow, too – sorry that I killed you off (at least you went out a hero!) – who was my first manager there.

The roll call of cheerleaders is immense, and too long to list in full, but special mentions go to Jay Stringer, Dave White, John and Evelyn Dingwall, Robert MacDuff-Duncan (Esq), and early reader (and awesome writer – go check her books!) Eva Dolan, who have all been privy to my doubts and madness during the writing of this book.

To readers old and new – what would be the point in any of this without you? Thank you!

Dot and Martin McLean – aka Mum and Dad – have always encouraged me with the writing, and as ever, I know I wouldn't be here without them. I know you're still waiting on that house in France ... just a little longer, maybe?

Mycroft and Magwitch – because, yes, I am the author who thanks his cats ... (And in memory of their departed brother, Moriarty.)

And finally, of course, my incredible wife (and brilliant author in her own right.) Lesley McDowell ... You are amazing – *Je t'aime*.

© Bob McDevitt

R.D. McLean is the author of eight crime novels and a number of short stories in anthologies and magazines, including Alfred Hitchcock's *Mystery Magazine, The Book of Extraordinary Sleuths and Private Eye Stories*. His debut novel, *The Good Son* was shortlisted for the Private Eye Writers of America Shamus Award in 2010. His latest novel, *Ed's Dead was called* "A really authentic and remarkable read!" by bestselling author Martina Cole.